Books by John Updike

POEMS

The Carpentered Hen (1958) · *Telephone Poles* (1963) · *Midpoint* (1969) · *Tossing and Turning* (1977) · *Facing Nature* (1985) · *Collected Poems 1953–1993* (1993) · *Americana* (2001) · *Endpoint* (2009)

NOVELS

The Poorhouse Fair (1959) · *Rabbit, Run* (1960) · *The Centaur* (1963) · *Of the Farm* (1965) · *Couples* (1968) · *Rabbit Redux* (1971) · *A Month of Sundays* (1975) · *Marry Me* (1976) · *The Coup* (1978) · *Rabbit Is Rich* (1981) · *The Witches of Eastwick* (1984) · *Roger's Version* (1986) · *S.* (1988) · *Rabbit at Rest* (1990) · *Memories of the Ford Administration* (1992) · *Brazil* (1994) · *In the Beauty of the Lilies* (1996) · *Toward the End of Time* (1997) · *Gertrude and Claudius* (2000) · *Seek My Face* (2002) · *Villages* (2004) · *Terrorist* (2006) · *The Widows of Eastwick* (2008)

SHORT STORIES

The Same Door (1959) · *Pigeon Feathers* (1962) · *Olinger Stories* (a selection, 1964) · *The Music School* (1966) · *Bech: A Book* (1970) · *Museums and Women* (1972) · *Problems* (1979) · *Too Far to Go* (a selection, 1979) · *Bech Is Back* (1982) · *Trust Me* (1987) · *The Afterlife* (1994) · *Bech at Bay* (1998) · *Licks of Love* (2000) · *The Complete Henry Bech* (2001) · *The Early Stories: 1953–1975* (2003) · *My Father's Tears* (2009) · *The Maples Stories* (2009)

ESSAYS AND CRITICISM

Assorted Prose (1965) · *Picked-Up Pieces* (1975) · *Hugging the Shore* (1983) · *Just Looking* (1989) · *Odd Jobs* (1991) · *Golf Dreams* (1996) · *More Matter* (1999) · *Still Looking* (2005) · *Due Considerations* (2007) · *Hub Fans Bid Kid Adieu* (2010) · *Higher Gossip* (2011) · *Always Looking* (2012)

PLAY

Buchanan Dying (1974)

MEMOIRS

Self-Consciousness (1989)

CHILDREN'S BOOKS

The Magic Flute (1962) · *The Ring* (1964) · *A Child's Calendar* (1965) · *Bottom's Dream* (1969) · *A Helpful Alphabet of Friendly Objects* (1996)

SEEK MY FACE

John Updike

SEEK
MY FACE

A Novel

Random House Trade Paperbacks • *New York*

2012 Random House Trade Paperback Edition

Published in the United States by Random House Trade Paperbacks, an imprint of The Random House Publishing Group, a division of Random House, Inc., New York.

RANDOM HOUSE TRADE PAPERBACKS and colophon are registered trademarks of Random House, Inc.

Originally published in hardcover in the United States by Alfred A. Knopf, a division of Random House, Inc., in 2002.

ISBN 978-0-345-46086-8
eBook ISBN 978-0-307-41659-9

www.atrandom.com

You speak in my heart and say, "Seek my face."
Your face, Lord, will I seek.

—Psalm 27

Books were still governed by the old rule,
Born of a belief that visible beauty
Is a little mirror for the beauty of being.
—CZESLAW MILOSZ, *A Treatise on Poetry*

What will our children's children say
About our art-monsters in future years
When Christian quiet relaxes the nations
And, as in the sunburst of the Renaissance,
Paint shall be gorgeous and, I hope, holy?
—KARL SHAPIRO, *Trial of a Poet*

This is a work of fiction. Nothing in it is necessarily true. Yet it would be vain to deny that a large number of details come from the admirable, exhaustive *Jackson Pollock: An American Saga*, by Steven Naifeh and Gregory White Smith (Clarkson N. Potter, 1989), or that some of my fictional artists' statements are closely derived from those collected in *Abstract Expressionism: Creators and Critics*, an illuminating anthology edited and introduced by Clifford Ross (Harry N. Abrams, 1990).

J.U.

SEEK MY FACE

"LET ME BEGIN by reading to you," says the young woman, her slender, black-clad figure tensely jackknifed on the edge of the easy chair, with its faded coarse plaid and broad arms of orangish varnished oak, which Hope first knew in the Germantown sunroom, her grandfather posed in it reading the newspaper, his head tilted back to gain the benefit of his thick bifocals, more than, yes, seventy years ago, "a statement of yours from the catalogue of your last show, back in 1996."

As a child Hope would sit in the chair trying to feel what it was like to be an adult, resting her little round elbows on the broad arms, spreading her fingers, a ring of fat between each joint, on the dowel end, which was set in the softly curved arm, a kind of wooden coin with a pale stripe in it, the butt end of the wedge that tightened the dowel. The chair's arms had been too far apart for her to rest more than one elbow and hand at a time. She must have been—what?—five, six. Even when new, in the 'twenties or 'teens, the chair would have been a homely unfashionable thing, a summer kind of furniture, baking in the many-windowed sunroom with the potted philodendron and the lopsided hassock, the hassock's top divided like a pie in long triangular slices of different colors of leather. When her grandmother's death in the 'fifties had at last broken up the Germantown house, Hope coveted the old chair and, her amused surviving brother making no objection, brought it to Long Island, where it sat upstairs in her so-called studio, where she would sometimes try to read by the north window, the sash leaking wind howling in off Block Island Sound while Zack played jazz records—Armstrong, Benny Goodman, a scratchy Beiderbecke—too loud downstairs; and then to the apartment with Guy and the children on East Seventy-ninth, in the dun-walled back spare room by the radiator that clanked like a demented prisoner while she tried to set her own rhythm with the loaded brush; and then to Vermont, where she and Jerry had bought and renovated and dug in for their last stand in life, a chair transported from muggy Pennsylvania to a colder, higher climate yet hardly incongruous in this plain, prim, low-ceilinged front parlor, the chair's round front feet resting on the oval rug of braided rags in a spiral, its square back feet on the floorboards painted the shiny black-red of Bing cherries, the browns and greens and thin crimsons of its plaid further fading into one pale tan, here in the sparse blue mountain light of early April. Strange, Hope thought, how things trail us place to place, more loyal than organic friends, who desert us by dying. The Germantown house became overgrown in Grandmother's lonely last years, its thick sandstone walls eaten to the second-story windowsills by gloomy flourishing shrubbery, hydrangea and holly and a smoke tree whose branches broke in every ice storm or wet snow, the whitewash flaking and the pointing falling out in brittle long crumbs lost down among the stems of the peonies, the roots of the holly. She had loved living there when so small, but after her parents moved to Ardmore visits back felt strange, the huge droopy-limbed hemlock having grown sinister, the yard with its soft grass smelling heated and still like the air of a greenhouse, the swing that her spry little grandfather, the first person Hope knew ever to die, had hung from the limb of the walnut tree rotting, ropes and board, in an eternally neglected way that frightened her.

The young woman, a narrow new knife in the chair's fat old sheath, reads in her edgy New York voice, a voice that leans toward Hope with a pressure of anxiousness but also with what seems, in this shaky light of late life, a kind of daughterly affection, *"For a long time I have lived as a recluse, fearing the many evidences of God's non-existence with which the world abounds. The world, it has come to me slowly, is the Devil's motley, colorful instead of pure. I restrict my present canvases to shades of gray ever closer together, as if in the pre-dawn, before light begins to lift edges into being. I am trying, it may be, to paint holiness. I suppose I should be flattered when some critics call this phase my best—they write that at last I am out from the shadow of my first husband. But I have, miraculously it might be said, ceased to care what they think, or what figure I cut in the eyes of strangers.* End quote. This was five years ago. Would you say it is still true?"

Hope tries to slow the young woman down, dragging her own voice as if in thought. "True enough, I would say, though it does sound a shade self-dramatizing. Perhaps 'fearing' is strong. 'Feeling dread and distaste in regard to' might have been more accurate and—and seemly."

It makes a lump in Hope's throat to have this nervously aggressive intruder here, with her city-white face and her dark-nailed long hands and her doctrinairely black outfit—black turtleneck, black imitation-leather jacket with a big center zipper, black hair held off her ears by a pair of curved silver combs and falling in a loose and silky fan-shape down her back—finished off so ominously with heavy squared-toed footgear, combat boots of a sort, laced up through a dozen or more eyelets like two little black ladders ascending into the flared bottoms of her slacks, the slacks made of a finely ribbed, faintly reflective fabric Hope has never seen before, a fabric without a name. The boots, with that new kind of high heel, wide sideways but narrow the other way, front to back, couldn't be very comfortable, unless mannishness was always comfortable now. It is a new century—more appallingly yet, a new millennium. This millennial fact for Hope is a large blank door that has slammed, holding her life behind it like a child smothering in an abandoned refrigerator.

The visitor's voice, insistent with a certain anger yet femalely flexible, insinuating itself into her prey's ear, asserts, "You were raised as a Quaker."

"Well, 'raised' is a kind term for it. My grandfather was an elder, true, but my father, especially after we moved to Ardmore, attended meeting only once or twice a year. The Ouderkirks had been Dutch Quakers; Dutch Quakers settled Germantown, a misnomer really, it should have been called Dutchtown, just as the Pennsylvania Dutch should be properly Pennsylvania Germans. Pockets of these Dutch Quakers had been living in the Rhine Valley; the Ouderkirks came from Krefeld; Penn himself had visited them in the sixteen seventies, telling them of his lovely colony, his 'holy experiment' across the sea. When they first came over, in the sixteen eighties, some lived in caves until they could build their houses. My mother, though, was quite Episcopalian, typically lukewarm, but she would never have called herself irreligious. We all went to meeting together a few times, it seems like quite a few but in a child's mind a little does for a lot. I remember mostly the light, and the silence, all these grown-ups waiting for God to speak through one of them—suppressed coughs, shuffling feet, the creak of a bench. It upset me at first, you know how children are always getting embarrassed on behalf of adults. Then the quality of the silence changed, it turned a corner, like an angel passing, and I realized it was a benign sort of *game*. The Friends speak of 'living silence.' Actually, someone did eventually speak. It had been arranged. The Quakers *did* make arrangements, but left space for God, so to speak, to upset the arrangements. There was a kind of elaborate courtesy to it all. Once there had been a bench up front for the elders and recorded ministers, but by the time I remember, the late 'twenties it must be, the very early 'thirties, I would have been ten in 1932, the benches were arranged in a square, so no one had any priority in the seating. Though my grandfather never led us to a back bench."

Be quiet, Hope tells herself. This has ever been her fault, talking, giving, flirting, trying too hard to please, endeavoring to seduce. Her grandfather would use a Quaker phrase, "of the creature," for anything that was too much, too human, too worldly, too selfish and cruel. War was of the creature. Lust and intemperance of course, yet reason and excessive learning and disputation, too. The arts—save for the domestic, Edenic art of gardening, and the hidden art of making money—were of the creature, howls for recognition and singularity. Things of the creature were weak and dirty and unworthy; they were a form of noise. As a child Hope had chattered too much, feeling her round freckled face redden with excitement, her heart nearly bursting with its own beating, wanting within her ribs all of her, head to toes, scalp to footsoles, to be loved, to be held, to be desired. Even now, on the grave's edge, seventy-nine last month, the unmerry month of March, she is trying to charm the lithe black-clad stranger, charmless though she herself has become, in her baggy brown corduroys and slack-necked yellow cotton turtleneck and thick wool lumberjack shirt left untucked as if to hide her belly but in truth calling attention to it; her belly bulges but her breasts and buttocks are sunken, she has become beneath her clothes a naked witch by Schongauer, with imps of arthritic pain her familiars, or Rembrandt's dreamy Saskia several decades further lost in sags and wrinkles. Her shiny auburn bangs, her signature when a young woman, are not even gray now but white, so thinned and dry and lacking in body, each filament sticking out with a mind of its own, as to be a mere souvenir of what once covered her forehead with the smooth bulge of a coppery cuirass. Her hair was cut short then, two points curving in to touch the angles of her jaw, the wide jaw defining the pale pentagon that looked back at her from a mirror with a deceptive calm, firm in its freckled hazel gaze, the nose small and straight, the lips not quite full but tidy and quick to express receptivity, to laugh, to smile, even at herself so earnestly appraising her face in the mirror, a dimple leaping up low in the left cheek. As a child she wondered where the reflection went when she walked away; mirrors hung on the Germantown walls like paintings that kept changing subject. The 'sixties liberated her from lipstick and those frizzing 'forties and 'fifties perms as well as from girdles and garters; she let her hair grow long and flat down her back, bundling it into a quick ponytail to paint or do housework, she had all sorts of artful clips and hinged round combs, tortoiseshell, and ivory before endangered elephants became an issue. The gray ghost of this ponytail now is gathered at the back of her skull in one of those candy-colored elastic circlets they sell at the Montpelier five-and-ten (one of the few five-and-tens left anywhere, they don't call it that, just the phrase dates her, a dime gets you nothing now), and on her feet she has thick socks the color of lint and cradling soft Birkenstocks, which date her also. The 'sixties had been for her a grateful release, a joy, though she was in her forties for most of them. Money worries, mating worries were behind her, she was a Manhattanite with a horse farm in Connecticut, married to Guy Holloway, Pop Art's super-successful boy wonder, and, more amusingly still, a mother of three young children, pushing in her denim miniskirt and auburn bangs a wire cart with little Dot in the infant seat in corduroy overalls (the pocket a staring teddy bear or a round-eyed canary) and the two boys trailing behind whining for this and that through the aisles of the Lexington Avenue Gristede's, all those clustered consumeristic colors under the blazing cool ceiling, such uninhibited colors, Day-Glo oranges and phosphorescent greens and acid persimmons, a decade of brazen rainbows, of gold leaf and silvering returning to canvases, of shimmering psychedelic trips. Yet these interviewers always asked her about the dreary, fearful 'forties and 'fifties, the first decade a gunmetal gray and the second that sickly powder blue you can see in the washed-out 'fifties movies on television.

"Like your first husband's canvases," the voice proposes, pleased with the connection. "Attacked from every side of the canvas. Without priority."

She is referring, Hope realizes, to the Quaker meeting house. "Zack wasn't anything of a Quaker. He had no inner quiet, none. His mother, after Zack's father left, had tried to enlist her family in one of those grotesque Western sects, where they go up on high hills and expect the Lord to come down and end everything. It was one of the things he didn't like to talk about. One of the many things. He was still resentful."

"Resentful because he was made to go up, or because the Lord didn't come down?"

This is amusing, Hope sees. This young woman perhaps does not need to be utterly resisted. She is going on, her voice both spiky and silky: "The lack of priority also suggests to me *your* paintings, the later ones. Everything even, nothing too intense. Every square inch equally important."

"I've never made that connection," Hope tells her flatly. The flatness would have been softened with the addition of the young woman's name. Her name . . . What *is* the name she gave, in letters and e-mails that Hope's gallery on Fifty-seventh Street forwarded and then over the phone and finally at the door? There this living body was, incongruous with the everlasting mountains behind her, startling, a tall black-haired person, her face city-pale, in a purple cloak with a huge hood, like an apparition of death in a Bergman film. Hope pictures the "K" jutting above the line, the "y" swooping below it: Kathryn. That odd, mannered spelling. People now that they've gotten away from ancestors and the Bible give the oddest names, names they invent, black welfare mothers naming their dolls: Luceen, Baylee, Mary-vonne. Her own grandchildren, five of them and not a John or a Mary among them, or even a Bill or a Barbara. Barbra now. Ardmore and Shipley had been full of Barbaras, and Mary Anns. Hope wonders if her visitor is Jewish. She has never developed the skill that anti-Semites and Jews themselves have in spotting who is Jewish. In art circles you assume anyone with any dash or presence is, any fast talker with a certain tang to the consonants, sounding out that concluding "g," but even that doesn't always work. Around Philadelphia the only Jews they knew were their dentists;

though Quakers and Jews had both been persecuted and were closer to biblical religion than, say, Roman Catholics, they belonged to different law firms, different country clubs. Hope's family belonged to the Germantown Cricket Club, because unlike Merion Cricket Club it had a swimming pool, though its dining room had that depressingly low ceiling. There were whole mock-Tudor, fat-lawned, high-hedged enclaves where invisible real-estate agents kept Jews out. Bernie Nova, for instance, with his poseur's monocle and curling mustache with waxed tips, she thought to be a German or an Armenian even, as the great and crazy Korgi truly was. Bernie and Roger Merebien were the ones of Zack's crowd of competitors she felt easiest with, most fraternally cherished; they were the most articulate, writers of statements and letters to the editors, formulators of credos and haughty letters to the press, and on account of that rather condescended to by the others, by Zack and Phil and Seamus, as too glib for sublimity, lacking in the proper American passion, beyond words. Kathryn's skin has the matte lustre, the racial suppleness, but so much is makeup now, she might also be of Mediterranean descent, or Eastern European. We are all so assimilated. Last Saturday, Hope was watching the evening news and the weekend newscaster instead of Tom Brokaw was a perfectly stunning young woman, light topaz eyes as far apart as a kitten's, sharp-cornered wide mouth pronouncing everything with a perfect rapid inflection, more American than American, crisper, a touch of that rapid barking voice of 'thirties gangster films and romantic comedies, and when she signed off her name wasn't even Greek, it was more like Turkish, a quick twist of syllables like an English word spelled backward. The old American stock is being overgrown. High time, of course: no reason to grieve. On the contrary. She and Zack had been old stock—Quaker, Yankee, Western pioneer, Protestant, each a priest on his or her own, out of the Northern European mists to this land of sharp, cancer-inducing sun. "Kathryn," Hope says, cementing her hold on the name, "is this really one more article about Zack? Haven't there been too many already?"

"Not Zack, you. All of you. The moment, the historical moment, the explosion, when everything came together, and America took over from Paris, and for the first time ever we led world art. Why? How?" She sounds like a news-caster, reading the prompter as it unscrolls. Hope's bones feel leaden, heavy with the reality this young person is assigning her—*needs* to assign her, to justify her time, her spent energy, the boring trip up the Thomas E. Dewey Thruway on into Vermont, winding through the fading farms of cows in stony pastures and the overbuilt develop-ments of A-frame ski houses and the pretty little experi-mental colleges for the difficult children of the rich, the gas stations that are also mini-marts, the little lunch restaurants trying to be homey with white curtains at the windows and usually closed this time of year, and then the night of fitful sleep in the motel so as to be at Hope's door by nine-thirty; Hope told her over the phone her days began early, with some hours after dawn in the studio, and ended early. The young woman fears not getting enough for her mileage.

That "all of you" was kind, though. Hope was never considered a significant soldier, just a camp follower, one of the many, and then a wife, which few camp follow-ers achieve. Her painting embarrassed Zack, somehow a subversion of his manhood, and he hid her as a painter upstairs like the mad Mrs. Rochester. "Well," she offers, "to be simple about it, the war had left the other coun-tries ruined. They were exhausted. The same way we dominated the '48 Olympics—everybody else was still weak with hunger."

Kathryn brushes this aside as facetious, as unworthy. She can't imagine hunger and poverty as real cultural factors. Her face presses a few inches deeper into the space between Hope and herself, she in the soft old sunroom chair and Hope in her hard rocker, a rocker made by former hippies in Burlington of no less, the nicely printed (in green ink) leaflet that came with it said, than five different woods; they shrank at different rates and made the fit tighter as the chair aged, so the leaflet claimed. She had given the chair to Jerry for his first birthday up here and the claim is not yet disproved. It supports her weight, as she leans back to keep her inquisitor at a distance. The unkind clarity of the morning light—not a cloud in the blue sky, a glisten of mud on the bare earth outside the kitchen door when she had loaded up the bird feeder ten minutes before Kathryn too punctually arrived—strips the interviewer's face of beauty and shows it to be horsy and humorless, its plummy eyes astride a long nose with a slight bump in it, its lips downturned in determination not to be distracted or too easily charmed, lips that might melt if kissed but are in danger of settling into a permanent sour frown of unfulfilled ambition. Kathryn glances down into the sheets of paper balanced on her black lap, her thin thighs pressed tightly together, pages of computer-typed questions to help her as the interview tape unwinds in the little machine, a Sony of two tones of gray, its purr tinny in the silence, on the low table between them, not a table but an old wooden sea-chest Hope bought in Riverhead in the 'forties for twenty dollars and sanded and varnished, those first few years when she and Zack were enthusiastic about making a home together on the light-soaked windy tip of Long Island, worlds removed from what he called, euphemistically, covering his from-bar-to-bar binges, the "wear and tear" of Manhattan. Kathryn says hurriedly, as if Hope were sensitive to such matters, "The triumph was exploited, I know, politically, by the Rockefellers and the CIA among others, but I don't see it as a political movement, originally. I see it as innocent, the last flare of our idealistic innocence."

"Oh dear," Hope responds. "We didn't feel innocent to ourselves. We felt very sophisticated and a bit wicked. And the painters didn't all know each other equally well, or should I say like each other equally. A number of the others, the more intellectual and better organized, didn't like Zack much, especially after his paintings became so famous and his drinking became terrible again. Zack wasn't easy to like, or even, after a while, to love." She lets that float a few seconds, tantalizing this other, tempting her to pounce prematurely on that belly-up word "love," but Kathryn ignores the provocation, and Hope has to continue, explaining, clarifying what would have always been better left mysterious. Interviewers and critics are the enemies of mystery, the indeterminacy that gives art life. She flutters a hand—knobby, freckled, smelling of paint thinner—at the end of her man's lumberjack-shirt sleeve and says, "Everybody now is expected to turn inside out on command, like impatiens seeds when touched, or—what is that plant called?—squirting cucumber. Zack hated being interviewed; it offended his lower-class sense of dignity, of there being things one didn't say. We all—me, Clem, Peggy, Betty, Herbie Forrest—used to coach him on what to say, but when the time came he refused to say it, or mumbled it. It was his arrogance—he thought you shouldn't chase recognition, it should come to you without being asked. He was wild for it yet despised playing the game." He is gropingly coming back to her, his squarish puzzled bad-boy face, its three muscular dents, deep dimples as if in amplification—a stronger restatement—of her own lone dimple, and with his face the look of the Manhattan streets back then, before glass-skin architecture and plastic garbage bags: the curbs of East Ninth Street crowded on collection days with corroded galvanized trash cans, angrily dented on the dump truck's hydraulically lifted lip, and the huge metal noise they made in the middle of the night, the trash men getting their own back at all those sleeping safe above them. The cans smelled plainly of garbage then, and class war was unconcealed, unions versus management, the Reds against the rich. You were not asked to have a nice day; buildings looked much the same in Manhattan as in any city, brick and four stories high; each block formed a little village, with a shoe repairman, a barber shop, a notions shop run by a pair of sisters, a Chinese laundry, a coal-and-wood cellar, a drugstore with a marble soda counter. Eighth Street was a kind of *souk*, where you were jostled down into the gutter, and the area north and east of Washington Square had a furtive European quality, Grace Church with its waffle-pattern gray steeple presiding where Broadway slightly bent like a medieval street sneaking along, and Cooper Union standing afloat in its square like a brown Venetian palace. University Place was a string of bars, including the Cedar, which when you opened the door always seemed warm, and dim enough so that your defects were left outside. It smelled of smoke and sawdust.

"He was," Hope says, halting, conscious of herself as the possessor, in this other's pendulous black eyes, of a wandering, frayed old mind, beyond any usefulness but some shreds of memory to be woven into another's story, "he was self-indulgent and hardly even self-educated. And of course drank too much. But we all drank too much, it was part of the war, the blackouts, our desperate dingy mood, all that death, the newspapers dealing every day in death, hundreds, thousands, numbers that would make screaming headlines now. It was a man's world. Art was a man's world. They could hardly make room for women, even when they married us. It was a tough, man's world. You speak of Zack and the rest as heroes of this historic moment you have—what's the word now?—constructed, you see them as Titans in the clouds, but the Titans were a sad group actually, who came to a sorry end, if I remember my childhood Bulfinch. Except for funny old Bernie, who had married money, and Roger, who had a trust fund, and Onno, who began to sell before any of the others—he had that European flair that dealers and buyers could already understand, not our poor American groping, up from the depths, Jung and all those archetypes—*everybody* was poor and had been for years, living off the Project, the Federal Arts Project, before the war and even during it, though the dole was drying up. At the moment you mention, post-war, even after the publicity had begun to come in, Zack was still not selling paintings. A few prints and works on paper but not the big paintings. He was getting to be famous, but we stayed surprisingly poor—it maddened him. Peggy's gallery gave Zack a dole, we had to borrow from her to buy the house, a house and three acres for four thousand dollars, think of it, the land alone would be a million now, out there close to the Hamptons; he never earned it out, and so the gallery kept his paintings. Just kept them, for years. Most people had no idea anything wonderful was happening. They didn't know there was a moment. They were still thinking Picasso and Miró and the Surrealists. Not Dalí—he was as much despised as Benton, standing for everything we hated."

"Of course," Kathryn murmurs, placatingly, sensing a kindling, wanting Hope to run on.

"Dalí was a one-man circus, department-store window-dressing. He actually *did* some windows for Bonwit's, and then fell through the glass tearing up the display when the management insisted on putting clothes on the mannequins, who were, I don't know, stepping into fur-lined bathtubs and lying on beds of red coals, a lot of feathers and disembodied hands holding mirrors. It made all the papers, which of course is what he wanted. He understood publicity, and was shameless. Europeans are, when they get over here. This was before I moved to New York, but Zack somehow had been there and would describe it and laugh, but it also offended his sense of dignity that an artist would sell out like that. Zack could be in rags, filthy from a night in the gutter, but he had this ideal of dignity, of, I don't know, the artist not as some performer and society leech but as a *worker*, and at least as worthy of respect as a preacher or a banker. It was one of the things about him I loved." Hope feels herself roused, her face reddening, her heart pumping, striving to please, stung by the fear of appearing doddery; the old deprivations and ridicule seem as close as if this interloping girl had been one of the glib art journalists who had served up easy wisecracks in the 'forties *Time* and *Life*. But by the time these publications were taking any notice, a tide had turned. "You speak about a historic moment, Kathryn, but the attention was all in a few galleries, with a few critics, who had their own fish to fry for that matter, their own names to make—Clem used Zack to make his own name, and when Zack faltered Clem was the first one off the boat. The canvases, the ones that later everybody could see were magnificent, and that went for millions—what good were they? They were too big.

They were public art without a public. Zack—it was pathetic—when he was in his cups used to tell people what a great investment his work would be, and of course he was right. One man in the Flats—Jimmy Quinn, who ran what was really a glorified vegetable stand—took a little thirty-by-forty fiberboard of Zack's in payment and ten years or so ago finally sold it for two million dollars. He still drives around in his beat-up pickup. Zack would have liked that."

Hope pauses, and Kathryn's lips part to spit another question into the tape, but Hope is not done with her long, looping thought; there is a picture of Zack she wants to finish, though the memory of him threatens to suck her back, out, down, like waves foaming at her ankles at one of the beaches, one of the remote rocky ones past the bluffs, past the old fish-factories, toward the Point, where they would stand as the afternoon gave up its strong light and turned ruddy and the breeze picked up, there being nothing to the south but the Atlantic, a few gray ships on the horizon like index tabs in a filing cabinet. "We all drank," she repeats, "but for Zack it was a poison, it released demons. Like many a famous drinker, he really couldn't drink. I held my liquor better than he did, and I was just a slip of a thing in my twenties." Zack was in his thirties when they first went together: his narrow hips, his chest and shoulders coated with blond wool, even his bare feet were beautiful, knobby and broad across the toes, and the insteps as white as the skin inside a woman's arm. She stood beside him feeling the suck of ankle-high surf, the way it pulls the sand out from under your heels. There had been the white noise of the waves and the far-stretching scent of beach, salt and iodine and rotting marine bodies, fish and jellyfish leaving their round ochre corpses like puddles of varnish on the rocks, collapsed, unable to get back to their element, their anatomy dimly seen within the puddle, useless, wasted, something like breathing still taking place, poor doomed creatures, so we all. She had liked the way Zack was not too much taller than she, like some men, including Ruk; she felt like an Eve matched to him, as in those marvellous Cranach panels in Pasadena, or the two frescoes in the Brancacci Chapel, the Masaccio so anguished and ashamed, the red angel over their heads banishing them, and the Masolino so serene and stately and haughty, the little benign female snake's head above Eve's, Eve cool with her centrally parted fair hair, unrepentant, before the Fall, the cleft of her sex not hidden, nor Adam's penis. Face it: this young woman, too, is beautiful. Hope imagines Kathryn's naked body—the swing of hip into thigh, the rose-madder-tipped breasts floating on the rib cage, the pubic triangle pure ivory-black and oily as in a Corot—all in a flash, then renounces the image: *of the creature.* Her susceptibility to beauty, Hope has always known, is what has kept her minor as an artist. The great ones go beyond beauty, they spurn it as desert saints spurned visions of concupiscence and ease: the Devil's offer of the world as reward.

She tells her interrogator, "The moment you describe, when America came into its own in terms of art, artists had been saying ever since the Armory Show that it must happen; what was Regionalism but an attempt to make it happen?—Benton and so on, the WPA murals. We were terribly marginal, abstraction was a pipe dream like Communism. The media—they weren't called that then—played us for laughs; we were mad fools. America was titillated. Those pictures of Zack in *Life,* and then the little movie that terrible, bossy German made, Hans something—those were what killed him, really. He hated himself for becoming a celebrity, the new Dalí. For being made to see, I suppose, that becoming a celebrity was what he had wanted all along. He really had very little talent, the way most art students have it—just this terrible drive to be great. He was desperate to be not just good but *great*. Others thought they had it, too, the drive, but they didn't stick with it, they got distracted by their talent. Zack wasn't distracted that way; he *stuck*. He had nothing but this—" She does not want to say "hope." She goes on, "He was terribly clumsy with a pencil, with a brush. His hands seemed to be too thick for them. And he didn't *know* anything, compared with most people. He'd gotten in with Benton at the Art Students League; Benton saw himself in him, I suppose, the braggart part of him, the west-of-the-Mississippi thing, and Zack's talent was no threat, and then when back in California Zack had actually met Siqueiros, and picked up on the messiness, the new industrial paints, the social protest or whatever, everything messy and new, and he had driven out to Pomona College to see a mural Orozco had done of Prometheus; when he was east again he drove up to Dartmouth to see those Orozcos, he loved them, those earth colors, the bad drawing, and like everybody in New York in the 'thirties he inhaled Surrealism, but without having much sense of the psychological theories behind it, it was all just as it applied to him, the would-be great Zack McCoy, personally. You mentioned politics, but I don't remember that we much noticed it, the things people talk about now. Truman, and the Marshall Plan, China going under to Mao, and Europe on the brink, and all those tests, the test sirens, the talk about annihilation: it didn't have to do with us. We were utterly selfish. Even the war—though not everybody got out of serving, many did. The board doctors classified them as crazy or homosexual, even when they had wives. I was so shocked, coming to New York when I was twenty, by how nobody mentioned the war, in the worst year of it, when it looked like we really might lose and Hitler and Tojo would rule the world. All we talked about was painting and who was fucking who."

"But a lot of the group," the interviewer objects, with her prim book-knowledge, "were *very* political. Very 'thirties lefty. Bernie Nova and Jarl Anders, especially. If you read their post-war manifestos they're downright—what's that word?—apocalyptic. They saw what they were doing as a revolution. Anders said—I don't have the quote right here—he said he was going to undo two thousand years of mendacity and betrayal of the human spirit."

Why is this young person reciting Hope's own life to her? And not getting it quite right. Bernie loved to issue pronouncements, the more outrageous the better, but was also a terribly funny, enfolding, kindly man, a bear with his waxed mustache and clownish hip-hip-old-man monocle, words just flying from him, avuncular touches and hugs quickening her when she stood close. Jarl was more distant, more limited, gray and gaunt like a corpse unearthed, a bit paralyzed in his motions, staring out of those eyes, eyes shadowed like a movie vampire's, monomaniacal but capable, too, of a certain hawk-swoop tenderness, a sudden seeing into a woman, in a way impossible for Zack. Zack saw only a mother, an intimate enemy, whoever the woman was he looked at: a threatening softness, a suck underfoot at the rocky beaches, where he would make impromptu sculptures of the rocks, especially if there were other people's children there to entertain. He did love children, but with no sense of responsibility. He thought his own would be like somebody else's, you turn your back on them when playtime is over.

Hope admits, "They were all older than I, I was the baby,

they had struggled through the Depression trying to be artists, they might have starved or turned to something else but for the government and the FAP. Twenty-three dollars a week was a fortune back then. They were a generation older in some cases, and, yes, there was a lot of the Old Left left in them. They believed there must be a better society than this one, with a third of the men out of work and the rich wearing top hats and being vile about Roosevelt. The war suppressed all that. But not really. It persisted underground, the need for revolution. It moved into art. Wartime was deprivation, but so was the artistic life. The news all somehow glided by, apart from art. I was so surprised, coming to New York at the age of twenty, by the fact that art schools were still going so strong. Rationing and war bonds and propaganda everywhere you looked, and the streets full of uniforms, and nevertheless . . ."

"Of course," Kathryn smoothly interrupts, mistaking Hope's pause for a senile trailing off, "there were all the émigrés, Duchamp and Mondrian and the Surrealists, Breton, Max Ernst—"

"Yes," Hope snaps. "We—I, at least; *you* might have gotten to them—never saw them. The rich made pets out of them, they hung out in Connecticut and the Upper East Side, of all of them only Mondrian wasn't a snob about American life, thought he might learn from it—but they were there, yes, on our side of the Atlantic, upping the ante, making an *atmosphere*. There were exhibitions. That was one of our complaints, that the galleries gave all their space to Europeans. And Barr at the Modern of course could only think European at that point."

Who was this young woman, Hope wonders, to come pushing (she *must* be Jewish) into her life, reading it back to her from her studious sheets of printout? As Hope ages, the

outer facts of her life, including her legendary marriage to
Zack, seem to have less and less to do with her inner life, a
life that began with her noticing the paintings and reproductions that hung in the Germantown house, quaint
things collected by a timid Quaker taste—a few examples
of Pennsylvania Dutch Fraktur, crabbed wedding certificates with the doll-like figures watercolored in spots,
framed magazine-quality oleographs of Lawrence's *Pinkie*
and Vermeer's *Woman with a Water Jug* and pink-cheeked
heads with powdered hair, possibly Copley portraits from
the big brooding caramel-colored museum in Philadelphia
she could see from the back of Daddy's Packard as they
drove to Center City along the coal-black Schuylkill. And
her grandfather's house held some original paintings: hanging hushed in velvet boxes, oval miniature portraits of
Ouderkirks long dead and crumbled in graves, tiny shiny
stippled presences with eyelashes and ear folds and ringlets
if she looked hard, and watercolors of tumbling nasturtiums
or the Brandywine glimmering between heavy overhanging
trees whose reflected shadows she could trace on the water,
the work of some cousin or aunt of her grandparents who
had taken art lessons at the turn of the century and was considered among her gentlewomen friends very gifted, and
oil paintings holding visible peaks and ridges in the hardened paint, there had been one of a bowl of fruit posed
on a checked tablecloth, which Hope even when very little
could see would be very difficult to get right, the checks
going up and down the folds and wrinkles of the cloth, and
larger ones of woods, of fallen trunks like crusty rotting
bodies, dark paintings these, not pleasant but powerful in
that the child could feel the damp gloom, the strange truth
that this mossy shaded tangle, this loose scatter on yellow-
brown leaf mulch, this untended patch of forest, of Penn's

original Indian-haunted wilderness, would be here whether anyone was standing here with an easel or not. The paint *hardened,* Hope saw, touching (the child was alone in the room, there was nobody to tell her not to touch) its little rough spines. The hardened paint carried a glimpse forward into a radiant forever, along with the groping, stabbing movement of the painter's hand and eye. She felt an infinite, widening magic in this, and also the element of protest which made people want to nail down pieces of a world that was always sliding away from under them; the world was an assembly line that kept spilling goods forward, into a heap of the lost and forgotten. With the protest came a gaiety, that of small defiant victories over time, creating *things to keep.*

It was her mother who kept her careful drawings and suggested that a neighbor in Ardmore, where they had moved from her grandparents' Germantown house to a newly built big mock-Tudor on a curving shady street, come give her drawing lessons. She was eight, nine. However hard Hope looked, she failed to see what this thickset man, with his unaccustomed smells of pipe tobacco and cooking sherry and tooth decay, saw in the shadows, the greens in the reds, the blues hidden in the browns. Her little "gift" tended to crumple under the heaviness of his masculine attention—his name was Rudolph Hartz—and it relieved her when her family's summer rentals in Maine ended the summer lessons, held in the head-hurting hazy Philadelphia sun in the side yard or in the shade of the willow or English walnut, vegetation crawling with subtleties of color like garter snakes and toads. Their indoor lessons occurred in the library; pages of the *Evening Bulletin* were spread over the coffee table, whose inlay formed a long square chain of paler bits, triangular and rhomboidal, of wood. It was as if her slender, quiet father had grown thicker and put on an odor of German vices and brute force and was leaning over her shoulder, a hairy hand seizing her brush and impatiently dabbling in the water glass and the scooped rectangles of raw color in the watercolor set's little folding tray and mixing up a muddy color that looked all wrong but when dashed into place did make the subject— the vase, or the Kewpie doll, or the yellow pepper—jump somehow into solidity. Little Hope felt too slight to bear up under Mr. Hartz's passion, she felt herself a waste of his time, she smelled along with tobacco and stale armpits his mediocrity, his disappointment; he was one of Philadelphia's legion of frustrated illustrators, consigned to an occasional portrait commission from a friend or a set design for suburban amateur theatricals.

The lessons, even on winter weekends, ceased. Her parents must have spoken, politely, as grown-ups do, to Mr. Hartz. Hope tactfully let herself drift away from art, its muddy yearning—the water glass clouding from the dipped brush, the slick lindenwood palette with its circlets of stirred oils going gray from mixing with each other— as from a boy who, however fascinating, would never be a suitable husband. She was ten, eleven. As part of a proper upbringing she visited museums: the treasure house on the top of Fairmount felt inside like a great marble bank with a few customers shuffling and whispering under the skylights while high out of reach a naked slim Diana balanced on the ball of one foot; the more churchly—Daddy said "Byzantine"—Pennsylvania Academy of the Fine Arts had long stairs rising up between the two frightening big canvases by Benjamin West that somehow came out of the Bible, and beyond them rooms of white statues naked because they were goddesses instead of real people and of old pictures of cliffs and waterfalls and portraits of Ben Franklin with his mischievous little lips and George Washington looking pained and flushed; the farthest rooms displayed Academy student work, charcoal drawings of Negro faces monumental and sullen and staring and industrial workers posed outside closed factories wearing thick cloth caps whose bills were lowered over brows shamed by unemployment, creased by injustice, the foreshortened perspective working to hunch and dwarf their bodies like an unseen industrial press squeezing all color from the world; in nearby Merion a certain Dr. Barnes had turned his Argyrol millions into a painting collection and to house it had built a Doric-columned mansion wherein, admitted by careful pre-arrangement, a select few, including tittering classes of Shipley girls in their pleated green jumpers and matching green kneesocks, could view walls covered as many as four paintings high by French flesh and Provençal sunlight, Impressionism and its wilder children, polychrome thrusts into a new paganism, art disrobed of its duties to history, to piety, to anything but the glory of each day and its dappled skin of color. These hushed visits, these sanctioned contacts, kept Hope in touch with her childhood wonder at the glimmers called art.

At Bryn Mawr, in the first two years of the new decade, with the European war blackening the horizon beyond the Atlantic, the art history department, still haunted by the recently departed Georgiana Goddard King, a personal friend of Gertrude Stein, revived Hope's interest in man-made beauty—revived it enough for her to realize that Bryn Mawr was not enough, studying and admiring was not enough, there was a world not two hours' train ride away where art was life, where her virginal young body with its brain and eyes could be an instrument, could do and make and *be*, somehow, in a style that her faded, gentle Philadelphia would never allow. At the end of her sophomore year, while her mother was dithering over the details of this year's move to their Maine island, where, tired of unprofitable rentals, her father had bought a shingled property whose upkeep cost more than rentals ever did, Hope headed to New York, at the height of the summer heat, to become an artist. Her parents were shocked, but it was a time of shocks, and she was twenty and it was 1942. Her older brother let himself be drafted; her younger had already enlisted. Quaker pacifism was superseded, and female passivity too. She went forth with a retrospectively absurd panoply of matched blue luggage including two drum-shaped hatboxes to engage the creature, colorful life, its pigments and snares. As she walked the dangerous streets, making her way among eyes in which she registered with a flick like that of a brush, her freedom enthralled her.

Kathryn's voice overtakes her on those crowded evening pavements; it is keeping pace with Hope's mind. "Let's leave the galleries and the Modern for later." She looks at the printouts in her long black lap. "You were a student first at the Women's Art School of the Cooper Union for the Advancement of Science and Art."

"I was. They were doubtful but let me in, on the strength of some sketches I had done at college, and a self-portrait with bared breasts, in acrylics. Cooper Union in those days was very academic, very practical-minded. The training was organized in 'alcoves.' In the first alcove, students drew from plaster hands and feet. In the second, from casts of torsos. For the third, they had casts of the full figure. Not until the fourth alcove did you get live models. I dropped out before we got to the live models. The second-alcove instructor, I forget his name, didn't even want to promote me to the third alcove; he said I was too linear. But he promoted me to get rid of me. I was trouble, I suppose. I was so thrilled to be in New York, in the Village."

"The instructor's name was Leonard Wilton, the sculptor," her interviewer tells her, having consulted the notebook. "But before you left you, uh, became involved with another instructor, the portrait-painter Gregor Rukavishnikov."

"Ruk was really only a substitute instructor, the other had been drafted." Hope suppresses a longing to be outdoors, bathing her brain in colorless fresh air. Through the window, beyond her imprisoner's head of hair with its silver combs, she sees in the forsythia bushes that arch against the sills a set of birds abruptly beginning to flutter and fuss, excited by some current among themselves: it is the animal kingdom that feels the excitement of spring first, a stray squirrel emerging from nowhere and managing to find a nut he or another squirrel buried in November; sitting on a warm flat rock in the wall, he holds it in two paws corn-on-the-cob style and chitters at it like a tiny electric typewriter.

"I mean," she tells Kathryn, "he made enough doing society portraits, his stuff was *chic*, he didn't need to teach, unlike so many artists. He did quite well, actually, until drink got to him. As a teacher he didn't try to conceal his indifference but was kind, one on one, flirtatious enough but never gross—we girls all loved him, needless to say, though we distrusted his painting style. It was com*mer*cial and, by the 'forties, rather sweetly old-fashioned—long necks, fine outlines, sheaves of sculptured hair in stylized stripes, an Art Deco bas-relief look. Streamlined. His portraits had, how can I say, that false roundedness you used to see in *Vanity Fair* caricatures."

"The pastel he did of you, now at the Corcoran, is lovely."

"Yes, the profile. Those gleaming metallic bangs. The muscles in my throat, I suppose. But it seemed to Ruk, his facility, too much of a trick; he sneered at his own work and admired the rough brutes—Soutine, Kokoschka, Picasso when he wasn't neoclassical, the late half-blind Monet. He thought Dubuffet, who was getting some notice in America, was on to something. He told me to loosen up."

Hope senses that Kathryn is dissatisfied. She wants her to do more, somehow, with poor dear aimless Ruk. Does she want her to tell her how it was to fuck him? That was not what Ruk was about—his lovemaking was good, when he was halfway sober, but had less heart in it than his dancing; he had to be on show, that was his weakness, and even though he was Hope's first lover she soon felt herself bringing the greater conviction to their bed, the greater willingness to risk embarrassment for the sake of sensations that couldn't be sprayed with fixative and put on display, that were beautiful but not lasting. She says, "He was beautiful," which was what he would have wanted her to say. "He was the most beautiful man I had ever seen. Six foot four at least, high white forehead, these almond-shaped Russian eyes, pale blue like those of a husky dog, frosty around the pupil. The hair on his head was as lank and pampered as a woman's, and he loved his own legs, they were so long, the ankles so skinny. He was always taking off his pants at parties, not to be sexy but the way a male ballet dancer shows his legs. He said he was White Russian, but, then, that means so little to an American, all the Russians one met back then were White, as opposed to Red. The Red ones were in Russia, slugging it out with the Germans. Does that do him for you?"

Kathryn lifts her luminous matte face and bats her lubricated eyelids one beat, to register Hope's hostility and to show that she can take it. "Not entirely," she admits. "Did you love him?"

"Oh, of course, I'm sure. Isn't that what one does, a young woman, early twenties, romantic about art and artists? I will say this for Ruk—he showed me things. He showed me New York. He had a yellow Lincoln, God knows how he got gas for it. He drove me up and down the avenues, all the way up to the spots in Harlem, the cafés, the parties. He would dress me. I absolutely submitted—he knew what he was doing. One costume party, he had me go as a nun, an outfit he had made or stolen. Maybe he stole it from a real nun—he told me his sisters were Russian Orthodox and very fanatic, like the Empress Alexandra. He liked me in black dresses, with bright stockings to show off my legs. Legs—though I wasn't tall I had a tall woman's legs, he said. He would paint stripes of color on my face, and put a few feathers in my hair; he called me his Quaker Pocahontas. He made me a *presence*, in our little set at Cooper Union. He took me to openings, and told me what was good, what was not so good: Picasso not so good, he could do too much, too easily. Matisse was good because everything was at the outer limit, attained with effort, by a simple bourgeois man. Picasso was a gypsy, a bandit, a Bolshevik." She can begin to hear Ruk's voice, his skimming voice with its deep tonic, a Russian choir voice, vibrant through his screen of sophistries. "He said the Surrealists were right in that the subconscious must do the moving, the talking, but wrong in that they were all literary, and wanted just to play word games and politics. At the same time, he was turning out these society portraits of pampered women and their pretty children and even their pretty dogs. Ruk was at his best with dogs, certain breeds. But he drank. I had never seen a man drink like this, my grandfather didn't drink at all and my father just wine at the occasional special meal; the fathers of my friends maybe had a whiskey in their hands when I'd peek into the library, but I thought it was just a prop, I didn't know it could be a religion, drinking. I drank, too, as I said. But if it isn't a religion to you you aren't a real drinker. At any rate, Ruk—I was too young to see that he was going to seed, getting puffy, his hands shaky, yellow from nicotine, despairing that he wasn't a rough genius, one of the great brutes. Also, any man of that time who wasn't in the armed forces, it made you a subspecies. Men felt it, even if they laughed at feeling it. Ruk had a rheumatic heart, I guess. Rheumatic as well as romantic. There was a lot he didn't tell me, or made up lies about."

"I have read," Kathryn interposes with a considerate smile, adjusting by an inch the Sony's position on the varnished yellow sea-chest, "that he bragged of sleeping with the society women he painted."

"He did sleep with some of them. I knew it, though I didn't want him to describe it to me. He wanted to. That was his thing, showing off. But it wasn't meant to be a big deal, I had flings too, those two years we were together. Maybe I was trying to make him jealous. Or just doing it for its own sake. I had come late to sex, and it was like a glorious toy. It was power and submission and danger, it was a way of getting to know somebody and having them know you. It was a way of weaving a kind of costume of secrets. Isn't that how it still is?"

Did Kathryn blush? Certainly she moves her head a bit away, adjusting its angle as she had that of the tape recorder. "Yes, perhaps," she says, "I suppose. But we have AIDS now, and there's very little of the glorious-toy feeling left. The idea of its being part of some revolution is quite gone. The quality-porno-film idea. Sex as a cause."

Hope says, feeling rebuked and taking a brisk chastising tone in self-defense, "Well, my dear, we didn't have AIDS, but we had pregnancy. And the clap, they called it. There wasn't all that talk of crabs, as there was in the 'sixties. And syphilis if you were ever so unlucky. I was always lucky, I figured because my heart was pure. And I didn't sleep with just anybody, as some of the girls and models did, I had to respect the man. I had to think he was serious, at least about painting. Anyway: Ruk, whom you seem to care about a great deal. He was kind to me, as kind as a self-infatuated alcoholic can be. He broadened me, he showed me around. God knows what he saw in me."

"If he was sinking, as you say," Kathryn supplies, "you were a straw he was grasping. You were Hope." Another joke; her eyes, heavy and opaque like plums, widen and glisten, watching the older woman's response. Kathryn's jokes are spoiled for Hope by the suspicion that they are maneuvers and not the spontaneous, selfless embrace of absurdity that humor should be. Ruk and she, on a night of champagne and vodka, would laugh and laugh; everybody looked ridiculous and pathetic, his rumbling choir voice with its slurred consonants slipping one caricature after another into her ears. "His portrait of you shows what he saw. You look extremely vital and confident."

The closeness of this approach—the fact of another person in the room breathing, like a humidifier softly hissing—makes Hope uncomfortable. She is used to the dry quiet of solitude, of parched pure winter days. She says, to restore a distance, "It was through Ruk that I first met Korgi, and Onno de Genoog."

"And what were they like?"

These vanished dead men, why does Kathryn's voice grow warmer, evasively slack, as if contemplating stealing them for herself? "Alike, really. They were both immigrants, and had that Continental élan; they assumed the world was made for human pleasure, a very snobbish and barbaric view, of course, but it made them attractive; it gave them swagger and freed them up to paint in those lovely light colors they used. They were the same age, oddly, though you think of Korgi as a generation older. He got there first. I mean, there had been Kandinsky and Malevich and Mondrian, of course, doing abstraction, but they were like flares at sea, lonely signals, religious in a crazy way no one could be seriously expected to imitate—I mean, *think* of Theosophy and Madame Blavatsky, what we are being asked to swallow! It all goes back to Kandinsky—his essays, and Der Blaue Reiter, spiritualism rescuing us from materialism and the dreadful perspective-mad Renaissance and so on, as I'm sure you know better than I, since you've just been studying everything. But all it brought Kandinsky to was a lot of ugly, jumpy geometry, whereas the place that Korgi got to turned out to be an island, a large island full of these fantasic, edible flowers. I mean, everybody could eat them, and grow and grow. After Korgi committed suicide—when was that? '48, just when his influence was triumphing, really—Onno would talk about the first time he visited Korgi's studio, in Union Square, sometime in the 'thirties. He said the atmosphere was so saturated with beauty it made him dizzy. 'Dissy,' he pronounced it. It was a revelation he never got over. You can see it in the colors both men used—those coral pinks, those baby blues, the darting strokes between oval forms like amoebas or lily pads, floating across the canvas like, what?, those things in the vision when you look at a blank wall, in the vitreous humor—though in Korgi of course it all becomes transparent, whereas Onno tried to thicken everything, a ferocious thicket of strokes, but the colors are still playful, childlike even. Korgi, like Ruk, was strikingly tall, almost freakish, and his English could be witty. He called the Regionalist School 'poor painting for poor people.' "

Hope laughs, remembering the velvety accent, the cape and broad-brimmed hat, the haughty indignation, the searching light in the Armenian's mournful long-lashed eyes as he respectfully searched Hope's face for his opportunities there. He was, through maintaining a parasitic connection with the Art Students League, a considerable harvester in the ripe fields of the art-struck. He would say to a girl, "Come to my studio, be my *vooman.*" But Hope would laugh. She was never tempted. He was simply Ruk again, though with a naïve, unnegotiable genius that Ruk lacked, and she sensed in him reserves of nihilism that Ruk's butterfly nature did not threaten her with. She was too young, she thought, to take on a troubled man, though in a few years she would take on Zack.

"And it was Ruk," she informs Kathryn, "who put me on to Hermann Hochmann and his little school, where the real action was. I don't think we said 'where the action was' then. Or 'cutting edge.' What did we say? 'Most advanced,' maybe. There was this military notion of advance. Hochmann had set up shop in a single big third-story room on West Ninth Street. The day I walked in, the whole school, about twenty at their easels, was gathered around this most odd still life—some broken pottery, a crumpled Kleenex, a playing card, and a ball of string from the hardware store, with the paper band still on it, and the whole thing backed by cellophane raked by a side light so that it all was fragmented reflections and shadows. It was almost impossible to look at, let alone paint. Yet, everybody was painting away, and after a year of drawing plaster casts at Cooper, the smell of real paint was heavenly. Like wind on your face when you ice-skate."

"What was Hochmann like?"

"Oh, Kathryn, you'll think I'm so silly to keep saying this, but he was handsome. Every man I ran up against in those days seemed to me handsome. Even though Hochmann was over sixty by then, he was tall and broad, with hair left long like a musician's and tremendous big features— a wonderfully sensual, imperious mouth—and still very Germanic, very solemn, very hard to understand. Both his English, and what he was saying with it. He hadn't come here until he was fifty, and then to the West Coast. He was a missionary, bringing the gospel of modernism to an art scene that, of course, was very much American Wave— Benton's farmhands in the style of El Greco, Grant Wood and Rockwell Kent and that mock-epic stylization. Mural style for the Common Man. Hooray for democracy. Some of it, John Steuart Curry, the Soyer brothers, doesn't look so terrible now, it's become art history, but at the time we *despised* it. The thing about Hochmann was, a lot of people were vaguely talking about abstraction as the only ethical way to paint, but he offered a concrete prescription. He said astonishing things—astonishing to me, at least. He said when you put a single line on a piece of paper there is no telling what its direction is. But if you put a shorter line under it, the longer line *moves*, and the shorter one goes in the opposite direction. He said the piece of paper had now become a universe, in motion. He said the edges of paper became lines, too. And—this must have been Hegel, or Kant, thesis and antithesis and whatever—that when there was a third thing, as in music when two notes combine to make a third sound, this third thing was spiritual, non-physical, surreal. This was magic, he felt. The two lines

: 35 :

moving in different directions had tension between them, and that made them a living thing, what he called 'a living unit.' With color it got more complicated. Color, he said, made us feel certain ways—buoyant, depressed. Some colors receded, others came forward. He kept talking about 'push and pull.' *Poo-oosh und pool.*"

Hochmann's ponderous slow English, like concrete dripping in clumps inside a turning mixer, the handsome big face vulnerably lit by his daily hope of communicating to the students the spiritual depth of paint, the students in their dirty smocks, salmon or oatmeal in color, white socks and penny loafers and saddle shoes peeking out below, the boys leaning against the smirched hallway walls smoking, the girls in stiff 'forties imitations of Hollywood hair as it was then, pageboys, bangs, stiff waves done with those long-nosed curling irons, you plugged them in and they opened like birds' beaks, all those listening young heads buzzing with hopes, with frayed connections to the past and future, the streets outside brown and gray and jostling in her mind's eye like village rows in a Chagall or a Kirchner, even the spires in distant midtown—the Chrysler Building, the Empire State—caught up in the soot, the toxic war clouds, while Hochmann strove to impart his saving message: "*Begrenzung.* What do you say in English? Limitation. The canvas is a limitation. Without consciousness of limitation there can be no expression of the Infinite. *Unendlichkeit. Ewigkeit.* Beethoven creates Eternity in the physical limitation of the symphony. Any limitation can be subdivided infinitely. This involves the problem of time and relativity. A single star seen alone in space tells us nothing about space. Space must be vital and active. The space on the canvas must have a life of the spirit, the life of a creative mind. Pictorial space exists two-dimensionally, only. When the two-dimensionality of a picture is violated, it falls, how do you say, into parts—it creates an effect of naturalistic space, a special case, a portion of three-dimensionality, and this is an incomplete expression of the artist's experience. Thus it is inadequate. The layman has difficulty in comprehending that plastic creation on a flat surface must not destroy this flat surface. Depth is created by a recession of apparent objects toward a vanishing point, as in Renaissance perspective, but in absolute denial of this doctrine by the creation of surface forces in the sense of *push and pull*. Nor should one try to create depth by the use of tonal gradation, any more than one should create depth by carving a hole in the picture. To create the phenomenon of *push and pull* on a flat surface, one has to understand that by nature the picture plane reacts automatically in the opposite direction to the stimulus received, as long as it receives stimulus in the creative process. The function of *push and pull* in respect to form contains the secret of Michelangelo's monumentality. Cézanne understood color as a force of *push and pull*, and in his pictures he created an enormous sense of volume, breathing, pulsating, expanding, contracting through his use of color. Color is a plastic means of creating, ah, *Abstände*. Intervals. Intervals are color harmonics produced by special relationships, or tensions. The whole world comes to us, as we experience it, through the mystic realm of color. Our entire being is nourished by it. The mystic quality of color should likewise find expression in a work of art. The life-giving zeal in a work of art is deeply embedded in its qualitative substance. The *Geist*, the spirit, in a work is synonymous with its quality. The Real in art never dies, because its nature is predominantly *geistig*, spiritual." On and on he would preach, pausing where a German word, a

Kantian concept, occurred to him first and had to be painfully, inaccurately translated.

"Still," Hope tells Kathryn, "he had us believing that to make art was the highest and purest of human activities, the closest approach to God, the God who creates Himself in this push and pull of colors."

Yet his lecturing, his handsome, fervent, weighty presence, had a hollow side. He did not let students see his own work. He was shy, the enterprise was so great, the Ideal was so stern a taskmaster. As he aged, and others reaped the glory he had foretold, his own work went oddly dead in its cradle of theory: squares and rectangles of raw color looking like manufacturers' samples, without push or pull. At the time of his teaching her, his forms were still organic, bulbous and swooping like early Kandinsky but without that Russian wandering, those wandering drifts of brushwork, all the colors at once, like peasant decoration. "Flat, flat," Hochmann would say over her shoulder. "Keep the picture plane *flat*. You're losing the plane. You're growing *holes*. Make the colors," he would say, "sing." Sing like Beethoven, those shimmering doom-laden chords impossible to do in paint, in palette-knifed rectangles. In the late 'sixties, after his death, Hope went to a giant Hochmann retrospective, a whole floor of the Whitney, and the paintings around her didn't exist. They had evaporated, they had become walls of dust-catchers. Zack had not evaporated like that, though Hochmann had looked down on him, as an American ruffian, an out-of-control ignoramus. As Ruk would have said, a bandit.

"Push and pull," Kathryn repeats in polite bemusement. "Did you feel, ah, close to him as a man?"

"Did we sleep together, do you mean? Please. He was over sixty, I was—what, twenty-two? Yet you're right, I would have if he had asked; I loved him. He made us see what a noble calling painting was. Someone of your generation probably can't believe how crucial, how important, how *huge* painting seemed then. It was like sex, yes, you're right to suggest that. It hadn't been domesticated yet. It hadn't been put in its place, its page of the Living section, with a pat on its little fuzzy head."

Her companion snorts, so vigorously that a liquid snuffle emerges in follow-up from the long white nose. Kathryn peers down and fishes in her black pocketbook, almost as big as a tote bag, which sits gaping at the side of the plaid chair, for a Kleenex. Hope likes her the better for this embarrassment. Snot is human, one of our secretions. She likes Kathryn less for being too ready to laugh, for finding this old lady being interviewed too amusing, a husk of a person in which any rustle of sauciness or pert phrasing is a comic surprise. Such readiness to laugh betrays a nervous jealousy. Hope had been alive in a naïve, blunt, fruitful way this young woman is being denied; Hope had loved herself, having been raised in the illusion of a loving God; she had found the facts of her body amazing, as they emerged from beneath the quilts and the Quaker silence concerning such matters. She would stroke her own naked, silken skin, leaving yellowish ovals of fingertip impression on her freckled pink surface, standing fresh-bathed before the cloudy spotted mirrors of the apartment on Jones Street she shared with Cindy Jasinski, the roach-ridden, cramped bathroom floored in tiny hexagonal tiles, its narrow window left open an inch or two like a mouth breathing the Village's air with its morning smells of coffee and emptied garbage cans and its night sounds of jazz and taxis honking. Each new day, she wondered what marvel might befall her. Kathryn's world is marvel-proof, pre-processed, all emotions and impulses analyzed and denigrated before they can blossom, chopped up into how-to books and television, everything reduced to electronic impulses, bits, information, information increasingly meaningless as brains shrink too small to gather it in, the processing all done outside the mind, the heart, by cool and noiseless machines. Kathryn's nostrils do look a little pink as she pokes the balled handkerchief back into her big black purse. She has the sickliness of the city: the subways, the elevators, other people's breaths, forever running tired, New York people have colds all winter long, Hope did too, when the children were bringing home germs from school, but, living alone in Vermont, in the antiseptic crackling cold, the mountain air rich in ultraviolet rays, she almost never has so much as a sniffle, her old system a hoard of antibodies on the far side of fertility and its chemical storms. Kathryn has brought into this chaste parlor the stains, the imbalance, of fecundity—the monthly egg flushed away, the hysteria of entanglement with males. It is good, Hope tells herself, to be beyond all that.

It is that time of morning, toward eleven, when the sun in its overhead slant outside triggers a thought of relief, of enough momentarily done, and her custom is to make herself a second cup of tea, with the used bag, carefully saved in the stainless-steel sink, sitting upright like a tiny black-brown handbag beside the round drain. Her first run of concentration would have slowed down and blurred since breakfast, and the re-used bag would fuel a second go, an attempt to squeeze some further good out of herself before noon joined her with humanity in the gross chores of daily maintenance, of shopping and tidying and tugging by telephone on the few threads left in her life, many of them tied to medical specialists. Her dentist keeps telling her her teeth, the few front ones still lacking root canals and

crowns, would be much brighter without that daily drench-
ing in tea, but always there is, each morning, a hump of
anxiety for the first cup to lift her over, and then, with the
paler second an hour or two later, she can contemplate her
still-wet work with the dazed self-adoration that so strangely
alternates with her certainty that nothing she does is good
enough or amounts, really, to anything. She is often seized
by a dread that she has wasted her life up to now, a dread, at
bottom, that she has displeased God, who is not there, or is
there only in the form of light, which she rationally understands as a senseless rain of photons, a universe of particles
that once upon a time burst into being for absolutely no
reason. But she has a long life behind her that can't be taken
away, five grandchildren with some facet of herself embedded in them, works on display at the Hirschhorn and the
Whitney, in Tokyo and Zurich and São Paulo, and a filing
drawer full of reviews that are some of them very flattering,
even adoring. Poor Zack had none of that, going out to the
little barn, its loose and gappy boards leaking heat as fast as
the woodstove could produce it, those first winters on the
Island, for the single hour before the cold got hopelessly to
his hands in the rough work-gloves he had cut the fingertips off of; he had only this desperate creative drive, this
appetite for something even beyond fame and wealth, as
blind as a sick animal's instinct to seek privacy beneath
the porch. He drank less in those years—he saw how she
responded to his sobriety and still wanted to please her—
but his smoker's hack would take hours in the morning to
clear.

Hope confides to this girl, to keep her off-guard, "You
do understand that to have a real artistic advance there
must be not only individual stout hearts but also a certain
widespread—how can I say?—*rottenness* in things that only

an initiated few suspect. It's this nose for the rotten, I sometimes think, that takes the sensitivity, and the courage." She would get dread in her stomach before each of Hochmann's classes, too—before her mind lost itself in the paint, in that druglike rapture of self-forgetfulness when things began to happen on the canvas, *in* the painting, Zack used to say. The push and the pull. Since Kathryn, lurching forward in the chair to inspect her tape recorder, gives no sign of having heard this abruptly issued oracle, Hope asks her, more kindly, "Would you like a cup of tea if I made it?"

Kathryn casts an annoyed eye at the little gray machine purring on the refinished sea-chest with its rows of brass nailheads. "Could we keep going," the younger woman insists, "until the tape runs out? Would you like to tell me how you remember meeting Zack?"

Feeling pushed, feeling the other woman has been deaf to the subtlety of what she has said, letting the little machine listen for her, Hope says, modelling attentiveness, "I *like* the way you put that. How one remembers slowly replaces what really was. Like fossils." She thinks she is unclear, and amplifies, "The same way that mineral particles fill in the shape where a body has rotted away—a kind of lost-wax casting process, as I understand it. Zack," she restates, nettled to think that the girl will see her as an old fool wasting precious tape. "As I remember it, it was at one of the Saturday dances at the Artists Union loft at Sixteenth Street and Sixth Avenue. This drunken man grabbed me and asked me if I wanted to fuck, that was his word, considered quite rude in those days, even among so-called bohemians. Pretending to dance, he pushed his body against mine to show me he had an erection, and I slapped his face. It seemed to wake him up, because he became suddenly very polite, like a little boy. He kept begging my pardon, and I couldn't get away from him. He was too drunk to remember me afterward, but I remembered *him*, and would see him at the Cedar Tavern, where Ruk used to take me before he suddenly deserted New York and joined his family in Minneapolis, where they had somehow landed on their feet. Or their boots. Their White-Russian boots. Did I tell you I never understood how his family got their money out of Russia? I mean, that yellow Lincoln cost somebody a bundle. Jewels, I supposed, sewed into their girdles. You know about the Cedar, I'm sure—it was a perfectly plain bar, painted one dismal shade of green inside, and looked from the outside just like a dozen other bars along University Place, but the painters took to it for some reason, or because there was absolutely no art on the walls, or because the management had made the decision to put up with temperamental artists. They would gather in the back, in the dark leatherette booths there, and argue about art."

"Who, exactly?"

"It varied. The ones who liked to argue best, who were best at it, were Bernie Nova and Roger Merebien. And Mahlon Strunk, though he had a slower tongue and seemed older, it may have been more that he was getting some serious attention from the critics and galleries while the rest were still pretty much ignored. Mahlon was the one who took the Surrealist theories most seriously, even though he was from way upstate and very quiet and down-to-earth and *married*, which was a little surreal in itself. He and his wife, Myrtle, walked around in the Village like a working-class couple on a Sunday stroll, in matching gray overcoats. He always carried an umbrella, that's the kind of cautious person he was, but he believed in automatism. Masson was in this country by then, and had an exhibition at the Buchholz

Gallery, and he was the Surrealist we could take seriously, as opposed to Dalí, who as I say was technically everything we despised, though after Photorealism I wonder now why we all felt so superior. He was such a different kind of Spaniard from Picasso might have been the problem, though both were showmen, in their ways. I'm sorry, this isn't the kind of thing you want, is it?"

"I want anything you can give me. It all helps make a picture."

"It's so hard, to remember honestly. After over fifty years, nearly sixty. Mahlon was quite nice to Zack, I remember that, and of course the idea that by letting accidents happen on the canvas you could let your subconscious speak was appealing to Zack, who was so messy anyway. Even in the 'thirties, he would draw right on the canvas with the tube. And go over and over a painting till its original image was totally covered up. We were poor but didn't scrimp on paint. We weren't so much interested in the craft or the finished product as in what the painting did for the painter. That was the thing, back then, that everybody talked about—getting the *self* out, getting it on canvas. That was why abstraction was so glamorous, it was all *self*. I know it must all seem very naïve to your generation, who don't believe in the self, who think the self is just a social construct, just as you don't believe there are writers, just texts that write themselves and can mean anything." Feeling guilty over her resistant, counter-transferential feelings toward her interviewer, Hope does try to cast her mind back, into that opaque murk of the past.

In the dim back area of the leatherette booths, Roger Merebien's puffy round face, younger than his years, seemed a white moon, glazed with sweat, insisting on itself in the haze of cigarette smoke and beer vapors. "The so-called 'aesthetic,' " he stated in his rather high, affected voice, honed on years of education, Stanford and Columbia and with some English vowels picked up from a post-grad year in Oxford, concentrating not in art but in philosophy, back to the Greeks, back to ontology, "is merely the sensuous aspect of the world—it is not the end of art but a means, a means for getting at, let's call it, the infinite background of feeling in order to condense it into an object of perception. These objects of perception are basically relational structures, which obliterate the need for representation. The impulse from the unconscious, the automatistic moment, is only a moment, a way to get the painting mind going— probing, finding, completing. Collage is another way of enlisting the random, but how the scraps are manipulated depends on *feeling*, and here an infinite subtlety enters in, a really quite *breath*taking"—his round head seemed to rotate on its neck like a lighthouse beam, as if he dared objection to this girlish word—"play of body-mind trying to free itself from mechanical social responses, and in this becoming essentially moral, in subverting and even over-throwing an established American social order which is inhuman in its drives and responses. Our own Fascism, you could say."

"Exactly!" Bernie Nova pounced. "Regionalism is Fascist painting; it appeals to the same *Lumpen*, it labels everything else degenerate, just like Nazism it caters to injured pride and a warped national ego. It hates the French, it hates the immigrants, it's rural America—the pitchfork, the fat cat-tle, the cotton fields, the Okie in his jalopy, the good simple straight-standing farm folk, good Christ, the tidy rows of corn, the tornado lowering on the horizon—rural America in all its anti-Negro, anti-Jew, anti-city isolationism. The war, bless it, has swept isolationism away; ditto American

Scene, though its cartoon populism makes good war propaganda. And good leftist propaganda, too."

"Not propaganda, expression," mildly objected Mahlon Strunk, who for all his stodgy appearance was a doctrinaire Socialist. "What the Urban Scenists said was there, was there. Poverty, crowding, tenements. Give them that, Bernie."

Several painters began to object, to be sardonic, but Bernie's staccato voice, a Bronx native's undrownable-out voice, cut through them; settling his monocle in place with a lifted eyebrow, and switching his mustache back and forth with a sideways pursing of his lips, he continued haughtily, "Pittsburgh factories, breadlines, long-legged coons loping along A Hundred Twenty-fifth Street—face it, it's all cheap genre painting, Benton and Grant Wood with their bib overalls off. American art has become a picture-postcard factory. Every nation has its commercial artists," he stated resolutely, seeing that others wished to speak, "but not even the Nazis claim to have made art history with them. Americana doesn't make good American painting; the American project," he said, removing his monocle and gesturing with this disembodied emblem of vision, "is to create the conditions out of which great painters—great minds, great *seers*—can emerge. It is time artists refused easy success, refused isolationist-philistine money, repudiated the art dealers and museum directors; it is time we forgot about success."

This was proclaimed, the last phrases with the drumbeat sonority of President Roosevelt's high-toned broadcasts, to a group that had known little success. Their paintings—weak, coarse, modest-sized echoes of Miró and Mondrian, with a muddy impasto borrowed from the Mexican muralists—

held yet only the wish for revolutionary action, not the achievement. Jarl Anders, gaunt and pasty, a Minnesota preacher's child, a humorless shaman, cried out, hoarse with wrath, in the Cedar Tavern of Hope's recollection, "Swill! Ever since the Armory Show, synthetic tradition and unredeemable corruption! The Armory Show was swill, the spoiled fruit of Western European decadence, dumped on the American yokels with all its labyrinthine evasions, and it's been total confusion ever since. No shouting about individualism, no manipulation of academic conceits or technical fetishes can truly liberate. No literary games and idiotic automatism, no Bauhaus sterilities, no pseudo-religious titles, no obscene toadying to the smooth-tongued agents of social control can rise as high as even the toenail of the sublime."

"My goodness," Myrtle Strunk had to exclaim, sitting wedged against her husband. " 'The toenail of the sublime'— Jarl, how high would you say you have risen? The ankle? The kneecap?"

"You mean to mock," he stated, his torso as rigid as the dark near-abstract shaman-figures prominent in his work, "but I will repay your discourtesy with an honest answer. Since 1941—I date the year precisely, as more momentous than any puffed-up events at Pearl Harbor—space and the figure in my canvases have been resolved into a total psychic entity, freeing me from the limitations of each, yet fusing into an instrument bounded only by the limits of my energy and intuition. My feeling of freedom is now absolute and infinitely exhilarating. A *single stroke of paint*, my mocking Myrtle, a single stroke backed by a mind that understands its potency and implications, can restore to man the freedom lost in twenty centuries of apology and pictorial devices for subjugation. Imagination, no longer fettered by the laws of fear, becomes as one with Vision. The Act, intrinsic and absolute, becomes its meaning and the bearer of its passion."

Anders' vatic rapture roused a murmur, and then a clatter, of earthier commentary, including drink orders to the waiter, but all were, Hope felt in the rosy flush of her youth, touched, like a crowd of doubtful churchgoers, by the possibility of any such absolute. Bernie, quick-tongued, a dapper big tout in his suit of small black-and-red checks, cut in, "Roight. The recognizable image—dead. Sensation, plasticity—dead. Beauty is dead: Impressionism began to kill it, the rediscovery of primitive and archaic art finished it off. Beauty and comedy belong to the same Christian lie. Nietzsche said it: 'Truth is ugly.' He said, 'We possess art lest we perish of the truth.' The only virtue left in this day and age is courage before the hopeless. The only art is one whose symbols will catch the fundamental truth of life, its tragedy. Primitive art is magical because it is shaped by terror. Modern man has his own terror, and we—"

Strunk objected: "There's more than that, Bernie. There is, as Roger said, everything we feel, including joy. There is a realm within; painting draws it out of us. Our self discovers its laws in what Jarl called the Act."

Bernie snapped, "Self—a rag doll, a fetish. The painter's feelings, personality—who cares? Your Surrealist friends are French playboys, playing with Freud, who was playful enough. Who says that being asleep is more profound than being awake? Dreams are a muddle—brain-slime. What matters is not the psyche but metaphysics. Penetration into the world mystery; for this the painter's mind should be as pure as the scientist's and the philosopher's. I call the process *plasmic:* the purpose of abstract art is to convert color and shape into mental plasma."

"My God, what pseudo-European swill," Jarl Anders protested.

Bernie Nova persisted: "The canvas enlists the viewer in sympathetic participation with the artist's thought. It expresses the mind foremost, and whatever is still sensuous is secondary, an incidental accident. Truth before pleasure."

Roger Merebien's luminous round head emerged from a huddle with his bushy-haired girl of the evening. Flutingly his overcultivated voice announced, "I find I ask of the painting process one of two separate experiences. I call one 'the mode of discovery and invention,' the other 'the mode of joy and variation.' The first embodies my deepest problem, the bitterest struggle, to reject everything I do not feel and believe. The other is when I want to paint for the sheer joy of it. The strain of dealing with the unknown—the absolute—is gone. When I need joy, I find it making free variations on what I have already discovered, what I know to be mine."

"Just watch it," warned Bernie, "you don't get decorative."

The worst word they could bestow was "decorative." Zack so dreaded being decorative that he threw dirt and broken glass into his wet canvases; he walked on them in his filthy shoes.

Phil Kaline, a millworker's son from Detroit who had yet to discover his signature, big paintings in black and white, offered, "Come on, you turds, it's not about *knowing*, it's about *giving*. When you're done giving, the canvas surprises you as much as anybody. For me, it's free association from start to finish; it's procedure that leaves a result finally. Sometimes I make preliminary drawings, but the painting tends to destroy them. Paint never seems to behave the same. It doesn't dry the same. It doesn't stay there and look at you the same."

It hardens, Hope thought. None of this would be important if paint didn't harden.

One painter was conspicuous by his silence. His eyes darted from face to face, tawny slitted eyes the raw sienna of dead grass in blond-lashed lids rubbed pinker and pinker as the beers or whiskeys accumulated within him. At times Hope saw him take in breath, or tense his lips as if to speak, but nothing came out, and an affecting look of congestion knotted his face, his forehead. His face had more muscles in it than most. His forehead knotted easily into ridges, and circles of muscle formed dimples beside the creases at the corners of his pensive mouth and in the center of his chin. His head sank a little lower into his shoulders when his numb-looking lips moved forward to engulf a cigarette; he hunched at each puff. He was not old, though older than she by ten years, she guessed. His fairish hair was thin on top and his scalp was tan, and he wore a white T-shirt beneath a scuffed leather jacket which he had taken off, so this image of hers must attach to warm weather, the summer of 1944, when, after D-day, eight-column headlines followed the advance of the invasion and every day brought its hundreds of American deaths. As she had said to Kathryn, it was strange that while all this slaughter was going on and cathedrals and palaces were being bombed they could have been so blithe, so autocratic, so oblivious in their pontifications about the redemptive mission of paint, but so it was: the duty of the living was to live, and the brave and valid part of their lives was painting. At this time she was working through the benign but ponderous influence of Hochmann by doing collages and Oriental-looking black brushwork

like Merebien, who reworked his few images—a rectangular doorway, a row of black ovals like giant beans squeezed
in a pod—in a mood of joy and variation, and whose round
bland face was sweating amiably in their midst yet on its
long child-thin neck also floating above them, willing to be
their leader, their theorist. If Hope had ever been attracted
to intelligence she would have been attracted to Merebien.
But her own father had shown her the limitations of refine-
ment, of well-bred intelligence.

She is not eager to share Zack with Kathryn. She has
already shared him with so many inquirers, with the multi-
tude that still look to art to save them. She suppresses her
recollection of this night, compounded of many such talky
nights, at the Cedar or at Stewart's Cafeteria or the Waldorf on Sixth Avenue off Eighth Street, at the San Remo or
Romany Marie's on Grove Street, Ratner's on Delancey or
the Jumble Shop at Eighth and MacDougal Streets, nights
wherein Zack's face seemed to yearn toward hers in its
bleary puzzlement, which seemed more and more her con-
cern, his face aimed at her and lodged within her inner
gallery. "Self," she repeats, and tells the other woman, "But
we—they—didn't just shout theory at each other; really,
that was rare. What did Matisse say, 'Artists should have
their tongues cut out'? Mostly, everybody was burrowing
away in their own studio, jealous of everybody else's imagined successes. When we got together it was to drink and
have fun. The Artists Union had dances every Saturday,
and I remember going to one of them—a Christmas costume ball, after Ruk had cut out of town, me and this
other girl, Cindy Jasinski, I was rooming with on Jones
Street—as Hottentots, it would be considered too racist to
do now but then there seemed no harm in it, we went as
Hottentots, covered in grease and coal dust and big glass

beads and not much else, our hair up in knots with a pretend dog-bone from the pet shop through them, and I felt
pretty good about myself—I had a nice tidy little figure
then, nothing big or floppy, so I could have been wearing a
leotard—until, late in the evening, I looked down and realized all the men dancing with me had rubbed my coal dust
off and I was just about naked in the front, except for this
little lavender G-string Cindy had produced from the time
when she was doing burlesque in Jersey City to support a
boyfriend in law school!"

Kathryn blinks. She senses that this image, of Hope nude
but for coal dust, is meant to tease her, to taunt her. With a
brisk distaste she glances down again into the notes on her
lap. "You told *Artforum* in the 'sixties," she said, "that if you
had known how much trouble Zack was going to be—"

Hope can't let her young self clothed in coal dust and
grease and blacking in her hair go. She can still feel the cool
air of that upstairs loft washing across her front when she
and her partner parted, whoever he had been, dead now no
doubt like all the other witnesses of her youth, dead like
all who had held her at those sweaty dances in the 'forties,
the war outside the windows, beyond the fire escapes, darkening the city in which civilian life yowled on like a party of
backyard cats. "Of course it was no big deal, nudity, a lot of
us modelled, at least for each other." She realizes she has
fallen a question behind. Something about Zack and trouble. She says, "Anybody could see at a glance how much
trouble he was going to be. He would sit there not saying a
word, as if he didn't know the English language, then he
would have drunk enough to get his courage up and start
shouting 'Fuck you' at everybody, things like 'You're all
pretentious shits' and 'Some day all that matters about you
will be that you got close enough to me to kiss my hairy ass'

and then mumble and stumble off and go pee in the corner or Peggy's marble fireplace or anywhere. Zack did a lot of peeing, as anybody who drank like that would, of course. But he did more of it in public than necessary. It was like he was saying, 'I'm not that good with this thing in bed but I sure can pee.' "

"Peggy Guggenheim?" Kathryn's voice grew an anxious little tip when a name came along, a scandalous famous old name, it was rather disappointing to Hope, this susceptibility to celebrity. She would have preferred for Kathryn more of the *je-m'en-foutisme* she imagined for herself at this tender age. Before she possessed it, Hope considered celebrity vulgar, and an affront to the proletariat, whose anonymous dictatorship was coming, once the war cleared the air of plutocrats and princes. Would the air also be cleared of movie stars? They were what the proletariat seemed to care about; they hung over the war-darkened nation like silvery blimps.

"I think so. I forget whose marble fireplace, there was certainly more than one Zack peed in. He was pathetic when he was drunk. He had no gift for alcohol, not like Ruk, who was always aware, always civil. Zack reverted to infancy, this drastic insecurity and megalomania, burbling, showing his penis, doing whatever it took to make himself the center of attention, punching somebody. He liked upsetting a table with all the food on it. He did that to me more than once." The Thanksgiving feast with his family from California; the gallery party after the *Life* article had come out and celebrity had turned him ugly: the incessant ornate humiliations of those last Long Island years, all her attempts to make a decent home overturned and rebelled against, have unexpectedly affected Hope's eyes. Old age does that: senility of the ducts. As a young woman she took pride in never crying, no matter how stung or insulted—in not giving the evil, creaturely, colorful world the satisfaction.

Kathryn's voice softens, retracts its hard tip, becomes almost idle in its helpful prompting: "It was Herbert Forrest who kept bringing Zack to Peggy's attention. She didn't like his work for the longest time."

"She *never* liked it, really. Poor dear Herbert, yes, I think he loved Zack, much the way I did. Except he also liked those muddy Picassoesque 'forties paintings of Zack's, all those scribbled Jungian symbols. I didn't. Herbie was a miserable person, poor soul—overweight, queer, terribly epileptic, which he tried to hide, but he had the training, he had been to Paris, he had the eye to see the genius in Zack. He called him a genius from the outset. For me in my ignorance there was too much groping and searching in Zack, not enough finding. Zack couldn't draw really, as I was saying, and until he began to use industrial paints right out of the hardware store his color was dismal, I thought. But what did I know? I was timid and tidy; I hated to dirty a clean canvas, the first strokes that Hochmann said were so important. No, it wasn't Zack's painting I was attracted to, it repelled me actually, it was Zack himself, his body, his face. He was beautiful, and it was a beauty that, unlike Ruk's, took some creativity to discover. You'll think I thought all men were beautiful, I was your usual de-repressed ex-Quaker hotpants, but no . . . it was Zack. Something about the *knit* of his face, and its color; he had skin, Western skin I thought of it as, leathery-soft, it didn't wrinkle, it *creased*, and he kept a sallow sort of tan through the winter, and in summer he never used lotion; his face had these lovely low-relief episodes of muscle, even in his forehead, the two diagonal high places up from the deep creases where his eyebrows frowned in, he was always frowning; as his hair thinned more and more, he looked less and less as if he had *ever* had hair, it was the most natural and becoming baldness I ever saw. When I was shown snapshots of him with this blond mop from boyhood I felt a kind of disgust. His dimples are always mentioned in descriptions of him, but there was something in the *planes*, a kind of perfectly symmetrical push-and-pull that may have been what Hochmann was always talking about. And perfect ears—look at the photographs, they're rather amazing, big but perfect, without lobes. And the rest of him—we never talked about men's 'bums' back then, but his was tight and quite lovely, he couldn't see it so he was un-self-conscious about it, the two buttocks tight against each other with this fuzzy innocence—he had a lot of body hair but it was pale hair—and the legs looked almost bowed out, the calf muscles were so rounded, he was always telling people he had been a cowboy and it was a lie but his body looked it. You can't do a beautiful person item by item, there's the unity, there was a *swing* to his body, a *thrust* I guess we can say without getting too Freudian, that used to take my breath away when he wasn't aware I was looking at him. You know those male bodies they used to do in murals, like in Rockefeller Center, not the ones bringing the electric light bulb or whatever but the workers operating the capitalist machinery or hauling bales of cotton up from the docks? Zack had that kind of body, but because he never did exercise if he could help it there was nothing preening about him. It would have violated his sense of manhood to be pleased with his own body. His art was strangled by self-consciousness, before it got great suddenly, but his body just always happened to have this grace. Except, come to think of it, he couldn't dance. He just couldn't match his steps to yours, or let you match his."

She feels emanating from Kathryn an opinion that this is enough on the subject, but Hope continues with a superior insistence, "He was trouble, yes, but, dear, *life* is trouble. Bernie used to say that life disturbs matter's unconscious mineral calm, that's why we have a death wish." To bring herself back within the bounds of an interview, Hope tells the young woman, offhandedly, "I've been trying to remember the year of that dance when I went as a Hottentot, the New Year might have been 1944, but the mood, the temperature of the war outside feels more like '45; we were no longer so afraid, the end, in Europe at least, was in sight, though people forget how grim that drive toward Germany was, it still didn't seem impossible that Hitler would roll us back into the Channel. Hitler *did* the impossible. He was surreal; he was the bogey who had escaped the collective subconscious and found a country to run. The Germans followed all his orders, however mad, right down to the Berlin bunker; it all seems quite unbelievable now. Meanwhile, we had this aristocratic cripple to lead us, and Britain an old brandy-soak. Stalin, it turned out, was better at killing Russians than even Hitler was. It was the biggest, baddest fairy tale the world had ever seen, the kind of carnival that has those giant papier-mâché heads."

Kathryn, perhaps stupid after all, seems tensely intent on nailing down a point she can use: "Did I understand you to say you didn't think Zack had a future as a painter?"

Hope searches for a way to avoid giving her satisfaction. "It's hard enough to remember what you did, let alone what you felt. I wanted to like him as an artist because I came to like him as a person. He did have his champions, like poor

Herbie, and in '43, before I got involved with him really, he was in this show at Peggy's Art of This Century—who could have dreamed then that This Century could someday become That Century?—and he got the famous nod from Mondrian—though there may have been some politics behind it, it turns out, there was another artist in the show who had helped Mondrian escape from Paris, and that's why Mondrian came to the show at all, he wasn't well, he died the next year—but I was really impressed less by Zack's work than the dogged way he kept at it, against all these odds. Still, he was losing heart, his binges were getting worse, he would be gone for two or three nights, if I was to keep on with him we had to get out of the city."

"Is it true he insisted on a church wedding?"

"I had insisted we get married, it was one thing to live in sin with a man in the city and another to do it in rural Long Island in 1945. I would have been happy with City Hall, my snotty family had pretty much given up on me, my younger brother's being killed in the war had left them just shadows of their disapproving old selves, but, yes, it was Zack who insisted on a minister, I thought he did it mainly to make it so difficult I would give up, but Myrtle Strunk and I found this little old Congregationalist preacher in a musty sad church down beyond Bleecker who didn't terribly mind that I had never been baptized—Quakers don't do it, you know—and Zack couldn't say if he had or hadn't, his religious upbringing had been so end-of-the-world, off and on. The minister kept smiling all the time, like a demented person—his face had absolutely no color, you felt his whole life had been lived under this rock of lower Manhattan—and with Myrtle and Herbie there as our witnesses gave an oddly lovely short sermon telling us about marriage, and Creation, and how beautiful, now that the war was ended, all our lives were going to be. The only thing he asked from us was that I wear a hat and Zack a jacket and tie, so, luckily, I still had my hatboxes, with the rest of my blue luggage, in a closet behind all my dried student paintings. What *I* asked of Zack was that he stay sober, and he did. He took it seriously. It's hard to say what he believed, but he definitely did *not* believe in nothing; he had been to a number of shrinks about his drinking, and they had all been Jungian. It tied in with his painting, of course, the archetypes, the magic of symbols, the unearthing of the deepest self. What it didn't do, for very long ever, was cure his drinking. So, yes, in answer to your question, it was a church wedding. A wistful little linen-white interior with box pews and tall clear lozenge-pane windows, one side blocked from the light by an adjacent building, like Sainte-Chapelle, and high above the altar a circular stained-glass window of Jesus with a lamb. Jesus in a grape-colored cloak and an ecru lamb. Oh my, my mouth is dry and my head feels light from too much talking. *Much* too much. I *am* going to make a cup of tea now. Please, could I make one for you too?"

Kathryn leans forward to frown at her tape recorder and reluctantly switches it off. "I'd prefer coffee if you had it," she says, perhaps she doesn't realize how ungraciously.

"Coffee. I gave it up so long ago—they said doing that would lower my blood pressure and prolong my life, and I suppose it has—that I have no coffeepot. Or grounds. There may be some instant in one of the cabinets, if you could look for me in the upper shelves; you're taller than I."

But when the two women stand together Kathryn even in her boots seems not incommensurately taller; her eyes come to the top of Hope's head. She surrenders: "Tea would be fine. I've never been a fan of instant. These percolators they have now with clocks you can set for the next morning spoil you, I guess."

"It's Taster's Choice," offers Hope, feeling sorry for the little red-labelled jar gathering dust somewhere at the back of a shelf that she hasn't gotten out the kitchen stool to look into for years. Her hand remembers how the jar had a subtle, friendly waist, to make holding and tipping it easier.

"No, really, tea would be nice. My mother used to give me tea, half milk and half tea, when I was sick."

"Good," Hope says, "if you mean that." She pushes up from the rocker and takes her first steps carefully, in case her knees have stiffened or a foot has fallen asleep. The rag rug has tripped her more than once, hurrying to answer the front doorbell, which nobody who knows her or the house ever uses, or getting to her feet after losing herself in a book in the plaid chair, a good sleepy-making mystery or international thriller written by the child of some old friend; imagine being young and believing the world is such a conspiracy. On one occasion not so many years ago she sprawled right onto the floor, its black-red sheen swimming under her eyes as she mentally checked her body for the signal, first dull and then frantically pulsing, of a broken bone. She knew the sensations because she had broken her tibia skiing in the Poconos when she was sixteen, the bindings had scarcely any release then, the tows were merely rope tows and single metal chairs, icy-cold right through the ski pants and the woolen long johns, it was all very uncomfortable but boys did it and so you had to.

"I'll heat up water in a pot, since there are two of us. When I'm by myself I just microwave a mug, though the heat in the water for some reason doesn't last as long. The way it agitates the molecules, I suppose." One of the reasons Hope doesn't like talking to young people is her fear of being stupid about all the new technology that has come along—not since she was a girl, but since about 1980. The VCR was a dividing line; until then, it was *her* technology, and she could handle it, but she never has been able to program a VCR, even with reading glasses on.

Now that she is standing upright, her voice sounds as if it originates, crackling and indistinct, some distance from her head, like one of those little radios that used to be everywhere, playing daytime serials in shops and dentists' offices and front desks at dry cleaners, before people had cell phones and television sets to make themselves feel connected. When she goes into Montpelier now, she is astonished by how everybody has cell phones, even the schoolchildren walking along with their knapsacks on their backs, and in summer there are all these earnest girl hikers in very short shorts clutching in one hand a cell phone and in the other a bottle of water, suddenly everybody in the new millennium has to have a private bottle of water. There do seem to be fewer and fewer public drinking fountains, they used to be everywhere, that had been one of the great things about America, you could always get a free drink of water. Behind her grandfather's house, near the giant droopy-limbed hemlock, down some slippery boards, there had been an open spring lined with mossy stones, and a tin dipper for anyone to use, even someone off the street if they cared to venture in on the brick walk alongside the house. Strangers might be angels, was the old superstition.

The way to the kitchen leads around a table with an old-fashioned black dial phone on it and beside it a cane-seated ladderback chair in case the conversation is so long and important Hope needs to sit down, which ever fewer of them are, and down a short hall past the narrow and steep back stairs on one side and on the other the back door and its storm door. Through the double glass—nine six-by-nine panes, both doors, though they don't quite line up—the outdoors calls to her, bright and bleak and still wintry, pieces of snow visible in the woods like scattered laundry, the side lawn beneath the feeder gray with sunflower husks the birds or the squirrels have spilled. The beech tree from whose lowest limb the feeder hangs seems, at a quick glance that flashes through her eyes upon a brain still displaced by its effort to remember the past, a photograph of a silvery explosion, monstrous, multiform, spraying outward like a Richard Lippold construction, the beech's narrow white-tipped leaf buds still tightly sheathed but taking on a ruddy, sappy tan. And the woods beyond have a russet tinge where the maples cluster, and the bleached lawn shows in bare spots, a dark gleam of thawing earth though mud season is not quite here, in this part of Vermont. The lawn still looks hard enough to walk on. Hope imagines it rocky and crunching beneath her feet. Where patches of snow linger in the shadows of the woods they look, she has often noticed on her walks, like smoke; so do, oddly, distant mountains and a lake and even a blue house, seen through branches: to a painter's open eye the world abounds in optical illusions. The other day, by the dining-room window, she was trans-fixed by what seemed to be a piece of translucent paper, wax paper, caught in the brush at the edge of the lawn and trembling in the breeze, and she wondered what impudent litterer had flung it here, then realized it was a gray squirrel, clinging to an alder shoot thick enough to half-hide the little animal body but so slender it kept swaying.

This is burning season. If the girl would only go soon, Hope could spend an hour outside picking up dead sticks—the beeches and hickories drop them endlessly—for the brush fire Jason Warren would light when he came this Saturday, if the wind wasn't high. Though he is one of those men to whom women are always in the way, strange two-legged incessantly talking animals found now even on the mountainsides, Hope likes to stand with him, adding to his blaze with garden stakes and dry stalks and feeling the heat on her face, enough to singe her eyebrows if her eyebrows hadn't faded to wisps ages ago. Until she turned seventy she did almost all her own yardwork, Zack, much as she maligns him, having shown her what a person can do on their own; they had been too poor to think of hiring many workmen there on the Flats. Zack knocked out partitions and replaced shingles and porch supports and moved the barn uphill, out of the center of their view of the marsh and the distant strip of saltwater that was really a small harbor. Zack got neighbors—Andy Silcox, Glenn Urquhart—to help push the barn on rollers, it moved five inches each time they leveraged it up, less as the uphill pitch increased, they finally had to get a fisherman with a seine-hauling winch on the back of his truck to pull the big dilapidated thing onto the cement foundation Zack had laid by himself, spraining his shoulder in the process, spreading the hardening concrete. The Flats had been a frontier to them, though English sailors and their inbred descendants had been farming and fishing here since 1640. Neighbor helped neighbor, Zack paid back his labor-debt with labor on their places—rebuilding the Urquharts' porch, helping harvest the Silcox potatoes. "It was the end of the world," Hope says aloud. "Just the elements."

"What was?" Kathryn asks, behind her. Too close behind her, Hope feels, wary of having the heel of the Birkenstocks stepped on and a strap ripped. Birkenstocks are harder and harder to find to buy, the real ones, not imitations that stretch and loosen up right away.

"The Flats. Sorry. I was thinking aloud. One does that, living alone. Here is the kitchen, but there's a bathroom to the left, under the stairs, if you need it."

"No thank you, Hope. I don't need it yet."

Hope, is it? How the young do presume—all these letters one gets without a Mrs. or a Ms., Hope McCoy as if there hadn't been two husbands since or she didn't sign her work "H. Ouderkirk." And flaunting their superior bladder control. She really shouldn't let them in, they take your day and send you to bed dizzy and then write what they had determined to write before they came. She had sat some years ago with a nice young man till near midnight, a professor of fine arts somewhere in the Midwest doing his first book, an expansion of his thesis, and when it came out all she had told him was reduced to a footnote contradicting somebody else. But it had been a while since anyone had asked, not only was Zack fading from what people in art talked about but Guy, too, which she would have thought would never happen, his ideas were so youthful and gay in the old sense, so impudent and fresh and tireless, he was an art movement by himself, until carrying it all began to weigh on him. Zack had felt weight only for a little while, and had got out from under. "When we moved, right after the war, most of the houses in the Flats still had outdoor privies. When we'd try to get to ours that first terrible winter, we'd be blown nearly off our feet, into that big silver maple, and when you were in there the wind would howl from underneath, quite alarmingly."

They enter the kitchen, and Hope worries that the girl will think she was talking about this house, which she and Jerry had acquired in another era, another marriage. They ripped out—they paid workmen to rip out—the linoleum floor and low stone sinks and leaky old Frigidaire and put in everything new, but that was a generation ago, and the fashions in stoves and sinks and ovens and countertops have moved on. The suspended cabinets, spray-painted a cream as smooth as a car finish, show loose handles and grubby patches where her fingers touch most often, and the ivory Formica on the long counter below the cabinets has split where the woodwork underneath has settled and shrunk. The black prongs of the burner she uses most often have chipped, and the big Andersen windows that provide a wide view of the old apple orchard staggering up the slope to the north don't easily crank open and closed any more, rain and snowmelt have dripped down through the casing to swell the frame. It is an expensive airy kitchen turning shabby. Only the green serpentine top to the island holding the gas burners has proved impervious to time, its veins preserving the eddies and ripples and mica flecks of metamorphic flow molten in a moment inconceivably remote, millions and millions of years, time enough for the human species to go extinct a hundred times—metamorphic rock older than these Green Mountains eroding around her but at this moment cool and sleek to her touch as with the other hand she sets the spouted round kettle on the chipped prongs of her favorite burner. Her hand stretches grotesquely in the kettle's mirroring aluminum; her face is a distant pale spot with pathetic white bangs, a snatch of smoke, white straw too dry to be tamed.

Hope turns on the gas, holding the knob pointing to noon until its rather frantic little clicking ignites a blue rush of flame that she subdues by turning the knob to where eleven o'clock would be. She feels Kathryn looking about the kitchen, its flaking surfaces and pockets of jumble, and wondering where Hope's money has gone. She will not ask that, but Hope has a ready answer. She has kept the money, and invested it conservatively, to leave to her children, the major share to her daughter: conscience money, but she won't go into that. Her father had dribbled *his* father's money away, so she is proud of her shrewdness and thrift. She held Zack's paintings back as their value went up and up; then Guy was an astute and industrious exploiter of the fat art market in the 'sixties and 'seventies; and Jerry was generous, leaving her the same share of his fortune as each of his children by the former wife and listing the Vermont house in her name from the start. It had been hers as the search for silence and country simplicity had been hers. Zack was her partner in that search for a while; a child of Western spaces, he needed room to roam in, as he had that first summer, the one of '46, dazed by the marshes and dunes as they came into bloom. "What I loved about the Flats," she tells Kathryn, "was the light, the way the land accepted it, as if it were the flat palm of a hand at the end of an extended arm. It felt like the end of the world. You've been there, of course, as part of your research, but not then, right after the war. Nothing had changed for so long. Farmland had that treeless look then, though our own land had the silver maple on it, and a tropical-looking tree with gauzy pink-and-white flowers and feathery locustlike leaves that when you handled them wanted to close up like the page of a book. An albizia, or silk tree, though people called it a mimosa. One of the farmers who had owned the place must have planted it, for an ornament. That far out on Long Island there were almost no houses that weren't farmhouses—a church, a Masonic lodge—and the potato fields stretched everywhere. The land where it wasn't culti-vated was sandy and marshy, and here and there great stray boulders had been left by the glacier. Montauk had been an island until the glacier filled in the gap with a moraine.

Looking east as we did, we saw a strip of blue saltwater—McGonicle's Harbor—a strip of land beyond, and a huge windy sky. Water, air, sand, the sun. But I bet you wish I wouldn't talk without your tape recorder being on."

"I *would* prefer it, though my memory is pretty good. Still, it's better to have your exact words."

"Oh dear, does it really matter? I hardly trust my words any more, it's always been a failing of mine to say what I think people want to hear. And I do doubt there's anything I can say I haven't said someplace already. What would you like in your tea?"

"My tea? Oh. No, just plain, thanks."

Why had this simple request startled her? The interviewer's mind had been elsewhere. Hope finds she is hurt by this, this inattention when she is putting herself out, making tea, talking so freely. Yet this female stranger must have a life, back in the city—men friends, job worries, rent to pay, or condo fees more likely in this day and age. When Hope was young it was easier, you paid by the week and ducked the landlord when you were late. He was stuck with you to some extent, eviction was a legal procedure, so there was some play in the situation. Kathryn is looking around, disappointed by the plainness—the Redouté calendar such as anyone could buy in a book-and-card shop, the cabinets with their soiled handles, the appliances twenty years out of date, the fading photographic keepsakes—vacation snaps and official school photos of grandchildren taken in a curtained booth one by one and tacked to the refrigerator door with magnets in the shape of vegetables. "Would you like to see my studio?" Hope asks the interviewer.

"Oh, yes. Very much." Yet the young woman's enthusiasm lacks the fervor Hope thought the offer deserved: the sorceress's workshop, the scene of the daily miracle.

The farmhouses in northern New England feel like trains, one car linked to another to spare the farmer wading out into the snow. When she and Jerry had bought the place, a collapsing, disused cow barn was connected to the kitchen by means of roofed storage space filled with ten-gallon milk cans and other apparatus for the defunct dairy operation; this long, low space now holds the tools of lawn and bed care that Hope has gradually yielded to the weekly crew of Warren offspring. Even the little implements of flower gardening—trowels, scratchers, asparagus forks, hand clippers, wire peony supports always maddeningly tangled like Chinese puzzles—are touched by her less than she intends; it seems that making her body move out of bed and doing her morning time in the studio is all she can do, though this spring she firmly intends to make a fresh, more energetic start. The musty odor of last year's fertilizers—Milorganite, Holly-Tone—and bags of buckwheat-hull mulch fills this long, unheated space with a distilled essence of earth under cultivation, the scent of a season ahead but still out of reach. Past a bench of clay pots and tarnished hose nozzles and bundled green garden stakes she leads the city girl, who cringes to keep her smart black outfit from a dirtying contact, her square-toed boots feeling their way along the cracked concrete floor as if over stepping-stones, through the electronically controlled double doors of the elegant studio Jerry had built for Hope, for her sixtieth birthday, where the old barn once listed sideways on its tired beams, bindweed interwoven with its side boards, a row of hollyhocks, in fainting Kate Greenaway colors, eight feet tall along the south side lost to the reconstruction. The high square space is thickly insulated and illumined by a northward-tilted Plexiglas-bubble skylight brimming this morning with a blue so deep it attains indigo, layer upon layer of atoms of pure illusion. Zack never had such a perfect setup, though in planning it Hope could not but reconstruct his old studio, doing it better. Overhead tracks support long fluorescent fixtures; she flicks several of the switches on a panel just inside the doors, and a sharp artificial brilliance, after some blink and flutter, intensifies the natural northern light.

"Oh," says Kathryn. "So bright."

"The better to see you, my dear."

Hope's visitor—whose posture could be better, as if when she got her growth spurt she cringed and stooped so as not to tower over her classmates—approaches the canvas on the central easel, still wet with this morning's work, a canvas six by five feet, of horizontal stripes. Is she near-sighted? She peers so intently, at such close range, that a sideways lurch brushes her against the crusty table crowded with half-squeezed tubes of oil paint and jars of stand oil and the panes of glass, ordinary nine-by-twelves, that Hope uses instead of wooden palettes. Startled by the contact, Kathryn takes a hasty step back, and she and Hope together look to see if any wet paint has spoiled her black slacks, their exotic ribbed fabric. "I don't see anything," Hope reassures her.

"Me neither, don't worry." Not trusting the older woman's eyes, she has inspected independently, fussily brushing at the unsmirched spot. At last looking up, she changes focus. "The painting is lovely. So refined."

"I wondered, glancing at it just now, if the two shades of gray are close enough together. You don't want stripiness to be the first thing you notice, this isn't meant to be Op. You want them to be so subtle they *dawn*. Slowly."

"Like those Ad Reinhardt rectangles. He leads us into the paint, to see they're not quite all the same shade of purply brown. You get that in Seamus O'Rourke, too—the elusiveness, the quasi-thereness."

Hope flinches at the false note, the student note. But, then, did the painters themselves do any better, verbalizing? That had been one of Zack's beauties, his refusal or inability to verbalize. Artists should have their tongues cut out. "That was one of their ideas, I think," she says tactfully. "To immerse the viewer, to paint at such a scale that the viewer ceases to be conscious of the edges of the canvas."

"You've never gone in for the biggest scale," Kathryn tells her, and asks, "Does that have anything to do with your being a woman?"

"Probably. Also, the theory never seemed to me to quite hold water. Bernie Nova's huge canvases, one is aware of the edges *because* they're so huge, so far away on the wall. You think of the space in which he must have made it, and wonder where it can be hung, *except* in a museum. With Renaissance murals, the building itself is the edge, and it all melts in, flows into something not sharply different. But in a museum, with the white walls, the guard standing in the corner . . . only in some of Zack's biggest, the three he did in 1950, before his gift gave out, does it really happen, we lose ourselves in the paint, the way he said *he* did. And even then, we come up against something, a bumblebee, a sneaker print, a cigarette butt that got worked in, that reminds us of what we're looking at, a big piece of canvas, with edges. I think it's very hazardous to base any approach to painting on what a hypothetical viewer will do or feel. It has to be between you and the canvas—question and answer, push and pull, and let the viewer come in however he can."

Even amid the resiny, spiritous smell of fresh paint Hope catches a whiff of Kathryn's perfume, a sweet faux-floral gust thinly applied over a coarser scent, the chemically loaded aura of a young female animal. In the merciless light a small redness, not quite a pimple, burns beside a nostril wing of the long waxen nose; a blusher imposes chalky shadows of orange pastel at the cheekbones, and a henna rinse makes a rust on the metallic black filaments springing back from her brow. Her face is long, but her hair begins rather low on her brow. Hope imagines a fever of wanting pressing behind that brow, giving it its fretful texture, its shadows of tension; these young people know, as her generation did not, that however much is attained it will not be enough. Sex sours, wealth melts, fame is for fifteen minutes. The wet plum-solemn eyes—blue grease on the upper lid, a line of kohl on the lower, the lashes long enough to curl backward but almost certainly her own—dart toward the corners of the mercilessly lit big room, where other gray canvases of Hope's, dried, with their faint intimations of a beauty on the edge of an invisible quiet, lean against others, splashier, lesser, unsold works by her first two husbands, kept for their passive companionship and as insurance for her old age, as if it were not already here. Photographs of herself with others in other times going back to Ardmore in the 'twenties, framed certificates of graduation and commendation (*Commandeur de l'ordre des Arts et des Lettres, Erster Preis Kunstfest München*), the hideous trophies of crystal and painted metal one gets as tokens of recognition and public gratitude (the most ungainly of them handed to her sheepishly by the first President Bush, a tall and boyish Connecticut gent apparently as pleasantly surprised to find himself in the White House as she was; at lunch afterward, seated beside her, he pointed out for Hope to admire the daily flowers, the elegantly clad Marine guards, the splendid imposing punctilio which momentarily surrounded them, two proper children of the fading Protestant hegemony): these souvenirs, still in the hasty order of an afternoon's arranging when the studio was newly built, attract Kathryn's attention less than Hope expected. Only the old photographs tempt the interloper to move closer, her neck cranked forward in that unbecoming way. "How pretty you were."

"I never thought of myself as pretty, but I tried to be amusing and not lazy. If you're raised as a Quaker, the world seems terribly exciting, like a party you didn't expect to get invited to. The Devil's party, if we take that obsolete statement of mine seriously."

Hope thinks this was worth saying, and regrets that Kathryn doesn't have her tape recorder running. But, then, what kind of capture is it, the words on tape, words on paper, if nobody listens, nobody reads? It all just pours into the dark, the darkness that exists even in the midst of the light; the light itself is blind.

"This is the best," Kathryn says, her circuit of attention returned to the painting on the easel. The assertion takes Hope aback; who is this girl to judge?

Hope self-dismissingly sighs. "It's very like all the others, yet there are little differences that I can feel. Each is an adventure, even at my age."

"You must stop thinking so much of your age. I never think of mine."

"At your age, I didn't either." Is this true? Hope doubts it. It was part of the old way, the way still mapped by religion, to see yourself on a path, within a journey from which you might be called out at any moment, for an accounting. She cannot picture how this young woman conceives of her own, her only, existence—as an unaccountable present tense, an unframed *now* that imposes duties upon her, such as this interview, without a possibility of drastic, everlasting failure? Hope knows enough younger people, her children and their children for a start, who would never think of being *grateful* for existence; as best she can tell, the universe for them is a kind of joke to be shrugged off, a cosmic sneeze rapidly dissipating into the original nothingness. What's to praise? Who's to blame? Her father, Hope in her childhood came to sense, had a religious sense of failure, for all his nice home of false timbers and stucco and chalky bricks, and his office overlooking Market Street from a suitable height, and his handsome energetic wife organizing his party life and summer homes, and his perky auburn-haired daughter and his two sons, both of whom had inherited his good bones and fair fine hair and thoughtful, faintly melancholy calm. His pious ancestors, those fanatics risking hanging and exile in their zeal to strip Christianity back to its uncorrupted essence, made him feel a failure in his worldly status, a genteel offshoot of his more immediate ancestors' success in trade, in manufacture (a carpet factory whose vast clatter and heaving looms and sense of imprisonment formed one of Hope's earliest memories, a visit with her grandfather just before the plant closed under pressure from the South's lower wages) and investment (railroads, coal, slums). To "feed" his "face"—a favorite phrase of his—for decade after decade, to feed his children's faces, to put clothing on their bodies, and to drape them in the educational credentials needed to maintain membership in their social class, and to mediate, in a time when lawyers also served as financial advisers, between old Philadelphia money and the hazards of an ever-new world that played host to a market crash followed by a radical Democratic President who laughed at privilege, being himself privileged—none of this seemed, by the inner light that burned dimly within him, enough. He did not much protest when his daughter rebelled and went wild in New York.

She thinks Kathryn has seen enough of the studio. It was important to Hope that her studio feel secret, an extension of her brain, flooded with a thinking silence, a fluorescence wiped clean of the traces of visitors. "Where is your tea?" she asks.

"Oh! I forgot it and left it in the kitchen!"

"I don't think you're a tea drinker. Don't be. It stains the teeth. You have beautiful teeth. You should smile more often."

Back in the kitchen, past the bags of Milorganite and buckwheat hulls, Kathryn says, seeking something smiling to say, "It's warmer in here."

"The studio cools down; it's on a separate system, electric heat, terribly expensive, and I turn it down to fifty-five when I'm done for the day."

"I'm taking too much of your day. Kick me out whenever you have to."

"But we've only gotten up to 1946!"

"That's true." The girl sees, dartingly, with a bit of fright in her eyes, that the older woman is game for more. "I think I *will* accept your offer of a bathroom, before we—"

"Go back to work," Hope finishes for her. "Out into the hall, turn right, under the stairs, a narrow door on your left. We had to squeeze it in."

Momentarily alone, Hope empties the mugs—her own, nearly empty; Kathryn's, nearly full—in the sink. Then she swishes hot faucet water around in them and puts them mouth-down on the drainer to dry. The pets she and Jerry had have all died, but even these mugs, with their painted parrots and red-and-green stripes, have that quality pets do, of sharing your innermost domestic existence, so that you come gratefully home to them from a venture into human society. They give you back your self after others have dirtied and addled it. She stands at the double door leading to the side yard, for the thousandth time annoyed that the panes don't quite line up, and feels that this swaying feeder on its wire, this gray birch and the woods beyond, with its tinge of red and smoky gaps of pallor, are friends whose silent trust she is betraying with all her excessively eager talk to an intruder. She longs for solitude as if for Paradise. What did Freud say happiness was? Release from tension, of which sexual release was the model. How bizarre and unconscionable, really, her own sexual activity looks from the altitude of years. Bug-behavior, the repulsive intricacy of insect genitals and strategies, strategies in which the death of the individual is quite casually folded. Poking, biting, squirting, dying. Bernie, who relished Nietzsche's thought that truth is ugly, used to talk about such things; his parents had once given him a microscope, and he would draw for Hope insect genitalia, to see if it turned her off. It did not. What a chemical daze it must have been that allowed her ever to see male genitals, especially when erect and inflamed—the blue vein, the lavender head, the painfully stretched translucent skin—as beautiful, so beautiful she wanted the thing within herself, incorporated, possessed. What is the irritation female bugs feel, that they submit?

The toilet down the hall flushes: Kathryn rising from the seat, having patted her oily dark cleft with a pad of tissue. This downstairs water closet sometimes keeps running, the stopper balancing upright on its hinge and failing to fall, so that water runs without filling the porcelain box and making the ball cock rise and shut off the flow. Hope listens for the telltale change of pitch in the toilet's murmur that signals a fallen stopper and a seal. She imagines she hears it, through the rush of an open faucet: Kathryn washing her hands. Had Hope set out a clean hand towel? The other woman emerges with that curious stalking gait of hers, as if walking in her boots on uneven stepping-stones, a praying-mantis gait. Hope wonders if she should follow the younger woman's example but foresees that the seat will be warm, an uncanny undesired intimacy, and decides she can wait. The tea will want out in an hour or less.

Mustering an uncertain half-smile—Hope regrets having said anything about smiling more often, her tongue runs away with her, all from trying too hard to please—Kathryn stalks back into the front parlor, to Grandfather Ouderkirk's plaid chair. Irritably the interviewer peers at the little gray Sony, holding it nearsightedly close to her face to check if the fresh tape is turning, then replacing it on the old sea-chest, among the brass nailheads. "A church wedding," she prompts.

Hope bridles at this re-emphasis. "As I said, we could scarcely, in 1945, live together in a rural community like the Flats without a marriage license. You couldn't even do it in Hollywood, that's why all those stars like Lana Turner and What's-her-name—the one with the purple eyes—kept getting married. The locals were suspicious enough of us. They couldn't understand how Zack earned a living. And in fact he scarcely did—the agreement with Peggy paid him a hundred fifty a month, which was less than the twenty-three dollars and eighty-six cents a week he had been collecting from the Federal Arts Project plus the sixty a month my father had been sending me. That stopped, of course, when we got married. As to the church part, Zack had these touching pockets of conventionality. Maybe he thought it would please me. And actually it did. I got to wear one of my hats."

"Your work. How much were you painting at that time?"

"Some. By the fall of '44, I had dropped out of Hoch-mann and was waitressing at an Italian restaurant, Euge-nio's, south of the Park. Weekends and evenings I tried to paint, but once Zack entered my life there wasn't much time for myself."

"He was demanding?"

Hope sighs, feeling this to be tired terrain. "He had been the youngest of five and was like a child in that you had to be paying attention to him every minute; except when he was painting, he had no inner resources. Even when he wasn't there, you had to keep worrying if he was going to get killed, hit by a car or his neck broken by some guy in a bar he would pick a fight with. He was always picking fights and always losing. It was like his drinking—he was poor at it. My theory was, he had been the runt of his litter and being beaten up reminded him of home. I mean, he came home to it."

"Or perhaps he thought," Kathryn says, "that this time he would win."

Hope is enough accustomed to the subservience of inter-viewers to be piqued. Does this girl think that, through her research, she knows Zack better than his wife, who steered him up from those Village gutters into greatness?

Kathryn senses Hope's stiffness and says meekly, "It did happen with his painting. Winning."

"It did," Hope concedes. "But then he smashed it all up. He hated success, it seemed tawdry to him. It got him too much out into the open, he felt painfully exposed, though he had thought it was what he wanted."

"Your painting," Kathryn says, as if bringing Hope to heel. "Was it abstract at this time, around the time you moved?"

"I kept backsliding, how did you know? Fragments of the city—faces from the restaurant in Little Italy, neon light reflected on the wet pavements, the silhouettes of midtown you saw from the walk-up on East Ninth Street—kept working their way in, through what Hochmann used to call 'holes' in the canvas. Zack was contemptuous. 'What's this representational shit?' he'd ask. 'Who you think you are, Hopper?' He'd tell me, 'Let Levine and Ben Shahn do the political cartoons.' Jack Levine was big before the war and in the 'forties, and Zack had an especial dislike for him, I think because he could do all those Old Master–ish things—draw anatomy, work with shadows and light—that Zack couldn't do if his life depended on it, any more than he could assemble an evenly lit pseudo-Renaissance tableau like Benton."

"There was a lot that Zack couldn't do as you saw him."

She thinks she knows Zack better and loves him more. "But there was something," Hope says, "he *could* do, a kind of impacted emotion, a sort of strangled truth dug up from that hardscrabble childhood with that weird, dominating mother. Even Alfred, at the Modern, was made to see it, though his taste ran to the more European of the young Americans—Roger, Onno—who could speak French and do nice brushwork. In '45, Barr okayed purchase of one of Zack's messy Jungian canvases—the one of the wolf that looks like a cow. That six hundred dollars paid for a lot of building supplies our first year in the Flats."

"Tell me about the Flats. You were happy there, at least the first five years, before Zack began to drink again."

"Happy. Let me think. We were *busy*, which may come to much the same thing. The place had been left a total mess, chock-a-block full of dumpy sad furniture and old clothing, and the little barn crammed with rusty farm equipment that hadn't been used since the Depression. There was no central heating, no hot water, no bathroom, as I said. That first winter was brutal, the worst in years, the natives told us. When a storm blew in from the ocean it seemed our house was the first thing it hit. And we had no car, we went into the city by train when we had to. Henry Drayton, who ran the general store a half-mile down the road, loaned Zack two dollars to buy an old bicycle to get back and forth on. Henry sold everything, on credit in the winter—food, hardware, liquor, paints. A lot of Zack's painting was done with industrial enamels—Duco, Devoe—straight from Henry's shelves. The only other commercial establishment in the Flats was a bar called the Lemon Drop about a mile away. A little far to walk in bad weather, though Zack would do it. He complained nobody would talk to him, the way they did at the bars in Manhattan. The locals just sat there with their drinks, grunting at each other now and then. Of course, they saw each other every day, and were all intermarried. They called each other 'bub'— Zack at first thought they were insulting him, but it was their language. Women were 'dollies' and children were 'yowns' and summer people were 'drifts.' We were 'drifts,' poor as we were. They distrusted us, how could they not? Zack minded this more than I did. He worked at breaking down their resistance—somehow he and Henry amused each other, and the crowd at the Lemon Drop warmed up. But that first winter the wind and the cold were so ferocious we didn't go outdoors for days—just huddled by the woodstove in blankets drinking coffee to keep warm. Things kept breaking down—the pump in the basement gave out, the porch was collapsing, the windows all rattled like machine guns. We weren't happy, we were frantic. Zack hardly painted, it was too cold in the upstairs room he had cleared of junk. Still, it was lovely not to have him hungover most of the time. He was so innocently proud, to own a house. His family never did, after the father left. The buyers had wanted four thousand five, we got them down to four even. To raise the down payment Zack had to sell his soul, practically, to Peggy's gallery. Banks wanted nothing to do with us, though finally one in East Hampton came through with a mortgage, after Roger put in a word for us. He had come out to the Island, too, but of course on very different terms. East Hampton was seven miles away, down Fireplace Road, but light-years away socially, in those days."

"Weren't you lonely?"

Hope gives it a second's reflection. She wants to be honest but not to feed this young inquisitor's desire to come between her and Zack, to fit their marriage into a frame somehow flattering to herself. "I wanted to be. I wanted to be alone with Zack, because I loved him and because it was the best thing for him and his work. We were just married, this was our honeymoon."

"How old were you?"

"We moved in November of '45. I turned twenty-four in May of '46."

"Wasn't that terribly young, to be taking charge like that?"

"In the war, nobody seemed young. Zack was ten years older, but as I say he was a child. He was missing about half the components of a mature human being."

"Really?"

"Kathryn. How can you doubt it? You know what happened afterward."

This silences the doubter. Hope goes on, "And then, eventually, spring came. It came early that year, actually. In the dunes, there were all these tiny pink blossoms—

people called them bearberries. The farmers began to plow up the ryegrass for potato planting. The fishermen began to put out their nets for striped bass. The ocean, the ocean that had been such a bitter dark enemy while we suffered through the winter, softened in color, became a mild china blue. Zack was ecstatic. I could hardly get him to come indoors. He dug and planted a big garden for vegetables and melons, the way his father had done years ago. He brought home a mongrel dog one of the neighbors wanted to get rid of, he had had a piebald dog like that as a child. We walked with that dog, Trixie, for miles, and rode our bicycles all over, to Montauk and back, to East Hampton and back. It was a pleasure to bicycle, there was nothing like today's traffic. The last time I visited the Flats, to check on the museum they've made of our old house, I was struck by how stifling everything has become: stop-and-go traffic all along Route 27, the people from New York bring their congestion out with them, along with their laptops and Starbuckses."

Hope remembers the sense, new to her, of claiming a region, making a stretch of scenery and history their own, finding a leafy corner of America where she and Zack could taste freedom. The simplest transactions of country living pleased her — being greeted "Madame McCoy" by Henry Drayton at his store with a solemn ironical nod that said he knew what she was putting up with but saluting her undiscourageable youth and perkiness. He would add her purchases to their lengthening tab, and she would bicycle home fighting the front-heavy wobble from her loaded basket, between the new-sown potato fields and blossoming wild cherries beside the road. The most mundane signs of communal acceptance took her back to Ardmore, where the tradespeople had seemed giants at the back door, family members. The Flats' plumber, Al Treadwell, would let himself into the downstairs noisily, to warn them in case they were upstairs making love, as he installed, bit by bit, carton by carton, a plain but functioning bathroom to end forever their windblown winter trips to the outhouse. For two weeks later that summer, as the albizia dropped its feathery blossoms on the lawn, in whose center some previous owner had left a collection of six or so large boulders, she and Zack woke each dry day to the whistling, knocking sounds of Jimmy Herrick and his two adolescent sons arriving to paint the house's weathered shingles white and the trim and windows blue. Owning this house restored her to certain simplicities of childhood, when houses and yards demarcated territories of safety and drew upon deep wells, mysterious cisterns brimming with communal reserves. "Zack surprised me by being so handy," she tells Kathryn. "I didn't really know that much about his boyhood, just that his father had owned a twenty-acre dirt farm outside of Santa Fe and after the farm failed and the father faded away—he got road-building jobs, surveying jobs, and came home less and less, there was never a clear break—the mother took all these boys to California and kept moving from place to place, sometimes little boarding houses they would run, I don't know how many, as I say he didn't like to talk about his past, his family made him very uncomfortable, which may be another thing we had in common; what I'm trying to say is that he was fearless about doing things. Plumbing, wiring—he'd tackle it. He and Eddie Strode, a fireman he had met at the Lemon Drop, ripped off the whole roof of Eddie's house, right down to the rafters." In her mind's eye Zack sits silhouetted, shirtless and laughing, holding a beer can, his legs dangling down on either side of the bare ridge beam, the bright thunderheads of a coming storm piled behind him against a sky as profoundly blue as the indigo sky she has just seen through the skylight of her studio. His bald head glinted. "Neither he nor I liked the way this shabby barn came between us and the view of the harbor, so all by himself he laid down a cement foundation thirty yards up the hill, to one side, and he and some other men girdled the barn and its shed in two-by-fours and tried to push it uphill but finally had to get a local fisherman, his name was Brick, it just came to me, Brick Lester, he died not long after, to haul it up on the winch on the back of his truck." Has she already told Kathryn this story, or just passed it through her mind? An epic tale deserving to be oft-told, the moving of the barn: Hope can still feel in her gut and groin the sensation of release when the winch creaked, the cables tautened, the chocks under the truck's back wheels held, and the barn, big and hollow as the Trojan horse, budged and tottered forward beneath the great silver maple that sticky summer day, the watching men, having sweated their shirts wet in vain, cheering, shouting admonitions and encouragements to one another, dancing about to see that the girdle of beams was holding together, Brick's face reddening, his fat white hand bunched on the black winch lever; the sputtering engine fed its power into the cable reel and all the nails and rivets held as human ingenuity and good fortune majestically converted desire into movement. Brick had a great drooping gut, which dragged him down into death not long after. "I kept serving everybody lemonade, and then beer when they were done. If they hadn't done that, think of it," Hope tells Kathryn, "the barn wouldn't have been close enough to the house to use as a studio, and Zack's paintings would have stayed easel-size. He cut a big north window high in one wall, but when I suggested another window lower down, toward McGonicle's Harbor, he said No, he didn't want to be distracted by any view. He loved the view, he would spend hours sitting looking at the dunes, and the marshes, with the ducks and red-winged blackbirds, but he wanted the studio sealed off. He wasn't articulate but he was smart enough to know that—his painting now had to come entirely from within."

She arrives, thus, at an impasse, a sealed cul-de-sac, a kind of blank-faced monument to the something obdurate and shrewd that had lifted Zack, for all his limits, far above her. Freshly married, she thought she had rejoiced to see Zack regain health and enterprise, but there was a part of her that resented the way that he seized her initiative and accepted her services, those glorious first years on the Island, yet shut her out, leaving her as an artist far behind.

Kathryn tells her, "The paintings he did in '46 have a lovely outdoors feeling, like watercolors. Those clear pastel colors, Matisse-y almost, peach and lime green and powder blue. And the brush strokes," she goes on a bit breathlessly, getting her art-crit voice in gear, "are so free-flowing, transparent somehow, at the opposite end from the clotted, dark canvases he was doing just a year or two earlier."

"I had never liked those, though Herbie did," Hope says with deliberate crispness, curbing the other's rapture. "We were happy," she firmly states. "We would sleep as late as we could, spend time together in the garden in the morning, he would work in the studio in the afternoon and I might shop and do housework, we would take walks with Trixie in the late-afternoon light, and come home and eat, and listen to records, and make love. Making love had always been easy for me, but not for Zack. That was why he talked about fucking so much, and was so rude to women when he had some drinks inside him." *And would have been rude to you*, she does not say, *had you been there.*

Yet always, she remembers, and can almost taste it, a bitter nugget in the midst of this translucent happiness, there had been his ambition, and the fear that sealed his ambition in, and his insulting need for alcohol's spell of self-forgetfulness. Her eyes surprise her by feeling hot and watery. "I made love to him," she tells Kathryn, "to keep him from running off to the Lemon Drop in the evening. He would fuck me and put his clothes on and go off anyway. He would walk a mile in the dark to be with these ignorant men who wouldn't even talk to him."

"You made him into a heterosexual," Kathryn explains to her, as if in reproach, with that easy New York knowingness that withers all it touches.

Hope feels blood rush to her face in her eagerness to turn aside such an impudent implication. "Zack never thought of himself as anything but. Biographers have made much too much of certain minor incidents. In his teens, when his brothers were leaving the household one by one and his mother was working late hours and he was pretty much on his own in Los Angeles, and then when he first came to New York and hardly had a place to stay, but really, in that blue-collar world he came from, there was nothing homosexual about liking to sit around getting sloshed with other men, it was simply how men were. He was awkward with women, but not unresponsive to them. Believe me, dear. Don't ask me to spell it out."

"May I ask—was there anything, oh, out of the way about his lovemaking? Did you have to do anything unusual to arouse him?"

Hope can hardly believe she is being asked this, but then must admit to herself that she deserves it, for flaunting her sexuality before this young woman—rubbing her nose in it, as they say—with her talk of being wicked and of going to

the costume ball in little more than coal dust. It was a way
of teasing her, of keeping Kathryn from swamping her, but
there was no holding off her relentless, humorless demand
that Hope bare her life. And it was all so long ago, before
even the middle of the last century, when she and Zack
came to the sunstruck, wind-raked Flats and filled the for-
saken old farmhouse with the sound of their voices, aug-
menting the warmth of their bodies with that of the
woodstove, whose heat parched their skins and hair in its
close vicinity but died halfway upstairs to the cold bedroom. "He was an old-fashioned man in many ways," she
tells the other woman. "Just the sight of me naked was usually enough. There wasn't all this emphasis on oral and anal
there is now, though he did like to take me from behind. I
would give it to him as a treat, though of course it didn't do
much for me, besides the cuddling part of it. At times I
would be left unsatisfied—and angry, I suppose—but there
was still this notion in the air, which the war had reinforced,
of women *serving* men, because they were our buffers
against the real world, the cruel world. They earned the
money and fought the wars. I learned to cook, once we left
New York, because Zack's mother had always put these big
square Western meals on the table. In our sex, if you really
need know this sort of thing, I wore a diaphragm, and had
to guess ahead of time when it would be needed, and sometimes guessed wrong, which was humiliating in a small way.
Your intuition, Kathryn, is correct in that Zack did, in
general, have to be coaxed into sex, as opposed to being
always up for it, as they say now. The liquor acted as a drag
when he was off the wagon, and he was *con*stantly preoccupied by this need to be a great painter—not an adequate
and earnest one like Mahlon Strunk, or even a famous one
like Benton and Mondrian, but great in some deep, final—

'existential' was the word we all used—way that he couldn't come out and confess but all the painters we knew more or less shared. They were out for big game. Zack didn't have the facility, the intellectual background, of Roger or Bernie, and where someone like Onno was such a natural painter he could do his thing at the canvas for hours a day and then just forget it, like natural exercise, it wasn't a natural thing for Zack: he had to find, or *invent* would be better, a manner in which he could be fluent like the others, and though Herbie loved him and Peggy supported him in her Fagin-like fashion and Clem thought he might be a winning bet to make his own name as a critic on, Zack knew he hadn't found it yet, those outdoorsy watercolory Matisse-y paintings you were praising weren't quite there yet, though, you're right, they were closer, they were freer, he'd gotten away from those deadly brown Mexican muralists and that Miróesque Surrealist clutter. What I'm trying to say with all this—your poor tape recorder!—is that though he wasn't very self-reflective Zack knew that the move to the Island with me might be his last chance to be great. It sounds stupid and naïve to you, I'm sure, being great, but it was very real to Zack, this possibility, and to the other painters too, as I've said, a very American notion, no doubt, a kind of holy state—imagine if Picasso had bothered himself with so gross an ambition, how could he have *played* the way he did?—and time was running out. And he had me now to run interference for him and do a ton of scut work and get on the phone for hours trying to boost his stock in the city—I pretended to believe in him more than I did, and then, about our second year on the Island, I became a believer. So he had a reason to try to avoid the Lemon Drop and, when he went into town, the Cedar or loft parties; it wasn't just screwing me that kept him home. Zack got himself down to wine and beer on his own. Roger had a place in East Hampton, the Georgica section, and Onno and Renée had bought on Two Holes of Water Road a carriage house they painted this sardonic Easterish purple to annoy the uptight neighbors, and Bernie and Mahlon had followed by '48—Mahlon and Myrtle went all the way to Montauk, typically isolating themselves somewhat—so there was a real artists' colony growing up, with *lots* of parties and booze, and it was after Roger brought a bottle of Jack Daniel's to the place on Fireplace Road when we were giving him and Tasha dinner with two other couples and Herbie that Zack solemnly handed it back to him and looked him in the eye—there had always been a little bad blood between them, Roger was so much what Zack wasn't, so effortlessly *au courant*—and told him, 'Thanks, but I don't need this stuff any more.' "

Had she got it wrong? There *was* such a moment, but had it been Onno who had presented the bottle? Not Bernie, he was too sensitive. And her account left out the tranquillizers that the doctor in Southampton prescribed, and that made Zack so dopey and amiable he wouldn't go near the barn, just wander all day with Trixie over the fields and dunes. And the binges now and then that would leave him stumbling home at three in the morning, having passed out in the woods by the side of the road on the way back from the Lemon Drop. After two years of bicycling and begging rides they scraped up money for a car, a Model A Ford that cost ninety dollars, and Hope would lie awake upstairs terrified that he would run the car against a tree; his binges had gained a lethal potential. Still, he had joined her in the struggle against his drinking, they were on the same side of the problem, and if taming it took a little more rear presentation than she would have chosen for herself, then this was life, of the creature, and worth the potential prize. She would love this man's greatness up out of him. And, to be fair, Zack was beautiful, the blond furriness of him, curly small hairs pale against his tan, and the muscular push-and-pull of his torso in the summer light, from collarbones and nipples down to his pubic bush, that whole classic terrain of human anatomy symmetrically subdivided like the plaster casts of *kouroi* at the Cooper Union, a youth's abdomen only slightly pot-bellied in Zack at thirty-five, liquor's bloat counteracted by home carpentry and his walks and the work of their garden. With the tide of liquor ebbed out of his system, Zack smelled of cigarettes and linseed oil and garden soil and salt air. When Trixie flushed a skunk, the smell of the spray spread from the dog's hair to his hands and blue jeans and from them to her, and because they were so much alone those first glorious rough seasons on the Island they didn't care. She can see herself kneeling and washing his back, herself naked, in the claw-footed old cast-iron tub Al Treadwell had salvaged from another job and, saving them money as he kept pointing out, installed in their new little bathroom; she can see herself, her rounded freckled arms, her pointed tan fingers, lathering Zack's back and shoulders as he smoked a cigarette even in the tub, keeping one hand dry to remove it from his pensive mouth and tip the ash into the cocktail peanuts can that did in this room for an ashtray.

"He began to drip when?" Kathryn asks, then quickly answers herself. "Early in '47? What do you remember of that moment? Did it seem epochal to you and Zack? Did he talk about it as something revolutionary?"

Abruptly bored, touched as if by a clammy hand by the desolation of these same old questions, Hope looks for escape toward the window and sees that small puffy clouds, mere shreds, have appeared in the unflecked ozone-rich blue framed an hour ago by the skylight. As the sun warms the mountains, these wisps of vapor are stirred into visibility above the valleys. The front-parlor windows, curtained in a faded chintz of roses more brown than red, have delicately thin muntins, which were one of the house's charms when she fell in love with it and persuaded Jerry to buy. He couldn't see it as a big part of his future, but she knew in her bones it would be hers for life. Not just the sashes but the glass itself, the bubbled, faintly wavy, faintly violet-tinged panes, had seemed thinned, like the skin of an old person; at a blast of wind from a certain angle or even a moment of evening cooling, a window vibrates like a harp string stroked. The house talks to her. This girl is not avoiding the obvious, as her polite, factual telephone voice had seemed to promise she would; there had been something scattered and off-center about her proposal that led Hope to say yes and set a day well into the future, which has become today. If she were only outdoors, Hope could be silent, and the past would be left untouched, like mulch in the woods: scuff a few leaves, and the wood lice scurry, miserably exposed, panicked beneath the glare. There was in her years with Zack a considerable soreness that has not gone away; the unhealable soreness in him had rubbed off on her and become an area of shame, of guilt. She had drawn him out into the greatness he wanted—she had found him the space he needed—but perhaps to serve herself, not him. His nature had been too frail for success.

"The key thing," she dutifully told her interviewer, "was the barn itself, making it into a studio. He had never before had a floor big enough to work on. Ever since I knew Zack he would move his painting around on the easel, looking at it sideways or upside down and even painting on it that way—his instinct was to liberate the image from gravity. Even those figurative family scenes from the early 'forties—they're like a dinner party viewed from above.'"

"Or like the Navajo sand-paintings he had seen as a child.'"

"Zack," Hope says, rocking back a little and speaking levelly to conceal the hatred she is beginning to feel for this prying, self-serving intruder, "was never as much of a Westener as he liked to let on. He was an Angelino, if anything: his critical years in high school came in Los Angeles, and the first art teachers who were in any way inspiring. But, yes, once he got the canvas taped to the barn floor he could attack from all sides, and the dripping began to happen. Spattering was a way he could reach the center of the canvas. There are paint dribbles in the early work, of course—he painted with the tube even before the war—and the Surrealists had played with pouring or spilling to give them their automatic effects. You know, Matta, Masson. But Zack always insisted there was nothing accidental about his drips, that he intended everything. It was true, he learned just how to thin the paint and what tools—sticks, dried brushes, glass turkey-basters—could do what. Nobody had ever had to master exactly those skills before; he was wonderful to watch, so graceful and sure of himself in the very way he wasn't usually. I think it was that, the athleticism, that generated the publicity, the appeal to the masses: it was like what they saw in the movies. This beautiful torso in the black T-shirt, the tight dark jeans, the bald head, the intensity. He was not only uncharacteristically graceful, he was *decisive*. When that horrible German—I keep forgetting his name—"

Kathryn supplies it.

"Yes. When Hans took those movies, he complained that Zack didn't hesitate enough; he didn't *ponder*, he just jumped right in, spattering and waving his wet stick in the air. That was part of it, that speed, when he was, as he used to say, *in it*."

"How wonderful to watch!" Kathryn cries, spontaneously, Hope decides, and not to demonstrate that she loves Zack more purely than Hope ever could, this man dead twenty years before she was born.

"I didn't watch often. It would have been violating his privacy, disturbing the process." She pushes on with her complaint: "Hans had a director's idea of how a painter painted, with a lot of contemplation. Zack would go out into the barn and contemplate in the evening, I've known him just to look at the works in process all day and never touch them. But in action he had a tempo to keep up. Jazz of a sort, your feet can't hit the ground. The German interfered with that. There were retakes, and waits while the cameraman got in a new position, or reloaded film. Zack stood there waiting with his dribble stick while the German talked at him. It was being *directed*, and taking the direction more or less meekly, that drove Zack back to drink, I honestly do believe. An ordinary person would have shrugged the whole business off, as a route to making money — for we still weren't making money, a few sales for a couple hundred here and there, all through the 'forties, when thanks to *Life* he had become quite famous, 'notorious' I suppose is the real word — but Zack wasn't an ordinary person. He had this old-fashioned macho sense of honor, and putting himself on show like that — though Picasso could do it, in his little swimming shorts even, as an old man — was for Zack the betrayal of the only thing he believed in, painting. The paintings he did on camera were useless to him, he never looked at them or displayed them, they were failures because he wasn't *in* them, he was on camera. His way of working did produce failures, of course. Sometimes they got what he called 'messy'—too many drips, too many spatters, the whole surface covered, so any rhythm was lost. Then, to lighten it, he would cut away pieces, biomorphic Miró shapes, and mount what was left on fiberboard, and dabble on the fiberboard—I never much liked these, but it was his stubbornness again, refusing to give up, thinking he could pull something out of any mess he made. Those winters of '47 and '48, we were so hard up for canvas he would paint over some of my old work for Hochmann, pouring on these tangles and letting it dry, and then coming back to it three weeks later, going out to the barn even when it was so cold he could only stay an hour and would come back into the house scared his fingers had gotten frostbite, holding them close to the stove."

"Wonderful," Kathryn repeats, more weakly, watching Hope's face to see that she doesn't offend, doesn't trespass.

"Maybe because," Hope volunteers, "I saw how he suffered making them, those early ones, when they still had names and were more vertical than horizontal in shape, are among my favorites. *Galaxy*—they were all galaxies in a way. We could see the stars out on the Island in a way we could never in the city. *Full Fathom Five, Sea-Change*, when there was still some brushwork mixed in with the drips. *Cathedral, Phosphorescence*. He had discovered aluminum paint, gallons of it sold right off Henry Drayton's shelves. There had never been anything like those paintings he did in the cold those first winters. He said it was cold but the light, with the snow, in the barn was glorious. He was so excited how they were turning out, so proud that, as you know, one of the first mural-sized ones, he slapped his hand loaded with black paint along the top as if to say, 'I made this.' It became a cliché, painting with your body, but Zack was the first. All alone in that barn with his sticks and hardware paints, he was inventing performance art."

After a reverent pause, seeing that Hope for the moment has no more word pictures for her, Kathryn asks, "And what were you painting at this time?"

"Nothing. Zero, dear. Zilch. My easel was upstairs, in the little room Zack had vacated, but it basically gathered dust. I was busy with the sort of woman's work that leaves no trace. Cooking, as I said. Zack expected square meals like his mother made, and I had to learn almost from scratch, my own mother had always had cooks, and the cooks would chase me out of the kitchen once I had passed the age where my being there was cute. To be fair, other girls might have insisted on learning more but I liked being *out*, playing with boys. And then I married an artist and became a house slave for his sake. We would give little dinner parties, mostly in the summer, when we could have drinks outdoors, sitting on the boulders in the shade. Eight, ten people at most, counting us—maybe one other painter and his wife and a critic and his and somebody from the gallery world—all designed, you see, to advance Zack's career. I was on the phone a lot, trying to generate more sales; the smaller works on paper were the best bet, being cheaper, and you could hang them on a small wall, an entrance hall or a bedroom. They didn't demand all the oxygen in the room the way the big poured works did."

"Some of them are lovely, the smaller works on paper. Like Chinese ideograms. The ones where the black enamel dried with a silvery edge, the ones with an unexpected color like orange or teal. Quite Zen in feeling."

Hope agrees but resists admitting it. What isn't Zen in feeling, looked at blankly? "He didn't much like doing them, he thought they were gimcrack. I think that was his word. They weren't big enough for him to muscle himself *into*."

His airs, his vanity got worse after the *Life* article, and the world showed signs of coming around to his naïve overestimation of himself. Collapses would occur, sometimes at one of the dinner parties she so carefully constructed, sometimes in a trip to New York, where the sense of a spotlight on him, of bright lights and fortunes to be made as post-war prosperity seeped into the art market, panicked Zack and he fled to the dark depths of a bar and allowed himself to be found only when sodden and abusive. Bedwetting: Hope has tried to forget this aspect of his drunkenness, but it was for her the most humiliating. Her skin in her clothes shrinks from the remembered touch of clammy wetness, warm when issued out of his unconsciousness but cold when it reached and woke her, the liquefied mattress and sheets rendered impossible for sleep, and Zack impossible to wake in order to change the bed. She would desert him for the sofa downstairs or the guest room, her wool nightie half soaked and entirely unwearable, the blankets she could find not warm enough in the cooling house, the pre-dawn saturated with her humiliation and infantile discomfort. Her angry, churning mind would finally impale itself on her shame and defeat and wifely captivity, and in the morning she might rouse to the sound of Zack rustling and humming as he draped the polluted bedclothes on chairbacks for the revived furnace to dry. He took pride in awaking from however degrading a binge with his manly energy intact, hungry for breakfast, a fresh slate before him, his bedwetting for him a discharge, a release, a restatement of his contract with the earth. There is nothing more wonderful about alcoholics than the way they get the world to assume the burden of their misbehavior.

Hope decides to tell Kathryn, "When I did try to take up painting again, he accused me of imitating him. And he said I was lousy at it, any woman would be."

"When was this?" Kathryn asks sharply, her eyes darting down to make sure the tape in her Sony is still running.

" 'Forty-eight. 'Forty-nine. It kept happening. Everything kept happening. He would drink, he would paint, we would go to parties, we would give parties, we would both go to psychiatrists. His brothers and their wives and children would show up at Thanksgiving and Christmas, bringing their mother in tow. She was like a float in a parade, impressive and disconnected—you know, the crowd lining the curbs cheers, the people on the float smile and wave, the parade moves on, the same thing happens farther up the street. His mother had all these domestic skills—cooking, laundry, crocheting, découpage, doing all these dear little artistic things, setting up house in one rough Western town after another, trying to be above it all, creating this island, you see, ignoring the neighbors, drawing the curtains, ignoring the sand and dirt and desolation outside the door, ignoring the way her boys were running wild and her husband hadn't been on the premises for years. She was— what's the word?—'impervious,' she had this lovely shabby-genteel gift for denial, and I think Zack got his power of concentration, of shutting things out, from her. He got his artistic gift from her, if you think of his drip paintings as a huge kind of crocheting. I liked her, though she wasn't much of a conversationalist and had no way of pegging me. To her I was a silly rich girl from Philadelphia. The only reason she had for liking me was that I had taken Zack and his drinking off the family's hands. He was her baby, and big babies get to be a chore. She had this absolutely eerie way of calming Zack when she was around. I think as the youngest he had never got enough of her attention and was still hoping for it. She was like—oh, these words! never get old, Kathryn, everything flies out of your head—a 'basilisk,' isn't that what I mean? She had a *stare.* Anyway, you didn't ask me about that. You keep trying to ask me about me and my work, and I keep hiding behind Zack—the fact is, my work wasn't very interesting at the time, Zack had made this stunning breakthrough and there wasn't room for two interesting artists in one little farmhouse, I took up painting again mainly to give myself a little self-respect, a tiny space where I wouldn't be absolutely crushed by the tremendous thing Zack was doing, and the hangers-on who were beginning to crowd around, and the interviews he was supposed to give, and he was right, my attempts to do the big gestures weren't very convincing. I would get fussy, and try to retouch, to smooth out the holes as Hochmann used to call them, and it pained me to have splotches, it just didn't fit my philosophy to be that much out of control, some on Zack's canvases were so big and thick that the paint would curdle and corrugate in drying, these Duco enamels he brought home were never meant to be poured together like that, with sand mixed in, and cigarette ash, and bugs that made the mistake of wandering into the barn. Also, I didn't have a barn, I had a tiny upstairs room with one window the silver maple shaded so it was always dim, it would have made a great room for developing photographs on cloudy days, or a sewing room with a bridge lamp, so I was stuck with brushes, and collage, which is daintier still—I *couldn't* imitate him, I didn't have the equipment, which I suppose is what he was saying. I didn't have a prick."

Kathryn's long face gathers a waxy glow to itself as the clouding day shifts past noon. Hope back at Cooper Union used to struggle with skin and skin color, skin's translucence and the way it takes light at different depths and glows from within. If she were to paint Kathryn she would have to use a lot of green, to catch the matte dullness, the otherworldly tint. In summer such skin would take a deep even tan miles from Hope's pink freckles. The woman shifts a little in the big plaid armchair that Hope had measured herself in as a child, and clears her throat of a collected dryness. Perhaps she is framing a question to ask, but Hope continues rapidly to prevent her: "So I was floundering in Zack's shadow and got quite interested in what the *other* painters were doing. They had all come out to the Island, mostly all, here and there within ten miles of East Hampton. By '48 or '49, let's say, after Zack had made his breakthrough though none of them liked to admit it, they had each settled on their *shtik*, a signature style they hoped would be as identifying as Zack's drips were. I mean, they all still spoke of painting in terms of self-exploration and an agonized authenticity that would revolutionize the world and whatnot, but the results were a little like company logos, everybody working on the scale of nineteenth-century academic art but each of them having come up with some eye-catching simplification. Phil Kaline had his black-and-white girders, and Jarl these flaky flame-shapes in two or three flat colors, vertical canvases getting so tall he had to convert an old disused Methodist church in Amagansett to work in, and Seamus, poor sweet fat Seamus, who even when doing his 'thirties urban realism—his mar-vellous subway scenes!—painted in a kind of Thomist grid, you could say, had turned to these floating rectangular clouds in a fuzzy milky color, the same hardware paints Zack used but thinned way down, curators say they're desperately unstable, which could have been part of his intention: *vita brevis, ars brevis* too. Roger, who was always thinking so hard, and full of French theory—symbolism, existentialism, structuralism before anybody else had ever heard of it—really only had one painting, oval black shapes like giant beans squeezed between black upright bookends with swatches of color peeping out behind, and Bernie, the other very clever one of us, took to doing colored strips the width of masking tape between giant flat fields of color. It seemed to me and most other people rather arid and doctrinaire, but he always spoke of the great passion with which he painted, and actually Bernie's was the direction painting took in the 'fifties, he was the most influential and least arid in that sense. I loved Bernie, but felt closer to Roger as a painter, stuck with those huge squeezed beans, over and over, though in truth he had another thing he kept doing, he called them rather grandly 'portals,' they were rectangular, a single rectangle, partially outlined, on lovely big sheets of wove paper, each sheet must have cost *dollars*— well, you've been to museums, you've seen all this, but at the time it wasn't so clear that this was *it*, American art's coming of age, these big cartoony abstractions, to me it almost looked like a giving up, a reduction of a complex subjective process to *ideas*, compared with what Zack was doing out of his instincts. Two who wouldn't stop painting, painting the old way, with brushwork and variety and a sort of representation, and still giving titles to their paintings— *Dwarf, Woman*—were Mahlon and Onno, and they suddenly seemed quaint, neither here nor there. What's that thing from the Bible—*lukewarm I spit thee out*? I must have let something of my reservations show, because over in the purple carriage-house that Onno and Renée had inflicted on the landscape, I remember him putting his arm around my waist and pulling me close and saying, 'Dunt you vurry for me, Hope. Mondrian is dead, Picasso keeps on goink.' Meaning that what he was doing, these mad multicolored flurries you could just barely see were seated women, with crossed bare legs and high heels, would survive the devices invented by people like Roger and Bernie, who were intellectuals who really couldn't paint at all in the old art-school way. Zack he respected—he knew Zack wasn't taking it easy on himself, and didn't let it get mechanical. If Zack had been willing to turn himself into America's marvellous drip machine, he wouldn't have gotten stuck after 1950. He wouldn't have killed himself. Zack's behavior was repetitious, but not his painting. He wouldn't let it be, and it killed him."

Onno was handsome, in a pale-haired Netherlandish style, with white eyelashes and full lips and a long chin and bottle-green eyes whose glance felt like a flick on the skin of Hope's face. His hand around her waist was broad and workmanlike; though he drank and smoked recklessly enough to be one of the gang and had adored madcap, doomed Korgi, he was sane, Hope felt, sane as Zack was not. Onno's brushwork looked wild and was subject to such expedients of *dérèglement* as painting with his left hand or pressing a newspaper over a wet canvas and transferring the imprint to another canvas and beginning again, these were all rational maneuvers to suppress his natural facility, his Picassoesque childhood as a precocious product of classic European art-training. He had learned to imitate American violence; Zack, born into it, was its captive. Onno's hand rested long enough on Hope's waist to send a message. He and Renée were one of those Continental couples who looked too good in public to be true. Hope was twenty-six, twenty-seven, old enough to believe she deserved a genius who didn't need a nursemaid. She could do with a little care herself. The breath from between Onno's fleshy, inquiring lips possessed beneath the stale tobacco smell a sort of licorice sweetness.

"Onno de Genoog," Kathryn pronounces. "Would you like to talk about your relationship?"

"Not really. He was a dear, kind, hardworking man and a wonderful painter. He was supportive to me when I needed it, when Zack"—how to say it?—"was falling apart."

Kathryn leans forward to check that the Sony is still running and asks in a voice from which all fellow-feeling has been edited, "Is it true that he thought in the early 'fifties of leaving Renée for you?"

"No. Never. He and Renée were too much of an act, I would never have wanted to break it up. She has been the perfect great man's widow, chastely tending the flame, never remarrying, unlike me."

"You came to the role much younger than she," Kathryn points out. "What about the time in the early 'fifties when Zack broke his ankle wrestling with Onno. Were they fighting over you?"

"Not at all. My dear, as I said earlier, women didn't count for much in that macho world. They were drunk and fooling with each other, they had an artistic rivalry, and Zack came down hard on a low spot in the grounds around the famous purple house."

"Is it true," Kathryn went on, humorless and relentless not an hour after drinking Hope's tea and using her bathroom and appearing awkward and guilty in the corridor to the studio, like a lost child, "that Onno called Zack's work 'pissing on canvas'?"

Hope smiles. "That was not an unkind remark. Anybody who knew Zack knew he was always pissing, in public if he could. He used to tell of watching his father urinate off some rocky ledge in Arizona, it made a huge impression on him, in his child's mind it defined masculinity, the great golden, glinting arc of it. You will remember, Kathryn, that when one of the Pop artists, I forget which but it wasn't Guy, tried to parody Zack it was by urinating on canvas covered with copper metallic paint so the oxidation created patterns. The patterns were spattery and ugly, though, whereas Zack's drip paintings are beautiful, stunningly beautiful, don't you agree?"

"Oh, yes. Certainly." But Kathryn is affronted, being called onstage this way, to give an opinion into her own tape.

"The early ones, as I perhaps said—do forgive me if I repeat myself—are my favorites. The canvas on the floor but still cut to human scale, six by four or so, before he began to give them numbered titles. Before a show he would call me into the barn to help him name them. It was one of the things we did together, one of the few ways I could be a collaborator. He used a lot of aluminum paint early on, and there was a skyey, spinning feeling to them, so I would suggest names from a star book Zack had bought when we first went out to the Island and he could see the stars the way he had seen them out west. *Sirius*, we called an especially cold-looking one, and a reddish one *Betelgeuse*, and another I wanted to name *Cassiopeia* because I remembered that she had bragged about how beautiful her daughter Andromeda was, or perhaps she herself, but Zack didn't want people to look for constellations in the spatters, so we used more general terms like *Galaxy* or *Comet*—and there really is a comet in it, his drips were straighter then than they became in the 'fifties, when he got to do what he called drawings in air, which that German whose name I keep suppressing photographed. One little one done in blues and aluminum paint on a black gesso we called *Magellanic Cloud*. Zack had very little interest in travelling—one of his insecurities—but he did use to talk about going to South America so he could see the Southern Cross and the Coal Sack and the Magellanic Clouds from his star book. And I tried to think of fairy-tale names, like *Sinbad* or *Wotan*. He liked the Jungian idea of mythic prototypes but didn't want people to think his paintings were in any way portraits, so, beginning in '48, he and Peggy labelled them with numbers and the dominant colors: *Blue, Red, Yellow; Yellow, Gray, Black*. The sad truth is, which I'd tell only you, Kathryn"— a dash of irony, to see if her interviewer is still paying attention—"is that I liked the later canvases a little less in part because I was locked out of the naming. And it wasn't long after that that I began to take up my own painting again, which Zack interpreted, not altogether incorrectly, as a hostile gesture."

"Yes. I wanted to get back to that."

"You needn't bother, dear. It was rather paltry, the good wife in me fought the painter all the way. As I said, I tried being Abstract Expressionist, as people were beginning to call it—I think that big red-headed art critic *The New Yorker* had, Coates, Bob Coates, was the first, and he capitalized only the 'e'—but as Zack pointed out, I wasn't very good at it, there wasn't when I did it that eerie control Zack had, no matter how many beach pebbles or cigarette butts he dropped in; he had a sense of balance, of balancing rhythms, that critics since have traced back to his years under, of all people, Benton. The things I did, trying to be free, came out looking like I had burned the dinner, so I began to follow Roger's lead—imitate him, I suppose you could say—and do these austere collages, paper on paper,

with a few black lines in Conté crayon or a Japanese callig-
raphy brush, looking for the point of balance, the look of
quiet. The strange thing, Kathryn—I know you didn't
come all this way for my, oh, what's the word, *vaporing*
about works that have already had bushels of criticism
dumped all over them—the strange thing about Zack's drip
canvases is that, for all the violence of the details, the spattering, the gummy pooling, the overall effect has this, this
quiet. Someone somewhere, maybe it was Frank O'Hara,
funny old Frank with his poems scribbled on odd bits of
paper in his pockets, called Zack our Ingres. Our *Ingres*. It
made me think, it made me cry in fact, years after he was
dead, when the turmoil Zack always created around himself
had died down. There was this peace, this balance and calm,
in his paintings, and I can only think that that was his
mood, out there in the cold in the barn, away from me,
away from the clever critics, away from the bitchy rich
women and cagey foreigners who ran the galleries, away
even from his need to drink: he was at peace, drooling one
design on top of another until he had to stop and wait for
the paint to dry. And there is so much innocence in that
man dancing and kneeling around the piece of canvas on
the floor, such sweet childish absorption in the *doing*, that I
want to hug him and beg his forgiveness for bringing him
out to where he could wrestle beauty to a fall and yet being
unable to show him how to get any lasting happiness out
of his having done it." The image of Zack painting, and
then the two of them side by side bestowing names on his
canvases as upon a set of babies, afflicts Hope so that her
throat catches and she has to pause. Perhaps happiness cannot be lasting. Perhaps the nugget of woe and confusion
within Zack was beyond dissolving. Yet the memory of him
with his habitual scowl (that baffled crease of extra skin

between his eyebrows) and paint-spattered old shoes making those beautiful things in a style never before known, for a public that almost never bought one, for a gallery owner who was losing interest in him, while cigarette smoke dribbled back into his squinting eyes and the cold numbed his hands, seemed in her mind the image of life lost, beautiful life that erases itself, like her young body emerging into besmirched pallor as the coal dust was rubbed off by those hours of sweaty dancing.

To rescue Hope from her pause, Kathryn tells her, "Why would it be your job to show him how to reap happiness? His happiness was Zack's own responsibility, surely."

Hope clears her throat and smiles, tearily, to thank the other woman for giving her her voice back. "Oh, I know that's sensible, everybody is responsible for themselves, that's the theory now, it makes it easier to get out of a relationship, but back then the wife, even a child wife as I was in a way, ten years younger, was supposed to do everything for the husband, the way women did for their children, if anything turned out wrong for the child it was your fault, and Zack was very dependent, worse than a child really, since you got the blame and not any obedience, the guilt and not any credit. Women now talk about empowerment and have all these paying jobs, but back then a woman really was thought to be omnipotent, on no salary, and if anything went wrong in your vicinity it was all your fault. Any resentments about my own upbringing I had I always directed toward my mother, for instance, and not toward my father, who though he supported us was considered otherwise perfectly ineffectual, like a man in a Thurber cartoon."

"What resentments about your upbringing did you have?"

How quickly this lanky intruder can pounce! "Oh," Hope answers slowly, "not very many. Our comfort, I suppose—I thought of it as coming out of the hides of the poor. Our complacency, though I didn't pass up any meals, I noticed, and dressed just the way the other Shipley girls did. Our Quaker heritage seemed to me pretty dim and colorless—I used to daydream about being a Roman Catholic and having all those saints and painted statues. I thought my two brothers got all the *serious* attention, and were expected to do something serious, unlike me, who was just expected to catch a suitable man. The usual sort of resentments a girl of good family would feel."

Kathryn accepts Hope's implication that this is a dead end, for now at least, and shifts her black-clad weight in the broad chair where Isaac Ouderkirk would sit and read the *Evening Bulletin* with tipped-back bifocals. "Did you and Zack ever discuss having children?" she asks.

"We did. He claimed to be quite keen on it."

"Claimed to be?"

"Zack had his enthusiasms, but except for his painting he didn't much stick with anything. I told him I didn't want to raise children with such an unstable man."

She had in fact said, "I don't want a crazy man for the father of my children."

His face went slack. His eyes narrowed to a hurt glitter. "Who says I'm crazy?"

His pressure on her to have children made her tongue harsher than she wanted it, but she could not beg his pardon or she would find herself giving in. Zack had his ingratiating mode as well as his destructive one, the winning child who had grown from the frowning baby. He would worm his way around her, and her well-bred politeness was a weakness he used against her. "The draft board, for one," she told him. "You got your shrink to say you couldn't take Army discipline and they didn't argue."

This hurt him, as she knew it would. He could hardly speak. "You dumb cunt, it wasn't that simple."

She tried to cover with hurried words the wound she had inflicted: "I don't give a damn if you served or not, I was raised to be a pacifist, my brother wound up getting killed because he wouldn't hide behind the Friends, but I know you gave a damn, being stuck in New York with a pack of 4-F fairies all during the war. I don't think the worse of you for it, Zack, but I don't want a baby—your baby, any baby. We're artists. We're poor. You're on to a great thing right now and you don't want to be changing diapers. I'm not even sure you *could* change a diaper."

This was unfair. In small mechanical tasks Zack was often expert. And his feeling for children, his brothers' and those of their friends, for many painters do breed, was tender and quick to kindle. At beach gatherings or lawn parties where ignored children collected in the background, Zack would gravitate to them, shambling up, drink in hand, as if he were still one of them at heart, a reprobate indulgent uncle. But Hope had denied him, in the harshest terms she could muster, calling him unfit, 4-F as a prospective father. His wish for a child had come to her as a wish to make her a mother, stupidly caught up in the needs of an infant at the moment when she was seeking to recover herself as an artist, as an independent spirit. This was when, '49? Though he would be productive for another year, the sunny season of their marriage had passed; her refusal of his so normal desire stood between them. In her memory he took the rebuff by narrowing his eyes like a child who, having been unfairly struck by a cruel parent, stands his ground, expecting another blow, silently vowing revenge.

"It might have made him *more* stable," Kathryn presumes to tell her.

"Or it might not. Then there would have been two of us to suffer, to sit up all night not knowing where he was or if he had been killed."

"But this was in his least drinking period."

"There were still some nights."

"Was he ever abusive? Did he ever strike you?"

Hope tries to be honest. "Not till later, till the 'fifties and his work was blocked. It was I who occasionally hit him, he could be so frustrating, so pig-headed and unreachable. But I think, I'd like now to think, that we both understood I was violent because I loved him and couldn't stand seeing him destroy himself. That he never hit me was a way of keeping his distance, insisting on his superiority. Or that was how I felt it. Remember, I was only twenty-seven, twenty-eight, and still very romantic. Psychologists still spoke approvingly of female masochism. I wouldn't have minded being hit, if it meant real contact."

"You would have been twenty-eight in 1950, when he did those three huge canvases, so different from one another. I think of them as like the three last novels by Henry James."

Tall black laced combat boots, and a Jamesian besides. Perhaps letting her come here wasn't entirely a mistake, the young have their pockets of knowing, their surprising humanity. "Except," Hope says, "that James was sixty and Zack wasn't even forty. Do you think he knew he was going to die? People ask me that and I never know."

"I think," Kathryn states, as if the tape recorder is now for her too, her and her opinions, "he had removed the safety barriers. He was courting death. But that doesn't necessarily mean that death will say Yes. He was lucky, you could say, in being unlucky."

"That seems a cold way to put it." Zack, alive, even so bloated with alcohol his eyes were piggy, tawny slits, was betting in some quarter of himself on more of the same, a life long enough for the redemption that one more master-piece brings. He could pull it off, pull something off just as he had pulled off how to do away with image, how to paint nothing but paint. His hands, she remembers, were some-times startlingly warm, warm on her waist and buttocks in bed. Though she thought of herself as hot-blooded, a lit-tle tidy plump body too anxious to please, Zack sometimes jumped when she touched him, complaining that her hands were cold.

"How can they be cold?" she asked him, hurt.

"Circulation," he explained. "Women have smaller hearts than men. The blood doesn't get to the extremities." He so seldom offered to explain anything, it amused her to hear his practical, mechanical sense applied to their own selves, which she thought of mainly in hazy spiritual terms. Zack saw the two of them as upright instances of flexible plumbing.

Kathryn is smiling at her, seeking a concession. "I'm twenty-seven, as it happens," she tells the older woman. "Does that make me romantic?"

Hope feels a blush warm her face. "More than you real-ize, perhaps. Romanticism is a function not of the mind but of the blood; it's the fever whereby Nature gets her work done."

As before when Hope softens toward her, Kathryn hard-ens: "Did you see any contradiction between the love you say you felt for Zack and your refusal to bear his child?"

"Well, of course. But I was very sure I was right. For his good as well as mine. *He* was the child, he wanted what he wanted when he wanted it. Zack had very little capacity for reflection—for imagining, so to speak, beyond the edges of the canvas. As I told you, that German was shocked when he saw how little Zack hesitated or thought about what he was doing. He couldn't understand how such a mind worked. Neither could I, to be honest. If Zack had had a normal mentality, he couldn't have done what he did. He would have tried to think his way around it, like Roger and Bernie. Even Onno, for all his wild brushwork and Surrealist *dérèglement*, was thinking—was canny. Only Phil and Seamus had Zack's uncanniness, his style of plunging in, of staking his whole soul. And they both died young—both drank themselves to death, aided by pills in Seamus's case. He was always trying to diet. And look at his paintings— the paint gets thinner and thinner, until it's just a wash, a ghost of paint. They said they drank to feed their visions, but I think it was because they knew they couldn't keep it up, the intensity, the painting *for no reason*—nothing to hold on to but their own hands in front of them, moving."

Kathryn lifts her chin, her opaque protuberant eyes flash like those of a predator on the scent. She wants Hope's analytic mood to keep expanding, but already the effort has embarrassed the older woman with its immodesty. Who is she to speak for these dead men, just because she has outlived them?

"You wouldn't have children with Zack, and yet with Guy—"

"Guy was sane," Hope snaps. "He was exceedingly levelheaded. Pop Art was all about sanity, about modesty, about accepting the world as it was, flags and trash and ads and goopy hamburgers, and not trying to heave something impossibly momentous up out of the poor nebulous self. Guy was crisp and irresistible; he made me laugh, and he made our children laugh, when he paid some attention to them. As at first he did. He adored them."

"Before we get into Guy—"

"Let's not get into him. He's still alive."

"But he has Alzheimer's."

"I know. But our children don't have it. I don't want them hurt by their garrulous old mother."

Kathryn glances down, regrouping. Her nostrils draw in; her long white dark-nailed hand reaches out as if for the tape recorder, then withdraws to her long black lap. "Did I understand you to say that Zack's being disqualified for service created or emphasized his doubts about his own sexuality?"

"I don't think I said that, but others have. Apart from his painting, you must realize, Zack was not self-critical. If he had some homosexual experiences, he was possibly too drunk at the time to remember them. Any mouth in a storm, he may have thought. His having been 4-F bothered him less than I may have thought it should. He was beyond, or beneath, politics; if Hitler and the Japanese had taken over the country, I'm not sure he would have noticed for a while. His father had been one of those left-wing Wobbly types, and I think this came down to Zack as a mild contempt for the system, before it was called that. In his dealings with the Federal Arts Project, he took what they offered and gave as little as possible back. He never signed on for a mural project, though one of his brothers *did* work on the one they've restored at the Marine Air Terminal. The main thing Zack got out of the Mexicans was their scale and the archaic symbols."

"That isn't quite what I meant. I've seen interviews and

statements by men in New York during the war who claimed they had had sexual contact with Zack and that he participated in all-male orgies."

"Well, truly. How lurid." Hope finds herself repelled by this woman and her questions—so common, so scandal-mongering. And she dislikes being trapped into a topic where she must doubt her own honesty. "You're asking me," she tells Kathryn, "how queer Zack was. As I said already, he was shy, sexually, but there was nothing queer in"—she blushes, damn it—"in his approach to me. He was an American man of his generation, quite puritan. Once, when we were still in New York, he asked me to masturbate for him so he could watch, and after a minute or two he was so embarrassed he looked away." If this is the topic, she will slap the other with it, coolly punish her with it. "We had straight sex, quite often those first years on the Island, then less often beginning around '49, and the last years, when he was seeing that pathetic groupie, hardly at all. We were like trapped animals with each other, all claws and teeth. But the very day he died he telegraphed flowers to my hotel in Venice. The telegram said, 'Miss you.' He signed it, 'Hopeless.' "

"Where is that telegram? I'd love to see it."

"Oh my goodness, long gone. I don't think I even brought it home, because the next day I got the cable saying he was dead."

This is an unblushing lie. Both telegrams are upstairs in a steel drawer, in a filing cabinet, along with saved reviews of old shows of hers and Zack's and Guy's and brave worried letters from her family when she was young in wartime New York and the clipping from *The Public Ledger* covering her coming-out in 1939 and even her Shipley yearbook signed "Lots of luck" by the girls she knew. Why should she go rummaging for this common-minded intruder to see them, to paw them, these antique telegrams—strips of tele-type pasted onto crumbling yellow paper, the cheapest possible, meant to last a day—which had once had the force to knock the breath out of her? The second had been a blow she thought she could not outlive. The first, Zack had meant for her eyes only. Her heart had lifted at his overture, his shy pun, then sank back in weariness at knowing what her return to him would mean, the terrible soggy burden of his life laid on hers, a life he had lost the capacity to lead, pity and wariness warring within her there, in her front room at the Danieli, the Grand Canal outside her window churned by vaporetti and freighters and a few sails beyond San Giorgio Maggiore glinting within the sea-glitter and the tourist crowds, the Americans and the Germans already indistinguishable, in 1955, prosperous, bland, blond, the losers doing a perfect imitation of the winners, shuffling in their tours along the broad sidewalk for their dutiful look at the Bridge of Sighs, trying to imagine the passions of doomed and shackled prisoners.

Outside the thin-paned windows, birds cannot be seen, a hush has thickened the air. The small shreds of cloud have grown flat lead-blue bottoms and white tops shaped like cauliflowers. Hope wonders if giving this girl lunch would terminate the interview, which is turning ever more invasive. It is strange how, in this shameless day and age, a breach of privacy gives the breacher more and more rights, as if a burglar should start moving the furniture around and loudly ridiculing the décor: having to defend her sex with Zack as normal, and to describe herself naked but for grease and coal dust. Or had that been her own idea, bringing that up, feeling again the brush of air on her exposed abdomen at that overheated wartime dance? Ruk had thought her an exhibitionist, citing the careless readiness with which she stripped to model, his "Quaker Pocahontas," and Bernie, in his rural bedroom loft that smelled of fresh-cut wood, teased her as his red-haired Renoir. She *had* put on a few pounds by then, turning thirty, drinking to keep company with Zack, to muffle her married misery.

"Kathryn, could I offer you a little lunch? I don't know quite what I have—sliced smoked turkey for a sandwich, or a can of tuna I could make into salad. You must be starved. I am."

In a gush of innocent self-promotion the young woman says, "Oh, when I'm interested in what I'm doing I totally forget to eat. Then around four I wonder why I feel so light-headed. But you get up so early, and—"

Are old and frail, she doesn't say, *and have so few pleasures other than food.* Food and reminiscence. What is it, in our pasts, that we keep trying to recover, what misplaced marvel trod under in our haste to live the days, the days which, once gone, acquire the majesty of eternal testimony—*I was there, I did this, the times were such, I was beautiful and pregnant with my potential, my beautiful future?*

"I'm fine," Hope briskly assures Kathryn. "Let's go to the end of this tape. It will do our figures good. Ask me your worst."

"The 'groupie.' Have you ever read her memoir? It's better than you might expect, and presents rather a different image of Zack than the one you're presenting. Clever, suave even, a man of the world, not just the art world."

"Clever, so clever he would have killed her if she hadn't been thrown clear of the convertible when he crashed it into the woods. The friend she had along wasn't so lucky, she got under the car when it flipped. Not Zack—he flew straight ahead into the trunk of an oak like a human cannonball. The coffin was closed at the service because his head was such a mess." The word "mess" stops her tongue, it tastes and stings of something lost, a word Zack was fond of, using it of a painting in which his attempt to overpaint and efface the image had gone too far, to the point where he razored out sections to let life back in. "No, I've not read the groupie's book. It could only be self-serving and semi-literate."

Kathryn looks startled; Hope's tone is new to her, and her terms are outside the non-judgmental critical vocabulary she is used to. As if improving her hearing, she lightly strokes the long black strands of hair above her ear, and carefully responds, "It might not be entirely painful, if you could bring yourself to read it. She writes that, after you gave him the ultimatum and went off to Europe, she moved in expecting to take over, but after the first week of her living in the house, mostly in her underwear—it was especially hot that summer, evidently—he became quite unmanageable. He wouldn't eat the elaborate meals she cooked, he wouldn't defend her when your old friends snubbed her, he drank a case of beer a day. They didn't make love. When he looked at her he only saw you, she writes. She had told the friend who died under the car that it would never work, even though he was everything she wanted, a great artist. Her book keeps this starstruck tone, but she admits she can't imagine how they would have gone on together. You were still too much on his mind."

"As I said, 'pathetic,' " Hope says, her own tone pitiless. Kathryn really should stop feeding her this stale fare, fare once possibly delicious to scandal-mongers and art lovers but after nearly fifty years quite tasteless. Zack had re-enacted with—what was her name? a boy's name—Meredith for two weeks the inchoate callousness she had endured for ten years. Long before Zack stirred himself to find another woman, or she had found him in the celebrity-stalking grounds the Cedar Tavern had become, Hope realized that the marriage was ruined. As long as he was painting, gesturing with his thinned enamels above great rectangles of canvas that accepted swirls of aluminum, lavender, brown, and white to become shimmers of motion, atoms, breath, the speckled depth of air itself; as long as his annual shows at Peggy's and then at Betty's, after Betty had, very much against her own better judgment, taken over Peggy's miserly arrangement with Zack when Peggy upped and went to Europe, were faithfully listed in the art journals as among the year's best; as long as there were a few sales and his name penetrated the murmur of national publicity as an anointed one; as long, in effect, as there was work to do that only he in the history of all art could do, the dazed rapacity of his self-regard could be borne, and she could imagine herself a partner and believe that the daily gift of herself was in some heavenly gold ledger taken into account. But when, in the wake of that film by the directorial German, Zack began to drink in earnest again, and she resumed, in that ill-lit little room upstairs, her own painting, as her only path to an orderly future, then the true face of her marriage showed itself and terrified her. One mid-morning, at that time of day when, new to the Island, they would be bending and stooping in their garden, which was now a neglected weed-patch whose fencing sagged and whose half-rotted gate built by Zack no longer swung open, he came up the stairs, with heavy feet, to this studio of hers and looked at the wet canvas on the easel and the others stacked dried and hardened along the walls, and said, at last, his tongue thick, "Not bad. Not great, but not bad."

Her voice came out edgier, with more fight in it, than

she wanted. She was on her own ground, narrow as it was. "At least I'm giving it a try. I'm not hiding behind booze and bombing around in an old Olds bothering our friends. The few friends we have left." The Ford had been replaced by a great white boat of a second-hand Olds convertible behind whose wheel Zack had become even more of a hazard to himself and others.

"What the fuck're you talking about?" He seemed genuinely not to know.

"You, Zack. I'm talking about you."

"These so-called friends say I'm bothering them?"

"They don't have to say it. Just look at their faces when you stumble in. Look at the way people at parties move to the other side of the room to avoid you, because you want to pick a fight."

His eyes glanced down in embarrassment. "Fuck 'em all. Who are these people?"

"Roger. Onno. Bernie. Bernie said to me he tries to put up with you for my sake. Even Clem, who was your biggest booster not so long ago and thinks he made your name and gave you the theory you needed to function, even Clem avoids you."

"He screwed me in his last review."

"He's worried for you. He wants you to go back to work. Serious work." There was a heavy fragrant danger in his near presence; she heard his breathing—moist, strained by the climb up the stairs—close behind her as she tried to apply a long smooth stroke of alizarin crimson to balance a red spot high in the picture, like a sun burning through sea fog. She had wanted the canvas to be wild, full of push and pull, but it was coming out muted, foggy, composed with a strictness and care she could not shake.

"Clem's a shit. I made *him*, not him me. Roger's a pansy.

At least for Chrissake you've stopped imitating him, all that blank white and portal of life or whatever shit."

This had, in its rough humor, a muffled ring of conciliation. Hope took the moment of remission from Zack's clumsy pressure to try to gauge if the streak of crimson did spring the rest of the canvas into the life that Hochmann had believed arose from tension between colors.

Zack saw where her eyes went, away from him, and resented it. "It stinks, if you must know," he told her. "It stinks of landscape. There's the fucking sun, peeking through the fucking gray clouds. Look, here's our fucking house, there's the barn, these fucking wiggles must be our trees." In gesturing, his fingers scraped the wet paint, and he wiped his hand on her smock. The smock was covered in paint anyway, but it enraged her.

"Don't touch me, you stupid lush. And keep your fingers out of my painting. You don't know what you're doing."

The crease between his eyebrows deepened. "I'm a lush and you're a cunt," he explained to her with a lofty alcoholic calm. "Cunts can't paint. There are pots and brushes, pots don't paint. They don't stick out. Sticks and brushes paint. Look." With the blunt end of a brush resting in the trough of the easel he jabbed the wet paint, making one of his sloppy hieroglyphs.

"Zack, I said don't touch my goddamn canvas."

"I'm giving it some value. Here, I'll sign it, my piece of it. The priceless piece. This'll make it worth a million bucks someday." He bent over, wheezing through his nose, to scribble his scribbly signature with the wrong end of the brush across her wet streak of alizarin crimson. She had never liked his signature, it looked semi-literate to her. She knocked his head away, so a smear of paint came off her smock sleeve onto the glossy bald front of his skull.

Her elbow stung, and must have hurt him, for his eyes watered and narrowed so their tawny color disappeared. He said, still striving out of his daze to be her teacher, "You hoity-toity twat, the greatest painter in the world is giving you advice. Hang it up. Your stuff is crap. Pseudo-representational crap. You never got it, Hope. Your hero Hochmann was a kraut phony who never got it either. He could talk till it ran out his ass, but he didn't have the guts to be a real painter. You're like him, trying to think your fucking way in."

"Let me alone, Zack. Let me paint an hour a day and the rest of the time I'll be your idiotic slave. Just for an hour, that's all I ask. I'm stuck with you out here with nobody but those bums you meet at the Lemon Drop for company—you've offended everybody else, we never get asked anywhere, over at Onno's or Bernie's the whole room freezes when you stagger in."

She kept at this aspect of things because it pained him to think it true, he fancied himself a charmer in spite of everything, the baby brother, his mother's pet, and he kept at her painting because he knew this was the way to hurt her, her sore spot. He had one thought, to sting, to attack; he was like one of the bumblebees he painted into his own drips; the paint hardened and the bee's furry dry body was there forever, mummified. "You poor cunt, trying to think your way in. Stop thinking. Stop standing here. Nothing's going to happen. Go the fuck downstairs and do a little house-cleaning, the place looks like a pigsty. My mother when she was here last—"

"Your mother, don't throw her up to me, she kept house and that was all she did, it was delusional, she thought if she crocheted enough doilies it would make it all respectable, but you weren't respectable, you were a bunch of fatherless undisciplined riffraff who left home as quick as you all could, the only thing she ever loved was the appearance of respectability, of being a cut above what she really was."

"My mother was a damn brave woman. She kept us fed and dressed on the dole Dad sent and kept a damn nice home. Other kids used to want to come home with me, our home was so nice. She'd give them cookies she'd baked herself. She didn't live in any Main Line mansion lousy with servants, she did it all herself. What you can't get through your thick little head is that we don't have any servants, we're the servants."

"*I'm* the servant, you mean to say. I do all the cooking, the cleaning, I make the beds, I try to do the lawn since you've given up and do nothing but drink, if the house looks like a pigsty it's because a pig lives in it—*you.* A pig drunk as a skunk. No wonder our friends hate us. Our former friends. Your colleagues. They pity us, Zack."

"I'm the greatest painter in the world and they know it. That Italian paper said I made Picasso a painter of the past, what did it say, *povero Picasso?* Listen, you poor snotty cunt. My mother is six times the woman you'll ever be." Fury had momentarily burned the fog from his brain, but now he was rambling and stumbling again.

"Get out of this room, please," Hope said. "This is my *povero* little studio, it's dark and tiny but it's mine, the one place around here I can find some peace and self-respect."

Zack stood there, a bumblebee stuck in paint, his puzzled face seeking some distillation, some moral that the mention of his mother reminded him lay at the base of every circumstance. "A woman's place," he came out with, "is behind a broom or on her back." It sounded like something he had picked up at the Lemon Drop.

"Oh?" Hope said. "Is that how you want me? On my

back? Let's go, big boy, it's been ages. Just give me a minute to clean my brushes and slip in my diaphragm."

"O.K., never mind."

"Zack, can't you see, you can't even fuck any more? You must get help."

"The point of fucking is kids," he said.

"Oh, that again. As if you're in shape to be a father. The point of fucking is health, psychological-emotional health."

"Is that what it is?" he mocked. "Drop dead, Hope. You're not my shrink." But she had succeeded in chasing him away; he was turning his back. "Go fuck somebody else."

They would soon be beyond recall. "No, Zack. Wait. You don't mean that. I didn't mean half the things I said, I just get so frustrated, because I love you."

"Like I said, go fuck somebody else. Get off my case."

Half turned away, he heavily turned back to face her, to give her his face, puffy and with a smear of alizarin-red paint where her elbow had struck his high forehead, but still his, those three dimples, the rings of muscle, still giving an impression of amiability and masculine resource. "Get off my fucking case," he repeated, stuck, and tried to focus on her but failed, and the flutter of love, the urgent impulse of reconciliation, died within her in horror at what she saw: he didn't care. He didn't care about her. She had become a mere noise in his ear, an impediment to his vision; he cared only about the quest at the back of his brain, the quest in the barn, where he was finding nothing now. He used to sit and stare at the canvases in progress for hours, but then he would act, he would add paint. Now he did nothing. In his wounded alcoholic brain he was stuck, and she was no help, she was nothing to him, she was a figure in a haze so thick she could be there or not, if anything he hated her, because she made claims, as a fly buzzing makes claims, busily landing on your wrist and lips and creating an unendurable tickle; he needed silence and stillness, all he cared about was art, the fire at the back of the cave, and the rest of the world was illusion, bothersome distraction, he would flick her off like that fly and not even notice she was gone in his leaden dedication to something else, a sacrifice of all that was orderly and decent and daily in the world to the sullen, obsessive blaze of his art, his stupid, selfish art. In his stuckness lately he had reverted in some black-on-white paintings to imagery, faces and figures, doodles making clear again what the drip paintings had so dazzlingly concealed: he could not draw. The face which she had always thought beautiful with its puzzled frown and tawny watchful eyes struck her now as a wall, an ungrateful blankness at which she had thrown her young life and wasted it. Even now, the remembered revelation puts a caustic taste in her mouth, the taste of faucet water that has travelled miles through corroded pipes.

She says to Kathryn, "I suppose it should please me to know that he treated Meredith as miserably as he did me; but she got him, the poor dear, only when he was far gone, she never knew the sober Zack, the hardworking outdoors-loving Zack who was always so sweet to children. At the beach he used to take them aside and build towers of rounded beach stones; that German took photographs of some of them, as if they were works of art too. Am I repeating myself?" She smiles to conceal the taste in her mouth, of sorrow and defeat. "And maybe they were—Tanguys of a sort. There are times, Kathryn, when this whole art business, which has been my life of course, seems terribly transitory and disposable. I go into museums now and look at those oversize, boastful canvases by Zack and Phil and Jarl and it all seems *so* tired—Phil's paintings especially have cracked and puckered, the black looks like tar dried up on a flat roof in the sun, and Seamus's colors have chemically shifted, that marvellous *hovering* they used to do doesn't quite happen any more, the pinks and salmons have gone chalky and scrubby, they've sunk into dullness, and even the aluminum paint Zack used so much in the late 'forties has blackened, I've talked to curators and they say there's nothing to be done, I can remember when those elements *flashed* out at you." Hope looks directly at Kathryn as if somehow challenged by her, somehow doubted. She sighs and goes on, "They weren't Old Masters. They weren't even Picasso: those Cubist paintings he and Braque did side by side in that little village in the Pyrénées in 1910, what was it called?—Céret—are still as fresh as new, I looked at them the last time I was in MoMA a few years ago—maybe more than a few, come to think of it. Zack and the others got away from permanence, they didn't grind their own pigments or have apprentices do it, they took what materials were for sale around them, they didn't care about a hundred years from now, from them, maybe they didn't believe there *was* such a long future, with the atomic bomb; they were like performance artists in a way, going after the effect in the present and not pretending to be making something eternal. Bernie was a little different—he cared about traditional methods. He painted slowly, on sized canvas. When I visited MoMA that time, the two or three big Novas they have looked just the way they always did, they were dear old friends."

"You have gone on record," Kathryn tells her, "as having little use for performance art."

"Well, on the one hand, it's a—what's the word?—tautology: all art is performance, from the caves on. On the other hand, what is commonly meant by it goes against my every sense of what art is. *Life* is the performance; art is what outlives life. Which of course is why they do it—to upset old-fashioned souls like me. But it has gone old-fashioned itself very quickly, hasn't it?"

Kathryn doesn't answer; she poses another question, in a tone of voice meant to be just like that in which she couched the previous one but to Hope's ear coated with a glaze, a transparent hardening as if chemically to neutralize its entry into a more intimate region of memory. "How important to you was your relationship to Bernie Nova?"

Hope doesn't give her the satisfaction of more than a moment's pause. "It was important as a transition," she stated. "Bernie had always teased me, I knew he liked me, we all knew it, and after Zack's death there weren't so many of the old Cedar Tavern crowd who wanted, frankly, much to do with me. They were jealous of Zack's fame—he had become, almost the instant his head hit that tree, *the* painter of his time, the performer and symbol both, yet he had been such an impossible drunken boor toward the end that a kind of stink clung to his widow as well. I was just thirty-three when Zack died—I had this huge empty life in front of me." She tries to clear her throat of its sudden roughness, its lump of revived desolation. "Oh my goodness," she says, laughing as her eyes tear up and Kathryn's severe face blurs, "I've got this terrible frog suddenly. My throat isn't used to so much talking. We should eat."

"Before we do," Kathryn persists, "there's something I'd like to come back to. You speak of Zack's last five years as pure disaster, but several critics in the 'nineties have been looking hard at what he *did* manage to do. One of those semi-poured black-on-white biomorphs on canvas went for nearly three million at Sotheby's last year."

"Poor Zack, he never saw any real money. We lived on these grudging doles."

"*Angel Bower* was used on a postage stamp, as you know, the post-war artists series. I've always loved its return to Matisse-y colors."

"I named it, it was one of the last ones he let me help name. There was this shady corner he strung a hammock in, beneath the silver maple, this side of the barn. But it didn't seem to you to be—how I can put this nicely?—a doodle?"

"No, I find it very contemplated. And the big vertical panel he did as late as '54, *Number 61*, the flickering tongues eating into the black center, critics call it his homage to Jarl Anders but I think it's better than Anders, it has what Anders never has, a feeling of passion and doubt, a sense of *fighting through* to something, through something *else*. In Anders, for me, it all happens without enough resistance."

"Jarl had been a minister's son. He used to write Zack these insane letters, lots of Xed-out typing, telling him to keep his integrity, fight the good fight, revolutionize humanity, throw out the money changers, et cetera, and Zack took them as encouragement, addressed to his better self, which almost nobody else gave him credit for having, they were so jealous of his fame and disgusted by his drinking and rudeness. I think Jarl reminded Zack of Benton in a way—one of those crusty men's men from the heartland. And somehow Zack's difficulties after 1950 proved Jarl's point about the society being a totalitarian trap and the art community being hopelessly corrupt. He saw painting as a matter of conscience, and this appealed to Zack, with his intense, fragile way of working. But when Zack would get into the old Olds—he never owned a new car, *never*, think of it, just the Model A and then this overpowered heap that got maybe ten miles a gallon and took at least one quart of oil every time we stopped for gas—and would drive all the way over to where Jarl and Frieda had the Amagansett house and Jarl worked in this abandoned Methodist church, Jarl wouldn't come out from under his Jaguar, which he was always tinkering with. Frieda had some money, which I didn't. My father was still alive, and my older brother, the one that wasn't killed in the war, had the inside track back in Philadelphia; they both disapproved of me and my marriage to Zack, they saw him as a sozzled brute, they couldn't imagine what attracted me. And in fact, if you *must* know, Kathryn, there wasn't much of the family money left, my father had pretty well pissed away—I suppose it's acceptable English to say that now—what he had inherited from my grandfather. Oh dear, where was I? Jarl. He had this vision of eliminating European influence from American painting, which was about like trying to eliminate European blood from the population. He called Zack's work 'unravelled Impressionism.' He had quite a sharp and funny tongue, but Jarl was one of the few men, I must say, I knew in those days who *didn't* strike me as attractive. He was tall and gaunt and yellow in color, with dead-looking hair and protruding teeth. And a *glare*. Such a glare, I'd feel myself wilting under it. He didn't approve of me either. He saw me as a playgirl. He saw me as the Devil's party."

Kathryn gingerly leans forward to check the little gray tape recorder and satisfies herself that it is still purring. "Hope, could we get back for a moment to your relationship with Bernie Nova?"

Addressed with this sudden familiarity, Hope takes a, for her, violent initiative and stands up; the rocking chair of many woods, relieved of her weight, swings away from the backs of her legs. Her knees ache, her throat is parched, emptiness sits in her stomach like a pain pill she can't digest. "Oh my dear," she says. "It was all so long ago. Let's have something to eat, you must be frantic with hunger."

Though she is not tall, standing alters her perspective so that the room, this boxy, lightly furnished front parlor with its dainty-muntined windows curtained in faded brownish chintz, is jolted into strangeness: the undersized but formal Ionic-pilastered fireplace mantel, painted cream; its burden of a small gilt-cased clock and two brass candlesticks and a silver-framed color snapshot, its dyes ebbing, of her three children in bathing suits smiling beside a turquoise Connecticut swimming pool when they were all under ten, more than thirty years ago; the walnut piecrust table with its fat blue ball of a ceramic lamp-base and four stacked cork coasters like oversize poker chips; the plaid armchair and a rusty bridge lamp of similar ancient vintage, its paper shade darkened as if charred and bearing the printed image of a pointing setter; the oval rug formed of a coil braid of varicolored rags; the pine floorboards painted a dark red and broader than any you could obtain now; the bare and subtly uneven walls of real plaster, dressed up bleakly with a few small abstract prints, gifts from old friends now dead; against one wall, a bookcase whose lower shelves are too narrow for all the art books that jut out. It all seems charged with strangeness, the strangeness that the afterlife, however much like our life on earth it is, must have to the newly dead. She rarely sits in this room; the kitchen, her bedroom above it, and the studio beyond it contain her usual orbit. Each evening, having added the supper plate and glass to those already waiting in the dishwasher for it to be full enough to run, she thinks of coming in here and drawing the curtains behind the plaid chair against a draft and reading her book of the week, or even looking into one of the art books growing dusty, but she rarely does, drifting upstairs to the warmth of her bedroom instead. Climbing the stairs—"climbing the wooden hill," her grandfather used to call it—hurts her knees and left hip but helps keep her mobile, she believes, helps keep her for another year out of one of those assisted-living facilities with rubber floors and off-limits stairwells where her two sons would like to see her settled for the ease of their own consciences, it would make *them* look bad if she were to die alone and broken on the stairs à la Edna St. Vincent Millay. She so rarely sits in the front parlor that the space from her standing, momentarily light-headed perspective appears startled, its corners jarred into flight, elastic and awry like the corners in rooms by Van Gogh or Lucien Freud. There is something lavender, a psychedelic tinge, in the papered walls, in the thin warped windowpanes, that at moments enters Hope's eyes from the side, as if the room's inhabitants in the century now gone had breathed a tint of their lives onto these surfaces.

She turns to lead the way to the kitchen, and behind her Kathryn snaps off the little Sony, their faithful witness, impassive as a security camera whose fuzzy evidence is eventually tossed out of court. She sees, walking past windows, that the sky, this morning so blank and pure a blue, is closing down, the scattered white clouds expanding to crowd out the spaces between them, packing themselves together as tightly as gray flagstones, with something vaporous arising even in the chinks, so that the sunlight leaking through is tremulous, like the shuddering reflections from the windows of a passing train. When shadows return after these gleaming intervals, the light seems deeper, more enclosed, having dipped deeper into some darker element, so that the twigs and branches around the bird feeder look blackly wet. Hope switches on the rheostatted kitchen lights overhead, portholes sunk into a drop ceiling concealing the one of stamped tin, painted pumpkin-color and smoke-stained, here when she and Jerry bought the place twenty years ago. The digital clock on the microwave oven says in segmented red numbers 1:22.

"So long ago," she repeats, "and Bernie I know would want me to be discreet. He and Jeanette had the kind of tactful arrangement between them that Zack and I never arrived at. I was too young and idealistic; Zack was too primitive, too square in his way. Now, Kathryn. Let's think together. I could heat up some canned soup—split pea, or chicken with rice—and make a tuna salad. I know I have one can left, because I made a note to buy some more in Montpelier."

"What would you do if you were alone?"

"But I'm not alone. If I were, I'd probably go wander outdoors with a handful of Brazil nuts and dried apricots—there's a health-food store in Montpelier where everything is monkey-food, to be eaten with your hands, all sorts of nuts and dried fruits and yogurt-covered little pretzels, that you imagine must be terribly good for you but in fact are loaded with calories and sugar. People speak of natural foods as if nature isn't where everything bad ultimately comes from. I'm looking into the fridge, but we don't want to make sandwiches, do we? Too much starch, whoever said bread was the staff of life? Either Jesus or Mr. Pepperidge. And the canned soup, chock-a-block full of salt and preservatives. You must starve yourself to keep so lean, those drinks and heavy meals boyfriends make you consume, taking you out, trying to impress you with their fat wallets. Or are you in, what do they call it now, a relationship?"

"I run," Kathryn says, ignoring the last question. "I've loved to run ever since I was a girl."

"So did I, but then it wasn't considered proper after a certain age, away from the hockey field. Now exercise is so fashionable, in the summer people are running all over the roads up here, it's a wonder more of them aren't killed."

"I live on Liberty Street, near the World Trade Center, and can run in Battery Park City, along the river."

"Is it safe?"

"Oh, sure. My building's tacky but it's less rent than in TriBeCa. I'm above a mattress showroom and a hair stylist. In the daytime the whole area bustles with all these beefy young guys in finance, but when they go home to New Jersey or wherever it quiets down. It's a very safe area."

"Good. New York used to be safe everywhere, or so we thought, when we were young and foolish. Do sit down. Or would you rather look around, to gather details for your article?"

"It's not that kind of article, exactly."

"What kind did you say it *was*, exactly?"

"My articles aren't like other people's—they're more essayistic. Impressionistic, you could say. I never quite know what I'll say until I start to say it."

"An excellent way to proceed. I wish I could paint more like that. I must always look ahead, it's my timidity. Now, let's see—tuna salad. Here's the tuna. Would you like to open the can for me? My hands are still good for most things, but turning that little lever does set off my arthritis, I hope you never get it, it comes on knuckle by knuckle; I first noticed it when I would pinch a finger in the pages of a book to mark the place while I answered the telephone. It would hurt, and after that, any pressure sets it off, especially on days like today that are building up for snow or rain.

One of the reasons I thin now with stand oil is that the paint goes on easier. Celery. I know I have celery in one of the drawers, I hope not *too* wilted."

"Would you like me to chop it for you?" The young woman's face, above the round squat tuna can she has deftly opened, seems itself to have opened, to be childishly expectant in the stark kitchen light, the illumination that fills every crevice and forms a bulwark against the gloom outside, where cloud shadows dip across the dead lawn like swallows in summer. Kathryn perches on a stool at the serpentine-topped island, and the opened can releases a genie of oily fish-smell, tuna hauled flopping and gasping from thousands of miles away, out in the heaving Atlantic, everything pitching and sliding and flipping and dying.

"No, no—you just sit. You must be tired, on a poor night's sleep in a strange motel. Are you going back to the motel tonight?"

"Oh no, tonight I'm driving back to New York. I thought I might be on my way already."

Hope is relieved. This intruder will be leaving soon, or if not soon at least there is a definite end to her visit. Why can't Hope herself set the limit, asserting the prerogatives of her greater age and superior prestige? Her desire to please, to be loved, has plagued her all her life. Even now, who asked her to feed the girl lunch? From the look of her she can feed herself or skip a meal; if she's Jewish she was stuffed by her mama from Day One, they take care of their own, compared with Hope's own mother, who left it up to the cook or put the growing girl on her own diet rations, a little dry cereal for lunch, a canned pear on a leaf of lettuce, wolfing down cigarette smoke instead, loathing the fat Pennsylvania bodies around her; no wonder Hope was a nervous, imperfect mother with such a model to follow. She feels now the blood beating eagerly in her cheeks and throat, and her hands on the eight-inch knife trembling with the urgency of this quite unnecessary performance. Her back is to the girl, she is at the sink, at the chopping board next to the sink, under the ribbon lights installed beneath the cabinets, within a step of the refrigerator. She rips away the tough and stringy outer celery stalks and chops two paler inner wands into arches half an inch long and, her left hand pushing together a quick small heap, minces these arches into bits smaller than dice, her right hand pumping the knife up and down on the fulcrum of its lethal point. Then from a lower fridge drawer that holds a number of neglected delicacies—she must remind herself to keep cooking, to keep living, to fight slumping into a cranky senility munching nothing but nuts and raisins— she retrieves a tired, shrivelling red pepper, a wilted bouquet of parsley with its paper supermarket band still on, and a lemon going greenish-white at one end. She minces the parsley and cuts the lemon in half, dropping into the Disposall's rubber mouth the moldy half. She cuts open the pepper, gouges away the seedy interior, and carves the husk into strips she then chops crosswise. She takes the can of tuna from between Kathryn's idle long black-nailed hands where the girl sits watching at the green island of serpentine, and inverts the can into a drainer held over the sink, removing the excess water, and mixes the friable pinkishbuff fish-flesh, not too long ago supple and swift in the cold Atlantic, in a small Pyrex bowl with a dollop of mayonnaise, stirring in the fragments of celery and red pepper, many of the latter diamond-shaped, she cannot help noticing; from deep in her memory flickers the image of her mother's sinewy sportswoman's hands, the fingers too lean for her big diamond rings, swiftly fiddling at some kitchen task at the level of a child's eyes on an old wooden counter. So her mother did venture into the kitchen now and then. As Hope mixes, she squeezes in all the juice the unspoiled portion of lemon will yield to her own aching, ugly arthritic fingers. More than the pain she minds, vainly enough, the shame of her bent fingers, fingers no longer parallel; the way they rub together she finds disgusting. As she squeezes and stirs she tells her listener, "Bernie was consoling. He had his own sorrows too in those years, the early 'fifties. His shows at Betty's in '50 and '51 were absolute flops, they were ridiculed—these big canvases with a vertical stripe or two after all his heavy Nietzschean or whatever pronouncements of the 'forties. He wasn't included in the 'Fifteen Americans' show at the Modern in '52, which infuriated him. People laughed at him—his monocle, his mustache, his grand way of talking. He looked like an absolute washout, supported by his wife's money. Jeanette part-owned an interior-decorating outfit on Madison Avenue. She was in the city a lot; they had kept their apartment on Central Park West, they could afford to do that, whereas poor Zack and I . . ."

She can feel the tension in her listener, Kathryn fearing that Hope will spill the details of her affair with Bernie Nova while the tape recorder is idle in the other room. She leans forward at the green island as if to rise, asking, "Can I do anything to help?"

"No, dear, you sit. This is very simple." Hope has found a head of iceberg lettuce, pounds it on the cutting board to loosen the leaves from the heart, and tears off four large leaves to share between the two lunch plates—they have chipped pink rims and botanical images of wildflowers in the center, lavender *Veronica anagallis-aquatica* for Kathryn, yellow *Diplotaxis muralis* for herself—and with a sterling-silver serving spoon she has many times seen in her mother's glittering hand tries to measure out equal portions of mucilaginous tuna salad onto the overlapped lettuce leaves. She sprinkles on the minced parsley and, in a final inspiration, tops the mounds with a few walnut halves from a plastic health-food-store envelope on a fridge door shelf. "Tell me what you want to drink."

"What are the choices?"

Yes, her mother spoiled her, waited on her, as Hope is doing now. "Skim milk, cranberry juice, orange juice, faucet water, ginger ale but the bottle's been opened, I can't guarantee it won't be flat. I'm having cranberry juice."

"Doesn't it make you pee? I mean, people in general. I'm thinking I'll be in the car a long time."

Hope has to smile at how this young woman keeps holding out hope of her departing and yet keeps saying "pee" and appears more and more trustfully dependent. "I've not noticed that effect myself. But, then, I tend to be at home most of the time. You can have water, but it won't be the bottled water you're used to, the big plastic jugs are too heavy for an old lady to lug home from the supermarket, and the water here is from our own spring, farther up the hill, as pure as God makes it." She supposes that "God" from her lips is as gauche as "pee" was from Kathryn's. They are both growing too used to each other's company. They are like boxers whose reflexes are slowing in the late rounds.

"Is it filtered?"

"By the sand in the ground."

"I'd like to try it, please. Real spring water. The salad looks lovely. The walnuts are a jolly idea."

"I would have added olives and anchovies if I had them."

"I'm so embarrassed, I never meant to make you feed me."

"My pleasure, truly. I eat alone all the time. Let's sit over here." The kitchen table, under the Andersen window, is a five-foot circle of two-inch oak screwed fast to an octagonal column whose four long oak feet need a folded piece of cardboard—a matchbook is too thick—to level them; the table is a remnant of her marriage with Guy, from the kitchen in the Seventy-ninth Street apartment. They all ate on it—children, the help, Guy and she late at night. Now the table is permanently set with two straw placemats fabricated of a continuous braid on the principle of the oval rag rug in the front parlor. Hope brings forks and paper napkins and in a second trip the glasses of cranberry juice and spring water, continuing, "They say the old forget to eat eventually, but it hasn't quite happened to me. Food is—what?—the last intimacy. We don't want to give it up." The tuna, she thinks, beginning to eat, could do with salt. The lemon juice is sharp, on the edge of turning. She should have thrown the whole lemon away. "We could do with bread, I suppose," she says.

"I wouldn't mind," the guest admits. The girl is a taker; at her age, that is health. "Let me fetch it," she says, and quickly stands, with a scrape and clatter of boots and stool legs.

"In the big drawer in the middle at the end next to the sink," Hope tells her, "there's a built-in breadbox. The lid has little holes you lift it by, it's hard with my fingers. There's Pepperidge Farm rye." She realizes it may say "Jewish rye" on the label, but then decides it doesn't matter, the girl may not be Jewish, her black hair in the light here declares its reddish tinge, more blatant than just a tinge,

more electric, frankly unnatural, twenty-first century, this
seems to be the fashion, nobody lets their hair alone any
more, trusts it to be beautiful enough. Body-piercing, tat-
toos, how strange to her generation, for whom the unadorned
untouched body, as pure as unflecked marble (even in staid
old Philadelphia, Greek slave girls and Indian maidens
stood naked in the galleries, sculpted by American Victori-
ans in Rome, what *were* their names?), formed the ideal, the
ultimate beauty, so that her own freckles, on forearms and
shins and the sunbaked area above her breasts' blue-veined
white, were a flaw in her mind, forgiven by the shadows of a
bedroom. Bernie's bright house had discomfited her at first.
While the girl fusses at the breadbox and searches the cup-
boards for a suitable plate—as with most children, it would
have been easier to do it yourself—Hope sees through the
western window by the table as she controls her impatience
and waits for the bread to be clumsily fetched how the sky is
darkening behind its close-packed clouds, a sky has materi-
alized behind the sky, a blue-gray haze behind the cauli-
flower tops, a pattern of agitated streaks and tatters like the
mounting flakes in a Jarl Anders painting turned sideways
but, because mindless, grander than anything Jarl had done,
more merciful because unpremeditated, not indignantly
calculated to win glory or reverse two thousand years' corruption, serene in their aloof yet urgent movement, these
spacious eddies of atmosphere expressing a disturbance in
the west, a vaporous convulsion approaching from New
York State.

"Oh, thank you, perfect," Hope says, as Kathryn brings a
dessert plate holding more bread than three times as many
women would eat, and the cow-shaped butter dish discovered in its nook on the fridge door. In eating, Kathryn carefully swallows and more than once touches the corners of

her lips with her paper napkin to spare Hope any sight of gluey tuna salad being masticated amid her pretty teeth and tongue. "And yet," she says, "Bernie Nova's work was what led to the next stage—color-field painting, and Minimal—"

Hope is so eager to agree she doesn't let the other pronounce "-ism." "I know! Who would have thought it! The younger artists saw something in Bernie they could *use*, whereas Zack and Onno and Phil, there was nothing more to do in their line without being *them*. They were so individual, so furiously themselves, let's say—"

She is in turn interrupted: "They were so *hot*," Kathryn says, still watchful of her oil-soaked mouth, her tongue and teeth coated with the brackish scent of fish, but eager to arrive at some confluence with Hope's line of thought, "cool was the only direction left."

"Yes. I'm glad Zack never saw it, it would have enraged him, what came next, it would have seemed to him so trivial, so insincere."

She and Bernie would go to bed on some of those afternoons when Jeanette was in town working at a client's apartment, but not as many stolen afternoons as might have been, had lovemaking been the essence of their coming together. They were artistic waifs, lost here, toward the tip of Long Island, between Onno's flickering mastery and Zack's epochal liberation into dripping; even Roger, that perpetual schoolboy copiously producing his French-flavored collages and Zen-like dashes and blobs of black on princely large sheets of white wove paper, enjoyed a security within the well-heeled world of critics and collectors, museums and galleries, which magnified his modest talent and give him substance, a grip on slippery artistic fashion. Hope was demoralized by Zack's scorning her work as pathetically female and Bernie by the art establishment's dismissing him as foppish and "literary." In an hour's escape from a house where all was sullen hangover, inflamed resentment, daily blockage, and nightly binge, she took nurture in the Novas' newly built home—its shining floor-boards of pale maple, its bare beams of oak, its picture windows in which strips of gleaming sea and milky sky were mounted above a breadth of dusted green potato rows, its two-story studio where Bernie's mocked monochromatic canvases grew defiantly bigger and bigger, boasting Latin titles like medals the painter himself had bestowed. The second floor of the house was a huge loft; it gave, beyond a low balustrade, on the upper space of the studio, so the paintings were presences that shared the bedrooms, which were fragrant of new wood, and had the simplicity of a den, in Scandinavian shades of teak and blondness and unbleached wool, most starkly in the guest room, where, on a mattress supported by a sheet of plywood, Bernie played host to Hope's rounded body, which even through winter stayed drenched in reddish freckles, freckles so thick on her shoulders and shins as to merge and approach the Mediter-ranean tan of the other wives. Hope thought her bare body a fair swap for Bernie's cocky sardonic humor, the dandyish visual jokes of his monocle and tailored English suits, the fatherly rumble of his voice in his chest, broad as a Cos-sack's. He was a third-generation Russian Jew, his name a self-invented simplification of Novakhov, and his mustache like a detail from Gogol, with a life of its own. When he talked, the waxed tips twitched and it was easy to forget the rest of his face—the porous blunt nose, the bear-brown eyes, the rather feminine hidden lips, rapid and decisive in their enunciation.

"I don't give a rat's fuck if I ever show in New York again," he told her. "Why bother, it's all politics, all you get is abuse. They're scared of me, I'm too serious for those gossipy queer bastards. I frighten them by thinking seriously, by thinking religiously. They aren't ready to have their cozy little chattery world rattled by a revolution—a revolution arriving from within, out of an artist's passion. I've got my painting now so it's pure passion, high passion pure and simple, and it scares the stoops shitless. I scare them because, where they just talk, I *do*. Where they chew the old cud, the old pieties, I believe. I believe my art, if its principles were grasped in full seriousness, would mean the end of state capitalism."

"Oh, Bernie, how?" Hope drowsily asked. A breeze from the outdoors stroked her skin, dried the sweat on the side not pressed against the wrinkled sheet. Bernie when making love sweated like a man in a steam bath, and a partner took the bath with him.

"Geometry," he answered, emphatically. "Geometry is what imprisons us, and it has to be overthrown from within. It all goes back to Cubism; my geometry refutes Cubism. Where they drew edges, using outlines to set off shapes and spaces, my drawing *declares* the space. Instead of *segments* of space, I work with the *whole* space; I fill it to bursting with color. I've killed anecdote and set color free, for the first time in the history of man. No more anecdotes, representational or abstract. The critics don't get it. They're the last people equipped to get it. The art world lives under the capitalist table, happy to pick up scraps. The slaves don't realize that upsetting the table is the way to get fed."

"You sound so violent, for such a pussycat."

"The bastards have made me violent. They've put my back against the wall. It's the artist's lot to set himself against the world. The point is the painting, period. Being unknown and shat upon is the true heroism. Anonymity is the true and only thing. Look at your hubby. He's famous now—*Life*, the gossip columns—and it's driving him nuts, right over the edge. But being nobody is doing the same for me, frankly. It's a miserable trade, Red—how the fuck did we get into it?"

"Our love of beauty?"

"Beauty—nobody uses the word. That's not the category, my little Hottentot." She had told him that story from her flaming youth; he twirls his fingers at one end of his mustache and gives a villain's laugh. "Your category is doomed, my fair lady. The *sublime* is the category. If it ain't sublime, haul it to the dump. It's anecdote. Brushwork is anecdote. It's taken me twenty years to figure that out, that's how dumb I am."

Hope wondered how much of what he said was parody, employing a vocabulary he detested. Yet his canvases bore trumpeting titles like *Vir Heroicus, Crux, Spatialis, Ultimo Ratio, Animus Sine Termine*, grand names like *Solomon, Moloch, Guinevere, Azrael*. "The stoops say my canvases are empty but in fact they're full, full to bursting. Anybody who stands in front of them with eyes and a heart can feel the dome of sky over his head, the horizon at his back. They're full of *color*, not colors. You know as well as I do there's such a thing as false excitement. Spatters and swirls and dabbles that don't fill the void at all." This was a dig at Zack, but she, having betrayed Zack with her body, was in no position to defend him. "Empty activity," Bernie pronounced, rolling toward her so that an amber whiff of his aftershave washed across her nostrils, followed by a sadness of elderly sweat, the sourness men come to carry in the wrinkles of their neck. "You look, and there's a lot there, a lot of colors swooping this way and that, but there's no sense of fulfillment, it's anecdotes, it's like drinks, one demands another, they don't lead anywhere, it's *The Perils of Pauline*, each episode leaves us hanging. But the stoops in New York, the stoops in charge of reputations, they don't want fulfillment, they want excitement. Fuck 'em, I say. What do you say, Red?"

"To be honest, Bernie, I wouldn't mind some recognition. On my own, away from Zack."

"I hereby recognize you, Hope McCoy, as the sweetest tootsie to come my way since I hit forty-five. These sessions are saving my life."

"How you tease."

"I tease you not. Come live with me and be my love, and we shall something something prove."

" 'All the pleasures.' That's cruel teasing, now. Jeanette is a treasure, Zack is so jealous of—" She stops herself from saying, *of painters whose wives have money.*

But he sensed where she was going, and his fine little mouth, its sardonic small muscles, twitched the tips of his mustache. "Jealous of the bucks she brings in. I bet he is. When is the poor shmuck going to ease off the sauce? He's going to kill himself and take somebody else with him. I don't want it to be you."

"Bernie, you care. How dear. He needs the intensity," she tried to explain. "The way he paints, it's like playing jazz, he needs to drown out other noise. I don't think, when he's quiet, his head is quiet, if you know what I mean." *Who says I'm crazy? The draft board, for one.*

"Poor shmuck," Bernie said, and rolled himself heavily out of bed, launching them into the awkwardness of scuttling, *Vir Heroicus* and Hottentot, into their clothes. As she stood naked by the balustrade, spattered with freckles, the smell of paint and its chemical thinners rose to her from the studio a floor below, the vast monochromatic canvases, and she remembered the name of the once-famous sculptor of the Greek slave: Hiram Powers. Powers and his friend Horatio Greenough, who sculpted George Washington as a bare-chested Zeus. Through Bernie and Jeanette's huge glass wall she saw the potato fields in their sunstruck, industrious rows; orderly rows of things, from desks in a classroom to stripes in seersucker, always spoke to her in her private language of peace.

"Bernie was nice to me," she tells Kathryn, "at a time when I felt lost. Lost in regard to my own work, lost in regard to what to do about Zack. He was destroying himself, and for my own sake I had to stop caring so much."

"Did you and Bernie ever discuss marriage?"

"Never. He and Jeanette had a fine arrangement. He was happy enough with her and, happy or not, he was financially dependent. I wasn't happy with Zack, but I was bound to him. The worse we fought, the closer we were bound. He had done something great, and to me that made him a hero. Also, let's face it, where else did I have to go? Back then there wasn't this absolute freedom that your generation has grown up with, this almost *duty* to do whatever you want. We expected hardship. Depression and war and then the Chinese and the Russians to stave off. We were hardy, pious folk in our way. And yet, you know, I wonder if we didn't get more *fun* out of being American than you do. The oceans our people had come over were still huge, and things still felt new—banjos and streets on a grid and jazz and all those inventions we took credit for, like the airplane. The songs on the radio, the Sunday-night comedians, the soda fountains and patent medicines—they were *ours*." She is beginning to sound like a windbag; thinking back to Bernie has made her oratorical. He loosened her up. With each different person we are slightly different and, yes, she had liked the self he gave her. He kidded her, and she liked being kidded. Her grandfather used to kid her, gently.

"The, the physical part with Bernie—"

Oh my, this girl is determined to get into bed with Hope and her men, even without her tape recorder running. In a fit of impatience that shakes her old body like a creaky cat-boat in a gust of wind, Hope tells Kathryn firmly, "Bernie Nova was a sensitive, healthy man who didn't drink usually until six in the evening, and for me that was a very welcome change." At a softer, forgiving pitch, woman to woman: "He was a dandy but not a ladies' man. I think, as with a lot of men, he found sex philosophically embarrassing. He and Jeanette had grown out of it. Or so he told me. But, then, that's what married men do say. Now: there's a little more tuna salad."

"Oh no, I couldn't. It was delicious, but more than enough. I often just have a cup of yogurt for lunch."

"Then let me finish it up for you, right out of the bowl, if you don't mind. I hate to throw anything away, it's such a nuisance shopping for it and hauling it home, but then I hate filling the fridge with moldy leftovers."

Recalling Bernie has stirred her up, given her an appetite. Eastern Long Island had seemed young itself then, thinly populated, sparsely invaded by a few choice souls from the city, the marshes and beaches and rocky bays locked into communion with the days of the glaciers; the sun beat down even into November, unsoftened by the heavy green trees of Ardmore, those black walnuts and horse chestnuts and broad-leaved tulip poplars towering up out of the lawns and estate grounds like thunderheads, their shade making the grass thready and tender, even the tennis players hardly tan beneath the muggy white sky. Ostensibly off to East Hampton for an hour of errands, she would speed over the flat and sandy terrain in the Olds convertible like some noontide version of Emma Bovary running barefoot through the dawn meadows to her rendezvous; Hope sees herself skimming between the potato fields and farm stands to Bernie's elegant house—Bernie's great canvases of passionately blank color, Jeanette's smart subfusc Madison Avenue taste—while Zack, having bicycled to the Lemon Drop or in his baffled funk gone walking the marsh edges with Trixie, was lifted from her mind, the gloomy burden of him. She, in her flapping headscarf and sunglasses, feeling as weightless as an arrow, did not pollute the landscape but instead took innocence from the fields, the salt-bleached cottages, the shingled windmill at the end of Fireplace Road. Zack rarely stirred from his marital stupor to ask where had she been, why these few vegetables from Drayton's or a roadside stand, these toiletries and aspirin from Rowe's Pharmacy, had taken so long to purchase, or how she had spent two hours sizing up sweaters and pleated skirts at the Hamptons Department Store and not buying any. "Also," she would lie, if he asked, "I checked out the fall line at the Kip Shop. There was nothing for my figure, it's all for skeleton-types eighteen years old. I thought of looking at the stores in Sag Harbor, but halfway there thought better of it. The car, by the way, sounds funny underneath, when it changes gears. When did they last check the transmission fluid?" Having sex with Bernie, she wants to tell Kathryn, was like a woman serving herself lunch, taking pleasure twice, in giving the food and then in consuming it.

"No, I don't mind," the girl stupidly responds, as if Hope had really asked for her approval. Perhaps she was off in her own mental world, looking backward or ahead, beyond this interview, whose limits she had already gauged, though, strengthened by food, she would not give up on it quite yet.

"Dessert!" Hope proclaims. "I have some raspberry sorbet, absolutely hard as a rock but the microwave can soften it, or English oatmeal cookies. Carr's Hob Nobs they're called, from the health-food store, so they must be low on calories and full of whatever it is that's good for us—bran. Or you could have both."

"No, neither, honestly. Maybe half a cookie, if you can find a broken one. We should be getting back to the front room so you can get me off your hands."

"Well, to be honest, Kathryn, I was thinking of walking you around outdoors for a minute or two, for a change of air. It feels so stuffy indoors, a whole winter's worth of the same air. If we walk up toward the springhouse, there's a little meadow from which you can see clear to New Hampshire, the White Mountains."

"No, really, Hope—if I may—I don't have the right shoes, for one thing."

"You have sturdy boots."

"They're not sturdy. They're new Via Spigas, and they hurt, rather."

"Take them off."

"No, please—"

"Your feet wouldn't be my size, but I have some very roomy Wellingtons I live in in mud season. They might be a bit skiddy on the pine needles, though, going up the hill."

"You're *so* nice—"

"I bet you'd like some coffee now, even if it is ancient instant."

"No, honestly. I never drink coffee this late in the day. It gets to me. I get the jitters."

"How late is it?"

"Your microwave clock says not yet two."

"Two, oh my goodness, it *is* late. I wonder what else there is to say?"

"We've only gotten up to 1955," Kathryn tells her.

"So Zack is dead."

"But this isn't only about Zack, it's about you, you as an artist, and as a, a witness to the whole post-war—"

" 'An interested witness,' is how Clem would have put it. He thought my work was pathetic, and wasn't too polite to let me know he thought that. When I began at last to get some critical attention, in the late 'seventies, after Guy left me and before I married Jerry, and I had put myself on a schedule of working two solid hours once I had got Dot off to school, he tried to be gallant about it and told me he always knew I had the stuff. 'Stuff'! That said it all. He had set himself up to be the voice of Abstract Expressionism or whatever it was—the New York School, he liked to call it, as if nobody on the West Coast could do anything—and when it was dead as a doornail he kept huffing and puffing away, still thinking art had to be powered by testosterone. Don't you love that word? I'm just learning to pronounce it. It, and 'pheromone.' It turns out all that romance we all do and die for is pheromones—we're as brainless as insects. According to a nature show I didn't shut off soon enough, male lions go into a sort of zombie trance and kill all a lioness's cubs and then invite her to make love. And she does, poor silly soul."

And as she lets her tongue tumble on, Hope wonders what pheromones swimming in this young woman's fresh and oily system are infiltrating her own receptors, leading her to be giddy, flirtatious, girlish, in oblivious despite of her irreversible position on the grave's edge. But is she any less alive now than when measuring her fat little hand against the breadth of Grandfather's chair arm? The chair is still there. She is still here. *Where there's life . . .* How often she has had that quoted to her, as a friendly joke. However Godless her gaudy environment, she always harbored the cool white light, the tremulous shy miracle, of being herself, herself and none other. These people who say there is no self, that it's all a construct of the views of others—have they never been alive?

Kathryn, standing, hunching awkwardly, offers, like a child begging to be excused, "Shall we wash the dishes?"

"No, dear, leave them. When you're gone I can come in here and the dishes will remind me of our pleasant time."

Is she getting perilously close to a declaration of senile love? In old age, Hope finds, everything wears thin—the skin thins and declares its sun damage, the cartilage thins and bones grind one upon another, the membrane between what one feels and what one says thins. Sometimes, thrust into a public role, before schoolchildren or a group of professed art-lovers, she must fight the impulse to blurt out the nonsensical, the unacceptable; the ceremonies of polite behavior strain her system. Dry-eyed through most of her life, she can cry now just standing alone in a room, when some moment that will not come again flashes upon her or she finds herself gazing out at a moment of exceptional balance between the day's ebbing light and the familiar forms of the landscape while the barn swallows cheep encouragement to their young, teaching them to fly, because flight, catching insects on the wing, is the only way they can live. When the little ones first venture from the nest, they wildly career in the air, feathery cannonballs, and then cluster on the house gutter as if still crammed within the abandoned nest.

"I need"—her voice startles her, coming out croaky and

cracked, so that she must begin again—"I need a cup of tea if you're going to make me talk more."

"Just a little more," Kathryn promises. The girl hears the parental coaxing in her own voice and smiles at this as broadly as Hope has seen her smile yet, exposing a strip of upper gums and two symmetrical eyeteeth that, although she surely got all the orthodontia a middle-class Jewish girl deserves, were not brought quite into line with the others, instead making a strong, agreeably feral impression. The girl is gawky, the way she moves in the kitchen, her feet in their new boots a bit tender, her shoulders hunched as if to lower her height an inch or two, so that her arms slightly dangle, and her long white hands hesitantly hang between gestures. Hope would worry for Kathryn's future but knows there are men who are drawn to gawkiness, to a look of largeness in a woman, as to a big field to be brought under control and added to their personal domain. Her own efficient smallness, Hope sometimes suspected, had attracted men who wanted a woman who needed minimal tending.

"None for me, thanks. I don't want to—"

Don't say "pee" again, Hope silently begs.

"—feel stuffed. Gluggy. You're so generous with yourself, you throw out all these leads I want to follow."

Hope had not meant to be generous with herself, but instead sparing and judicious, every word being recorded on tape. Perhaps she would be dead before the interview and whatever gawky nonsense the girl made of it would be in print. What did Emerson say about death? No more trips to the dentist. She forgoes tea. The front parlor, now that she has given her light head the ballast of food, has firmed up its corners and seems as trim and transparently rectilinear as a factory photographed or painted by Charles

Sheeler. Precisionism: it keeps coming around, there is a fundamental pleasure, a primitive triumph, in capturing an appearance, whether with the frontal trompe-l'œil of a Harnett or the multiple angular reflections of an Estes. The women resume their chairs; Kathryn fiddles with the tape recorder, inserting a fresh tape, and sets it purring on the old sea-chest with its brass nailheads. "So," Hope begins, taking the initiative, wanting to get away from Zack, she has violated the poor sick man's privacy enough, "I'm a widow. At the age of Christ crucified, left with nothing but an old farmhouse and three acres and a barn-full of paintings nobody wanted to buy."

"But they did want to, once Zack was dead."

"Yes, some did. I was in no hurry to sell. I passionately believed in Zack's work now—at first, I hadn't—and there was only so much of it; the longer I could hold on to the paintings, the more they would be worth. I only sold them one at a time, and the buyer had to come to me. No dealers, no middlemen. The collectors who could have had them for hundreds when Peggy or Betty were showing them paid me thousands, tens of thousands. And even so they got bargains. When a Zack comes on the market now it goes for millions, he's bigger than Picasso, he lived half as long and didn't have all those decades of turning out self-parodies."

"But your being his posthumous dealer wasn't much of a career for *you*, was it?" Since relaxing her guard at lunch a little, Kathryn has turned stiff again, a touch accusatory.

"Well, no—but I don't believe I framed what I was doing quite that way to myself. I felt plenty busy, with Zack dead. I could paint longer hours, without his jazz blaring at me from downstairs. Some of my old friends—women I had known during the war, in the city—emerged from nowhere with husbands and children, and without Zack around to

embarrass everybody and pick fights all the time the other
painters and their wives were more cordial than they had
been for years. Bernie and Jeanette, Onno and Renée,
Roger and Linda—they were just married, she was twenty
years younger than he, a former student of his at Hunter—
Mahlon and Myrtle, though they were both showing their
age, he had never quite made it into Abstract Expressionism, he hung back in that suddenly very dated limbo of late
Surrealism, even Jarl and Frieda, though he was about to
move to northern California and in fact pretty much ceased
to be a part of the New York scene, as if he could keep mail-
ing in these huge canvases from sequoia country and still
make an impression, but out on the West Coast he became
one more pseudo-Oriental mystic painter like Tobey or
Graves, not quite shouldering, you know, the European burden, the strenuous tradition, copouts really, though Jarl
would have killed me if he heard me saying that, he always
saw me as frivolous, when in fact I was one of the few who
knew where he was coming from: the Christian wrath, the
terrible impatience with creatureliness. They were all nice
to me, and we had some good times, some lovely lawn parties especially at Onno's purple carriage-house and Bernie's
mostly glass house, and cookouts on the beach, though the
Island was changing, there were Levittowns farther in, and
tasteless new money in the Hamptons, building all over the
dunes as if no winter storm could touch them, these *nou-
veaux* kept inviting us constantly, but there were still nice
sunny barefoot times to be had, and the wives tried to be
good, especially Jeanette and Renée, about having me
along, though it was the 'fifties and it was unimaginably
important to be one of a couple, the men they found to
match me with at dinner parties were generally gay, we
didn't call them that then, we still called them 'fairies,' I'm

afraid. I wonder now that they bothered to include me, I had taken over some of Zack's manner, drinking more than my share and *liking* rubbing people the wrong way and becoming very combative about his work, I was passionate about it now that it was all I had left of him, and not at all interested in finding another mate for myself; it was the *women*, actually, that took my eye at those parties, the stringy, tan bohemian wives, ten years or so older than I, Europeans a number of them, and terribly funny and bangly and *wise*, the way women can be, that witchy offhand rather helpless wisdom. I kept wondering if their being so nice to me wasn't a way of rubbing it in, my being single again, as if a proper artist's mate should do what Jeanne Hébuterne did, throw herself out the window, pregnant or not, but the awful truth was that having Zack gone had its compensations: I could sleep at night without the police calling me up or Zack barrelling in at four in the morning, and eventually I moved my easel into the barn and had Zack's stuff inventoried and put into storage—it was hard to tell what was finished or unfinished, so I gave up on making the distinction—and painted bigger and bigger, I had the space now, big runny things in series, using rags and sponges, a rubber basting spatula, a Windex spray bottle I had enlarged the aperture of with a fork tine, anything to get away from brushes and palette knives, I wanted paint closer to liquid than that, I wanted it to soak *in*. I never primed and I never used the floor, in fact I covered it with linoleum, and ten years ago, when I gave the place to be a historic site, they looked under the linoleum and discovered all of Zack's spatters over the edge of the canvases like a final masterpiece, you can tell from the colors which paintings left what. In my own painting I felt for the first time this masculine thing about scale the guys were always talking about. Work so big you're not conscious of where the canvas ends—get *into* it, and fight for your life!"

Kathryn looks down at the notes in her lap; had Hope's outburst of confidences frightened her? She was a strange fastidious child, skittish with food and dressing like a neutered man and giving off an offended scent whenever Hope began to talk about sex, though her questions kept dragging them back to it. "Before we go beyond Zack," Kathryn says, acting the drillmaster now, the prim schoolteacher, "was there anything you wanted to say that you feel we've left out?"

"Oh, we've left out nearly everything. Did I talk enough about his beautiful body, the way his naked chest smelled *nutty*? We've left out the way he talked, so fantastically rude and yet timidly polite at the same time—the good boy peeping out of the bad boy. Drunk as Zack could get, he was always watching people's reactions. He was like me, surprisingly, in that he wanted to *please* people. In our family constellations, as they say now, we were both pleasers, not leaders."

"Leaders" reminds Hope of the nice intelligent young man from the State Department, a cultural officer, at the party MoMA gave in the spring of 1959 to celebrate the return of the travelling group show "New American Paintings," that had been touring Western Europe for a year, eight major cities. In the overly familiar art crowd, its smoky chatter of constantly renewed old acquaintance—curators and reporters for art journals and gallery owners and their slender henchmen and pallid handmaidens and the painters themselves, the grizzled, piratical stars—and its fug of stale envy and smothered grudge, the young diplomat stood out by virtue of a certain shine, in his gray flannel suit, white button-down shirt, and blue-striped tie, his hair cut shorter than any other at the party, almost a brush cut such as John Kennedy would wear campaigning for President a year later, sandy short hair with a straight part on one side and at the back a few short hairs boyishly standing straight up; this State Department cultural officer was visibly exhilarated by his sanctioned penetration of the artistic demimonde, with its chance to talk to a famous artist's widow, though he spoke about Zack with some constraint initially, since she was already remarried and hugely pregnant, the unborn baby (Paul, it would have been) obtruding on their exchange like an eavesdropper bulging behind the arras. Pink-faced, a bit breathless, his breath tinged by champagne, the nice young man in his rimless glasses took a half-step closer and told her, "Your husband—your former husband, excuse me—was the killer. You should have seen the young people, the Italians and the Germans especially, gathering around his canvases. Their silence, the look on their faces—they could have been in church. The whole show was a sensation; you could smell the electricity as those kids shuffled through. And the critical reaction—the USIA is drawing up a sheaf of translations we'll be sending you, but I can tell you now they were either rapturous or rabid. The left-wing hacks in Paris and Milan and Brussels went apeshit, pardon my French. They knew the jig was up with their pathetic *retardataire* social realism and Picasso peace doves and hokey peasant art and prole posters in Léger's clunkiest style. The Communists are funny," the young man in rimless glasses said, philosophically, trying to see it from the enemy's point of view, "they've had some good art—the Mexicans, the Constructivists—but these hard-assed establishment Soviets run absolutely the other way, they're terrified of anything with the smallest breath of originality, they know that anybody says 'Boo!' the whole house of cards will come tumbling down. Their stooges writing for *Le Monde* and *Corriere della Sera*—they didn't know what had hit them, but they knew a bomb had gone off in their faces: freedom in action, baby. Only in America. All that force, feeling, daring, simultaneous inwardness and outwardness. Hey, you want revolution?—here it is! In every city, even Madrid, the show was jammed. Europe had never seen anything like it—Surrealism without the smirk, abstraction without geometry, every painting a wrestle with God. *Self*—self and beauty, beauty and self. They weren't just impressed, they were *moved*. And these are tough kids— grown up hungry and bombed, brainwashed from both sides after the war, cynical enough to swallow Sartre and Brecht and their grotesque fellow-travelling. It may take a hundred more years of standoff, but this was a turning point. I'm telling you, Mrs. Holloway, the artists of this country have done a great thing. I'm just sorry Mr. McCoy didn't live to see it. If the fuddy-duddies down in Washington believed in recognizing artists, your husband would have a posthumous medal."

So Zack, too crazy to be a soldier when everybody else was, deserved a medal anyway. For being an exemplary American, in the muddy trenches of self-expression. The President himself in those days had been a Sunday painter. But Hope does not attempt to paraphrase for Kathryn the rhetoric of the young diplomat, old and pensioned now, if not dead, having served his empire in many exotic stations, gaining at each posting another language, another roomful of regional souvenirs. Remembering him has reminded her of what she does say: "During those early winters on the Flats, Zack came in after an hour in the cold and would admit he hadn't painted a bit, he hadn't opened a paint can.

I asked him what had he been doing and he said, quick as could be, 'Praying.' I don't think he meant to be taken seriously, but I did anyway. He prayed to be shown the light, and he was, for a while. Remember, he's the one who wanted us to be married in a church."

Kathryn uncomfortably switches her long black legs and says, reading from her notes, "It was through Bernie that you met Guy."

"I suppose. I actually forget the exact circumstances. As we've said, somehow after Zack died Bernie became the wave of the future. His flat colors, the Minimalism—the monocle, too, his touch of the dandy, the titles in Latin and the tinted cigarettes in the tortoiseshell holder—all this made him appealing where Zack and Jarl and even Phil seemed roughnecks who reminded the younger painters of everything crude and fanatic about the America they had come to New York to get away from. Bernie and Jeanette were great entertainers and befrienders of the young— with her business, she took every party as a write-off—and they had Guy and his pals up from downtown to Central Park West back as early as '56 or so. I think I met Guy in the summer of '57, but it wasn't at the Novas' apartment, it was at Guy's loft on Pearl Street, he was giving a party to celebrate Leo's signing him for his first one-man show, he had been scraping a living doing windows at Bonwit's and drawing shoe ads for Bloomingdale's, and a bunch of us, Bernie and Jeanette and Seamus and some girl he had at the time—Seamus never had them for long, they were mostly for display, he was a priest at heart—invited me to come along, it must have been August, the city had that dead just-us feeling I used to love. Guy had rented this huge space stuffed with all this junk he collected on the streets, though the area of the loft where he painted was a lot tidier than

Zack's barn had been, I noticed. He claimed he had met me before, at some opening or other—I was much more in and out of the city since Zack died, it would have been suicidal to sit out in the Flats all winter, Bernie and Jeanette had an extra room for me, I had become some kind of daughter to them since Bernie and I no longer slept together, that went when Zack went, another man's wife is one thing and a young widow is another. Men in fact were scared off: I was too available, and hard-up, presumably."

"Presumably?"

"I hope you never have a husband die on you, Kathryn, but if you do you may find that sex is the last thing you miss—not that Zack had been providing much. The urge just gets lost in all the other feelings, the guilt, not so much survivor guilt as what-might-I-have-done-differently guilt, and irritation at the sloppy state he left all of your affairs in, like the way men drop their socks on the floor and walk away, and the relief, frankly, of being disentangled. Taking on another man is the last thing you want. At least in my case. One of the things I liked about the younger painters was that most of them were gay, I think the word was 'queer' then, a nicer word really, not stolen from some totally different meaning, and even those that weren't gay were *fey*. Their stuff was deadpan and tricky, and when you asked them about it they would just shrug and act evasive; they came out of commercial work—window-dressing, advertising, design, sign-painting, billboards even—and didn't have that glowering theoretical passion, left over I suppose from Marxism, that Zack's generation did. These new artists acted as if it was all a lark, as if life was a joke, and painting too, though they worked hard, on the sly. Guy was tireless, I discovered. Once he got me set up with the children in an apartment and himself down at the Hospice, it was like being married to a Wall Street lawyer, he was never home."

"Did Guy remind you, when you first saw him, of Ruk?"

This surprises her, it feels assaultive, though of course a similarity had been noticed at the time, by friends from the 'forties (Bernie, Onno) who remembered Ruk, and had been picked up by scholars specializing in the era, even to tracing stylistic similarities—the smoothness, the undertone of mockery—but at the time the resemblance had not been prominent in Hope's own mind: she had been attracted to something new in Guy, a careless cleverness that she had not seen before in men, unless it was in some of Daddy's idle-rich Philadelphia friends, who would sit all day at the Germantown Cricket Club playing backgammon. "Well," she concedes, "both were tall, handsome, and fair, but Guy had this rosy smooth English complexion and Ruk that Slavic sallowness, a kind of fine-grained canvas color, and he was *soulful* and self-dramatizing in a way Guy would never bother to be; both men had a, how can I say, a *lightness*, but with Ruk you felt the lightness was a flaw, it would do him in, it was a doomed sort of lightness, his work for all its skill was society painting, à la mode, and modes change, whereas with Guy the lightness would help him float, he wasn't anchored to any one conception of himself. He would always be ahead of you, one step ahead, without even seeming to run. It wasn't a matter of irony, Ruk could be ironical, but it was half dark, a mistrust of the world, whereas Guy was, well, blithe—he came up with these ideas as if they were absolutely obvious, lying right there on the surface of things, which of course they were. But who else saw them? He was always picking up junk, everywhere we walked in the city, as if these scraps of paper and tin were flowers. 'Everything is so lovely'—I often heard him say it.

And he wouldn't laugh. Guy rarely laughed, and when he smiled it was the way deaf people smile when they don't quite hear what you say."

"So you are Mrs. McCoy, the real McCoy," he told her, at the party in his Pearl Street loft.

"I was."

"It must have been wonderful."

She felt her face jarred open by such cool, enigmatic, and cheerful effrontery. Surely all the art world knew that for five years Zack had been a torture to live with.

Guy smoothed it over: "Artistically, at least. The rest, mere life, we all have to lump. You should take pride in what you made possible. He's where we all have to begin now. The gorgeous corner he painted himself into. I love your new work, by the way—those big runny canvases like meals being cooked in a hurry. They made me salivate."

Hope decided she might as well enjoy this encounter with an apparently impervious, totally amused male. He had broad shoulders, a lilac turtleneck worn under a pink button-down shirt, a long upper lip, an unsmiling cool stare, and a slight English accent to go with his direct, clipped manner.

"Why is it," she asked him, "that when women loosen up they're called messy, and when men do it's considered forceful?"

"It's not quite fair, is it?"

"I've not thought so."

"By the same principle, though, a man knitting on the subway makes us look twice, and a woman knitting only once."

"Are you a knitter?"

"Oh, darling, no. I have nothing like the patience required. Everything I do I must do quickly, I think it pollutes it if a second thought intervenes. Contemplation kills—didn't one of the Greeks say that?"

"I doubt it," she said, brushing past him to inspect his arrayed work in this loft, with its eastward view of dreary brick buildings and, in the gaps between them, boats, water, and Brooklyn. His paintings were at first glance not easily distinguished from the street refuse gleaned from the curbsides and back rooms of lower Manhattan. There were a number of stuffed animals—a fox, an eagle, a rooster inflating his chest to crow—that a taxidermist or his widow had disposed of, and a stack of cans—beer, soup, oil—pressed into pleated shapes by onrolling street traffic, and broken umbrellas abandoned in mid-downpour, striped fragments of splintered police barriers, begrimed street signs fallen or torn from their poles, cardboard cartons bearing stamped logos and lettering, useless appliances, old magazines, discarded photographs, torn posters. Some of these things had been mounted on sheets of primed composition board and spattered and daubed with color that seemed random and scrubby yet worked to produce a chaste, fresh impression: a human spectator had covered this refuse normally beneath notice, these scales shed by the dragon of industrial excess, with gestures of paint. Most startlingly, yet to curiously seductive effect, a bed had been counterfeited on a vertical panel—quilt, sheets, and sagging pillow thumbtacked to the top corners, the pillowcase scribbled with soft pencil and all the fabrics attacked with thin, dribbling paint. It was a narrow bed, neatly made, as by a prim bachelor. A cool inscrutable taste like a preservative varnish overlaid these smeared *trouvés*, these three-dimensional collages, in orderly homage to disorder.

"What do you think?" Guy asked at Hope's side, his

clipped tone hurried a bit by a wish for her good opinion. They had moved away from the brighter side of the room, where the party went on, the New Yorkers clustering tightly, as if in a subway or freight elevator. "Pretty bloody terrible, yes?"

Instead of confirming or denying his boyish judgment, she cautiously said, "I see what you mean about beginning with Zack." She touched the hardened dribbles, the pasted cardboard and flattened tin. "Freedom," she said. "The freedom of paint, paint on anything. But there's an irony here that Zack never had. He was dead serious."

The young painter protested, "I don't feel ironical when I work. What did your late husband so famously say? 'I *am* nature'? I'm not nature, but everything in the city around us is nature—the garbage, the adverts, the junk culture."

"I like the bed," Hope allowed, wanting to like Guy's work more than she did. It mocked, at a fastidious remove from its materials that was the opposite of Zack's approach, and Onno's, and Hochmann's, and Korgi's. They each in their ways put themselves at the mercy of the evolving canvas, its active life. This same process with real objects intervening—spattered examples of taxidermy, or old-fashioned plastic radio fronts—took on quite another, a safer and more ingratiating, character. Having it, whatever it was, both ways. That was Guy. "It's a single bed," she observed.

"Like mine."

"You should get back to your party. I'm monopolizing you."

"You'll like these better, I bet. I did them a few years ago."

He led her to a set of canvases, not huge—four by six, six by eight—stacked in racks of pine one-by-twos and two-by-fours built with a neatness that Zack, for all his pretensions to being a man of the handy working class, would not have found the time for. As he moved close beside her, Hope felt Guy as taller than Zack, taller than she had first taken him for; his limbs and torso seemed to grow as he reached up to a canvas stored at the height of his head. He was careful sliding it out; little yellowing tufts of collaged newspaper stuck out from the paint, carefully buttered encaustic rather than slathered oil, with its shinier, more ridged impasto.

"What is it?" he asked her, holding the wide canvas in stretched arms, his pale face above its upper edge impish in its glimmer—the glass-blue irises, the downdrawn upper lip. His teeth were long, like an Englishman's.

"It's a—an American flag."

"Is it? It doesn't wave, it doesn't go up a flagpole."

"I see what you want me to say. It's an *image* of the flag, like Magritte's *Ceci n'est pas une pipe.*"

"It's a *sign*," Guy told her. "I find it easier to paint when the subject doesn't belong to me. When the image is as it were pre-established. I don't want the painting to be *about* me, to be a disclosure of my feelings."

Did he have feelings? She was curious. "But," said Hope, aware—as she had been when first exposed to Hochmann's lectures, and again when viewing in the drafty barn Zack's first purely dripped paintings, and even when visiting Bernie's house, where his great color fields and narrow vertical stripes vibrated in the wide light downstairs, the radiant gulf beneath their adultery—of seeing something new, "how can it not be? You're the creator."

"There are ways of creating without being the subject. I'm merely a means," the tall stranger told her, with that strange glazed modesty hard to distinguish from the height of conceit. "You—you're an end in yourself. You and Zack and those other agonists."

"Agonists. You see us as ancient. When were you born?"

"Nineteen twenty-five."

"Do you want to know when I was?"

"If you want to tell me."

"Nineteen twenty-two."

"Within range," Guy smiled, reading her mind unpleasantly but perhaps not inaccurately. From behind his shield of diffidence Guy saw shrewdly. She was sexually interested, excited by the fresh attack on beauty. When, at Leo's brand-new gallery in the fall, Guy had his one-man exhibition, Hope registered again, in a public light, the impact, the impudence of the counterfeit bed, the bespattered eagle, the deadpan flag, and a flag done all in white, only the brushwork and subtle differences in yellow tinge defining the stars and stripes, and targets and maps serving the same purpose of offering their outlines to be painted within, images drained of their purpose and filled with painting, strokes that, she could see especially where they danced and flickered over half-hidden pieces of newspaper, were as expressionist as Zack and Onno and Phil, but in the tone of an underlying joke, a layer in a sandwich of oblique meanings. Guy contained a cooled-off Zack, Zack without the congestion and menace and naïve greed for glory.

Kathryn, in an accusatory, getting-everything-straight voice, as if there is an unseen jury, tells Hope, "Zack had been dead for only two years, then, when you took up with Guy Holloway."

" 'Took up' is a rather absolute way to put it. We saw each other here and there, mostly at Bernie and Jeanette's but sometimes at Seamus O'Rourke's loft on Mercer Street.

Seamus was having his breakthrough right about then, the blurry rectangles, the floating patches of color, people spoke of them as modern versions of the Holy Spirit, there *was* that religious streak in Seamus, he was thrilled by the recognition he was getting at last, and of course began to drink much too much, I could see the signs even though it was a *happier* drunkenness than Zack's, he had a spiritual background that sort of sanctioned it, and I was quite slow to take it seriously when Guy began to—what's the phrase you use now?—'hit on' me, since I had assumed, as I told you, that he was gay, his scene was certainly gay, window-dressers and these minor actors not quite making it, and that was one of the reasons I let myself relax with him and enjoyed his company so. He was the best-tempered, most *mobile* man I had ever been with. We did silly things together, odd ethnic restaurants like Albanian and Ethiopian before everybody else was doing it, and there was a steam bath down below Delancey that had a co-ed section, which I certainly would not have done with a man I thought was straight. This was still the 'fifties, remember, and almost any little deviation felt daring. Early in '58, the winter after he had had his show at Leo's, which almost sold out was the amazing thing, despite the ridicule of nearly all the critics, Clem hadn't even bothered to come—I was letting Zack's poured works on paper go for a few thousand each, Guy told me I was giving them away, among his other skills he was an absolute wizard at knowing what the market would bear—that winter, I started to say, it must have been nearly spring, New York was cold and gray and horrible, he talked me into driving west with him, with him and a pair of younger men, one of them had a father who was in the movie industry, Hollywood was all falling apart, television was killing the studios, but this boy wanted a cushy job anyway, he wanted to be a director and later on did take part in some of Guy's happenings, and his buddy was a pale Negro, I don't think we called them blacks yet, who had been to ballet school and did have a *most* lovely body, we all saw enough of it, every motel with a swimming pool he would get into these French-style skimpy black bathing trunks, we'd be quite a local scandal, but I just *loved* seeing the country, especially the Southwest and southern California, it was another planet from the Northeast, all this light pouring down, and these straight, endless highways between purple hills like in O'Keeffe, and then vineyards and orange groves, and everything so open, including the manners. Maybe my impressions were enhanced because I was smoking pot for the first time, 'grass' we called it then, 'reefers' some still said, at least I wasn't putting on weight—when I was trying to keep Zack company the alcohol would build up in my hips, and in fact never did go quite away, the five pounds you can't lose becomes a platform to which after a decent interval you add the next five, right? But you're too young, or too naturally slim, to ask that of. It was during this trip, as early as West Virginia, that I realized Guy was straight, quite straight really when he took it into his head."

"You married him that same year," Kathryn further accuses.

"Dear Kathryn, yes. One didn't live in sin those days, and we were crazy about each other. He was everything Zack wasn't, and yet a genius of sorts too, and I—well, who knows what he saw in me? A mother he could fuck, I suppose, classically enough. His actual mother was from Rhode Island, descended from one of the refugees who thought the Massachusetts Puritans were tyrants. They weren't Quaker but something else—Antinomian, I think they were called, meaning they believed anything goes, or should go. Pearson had been her maiden name. His father, Mr. Holloway, had been English, that was how Guy got his accent, which he could turn on and off, and his feeling for America: he saw us as savages, really, full of vitality and appetite and an outrageous wonderful vulgarity, where my feeling about Americans is that what they are basically is conscientious, conscientious and usually exhausted, with the muggy climate and the work ethic and the expectations those heroic founding fathers saddled us with, though in fact they had rather low opinions of the common man, the founding fathers did. The average American is far less vulgar and bumptious than, say, the English themselves—we have nothing like soccer hooligans, for example. His father, Guy's, had faded away early. His mother still lived in Rhode Island, in Jamestown, a rickety shingled house on the Bay with a view of a bridge, and one of the things Guy liked about me, maybe one of the main things, was that I could stand up to her. Like me, she was short and feisty—she twittered away with this seductive malice you acquire living in out-of-the-way pretty places, and we got along 'rippingly,' Guy would say, his mother and I, when we met, which we tried not to make too often. She saw me as taking him in hand, and assumed he needed it, staying unmarried into his thirties; she imagined his life in New York as nothing but folly and Sodom and Gomorrah, and was such a materialist and snob she was oblivious to the really quite remarkable success he was having. I supplied *that* omission, too; I told her how I had never seen an artist produce work and make money like her son did. Especially in the 'sixties: it seemed every city in the country over two hundred thousand in population had these new high-rises with blank apartment walls, and they all had to have a Holloway filling the space. The things he painted to make his frightfully clever point about representation and reality—'This is not a pipe, or is it?'—they just took at face value; the flags and giant Coke bottles and blown-up comic-strip panels were things they knew and loved, American things. I must say— I can tell you this even though he's still alive, he's too Alzheimerish to be hurt—that I had my reservations about much of it. Those stencilled alphabet paintings, for example, with B-L-U-E spelled out in the color orange, and S-T-O-P signs painted green, struck me as Dada all over again; Zack and his generation had rejected the supercilious playfulness of the Surrealists who were here during the war, they were trying instead to extend, after Cubism, the legacy of Cézanne and Velázquez—the *majesty* of paint, of color and form. Guy had a good, professional eye—his compositions, even the combines with stuffed animals and so on, always balanced, and he knew when to stop, when enough was enough—but he was basically an idea man. After him, American art became one idea after another."

"Dripping paint was not an idea?"

"Kathryn, the tuna salad has made you so oppositional. Dripping, not touching the canvas, having it flat on the floor were all ideas, but the ideas were nothing without the execution. Nobody has ever imitated Zack without looking second-rate. Not even that—third-rate. Whereas Guy, once he got his full assembly-line down at the Hospice going, could give an idea to his assistant and have them turn out Holloways while he was sitting in the uptown apartment with me or going to a movie in Times Square. He reinvented the medieval workshop, he took art back from being a confession, something all yours, to being an artifact, something that belonged to everybody and anybody. In a way, he went beyond the concept of good or bad: if an assistant would use the wrong color or make a smear doing a silk screen, Guy would look at it and decide it might do fine, an artist wasn't a judge, he wasn't sitting there in robes and a wig ordering executions."

"I think it's marvellous," Kathryn says, leaning forward into the statement, her left hand with its black nails giving a twitch in her lap, "that you can be so enthusiastic about Guy after the miserable way he treated you, eventually."

"Was it miserable? There was nothing malicious about it. We had been useful to each other for seventeen years, and his use for me wore out before mine for him. He was a man who had to keep moving. The last time we met, before the Alzheimer's had quite taken hold, his restlessness had ceased to be debonair, he could no longer hold it in, his eyes kept darting around the room, he kept baring his long teeth. He looked terrified, he knew things weren't right. Poor Guy. I had never felt sorry for him before."

Her remembered insight into Guy's dismay spreads to her own situation; it attaches to the increasingly obdurate and surreal fact of Kathryn's presence—a presence becoming as monstrous, here in Hope's chaste and little-used front parlor, with its brown chintz curtains and lavender-haunted panes of glass, as a stuffed eagle spattered with thinned, dribbling paint. Guy once remarked to her, as they walked together one summer day down West Broadway, how everything, until you focus, looks like chewing gum. This seemed at the time a casual bit of nihilism, a tossoff from his depths of cultivated shallowness, meant to amuse, but the phrase stayed with her, as a clue to the intrinsic monstrousness of everything, its colorless, shapeless *thereness*. This girl has that quality, insisting on sitting there, on digging at Hope but with no clear concept of what she wants, or when she will have enough.

"What did he look like? In general."

Hope hesitates—the question seems so simple it must be a trap.

"I mean"—Kathryn blushes, winningly—"what did he look like to *you*. Accounts vary, and even no two photographs of Guy Holloway look exactly alike."

"Smooth," Hope brings out at last. "He had a smooth face that often appeared tipped back to me, maybe because I was so much shorter. His features were not very striking— a small straight nose, a long upper lip, lips that looked buttoned-down, somehow, and slightly pained, perhaps because he so seldom smiled—his keeping deadpan was a lot of his strength—and slightly bulging eyes this washed-out blue, like delftware. It was a face that presented little friction to the world."

"Unlike Zack."

"Oh, Zack. He was *all* friction—that's why he was stuck so much of the time. With Guy I had this wonderful feeling that I didn't have to push the cart, or keep pulling it up out of ditches—I just had to ride along."

"And then, very quickly, you bore him three children. That, to me, is the single most surprising fact about your life."

"But why? Nothing is more natural, it's Nature's business to make it happen. I would have loved to have begun earlier—it turned out to be something I was good at, childbirth. I had the pelvis for it, small as I was. And they didn't come so quickly, each took nine months—Paul in June of '59, Piet in November of 1960, and Dot in '62. We were thrilled to have a girl, we had agreed after Piet to try once more in the hopes we would, she came just a month before I turned forty. You used the word 'surprising'; *I* was surprised that Guy asked to name her after his mother, I hadn't thought they were that close, but maybe in his mind they

were, we had named the boys after favorite painters, Guy's
favorites more than mine, dry, cerebral painters—my father
had been a prick about my marrying Zack and his had abandoned his family, why reward *them*?—so it was disconcert-
ing to have to speak to the little innocent bundle, my own
daughter, with a name belonging to my rather intimidating
mother-in-law. But 'Dot' solved it, calling her Dot. And
Guy began his Benday series, comic-strip panels with big
mechanical dots, soon after, as homage of a sort. He was a
good, fun father to the boys, though noticeably competi-
tive, even when they were two and three, but having a
daughter absolutely melted him. He would even change her
diapers, something he was rather stuffy about doing for the
boys. He talked of beginning a series of canvases in baby
shit, and I believe looked into the technicalities, but never
did—I mentioned this morning the parodies of Zack that
involved urinating on copper plates, but it wasn't Guy, at
least my memory is that it wasn't."

Of course it wasn't. It was somebody secondary, looking
for a cheap shot of fame. Urine, feces, the first media. Hope
sneaks a look out the windows at the darkening April day. A
sickly wash of white light lies low over the horizon of the
mountains but no direct sunlight penetrates the clouds.
The darkness to the west has expanded and moved around
to the south as well, and against its blue-black a few dry
flakes of snow flutter back and forth, up and down, as if
never to touch the ground. But she knows in her sensitive
bones that the day is not cold enough to snow, at least at
this middling elevation. Up near the crests, where the
youthful skiers slide over the frozen granular toward the
end of the season, snow may accumulate, but down here it
will turn to rain. The tingle of suspense makes her rub her
arms through the woolen shirtsleeves. She wonders if it is

three o'clock by now. She never got the habit of wearing a watch, even when living in a world of city appointments. She knows time is more elastic than a watch says. Some activities—painting, playing tennis when she and Jerry were still young enough for sports—speed it, so an hour goes by as if your life has slipped a cog, and others—gardening, housework, making conversation with awkward company—stretch it as if life will last forever, like those snowflakes unable to touch the ground.

"Do you think," Kathryn asks in the accusatory tone her voice has taken on since Guy became the subject, a tone that reminds Hope of a daughter full of psychotherapeutically induced indignation, "that you and Guy were trying to prove something?"

"What would that have been?"

"In Guy's case that he wasn't gay, and in yours that you were still a young woman."

"I was, wasn't I?"

"Not for becoming a mother." The girl's voice has defensively retracted, she having never been a mother.

"Oh dear." Hope sighs mercifully. "I was half my age now. I must have been very young."

The children. Who would have thought that they would ever fall into place as part of the past, a chapter closed? For twenty years they had been present at every turn, not merely companions and dependents in her life but that life's justification, its near-total environment, their innocent ravenous egos filling every room where their cries could reach and their commotion speeding every day so that time flew by, at least so it seems in the backward glance through all those veils of change and outgrowing, growth with its fatal undercurrent of leaving behind, of leaving one set of toys behind and hungering for another, of shedding speech impediments and mistaken grammar, of learning away their enchanting misspeakings, their gains her losses, their breath her breath as she leaned over the beds where each small head slept, warm and damp to her touch in the fever of fragile new life, in the unearthly beauty of children asleep, their abandoned limbs palely flowing among the tossed covers, their dreams sometimes waking them to terror, their fears her own, their rages stains on her heart, their losses and gains hers as they grew day by day, inch by inch, into language, into social custom, into schooling, into ever more defined and limited personalities—Paul diffident and fair and cunning like his father, Piet excitable and malleable like her, and little Dot, who inherited the name Dorothy at thirteen when her grandmother died, a puzzling unstable mixture of genes latent for generations, full lips and dusky sun-loving skin and coarse black hair they could only trace to Hope's maternal grandmother, Virginia Lafitte, who came from New Orleans and had died the year Hope had been born, and to Guy's absconded father, whom photographs showed with a crown of upright dark hair and pronounced black brows above the milky-pale, slightly protuberant eyes. Dot tomboyishly insisted on wearing boy's clothes, to be like Daddy. Until she was six or seven, her nervous system woke her in the middle of the night and drove her into her parents' room for comfort. So often scolded for disturbing their sleep, she resigned herself to waiting out the wakeful spells herself; it would sadden Hope, with a sorrow that seemed close to the root of human existence, to find in the child's room evidence, in some scattered dolls, a disarranged dollhouse, or an opened picture book, that she had entertained herself in the pit of the night while her brothers and parents slept, safely tucked into their dreams. At some point in Dot's childhood, in the East Seventy-ninth Street apartment, they had acquired a cat, Pierre, a declawed Siamese with a silky small head that he thrust into a stroking with the force of a fist and a purr that could be heard in the next room: Pierre's purpose, neither Hope nor Guy admitted in so many words, was to provide Dot with another nocturnal creature while her parents self-absorbedly slept. How odd, the little that Hope's memory had brought out of that long, jostling pilgrimage of parenthood—the push of Pierre's purring skull; the sugar-sack dead weight of little Piet's body when she was nursing him in the big leather bean-bag chair (Paul the year before had felt so much lighter, though their birth-weights had differed by only four ounces); the linoleum smell of the clattering stairways of the non-sectarian pre-school over on Park on a rainy day; the endless picking up of blocks and Lego and broken plastic cars and undressed Barbie dolls; the kiddie meals of peas and fish sticks and sandwiches cut up in pieces the size of dominoes on plastic plates imprinted with fuzzy ducks and moles and hedgehogs and bunnies, in blue coats with big buttons.

In her mind's eye Hope sees a brown female hand with its pale thumbnail, Brenda's or Martine's or Josie's, setting such a plate before one of the children at the white kitchen table, and admits to Kathryn, "I had help. You're right, I was too old to have three children under four. Just the chasing after them made my back ache, and in winter suiting up everybody for the ten minutes at the playground in the Park before they began to whimper that they were cold. Luckily, Guy had plenty of money, ridiculous amounts after about 1962, so we could hire help, nursemaids though we didn't call them that, there was the day girl who cooked for the children and the girl from five to seven who fed them the dinner the day girl had cooked and gave the boys their baths. I did Dot in another tub, the boys got just too frisky and bumptious for me and she was terrified of soap in her eyes. I wanted to do it all, because my own mother hadn't, but I was too old, and spoiled I suppose, and preoccupied by wanting to get back to my own painting."

Her memory now serves up poor Dot at thirteen going off to Brearley and crying and screaming there in the foyer because her braces and acne humiliated her and she didn't want to go, ever, ever, she *hated* all those skinny smooth spoiled blonde bitches. Dot's figure in adolescence had become stocky and her sallow skin was breaking out and Hope felt so helpless, unable to change the body of her daughter as you would scrape down and redo a painting, and no father on hand to tell Dot she was still his beautiful baby, because by that point, in 1975, Guy had left. His mother died and he left, as if her distant will, her sense of propriety, had been holding him here, among the empty rooms and forgotten toys and female voices. Paul and Piet had gone off to boarding school. Jeanette Nova—Bernie too had died, a loquacious old master sheepishly basking in the limelight after a life of defiant obscurity, but Jeanette lived on and on, thinner and thinner, a thread vibrating on the city's loom, kept alive by interior decoration and gallery parties and gossip—said it was a compliment to Hope that he had stayed that long. She had been a saint, turning such a blind eye. Blind eye? But Hope didn't really want to ask her, *Blind eye to what?* Jeanette was spinning on, her shrivelled silver-ringed hands flickering in whatever bright room had housed this conversation, city lights splashed beyond the triple-glazed windows, a dash of vengeance in her animation perhaps, the two women's fondness for each other a mixture like Irish coffee, pulling several ways. "Nobody," she told Hope in her raucous, party-worn voice, "foresaw all those children!"

"People were surprised," Hope tells Kathryn, "that Guy proved to be as much of a father as he did, but that was his nature, to give everything a try, and to be productive. What he didn't have, I suppose, was staying power. His styles tended to last two or three years at the most, and he often would be working in two styles at the same time. For instance, at the same time as he was doing those hilarious huge plastic reproductions of junk food, all gloppy with paint just like a real Big Mac, mustard and ketchup and relish, he and his assistants were turning out those multiple silk screens of car accidents and electric chairs, after 1963 of Jackie looking stunned in her pillbox hat, with such a different, impersonal visual feel, in those icy Day-Glo colors. Though in everything Guy did there was a hospitality to accident, to the unplanned. It's a paradox: Zack, whose best work looks like *all* accident, as though a whirling dervish had gotten loose among the paint cans, in fact was very emphatic about his work containing *no* accidents, as I may have said before—forgive me, Kathryn, if I have. It was one of the few consistent things in his public statements, where Clem or I didn't have to put the words into his mouth. It had to do with the dignity of what he was doing, his masculine control over it. Whereas Guy, who made himself into a kind of factory, once he bought that town house on Twenty-seventh Street and called it Holloway Hospice and even signed everything with a stencilled 'HH,' *depended* on accident, on human imperfection intervening. I remember, before it became quite so clear that he didn't want me down at the Hospice—that he was quite happy with the gang of weirdos and druggies that were collecting there—my taking off an afternoon from the kids and helping with some acrylic silk screens, I was interested in learning the process, I hadn't touched a brush to canvas in years, I hadn't done anything but some charcoal sketches of the children asleep and a quick gouache or two out of our apartment windows. Anyway, down at the Hospice—Guy claimed the name meant art was on its last legs, this was where it had come to die—he looked at my results in that quick, almost frighteningly concentrated way he had and said, 'No, darling, you've done them too perfectly, you must let some carelessness in. Here.' And he smeared several with the side of his hand, and once I got over the shock I could see it looked better, the mechanical had been touched by the human, it made the whole idea of repetition, of a repeatable process, poignant. The imperfections are us, trying to break out. The smaller the imperfection is, the more poignant in a way. He went from putting pieces of torn cartons into his combines to duplicating the cartons themselves, as precisely as possible, but still you can see they are done by hand. I don't think his helpers at the Hospice understood any better than I did why doing one silk screen from a newspaper paragraph is just copying but doing a whole band of them, sixteen of them, all overlaid with cerise or turquoise, was a work of art that would say something on a museum wall. Zack was interested only in expressing what the painter felt, Guy more in what the viewer saw. He was as sophisticated a theoretician in his way as Bernie and Roger, but he never talked theory. At least to me."

Hope feels she is trying to sell Guy to Kathryn, as a worthy successor to Zack, but the other woman isn't buying, some taint or smallness clings to Guy in her mind, whereas Zack is all wide-screen glamour. The young woman's voice, growing huskier with a touch of catarrhal rasp as the room cools in tune with the darkening snow-spitting day outside, suggests she has heard enough about Bernie and Roger and artistic theories. "You bring up the Hospice," she says in an accusatory tone. "There was quite a lot of drug activity associated with the people who hung out there, especially when Guy began to make experimental movies. At least one of the staff died of a heroin OD, and an actress in one of his films—quite unwatchable, of course; that was the joke, I gather—committed suicide. How did you feel, while you were trying to raise three children on the Upper East Side, about Guy going off every day to the site of all this 'sixties– early-'seventies craziness?" A concluding sniff resounds in her long, stuffed-up nose.

"Well," Hope says. She feels the blood warm her cheeks as her Quaker blood rises to protest. "I never thought a modern artist could or should be a standard off-the-shelf member of the bourgeoisie. Art has no comfortable place in American life; the artist has to be outside the system. But Guy was never an addict. He didn't smoke cigarettes and hardly drank. Even on our West Coast pre-honeymoon, he was very measured with the pot—he didn't want to put any particle of his brain at risk, he had known from boyhood that he must live by his wits. And he had of course this beautiful ability to compartmentalize. Like most American men, he had an office life and a home life. We were like the sheltered spoiled family of a nineteenth-century sweatshop owner, who didn't bring any ugly details home. He would spend an evening with me and the boys watching *The Andy Griffith Show* and then put some Schubert on the hi-fi and play a game of backgammon with me and the next morning go down to where some of his tripped-out hangers-on were doing a threesome with cameras rolling. Squalor didn't bother Guy, he saw it as part of the urban reality we walk through every day. He had great faith in his ability to remain pure, a pure transmitter, turning everything into art. And he did this by simply saying it *was* art. And without ever raising his voice—that was what I marvelled at most about him, his good humor and even temper. With the children *he*, believe it or not, was the calm disciplinarian, I was too hot-headed and took everything they did I didn't like as a personal affront. When Dot would come in and wake us, in spite of our getting her a cat, it was I who would—what's the phrase?—'go ballistic' and Guy who would be the soothing one and lead her back gently to bed. At the same time, some of the art critics, who had gotten comfortable with Abstract Expressionism by now, just as it was quite clearly dead, were denouncing him as an artistic anti-Christ, a kind of King of Misrule recycling everything crass and stupid about American life and fooling museums into displaying it; Robert Hughes in *Time* was especially vitriolic. It was true, the museum directors liked what he did, it fit with everything outside the museum that the people had to pass through to get there; it connected with the life of the street. It connected with the gift shop."

"Well, you are certainly generous, talking about Guy."

"He was generous to me. Even at the end, in the settlement. Money was something that didn't interest him, except the actual *look* of it, he always said American money was the best-designed. I didn't have to marry Jerome Chafetz for financial reasons. I did it because we fell in love."

Kathryn yields up what sounds to Hope like a sigh through her nose, slightly liquid. Poor thing, she is fighting a cold, and with a long drive back to the city still ahead of her. And still waiting to catch up to this love that Hope keeps flaunting. Some women fall in love easily and have babies easily and their genes pour into the future, making the species ever more romantic. Then there is this other kind of woman, where it stops. The interview must be getting to the end.

"Your daughter, Dorothy. Did her eventual gender preference shock or disturb you?"

Now Hope gives a little sigh, refolding her hands in her
lap after rocking a beat or two, trying to think what an honest answer would be. Her dammed-up love for her lesbian
daughter makes within her a black swamp of sadness her
inner travels generally skirt. She stalls, she stonewalls. "No,
why would it?"

Her first and only daughter, necessarily neglected. The
boys were still toddlers, a menace to themselves and each
other; she would rest the baby between feedings in her
bassinet on the living-room floor like a parcel addressed to
someone else, and when her footsteps in hurrying past
would tell the infant someone was near, little Dot would
wiggle in her cocoon of blankets with, it seemed, sheer
pleasure to be sharing the earth with another live presence.
Taken into Hope's arms, her solid warm body would tense
and quiver with its unspeakable private bliss, like a song she
could not help singing; she would suckle avidly, clutching
and unclutching one of her mother's fingers in a wrinkled
palm that gripped as softly as a snapdragon. Her body
adhered and conformed to Hope's in a way the boys', resistant and thrusting almost from the start, did not. As in a
fogged mirror, her own spirit bent above the life-breath of
this other female, anticipating the games they would share,
the return to her own girlhood, at the same time consign-
ing Dot to the stoicism of their sex, and feeling justified
in neglecting her, for this interval while the demands of
the males in their family took precedence. Her brothers
continued to outrank, outshout, outshine her, and she and
her mother never did have the full-hearted union of spirits, the entry into affectionate conspiracy, that Hope had
anticipated. Instead, blockages, stagnation. When she would

wheel the child in her stroller around the windy corner of Seventy-ninth and Park, the fabled wide avenue would seem a huge treadmill hurtling with its yellow taxis toward the barrier of the Pan Am Building thirty blocks away and, like a treadmill, essentially not going anywhere.

Kathryn has not deigned to respond. She is waiting for her victim to elaborate, to fetch up another unshapely nugget from the mire of memory. Anything Hope says about Dorothy will be taped and possibly printed, although she doubts that this awkward, relentless interrogator, her spiritual substance so dense and unyielding, will ever place more than a tiny fraction of these recorded words in print, in this article she is doing for, Hope now remembers from their old telephone call, an "on-line" magazine that exists only in cyberspace. "She inherited Guy's clear blue English eyes," Hope tells her, "whereas the boys got my muddy hazel, with varying amounts of green depending on the color shirt they had on."

"Was she Guy's favorite?"

"As an infant, yes. But then as she got older, Guy seemed more at ease with the boys. He was friendly and teasy with Dot, but also slightly wary of her, afraid of getting too close to a mechanism he didn't understand. That was part of his personality, not wanting to wade in without understanding, without being able to foresee the outcome. He was unlike Zack in this. Zack waded in and then got restless. If Guy had been Zack, he would have trained assistants to turn out drip paintings until all the markets, foreign and domestic, had been saturated. That sounds cynical—*un*generous, yes?—but there was a *thrift* to Guy's inspirations, as well as an abundance. Art, which had been so hot and urgent and, yes, existential when I was a young woman, had cooled into ideas, one at a time—have I said this? What wasn't Pop was

Hard Edge or Color Field. Look at Bernie's big paintings compared with, oh, Ad Reinhardt and Morris Lewis. What has happened to Bernie's passion, those giant skies of pure color, the enormous gamble he took? It's become a flavor of ice cream."

Hope knows Kathryn doesn't want more painting talk from her but hopes to distract her from the topic of her daughter. Kathryn will not be distracted.

"How old did you say Dorothy was when Guy left?"

"Well, he'd been leaving for some time. Spending more and more time down at the Hospice, and going to events in Tokyo and Venice and Rio that lasted for weeks. Throughout the 'sixties, his projects had been getting grandiose. Guy became enamored of billboards, and got some real billboard artists to show him how to do it, and then produced these things so enormous they couldn't be gotten in or out of doors and had to be displayed in museum courtyards or the abandoned old railroad stations that more and more cities had in their centers. As if this wasn't grandiose enough, he took to designing public monuments—a pair of scissors the size of the Eiffel Tower and huge baseball bats and typewriter erasers and clothespins, no state or city authority could actually vote to build them, though a few actually did, mostly in the Midwest, hoping to put a little pizzazz into their dying downtowns, but even if they were never built they generated all these drawings and blueprints that were worth something, of course. As I say, Guy wasted almost nothing."

"You were going to tell me how you felt about Dorothy's gender preference."

"Was I? Or was I *not* going to tell you?"

In this impasse Kathryn's face glows with balked current; she tucks one strand of her sleek hair behind a white ear that is, Hope sees for the first time, not flat to her skull but cupped, like a boy's at the age before manhood begins to fill him in. Her hand still raised, the interviewer bends forward to check that her tape recorder is still murmuring.

"Shut it off," Hope says, with sudden sharp desperation. "I'll tell you if you'll shut off that poisonous little machine."

Kathryn's eyes, dark as plums or round wells of rust-tinged black ink, dart from her downcast face a startled, defiant look that shows a crescent of white beneath each iris. Her lips part, beginning to frame an objection.

Hope explains, "I don't want anything on the record that would ever hurt my daughter."

The younger woman stifles the daughterly impulse to argue and obediently reaches—a length of bony wrist leaps from her extended sleeve—to snap off the tape recorder.

Hope rocks back and speaks as if to a woman her age. "Guy and I had assumed," she confides, "that a daughter of ours would be beautiful. Why would we think that? Because we were both artists, I suppose, and deserved it. We thought of ourselves as—what's that wonderful old word?—comely. I imagined gangly and smooth plus tidy and pert and rounded would naturally produce a tall, elegant, womanly woman." It uncomfortably passes through her mind that Kathryn might be considered tall and elegant. "Instead," she goes on, "Dot had these skin problems I mentioned and coarse black hair and eyebrows that nearly met in the middle and a mulish, thick-lipped expression besides. She never got to be more than my height, and Guy's pale-blue eyes looked as if they had wandered into her face from some other planet."

"Still, you know," Kathryn surprisingly volunteers, as if her tongue, too, is freed by the Sony's being off, "a face isn't just an inventory of its features; if a woman has spirit, and a positive attitude, and uses makeup to good advantage—"

"Dot would not use makeup. She saw it as a sort of hypocrisy. Or else thought it was hopeless in her case, after the scarring. The sad irony is that if she had been born ten years later there would have been a cure, Accutane, which did wonders for the grandson of a partner of Jerry's, a boy who has the skin of an angel now. But for Dot . . ."

"Still, it's just a surface blemish."

"Easy for the unblemished to say. Most of what we see is surface. I agonized all the while she was growing up, after Guy had left, this miserable fatherless girl hating what she saw in the mirror, and she sensed that, my guilt, of course— when somebody is crying out to be blamed we tend to oblige them. My whole past—my friskiness, let's call it— offended her. She called me a silly, pathetic person who had traded all my life on attracting men, and to spite me, I suppose, she insisted on keeping up a relationship with Guy, right up until these last few years, when he's become impossible to communicate with, that beautiful cool mind of his . . ." Hope realizes she is drifting, skirting the reedy edges of that swamp in her mind. "Oh dear," she says. "Relationships are so sad, aren't they?"

Kathryn does not trouble to agree; she presses on, myopically. That pendulous, liquid strangeness to her eyes, could it be contact lenses? "When did Dorothy announce her gender orientation to you? When did it become apparent?"

Suddenly Hope is bored, with an icicle boredom that penetrates her soul to its black nerve of death. "She became active—flagrant, with short hair and men's jackets and so on—at Stanford, I don't think she began practicing at Brearley, she hated those blonde rich girls so, or said she did, but the first significant other she brought back from California in fact was a lovely tall blonde, the state is full of them, sun-bleached surfers, from La Jolla I think this girl was, a Park Avenue princess Los Angeles–style, a honey tan, slate-gray eyes, an enchanting total ignorance of anything cultural. . . . I was rather drawn to her myself, Marcy her name was, this was not too many years after Jerry had saved me from a certain experimental promiscuity of my own, I suppose in anger over Guy, is it still fashionable to think that everything we do is because of anger? A tan was becoming to Dot, too, it settled the issue of her skin, there was scarring but it went with her squat looks, a kind of bushy-haired menace she had developed, a version of 'black is beautiful,' I suppose; she looked *Chicana*, except for this rapid, intelligent conversational style she had inherited from Guy, she didn't have any of my dithering, rambly way of groping toward the end of the tunnel—to tell the truth, Kathryn, I fell in love with her all over again, my little nervous clinging Dot with this formidable new tough persona. She was tough with me, certainly. She accused me of seducing Guy away from his real orientation, which I had a hard time taking seriously, since he had remarried by this time, to Gretchen, this horse-trainer from Connecticut. Dot said Gretchen, who was hard and slim, like a jockey rather, was just a boy who happened to have a cunt, so there was really no winning against her in her new militance. By the time she graduated she decided my being married to Jerry was such a complete sellout to capitalism she didn't want anything more to do with me, and, to confess something truly horrible, it was a kind of relief, it was like when she would finally go back to bed as a toddler."

"How did you react to the seduction charge? May I switch the tape recorder back on?"

"Oh, go ahead. I don't suppose any of this matters; except to our children, we're all basically dead."

The click of the little gray Sony, and the murmur that sits like tinnitus in her ear, make an alteration in the room's atmosphere. The wooden furniture, the ceramic lamps with their wan, pleated shades, the fading chintz curtains patterned in brownish roses, the thin-paned windows all seem a notch more brittle and fragile. She has lived in this house so long she has ceased to see it, and with the help of this young woman's eyes now sees that it is waiting, rugs and curtains and staring pottery parrots from a trip she and Guy had taken to Mexico toward the end of their marriage, waiting for the purging and renovation that will follow her death. Paul and Piet and Dorothy will come together, formal at first with one another but falling quickly into the patterns of childhood; goods will be scattered and sold, there will be little they will want to keep, her paintings in progress will be trucked to the dealer, the children will be sad to see how sparse, when held up to a cold light, the residue of a life is. She will be beyond blame and love. Quaker quiet will be her haven and reward. Her early religious indoctrination did not include a vivid afterlife—a purity of absence, rather, a freedom from any creaturely distraction. Beyond the frail, warped windows, the snow has stopped spitting against the blue-black glower over Camels Hump. Upon the bare trees and evergreen bushes and brown lawn has come the greasy lustre, that exciting pregnancy of the air, which precedes a rain.

She stirs, trying to shake her premonition of death, her stab of boredom. "Within your own experience, Kathryn, does one person seduce another? Or is it that two people give off signals—surround themselves with atomic auras— which bring them closer? People are drawn together by the instinct that their lives can benefit, that there will be—how do physicists talk?—a net gain of order. Guy had a neutral sort of soul that was drawn to my positive energy, and of course he was turned on by my connection to Zack, who once he was dead shed all his pathos and obnoxiousness and became the, the—what?—the Holy Ghost of post-war American art. It amused Guy to subvert everything Zack and the others considered sacred and to take his wife besides. He liked—do I dare say this?—the sexual tricks I had developed to rouse Zack; neither man was easy to arouse, they would lie back and watch me do it all, and in the way of our adaptable gender I got to like doing it all, having them watch, having it happen almost despite them. After Zack, I was terribly attracted to Guy's lack of self-destructiveness. This bright, boyish creativity that no critic—not Clem, not Hughes or Hilton Kramer—could dent: it just flowed, idea after idea, one idea after another that nobody else had ever thought of, for the whole 'sixties, and into the 'seventies, until just a year or two before he left me, when his work got grandiose and lost its Pop modesty. That modesty was what people responded to, it had opened all that hermetic self-regarding 'forties-'fifties heroic art to the actual world around us. Guy's art cherished trash, it cherished America as it was, dirty and commercial and visually violent: he was foreign enough, alien enough, to love America. Or so it appeared to me. And he never seemed to strain; he made it look easy."

Kathryn asks, "How much of your own work did you produce in this happy period?"

"Ooh, that hurts: that 'happy period.' As you very well know, not much. Right at the start there were these very small children, even with the staff we could afford they took all my energy, and by the time I *did* have some time the art climate had changed so much that abstraction and every-thing Hochmann had taught seemed naïve and, to use my new favorite word, grandiose. There was an irony now that undercut everything, with or without Vietnam, just as Duchamp and Ernst and Breton had undercut everything when I first moved to New York, and I wasn't good at irony. Maybe women as a rule—what do *you* think?—aren't good at irony, what matters to us matters whole-heartedly, we don't have the luxury of distancing ourselves. It takes male power to mock and love at the same time. The only female who could do Pop was Marisol, and she had that Latin American folk-carving thing to give her a way in. She was a sculptress. I wanted *paint*, paint that came out gooey and then hardened and couldn't be pushed around any more. That was my idea of art."

Kathryn hesitates to ask the next question, so it must be loaded. "Did Guy give a reason for leaving you?"

"Do men need to give a reason? They just move on, like buffalo. At one point, as I remember, he admitted I bored him."

He had said, "Don't be boring, Hope. Don't keep pro-posing this and that, as cures. There are no cures."

"Why not, Guy, why not?!" She was fluttering up against him, in a flimsy chiffon nightgown; she could feel her swing-ing breasts exposed to the air, she had surrendered any thought of dignity or shame.

"Please, darling, don't give me a headache. I get these headaches lately; they're frightening. Your life will go on as before. You'll have the apartment and the children and plenty of money, you just won't see as much of me. You can start seeing other people."

"I'm fifty-three, you complacent idiot! That part of my life is over, I don't want to see anybody but you, you, *you*,

you bastard!" Even at the time she wondered why she burst into tears at the thought of his absence; in truth he had been more and more absent for years.

She tells Kathryn, "He poked fun at me for trying to think of a solution. I had proposed we leave the city—people were, in droves; cities were awful with the drugs back then, and not enough taxes for the schools and services, garbage everywhere—and keep a smaller apartment there, or make an apartment for us and the children when they visited on the top floor of the brownstone in Chelsea that housed the Hospice. Ha! The last thing Guy wanted was me down at the Hospice. I thought we could keep a little apartment and move to the Connecticut farm he had bought as a place to park his money, real estate in those years was a much better bet than the stock market, which people forget didn't go anywhere for a whole decade, it was like it is now, exhausted. Since we had the acreage, up beyond New Milford, another safe bet, Guy thought, and here maybe his brain was already starting to soften, he was investing in horses, and that was how Gretchen had come into our lives, as a horsewoman. Come to think of it, he did say about her, almost the first time I heard of her, that she was hard-assed as a boy, from all her riding. By the time he left me, it had all come out in the open, he wasn't bothering to deny it, I was so desperate, Kathryn, I begged him to keep her, to keep sleeping with her, just so he didn't leave me and the children."

"How had the sex between the two of you been going?" Sex again, Hope thought. It had been her mistake to touch on it; now the girl would not let up.

"I thought well enough," she tells her, lifting her chin, "but maybe I hadn't been paying enough attention. Guy had never made a big production of sex, the way Ruk had, or Jerry did. Jerry just lived for it; he snorted, he yelled, he wanted to have it every day. Every day, old as we were. Guy and I were down to, I don't know, less than once a week, maybe twice a month, when we'd come back from an opening a little high on the plastic glasses of champagne they give you and the evening still ahead of us but not enough of it for Guy to do anything at his desk or drawing board; he was very efficient with his time usually. The boys were off at Putney, and Dot stayed in her room listening to her tapes. She showed less emotion than she had five years before, when the Beatles broke up. Guy kept telling me how it wouldn't make a difference to anybody, except to me for a while, but I'd get over it—I'd find a new phase. He thought in terms of phases. And of course he was right in a sense. He was rarely really wrong, Guy."

And yet, in her mind's eye, he had cried with her, when she cried. His cold blue eyes produced tears that ran down his still-smooth face. He hugged her close, both their breaths hot, as he murmured, "I'm so sorry, Mickey. I'm so sorry things end. Life is rotten."

"Mickey" was a pet name left over from the days of courtship, when she had been the Widow McCoy. He thought it suited her better than "Hope." He shied from her real name's bluntness, its too-eager gift of herself. The tears he shed at the end of their segment of the road were genuine yet perfunctory, a tax he paid before moving on. His mind was always active, always ahead of her, ahead of the pack. Remembering how Guy had turned slippery in her grasp and politely slipped away, she wonders if her daughter was not right, she had seduced him, their getting together had been more her idea than his, more her wiles than his desire. In the heat of a new man, female instinct guides us to extremes otherwise out of bounds. She would blow him while he kneeled straddling her face on the tatty brown sofa in his Pearl Street loft, a sofa that looked like one more piece of street refuse, and then show him his pale semen inside her mouth, displayed on her arched tongue like a little Tachiste masterpiece before she swallowed it or disgorged it back onto his still-firm prick; even his prick was smooth, barely marked by the ridges and homely veins that other men had, like an ivory dildo or the erection in that Marisol masterpiece with the cigarette lighter.

Her grandfather used to quote, with his frisky twinkle, *"God is not mocked: for whatsoever a man soweth, that shall he also reap."* A woman, too, reaps. The seductress turned wife is replaced by the next. Yet Guy had not been basically about sex, his power was pre-sexual, his freshness, his art was never more beautiful than when it was childish— oversize Popsicles and wedges of layer cake worked out in vinyl, sewed together by slaves at the Hospice, stuffed with kapok, ten times lifesize, or else machinery like pay phones pieced together in canvas and left limp, hanging on the museum wall like the skin of Marsyas, or huge letters of the alphabet cast in bronze like men on horseback, or solemnly displayed bales of play money.

"The bastard shrugged me off," Hope tells Kathryn, not wanting to tell her about the tears they had shared or the semen she had juggled in her mouth where he could see it with a flicker of disgust that reminded her of Bernie, "leaving me with a stack of his money and three half-grown children. There I was. Looking up at this clever, sorry, amiable, perfectly opaque face, I had this panicky sensation—I'm sure you've had them—when you ask yourself, 'Do I know this man at all? Did I ever know him? Was I ever *anything* to him?' "

What she cannot share, because it too deeply shames her,

is the image in hindsight of her fifty-three-year-old body in its poses of fury and supplication, begging Guy not to leave, proposing to him open marriage, split residences, a reformed personality, an intensified subservience: an actress under the lights, seen small, the stage changing from the East Side apartment with its geometrical furniture and space-enlarging mirrors to the Connecticut farmhouse with its white fences and red stables and columned porch and dart-and-egg ceiling mouldings in the front hall. The stage lights are harsh enough to throw the gleam from the actress's unfeigned tears into the back balcony seats as she cringes and writhes in the invisible grip of humiliation, rejected once again by a man who in the end loves nothing but his art, whose personality is just a glossy shell protecting the artist, the immortal striver, eternally young at fifty.

"It was like dealing with a child," she tells Kathryn, "but then it made me realize how childish I was, too, what needy children we still are at any age. I had this sense," she goes on, "of Dorothy eavesdropping and judging me; I was losing her father, her only father. She didn't have the vocabulary for all the later judgments and dismissals of me, my pathetic male-oriented femaleness, et cetera, and I don't think she ever realized how much of my grief had to do with not failing her, her and the boys."

"The boys, you don't talk much about the boys."

"They were older than Dot. Paul once told me he was surprised it hadn't happened long before, Dad was such a cold fish. The boys were off at Putney, and Guy in the summer would take them in Connecticut, up there with hard-assed Gretchen, and for trips to Europe, which is more than he did very often with me, he didn't like to fly over water, he said; he said it added to his anxieties if I came with him to big shows in Venice or Brussels, they were pure business, meat markets of a kind, he came home as quick as he could; he said he needed to live in America, to know what was on television and in the stores, Europe threw his sensibility off, their art was like their manners—supercilious, high-end kitsch, he called it; it lacked a sense of crisis. If he hadn't been half English, I don't think he would have seen us—America—as amusing as he did. The boys loved their father, of course, though the degree of his fame made them wary when they were old enough to grasp it, and they shared that male whatever it is, silence. Maybe that's why I like men so much—they can hold their tongues, unlike me. Oh dear, I keep looking at the windows to see if it's dark yet, and it isn't, it's spring and the days are lengthening, behind the clouds."

"Paul and Piet are both in finance. In investments."

"Yes, isn't that surprising? One heads a mutual fund, and the other is in M and A, they call it, mergers and acquisitions, I forget which boy does which. Both make more money than I can imagine, they try to shelter me from it, but I can see from how and where they live, and how their wives spend. Guy was shrewd about money, and had that aesthetic fascination with dollar bills, so it isn't all that surprising. Both boys had the wonderful good sense to steer clear of art—they have the most pedestrian possible things in their homes, entirely their wives' and their decorators' taste, Guy used to complain about it before he went quite so gaga, but I think he was secretly pleased that they turned out to be so practical. *He* was practical, I suppose I keep saying. I'm nagged by a feeling there's something about Guy I haven't managed to say. It's hard to be clear about a man who's dumped you. Critics even now dismiss him as lightweight, but he wasn't; like Dürer and Leonardo, he was trying to improve our grip on the actual, he was the last

Mohican, in a way, of the pre-post-modern, when it was necessary to be light, when lightness was the only alternative to sinking, sinking like Zack and Seamus and Phil did, the only way to keep an identify afloat, post-modern, post-God, post-seriousness, really. When Nixon ended the draft and then resigned, those were the last serious things that the American people *felt* as serious, before news became all entertainment."

"And Dorothy? What does she do?"

"Poor thing, she stayed in art, pecking away at the fringes. Film scripts that almost get produced, working in a gallery in San Francisco until it failed, writing poems published in lesbian magazines. As I said, we don't communicate, she lives out there in Marin County, where the 'sixties never quite died, with a Dutch woman, the real thing, not some long-ago-transplanted Ouderkirk, but the real thing fresh from Holland, they met at some conference or protest on the West Coast, saving the redwoods or the salmon or the seals or the darter snail; when I last visited Paul in Brooklyn Heights, I saw on his bulletin board a snapshot of the two of them Dot had sent him at Christmas. Dot's hair was snow white, not yet forty and white as a dandelion, cut short enough to stand up all around and possibly dyed, some women when they go half gray bleach it all the way, their vanity won't let them dye it back to what it was, so they make this statement in the other direction, but I don't think Dot would do that. Her eyebrows were still dark, dark and broad over those cool, pale eyes of Guy's, and she still had that thickset look of clay pottery, her pockmarks like a mistake in the firing, but the look on her face jaunty and spoiling for a fight, my dear little Dot a white-haired dyke. Her friend had a toothy smile and seemed grotesquely tall, six feet at least, which is not how you think of the Dutch, certainly not the Ouderkirks. We were all on the compact side." She dabs with a middle finger at the tears on her face, still left over evidently from the day Guy departed.

Kathryn clears her own throat, she is running dry, and asks, "Did it ever occur to you that Dorothy's silence is a way of being kind to you, since she guesses that you see her as a failure? That she embarrasses you?"

"But she doesn't, she *doesn't*. I love her. I love her the most of—" No, that would be too hard on the boys, who put up with her now, as her brothers once did, and will have to deal with her when she takes the next step downhill and can no longer hold on here, where Jerry left her. To escape choosing, she turns her head and through the thin panes examines the sky. It looks like the underside of something, it has formed itself into rolls of nimbus clouds, breakers in an upside-down ocean. Yet the sky contains enough light to make her pupils wince. In the east, white wisps scud on a mottled grisaille. The distant mountain's hump frowns in a dip of shadow. Hope speaks as if making her way word by word. "I think she may have been right in accusing me of living my life in terms of men. But the art world then *was* almost all male; it was men who had the excess energy, the instinct for battle. This is terribly unpolitic to confess to you, but female artists have always struck me as hangers-on, whether genteel old maids like Cassatt or else layabouts and models like Valadon some man like Degas fed brushes and a pat on the head to. What do we remember best about Valadon? That she was Utrillo's mother and managed to nurse him along through his alcoholism so that he lived till seventy. I hate myself for saying this—these are my fellow-students, my bohemian sisters, much more fun than the men, more perceptive and harder-working, one of my spinster aunts used to do charming watercolors of nasturtiums and the Brandywine—but women don't go over the top; they're too timid and respectful, which is understandable enough, and easily distracted, again understandable. I loved Grace Hartigan, she was my exact contemporary, *so* confident, *so* unafraid of color, but even *she* couldn't quite let go and give herself to total abstraction, she couldn't believe she couldn't lean *just a little* on the scenery around her, for her titles and for sneaky little cute bits of pictorial allusion. She couldn't paint just out of nothing, out of herself, only a man would dare do that. And all these much-publicized women artists of the last thirty years, what have they been saying but 'I have a cunt'? Well, everybody knew they had cunts. Other women knew it, *I* knew it, and the news very quickly becomes boring. Men are the only ones excited by the information, so there we are again. Pointing ourselves at men. But is that so bad? Isn't it healthful, and fruitful?" *By their fruits ye shall know them* was another frequent saying of her grandfather's. And *Lukewarm I spit thee out*, said most commonly of his second cup of morning coffee. Hope's face feels hot, with that desire to please, to plead, which illustrates her very point, female weakness.

Kathryn's heavy dark eyes drop down to her long black lap, and study the sheaf of notes prepared in laser-printed lines. "You began to paint again," she says, "somewhat before Guy left you in '75."

"Yes, I did. The boys were up here in Vermont and Dot off all day at Brearley and Guy down at the Hospice with his mischief-makers, and I set up my paints in what had been a maid's little corner room. Its one window faced a dingy beige apartment building over on Park. The curious madness of people living different lives behind all these identical apertures and balconies—it led me, I suppose for the first time, to grids, to regular all-over patterns. Op Art had come and gone in the 'sixties, and all of its stars had been foreigners—Vasarely, Soto, Riley—but there was something still in it for me, something very American and Sundayish: the sidewalks in a small town, the front yards with nothing much in them, a calm emptiness yet full of American plenty. You see it in Sheeler, in Grant Wood. I loved the *quietness* of carefully painting horizontal patterns, the colors close enough together so nothing obvious jumped out at the viewer, nothing anecdotal. At first I tried putting things in, little variations, hiccups in the stripes, but they felt impure to me. 'Invisible painting,' some critics called a one-room show that Leo put on for me, not kindly. But I had to avoid strong color for fear of people comparing me with Zack, when I was married now to Guy. In deference to Guy, at first I put in bits of lettering or arrows to give a Pop touch, but it didn't please him. He thought what I was doing was like knitting, and maybe it helped turn him off." Hope laughs. "He said it gave him the creeps, seeing me fill in all these tiny spaces."

Kathryn says, "I don't think Bridget Riley fits your description of female artists. She's still going strong, too."

"No, I guess she doesn't. And, yes, she is. I admire Riley, of course. I've mentioned Marisol. Cassatt at her best breaks my heart—those little square feet being so solemnly bathed, the stripes on the woman's bathrobe. You shouldn't use my words against me—they were an attempt to describe my own self-distrust, and to respond to my daughter, whose accusations still rankle."

"Do I remind you," Kathryn asks, raising her eyes from the notebook so that again their whites flash in the gloom, "of your daughter?"

"No. Well, in ways. You both have—had—dark hair

with a lot of body. You both put me on the defensive. But you"—she doesn't want to say *are beautiful*—"feel to me successful, or headed that way, whereas I see Dorothy still in terms of the little girl begging to be let into our bed, and later begging to have a clear face."

"It's possible she doesn't see herself that way at all. In photographs I've seen of her, before her hair turned white as you describe, she looks triumphant. And rather attractive."

"That's kind of you to say."

Being charged with kindness makes Kathryn uncomfortable. Hope has overstepped, as so often in her life with men, presuming an intimacy that was not yet quite established. She is aware of a pain in her hands, the upper joints of her right hand, at the base of her fingernails. The body, attacked by itself, gives out a secret cry. She folds that hand within her left, to hush the hurt. Kathryn leans forward to check the worrisome Sony, as it sits drinking in their silence with a whirr, and shuffles through her six or seven sheets of notes and questions. "*I know,*" Hope says brightly, in what she perceives as a lull. "It's about to rain, let's go stretch our legs in the yard. You haven't looked at the view. Then we'll have tea, or coffee if you can bring yourself to drink instant, and maybe a snack, since you can't drive all the way back to New York on an empty stomach. I used to be able to eat only at mealtimes," she goes on, softening her firm proposal, blurring the edges, "feast or famine, but as you get older the stomach must shrink, because I've become what they call a grazer, nibbling constantly and being rather revolted by a full meal if one should appear, I keep dodging these awards dinners. Some evenings I don't even bother to heat up any soup, just mix what berries and nuts I have in the fridge in a bowl with a little milk, while I watch the news. I can get only one station up here without one of those unsightly satellite dishes, they're as bad in my view as having cars in the front yard with their tires stripped, it's Dan Rather I get, I can hardly make out his rumble, depending on the reception that evening. And he looks so often the way I feel, like a petulant old woman. I rarely watch to the end, the commercials are so insulting, all for iron pills and hemorrhoid medicine and incontinence diapers, it tells you how little the young care about the news, I'm generally upstairs and in my nightie before eight."

Had all this been only to hint that it was getting late? Hope feels light-headed with such an expenditure of breath, but she does want, so much, to communicate with this opaque, rather rejecting young woman, who is telling her, "Honestly, I don't need anything to eat or drink. You've been too generous already. I never meant—I have only a few more questions."

"But I'm nagged by the fear—the *terror*, Kathryn—that I haven't answered your questions at all, *at all*, as the poem says. Please. Let's take a break. It's after four."

So the thread-thin hands of the gold clock on the mantel state. Piet, her middle child, had had trouble grasping the principle of clocks, and in truth, when she tried, it was not so easy to explain, the big hand moving through twelve hours while the little hand moved only one, and why twelve hours when there were twenty-four in the day? The pathos of his puzzlement lasted in her mind for years beyond the unmarked moment—it might have happened at school, or perhaps Brenda or Josie successfully explained it to him— when the trick of it clicked into place and the child was saddled with knowing how to tell time, so that forty years later he was not late for appointments with multimillionaire clients who wanted to merge and acquire. Perhaps he got his mental block from her: though she was given years of piano lessons, at a time when modest artistic skills were still part of a woman's equipment in the hunt for a husband, the bass clef has remained for her something of a puzzle; when, to entertain her grandchildren, she attempts to peck out a Christmas carol or an Easter hymn on the piano, she has to locate the fingers of her left hand thinking, All Cows Eat Grass, A C E G, a munching, depressing reminder as opposed to the shining clarity of the upper clef, F A C E. How angry it used to make her when her little fat fingers couldn't stretch the octave the big yellow music book—arrangements supposedly *for* children—demanded. It wasn't *fair.*

"Come!" she cries to Kathryn, holding out her hand. "You *must* come outdoors. Put away those dreary sheets of questions reminding us of all we'd just as soon forget." Though her hand remains in midair some seconds, her guest doesn't take it in hers, instead using her own hands—long, pale, workmanlike, erotically charged with a serious intent at odds with her black (or are they deep purple, an aubergine?) fingernails—to switch off the Sony and lay her neatened pages of notes on the sea-chest, after balancing them on the chair's broad arm but thinking better of it, since the act of rising, even if done carefully, in a three-quarters unfolding move from one side of the broad plaid cushion, might tip the pages and scatter them on the floor. Hope has already risen from the rocker, feeling liberated at last, certain that her duties toward this awkward person are nearly discharged. "First," she all but sings, "let me put on the water for tea, so we'll have it as soon as we come back in. We'll just go out a moment. I know you're thinking of the time."

"No, I wasn't," says Kathryn, but hesitantly.

Heedless, unstoppable now, Hope leads the way to her kitchen, past back stairs narrow and steep with each bare

pine tread worn in two depressions as if by a double water-
fall of footsteps. Jerry wanted to replace them, they were
worn to half their original thickness in spots, but Hope
always said no, she loved them as they were, testifying to all
those laborious farmers' feet clomping up to bed at the end
of a weary day and then down again at dawn to begin
another in the odor of breakfast meats frying, sausages and
chops, oatmeal and dark bread, meals to get them through
the six hours to noon. Beneath the stairs a beaded-board
closet door hides brooms and a feather duster and an Elec-
trolux and cleaning supplies that smell to Hope like sugary
candy when she opens the door, which she rarely does, the
supplies wait for the weekly visit of Mrs. Warren, who is
always trying to give Hope a puppy, she and Jason breed
Labradors in the valley as a business. The narrow door and
its trim and baseboard and the window frame across this
hall are painted a warm medium gray, paler than battleship
yet darker than pewter, a low-gloss old-fashioned mole
color Hope had picked from a chart of Colonial Williams-
burg shades twenty years ago, when she and Jerry had
bought the house to be a place where they could get away
from everything, even television except for one channel, a
place where their mortality could find them at home when
it came knocking, though as it happened Jerry died in New
York Hospital, between the East River and York Avenue,
above but not far above the squawks of swerving taxis and
wails of ambulances arriving at the emergency entrance.
Hope sets the water kettle on the chipped prongs and blue
flame and at the far sink verifies her impression that the
rain has hesitated: the flecks on the Andersen windows
actually are drying. When Kathryn came in the front door,
which no one who knows the house would knock at, the
strange tall girl was wearing a hooded cloak of purple cash-

mere that got tossed onto the front-hall settee, but this is too fine a garment and perhaps not warm enough for early April in Vermont. However, the mud room off the kitchen, at right angles to the corridor to the studio, has pegs for holding skis and poles and snowshoes when these exertions were still feasible and lower pegs for parkas, of which Hope had a number, mustard and maroon and buff in color, all more or less dirty from rubbing around in car trunks and their goosedown stuffing somewhat flattened by the years, these outfits for vanished, more vigorous selves hung above rows of boots, high-ankled patchworks of leather and rubber and canvas, for snow and mud; there is no need for these, the lawn is still frozen, but she does grab the mustard-colored parka for herself and thrusts another, the maroon, which looks biggest and newest and fattest—it was Jerry's, she can see him in it for a moment, his curly gray hair, thick as wool, smartly dented by the elastic band of his yellow ski goggles before he hid it in the striped green ski cap that made him look like a chunky elf, his tanned face with its little scar off-center on the upper lip (a boyhood brawl; he grew up tough) which made him look rough-hewn and good-humored somehow; he thought she was *funny* was what she had loved—upon Kathryn, who stupidly drapes it around her shoulders cape-fashion, stepping warily, like a heron wading, out the back door onto the millstone that serves as a step and then down in her quite unsuitable Via Spigas with their ladders of laces and odd high heels onto the earth, which is a little muddy, here by the door, where the shaded lawn is thin on grass. Really, Hope thinks, the woman has the passive aggression of a child, whom nothing quite pleases, yet who can't articulate an objection you might argue her out of.

"There's the old orchard," Hope says, gesturing in the

chill dull air, in a direction up the hill past the house. "It still produces wormy apples and pears. Over here's the bird feeder, where squirrels terrorize the chickadees and a pair of cardinals that show up, though I haven't seen the male lately, there are runaway cats in the woods. I own twenty acres in that direction and fifteen more in this. Let's go around to the front of the house—watch your step in this section, the moles did a terrible job on it last summer, and yet my lawn boys refuse to roll it, they say nobody owns rollers any more, it's not part of lawn care now. When I was a girl in the Philadelphia suburbs every household had a lawn roller; you filled them with water from the garden hose and you could hear it slosh inside, it would slosh back and forth as you pushed it and almost knock you backward when you stopped, if you weren't paying attention. Do be careful, those boots of yours aren't as practical as they look, the soles are so smooth." Her mind runs on into the unspoken thought that it is she, Hope, who must be careful, at her age it begins with a single misstep, an ankle, a hip, a healing that is ominously slow. Her sons will take her into their hands and end her living alone as she does, unsupervised, free. She knows they discuss her, as her parents used to discuss her when she was in bed and going to sleep above the soothing mumble of their voices.

After hours of her longing to take it into her lungs, the outdoor air is less rejuvenating than she had anticipated. She feels the irresistible lassitude that comes over an old person toward the end of the afternoon. Jerry used to speak of "pick-me-ups." "Time for a pick-me-up," he would say, when Hope had been intending to spend another hour in the garden or at the easel, and she blamed the daily drinking he invited for the increase in her weight. Until her mid-fifties and her third marriage, she still had a figure she

needn't be too ashamed of in shorts or a snug black dress—
feminine, and thickening, and soft in the upper arms, but
with a waist still and hips that didn't look like a pair of duf-
fle bags packed for a long trip. She couldn't have landed
Jerry if she had been in the shape she acquired as his wife.

This is the present, Hope tells herself. This bare, raw outdoor moment. *I am still alive.* The air is moist and gray, not
quite freezing but with a breeze that cuts at her throat,
where the turtleneck is loose and she did not bother to zip
up her parka. The front lawn, as much hawkweed and dandelion and plantain as grass, all flattened by winter to one
dun color, ends at a drystone wall mended by Jerry's soft
city hands until he got bored and paid the Warren men—
Jason and his three sons and his twin bachelor brother,
Ezra—to finish the job. The driveway, such as it is, comes
off the road toward the house on the side with the bird
feeder hung on the big beech backed by pines; Kathryn had
driven her car, an orange Honda coupe with one unpainted
fender left over from, presumably, a city accident, up the
driveway and aggressively beyond it, parking at an angle
beneath the beech where neither Hope nor the Warrens
ever park. Beyond the wall, a dirt road with a high mane of
hay leads to the houses of her two out-of-sight neighbors,
one a retired Unitarian minister from the Syracuse area and
the other a once-well-known 'forties radio personality generally assumed to be dead. "We're up among the angels,"
Jerry would joke. Beyond the road a bumpy meadow falls
away, dotted with boulders and ghostly burdock stalks and a
few starting cedars the mowers last fall somehow missed.
The cold breeze is sharper out front, on this unsheltered
expanse open to the panoramic prospect of brown and
smoky blue and dull pine green from which faintly arises
a whir of highway traffic in the valley, cars and trucks

hurtling unseen on Route 89. She zips the parka up to her chin. The far mountains overlap in waves like viscid, studiously continuous blue brush-strokes on glass. The clouds above align in advancing rolls of mottled vapor. A few fine cold drops prick her face and the back of her pointing hand. "That's Camels Hump," she says. "A nice afternoon's climb twenty years ago, when I was younger." *This is it*, she thinks again, this drab present, this overcast radiance, colder and bleaker than April should be, this moist air sharp in her shallow lungs, this brimming vacancy of the seen. Witnessing the world alongside another makes her realize how little it all is, how brief and even negligible compared with our soul's expectations and bottomless appetite. A world made to our measure would go on forever. Instead, the million million molecules of H_2O overhead, and the thousands of leafless trees that from miles away blend into a tone of blue, a neutral yet delicately packed color like the blue-green-gray-pink background so frequent in Cézanne's later still lifes, and the myriad microscopic structures that bestow consciousness upon us all so quickly slip away.

"Quickly," she says to her mute companion. "You must see my garden. On the other side of the house." They make their way across the frozen uneven turf, where a few wrinkled shoulders of ledge jut from the lawn, frozen flow from a fire that turned rocks molten millions or was it billions of years ago, these two women unequal in age and height but yoked together by a sisterly determination to make the moment succeed, a moment like the thinnest possible skin of time, thinner than lichen, on the rocks' enduring unknowing. But the garden, lovingly extended and fenced while Jerry was still alive, and still tended by Hope to the extent her strength permits, with no more summer help than the Warren men can spare from more manly jobs and she can coax from Mildred and Jason's daughter, an overweight teen-age girl with her thoughts miles away, hopelessly stupid on boys and music, music she wears on her head in rustling earphones, music to drown out the merest sliver of a thought if any were to wander into her poor brain, Hope cannot believe she herself was ever that besotted, music came to her over her parents' radio and hardly grazed her consciousness, nasal men singing through megaphones, New York hotel music piping with muted trumpets, even in the war you danced when the music, the swing, was there but you didn't wear it on your head like a dunce cap—the garden presents almost nothing to see: the stubble of last summer's phlox and a few hosta leaves left flattened on the earth when she ripped it up hastily one unseasonably cold October day, her hands hurting, and a rusting wire peony-support unaccountably overlooked and then lost for months under snow. Dead, dead as sticks appear the writhing thorned stems of the pink rambler she has trained through the lattice of the green fence she and Jerry had the Warren twins put up to give the multicolored canvas of the garden, as it were, a frame. Jason was the outgoing bluff one, the salesman, but Ezra was the craftsman.

"It must be beautiful in the summer," Kathryn says, lamely, though Hope can't blame her for that, it is a lame occasion, she wonders now why she was so keen to get outdoors.

"It's English-style," Hope tells her guest, "that is, crowded and blowsy, and I tend to lose my enthusiasm toward the end of June, when it gets hot, even up here."

Already she sees, in the earth that has hardly begun to awaken, cracks indicating softening and refreeze, and the rounded tongues of daffodils and the pointed tongues of daylilies beginning to poke through. On the front of the house, the southern side, next to the sun-warmed Barre granite of the foundation, snowdrops and crocuses are already pushing up to flower. Green threads of garlic will soon appear in the lawn. The garden with its care seems a suffocating challenge, a cruel hill she must climb into the future. She cannot get enough of the day's darkening air into her lungs; her lungs are emphysematous from decades of heedless smoking. It wasn't until her marriage to Guy and its pregnancies that she stopped, Guy had never smoked and complained about the smell of ashtrays in the apartment, there was something prissy and whining about him that she refused to let herself dislike; the public that saw him as the embodiment of mad invention, of irreverent Pop revolt against the seven centuries of painterly tradition since Giotto would have been disappointed to know what an orderly and abstemious prig he in fact was. He drank in moderation, rarely anything stronger than wine, and smoked grass with her the last time when they took the vacation in Mexico, their marriage's last gasp; they arrived by 727 instead of by Route 10 in a sandy two-tone '56 Nash Rambler with a biracial, bisexual duo with great bodies and vague ambitions, but as soon as she and Guy landed in Guadalajara the moon did look bigger, like a piece of display pottery, and its pale light smelled of flowers, the tree flowers that soaked in the night dew and closed when dawn opened with cockcrows. Her husband scored a little pot from a kid on the street just outside the Hilton, and that sweet evening on the balcony in their underwear did carry her back to 1958. She had gone with Guy for a wild ride, but the ride had turned out to be tame and to end with a jolt. The jolt had been building; he knew that tameness was the undoer of art and that no twentieth-century art movement keeps its kick for ten years if that, the label dries up and curls off; though artists live forever with modern medicine, their moment becomes a corpse and there is no reversing the dissolution, resurrection flies in the face of molecular biology, Guy would have been sensitive enough to feel himself a walking corpse, with a wife well past fifty and three hostages to fortune receiving expensive private educations, no wonder he turned to tight-assed Gretchen, for a lighter ride.

"Kathryn, I was thinking," Hope says, her voice coming out tight and breathy under the pressure of being outdoors, "looking toward Camels Hump—Jerry and I used to climb it easily, even though we weren't young even then, with a lunch basket and a bottle of wine—thinking about human animals, how marvellous the biological machinery that gives us consciousness, and how we mostly just throw it away; even if we don't commit suicide, we presume to find life dull and be bored most of the time, and discontented, and just *waste* it; I bet that's why *Hamlet* appeals to us so much, out of all Shakespeare's plays, it's the one we take personally, it expresses this *disregarded* quality of life, the waste of our minds, our bodies, of everything that should make us joyful and careful. Am I making any sense?" For she can go too far, she knows; since childhood she has felt her overflowing spirit back up, meeting resistance in the faces of others, the blood in her own face damming in a blush.

The tall young woman pulls her borrowed parka, stupidly worn like a cape, tighter around her shoulders, her face looking chalky out here in the open, a pimple visible where her nostril wing meets the cheek, traces of plastery powder on her arched nose. Cautiously she responds, "I don't think anyone would say you've wasted your life. That's what makes it so interesting to me."

"Oh? Really? You're honestly interested? To me it all seems terribly scattered—as my daughter says, a lot of catering to men, and then painting in ways that the men said irritated them, and now that it's almost too late, painting in a way that seems true to myself but maybe is an es*cape* from myself, from the color of the world, which in that rather pompous statement of mine you read to me I said was the Devil—how weird of me to mention the Devil, I know you must think, but there *is* something out there, if you have any feeling for goodness at all, that resists it, that pushes the other way. I know you and your generation will think me quite mad, but God's non-existence is something I can't get used to, it seems *unnatural*."

Kathryn's lips—intricate braids of muscle, looked at up close in this cold outdoor light, designed to give her and others pleasure, if she doesn't fear contamination; but how can her generation not fear contamination, just as Hope's feared constraint?—fumble at her next words, her brain perhaps numbed by this un-asked-for venture into the great outdoors, where small cold raindrops are tearing little holes in the veil of sensation. Or perhaps, if she is Jewish, she is unable to put the question of God quite the way a Christian would put it, in urgent terms of either/or. For the chosen people the relation has evolved beyond the possibility of dropped acquaintance into that of a familiarity that breeds contempt: so Bernie once expounded it to Hope, his weary bulk redolent of sweat and cigarettes beside her in bed while his canvases below them sent up their unheard cries of flat, passionate color. Being Jewish amused him; he played with it, he heaped its ashes on his dandy's head and turned its tribal fury into visionary Socialism. Kathryn hesistantly states, "An old boyfriend of mine, studying at graduate school to be a physicist at Columbia, told me that with the thorough understanding they have now there's really no place for God in the universe."

"In us, dear. The place is in us, weak and silly as we are."

"As he explained it, it's a matter of energy, the equations. Eventually everything will get very far from everything else and trillions of years will go by, with everything dead and dark. There will be no place where we could be, even as pure souls. They need energy too."

The words chill Hope. Raindrops are unignorably falling on their hands and faces, and pattering on their Gore-Tex parkas. "I'm sure he's right, from one point of view," Hope says impatiently. "But look up there, in the woods, you can just make out a glimmer of the springhouse roof. And you can see the path that takes you up to it, and to an even bigger view. Every summer we have to take down some trees to keep the view open. I say 'we,' but of course it's men I hire who do it. A family of chauvinists who hate taking direction from a woman."

"I—"

"Can skip the view. I know. Let's go back in, before the tea water boils all away."

Still, it has done Hope good to be out in the cosmos, so different in feeling, so capacious, intricate, and benign, from the picture painted by Kathryn's old boyfriend. How old was old? Does this girl have a boyfriend who is not old, who is waiting to warm and console her, to listen to her story about this babbling old witch on her lonely hill it took forever to drive to and even longer to drive back from? Hope feels her face freshened by its brush with the outdoors; her skin is taut with that fullness she remembers from childhood, when it seemed too good to be true that she was she, her life a daily growing fuelled by food in the day and sleep at night, the moon and sun the same exact size in the sky though there was no necessary reason for it. She leads Kathryn back around the house, past the bird feeder hanging from the bare beech, over the gleams of mud by the millstone step up to the door of the kitchen; the mismatching storm door twangs on its rusty spring, and the real door, slightly sunk on its hinges, pops at a push from Hope's shoulder. Kathryn, too, despite herself, from the briskness of her steps and the speed with which she sheds Jerry's maroon parka, has had her spirit lifted. "How nice it must be," she exclaims, "to have so much space to yourself. The whole of my apartment I think is no bigger than your kitchen. And these boring towers absolutely dominating my view."

"My boys think it's too much space for one little old lady. Now, what can we give you to eat?"

"Eat? I don't need anything, but if I could use your bathroom . . ."

"Of course. You know where it is. But you *must* have something on your stomach before you set out."

"I still have a few questions. We're just up to the 'seventies."

"I know, but my main story is over. The unusual part, marriage to two men of genius. Jerry was no genius, but he was a sweetheart. First of all, is it tea you want, or that ancient instant coffee you turned your nose up at before?"

"The coffee, please. That was *chilly* out there." Her voice recedes and the door to the bathroom shuts, under the stairs. Hope, alone, feels the cosmos around her, as many stars under her feet as over her head, the endless galaxies and the trillions of dark years to come, and hurriedly gathers cups and saucers, a tea bag for herself—herbal, chamomile, from the health-food store, this time of day, a night of insomnia after being stirred up all day is the last thing she needs, she wants to start a new canvas tomorrow, a little broader in its stripes and a browner, warmer gray than the last, to sleep well she needs physical exercise and this sitting in a rocker talking is not it—and for her guest the Taster's Choice undecaffeinated with its red label and friendly little waist (the incurved glass sides in her bent fingers remind her of something; what?) and from the refrigerator the heavy loaf of rice-pecan bread (*No Preservatives, Fruit-Juice Sweetened*) from the same quaint store run by aged former hippies in Montpelier and from the cupboard beyond the double sink the squat straight-sided jars of Dundee marmalade and Skippy peanut butter. The girl must eat. It comes to Hope what the concave sides of the instant-coffee jar reminded her of: the curved walls of Peggy's Art of This Century gallery, designed by, what was his name, Fritz, one of those pushy Germans like that Hans who drove Zack back to drink, Fritz Kiesler, not Kreisler, Kiesler with his seven-way chairs that could turn into tables or lecterns or easels, an idea that didn't catch on but seemed perfectly adapted for the future at the time, wood covered in bright colors of linoleum, shaped plastic not yet invented, the floor turquoise. The future was here, in 1942, above a grocery store on West Fifty-seventh Street. There were contraptions, a pinwheel of Duchamps, a conveyor belt of Klees, Hope had just come to New York, it seemed such glorious giddy fun to her, all so new; the walls curved out, not in like the sides of the coffee jar, but it was the same idea, of curves where you expected straight sides, that had reminded her, the touch of them, taking her so far back it was frightening, that feeling returning that she used to get on the top of the cathedrals and the Eiffel Tower when Jerry began taking her to Europe, which Zack and Guy were too poor or uncaring to do, the feeling that she was much too high, that she might slip through the floor into all those uncaring galaxies beneath her feet.

Kathryn returns, having peed. Hope can see the difference on her newly relaxed face; how modest a lowering of tension it takes to satisfy what Freud called the pleasure principle. "This is a treat I sometimes give myself," Hope announces. "A marmalade-and-peanut-butter sandwich on this special rice-pecan bread. You must have one with me. It will get us through."

"I—"

"You don't eat junk, but this isn't junk," Hope finishes for her. "The bread is from a health-food store fifteen miles away, I risk my life every time I drive there. You must be starving, dear; I know I am."

Against the grain of her self-denying, ambitious, yet clumsy nature, Kathryn sits and warily consumes half the sandwich, its heavy dun-colored bread, its childish spreads, spread not too thickly or one's fingers, Hope has learned through experience, become sticky. The two women, who have been so busy asking and answering, eat in a silence new to them. Time presses; the digital kitchen clock says 5:06. Rain, gathering volume, runs down the far window through which Hope had earlier studied the tousled sky, its torment resolved into a pearly brightness beyond the rivulets of rain, the hidden sun lowering to the west. Kathryn sips at her coffee, though it must still be, like Hope's tea, scalding, and Hope takes pity on her: "If you're in such a hurry, we can take our cups back to the front room and the tape recorder. But do finish your sandwich. Isn't it good?"

"It is, it takes me back. Delicious. But I really can eat only half. It's funny, on weekends my boyfriend tells me I eat like a horse, it's a wonder I'm not fat, but when I'm on assignment I really have no appetite, I'm so focused. I didn't sleep much last night, either. The motel was just off 89, the traffic never stopped, you'd think it would way up here in the country."

So she does have a present, active boyfriend. Hope feels relief. And jealousy. "You poor thing. You must have been anxious. What about?"

"Not asking the right questions."

"Oh, I'm sure they're right enough. I'll tell you if we miss anything important. But isn't that what Freud's theory of psychotherapy claims, that it all comes around to the main thing even if you talk quite at random? What does your boyfriend do, may I ask?"

Kathryn lowers her lids, lids that seem in the fluorescent kitchen light gorgeously greasy, those of some sinful, defiant Biblical queen. The girl is offended to have the interview turned on her but has accepted enough of the other woman's kindness to see no way out. "He's in film, that's what he loves," she says. "He's on a team making trailers, part-time, but he wants to move to the West Coast and climb the ladder to be a director. He acts, too, but that doesn't turn him on."

"Doesn't it? How interesting," Hope says, not finding it particularly so. "He isn't a painter?"

"Oh no. He goes with me to openings and shows now and then and can't see what I see in any of it. He's a real philistine that way."

"You said he helps make what?"

"Trailers. You call them previews. There's an art to it, sequencing the high-energy bits. They work sometimes from rushes on a picture that isn't half finished and nobody knows the ending."

"Well, the ending is just what we don't want these— what are they?—'trailers' to disclose. Jerry was a keen

moviegoer, he liked going out, so we would bestir ourselves
and go, in New York up to Eighty-sixth Street and here
over to Burlington. But after a while every movie seemed
to be made for adolescent boys; they made you feel
processed—so many car chases you were supposed to care
about, so many explosions and narrow escapes, and that was
it. It must be a worry for you, to have him wanting to move
to Los Angeles."

"Well, not too much. It's less than six hours in the air. I
want him to succeed and be happy at what he loves."

"Of course. But what of you? New York is where you
must be, surely."

"I liked L.A., the one time I was there. The mild weather,
the Spanish flavor, the freeways. It feels like the future."

"You didn't find it . . . cheesy?"

"They do have art there. A very lively art scene, actually."

"They have those low-riding cars and some handsome,
virtually empty museums."

"*You* left New York."

"Not far. Not in my mind. I kept going back, until I got
too stodgy to travel. Don't sacrifice your own work, for the
sake of a man."

Kathryn does not say, *You did*, but both think it, Hope
with the reservation that she never betrayed herself absolutely, she postponed rather than sacrificed, she somehow
knew she had time to wait it all out, to get to this present, to
be herself in the end.

Kathryn surprises her by laughing—a prettier, lighter,
more musical laugh than her horsy face had prepared Hope
for. "You don't seem to approve of Alec, without knowing
him at all!"

"I want the best for *you*," Hope tells her, not smiling.
"I'm not sure a trailer-maker sounds like it. I've always felt

squeamish around people who want to be 'in film.' What doesn't your friend like about acting? It seems at least to be straightforward, an ancient art of sorts."

"He calls it a meat market. Alec is really very nice, you'd like him if you met him, even if he doesn't think painting amounts to much any more. Once pictures began to move, he says, it was all over for those that didn't." She shifts position at the table, looks at the remaining half-sandwich as if to begin eating it, and takes a sip of her rapidly cooling coffee instead. Microwave heat for some microscopic reason fades much faster than good old-fashioned boiling heat: the fact fascinates Hope. "You know," Kathryn tells her, not exactly rebuking, "most of us can't find these men of genius to marry. Most of us must muddle along in the middle, and hope at least it *is* the middle."

"Neither man attracted me because he was famous," Hope says, sitting more upright at the table, feeling her face warm. "Guy appealed to me because of his gaiety, his impudence. Zack was not unknown in art circles when I married him, but he was certainly poor, and going downhill fast. And I disliked his paintings, in fact. My family thought it was a ruinous match, as in many ways it was."

"Still, you were there when he broke it all open—you were part of it."

"I got him out to Long Island, that was good. For a time. But my being a small part of it gives me less satisfaction, I can tell only you, than if *I* had been the one to make the breakthrough."

Is this quite true? Welcoming Zack back to the relatively warm house after one of his freezing hours in the barn had had its satisfactions—a partnered wonder, a worried pride. This man hemmed in by clamoring needs, by chemical dependency and social incoherence, could nevertheless fetch back to her through the snow not a bloody kill on his back but the ghost, in his hands and eyes, his lovely tawny farsighted Western eyes, of beauty, beauty stretched flat in those great swaths of sized canvas taped to the floor with their swirls and spatters of pure paint drying. Then it was, as he spoke to his mate with breath still visible as frozen vapor, as if she *had* done it with him, ripped those imperishable hours from the perishing world.

"No more sandwich?" Hope says to Kathryn. She is a bit hurt, being rejected in this trivial particular. "I'll wrap it in Reynolds Wrap for your drive back. Really, it's not bad for you, though the marmalade has sugar in it. I've lived on nothing else some days up here, when I was snowed in."

"Poor Alec," the other woman says, off in her own world, where her lover has taken a wound. Hope forgets what weight her words have to these innocents dazzled by even a soft glow of fame. It was true, she had not liked the sound of a man who did not like galleries. To her they were Aladdin's caves, from her first glimpse of Art of This Century with its curved walls, and then, when married to Guy, of the Hansa and Reuben and Judson and Red Grooms', where happenings and playlets were staged that would leave the tiny audiences baffled but in some corner of their minds enlisted in a fresh way of seeing things, with less prejudice, with less expectation of familiar hierarchy, and then the midtown galleries, Leo's and Sidney's, which gave Pop its celebrity and opened it to the new collectors, the playful new American money, she had met Jerry in one of them. Galleries usually had an embattled, silent feeling to them, underpopulated, the girls at the desk fighting drowsiness, the paintings in their brightness and the sculptures in their savage stasis waiting for love, for the viewer, the buyer, while bored and idle noises leaked through from the back room.

These galleries housed works produced in loneliness and confusion but also in a mood of exalted contentment, of remove from the world's ruck, work done on the edge of usefulness, art undermining its own uses as fast as these could be identified, art at art's crumbling edge, fragments arrayed in these bare but for her far from desolate chambers of Manhattan; Hope was always stirred and happy in them, they were meetinghouses sacred in their silence, poised for visitation.

"Don't mind me at all," she tells her visitor, sensing but not greatly caring that the girl has been insulted. "Let's go to the front parlor. I can't offer you anything else? A quick little salad? Some Brazil nuts? How about a low-fat gluten-free oatmeal cookie?"

Kathryn rises, hands flat on the table to help her up, without deigning a response. Rain thrashes on the kitchen skylight. In the front parlor the sound is subdued. The two women, cups in hand, resettle into their chairs, and even as she leans forward and switches the tape recorder back on Kathryn says, "I'd like to return to Guy for a minute. His leaving you isn't very clear to me."

"Nor to me," Hope allows, sensing that her interrogator was going to dig deeper, to repay her for the doubt over Alec that Hope has sown. "He just seemed to sidle out of my life, and the children's, after seventeen years of being there, or at least checking in faithfully."

"Do you really believe he stayed uninvolved in all the drug use at the Hospice? What about amphetamines? Coke? Downers? In a lot of those experimental movies that were turned out under his name the actors are clearly tripping: the transvestite one, or one of the transvestite ones, *Sick Roses*, just the other evening I was watching it on video with Alec, and there's almost no interrelating, the actors are each doing their own thing with this tranced smirk on their faces, there is *no* attempt to connect with one another, let alone remember any lines that would advance a story."

"But, Kathryn dear, perhaps the point is that there isn't a story because there *shouldn't* be a story, because there aren't any stories any more, just as painting, you say, or Alec says, had to give up anecdote. That was why Hopper and Wyeth seemed to us such dinosaurs, they seemed to be still telling us stories. A story presupposes an author, moving the characters about from above, moving *us* about from above, to some morally intelligible end, and who believed that any more, after the Holocaust, after the A-bomb—"

Kathryn reacts so swiftly that the sheaf of questions in her lap slides and has to be slapped to keep from falling to the floor, its old boards painted the shiny black-red of Bing cherries. "Thank you for mentioning the A-bomb. In all this Cold War period, '45 to '89, did the threat of nuclear annihilation affect your thinking? Were you ever afraid?"

"A bit in '62, the Cuba crisis they just made a movie about, but not really. It was a lovely October day, that day when the world might blow up, with the Russian ships steaming toward ours. I remember pushing Paul and Piet in their twin stroller all the way over to the pediatrician's on East End Avenue and being much too hot in my new fall coat, and the television in his office being turned to a soap opera. People are optimists. They must be. I could never believe the world's leaders would be so stupid as to blow it all up."

"But—"

"Hitler would have, you are going to say. But the Russians, the Soviets, were like us—big bumbling countries with no need for *Lebensraum*, not little overachieving countries like Germany and Japan, driven crazy by these racist, death-loving myths they had. The Russians love life—read their novels. They were Communists, the ones running things, but so had been most of the older painters I knew, even into the war. In describing the post-war period you younger people keep telling us how haunted we were by the threat of nuclear Armageddon, but the fact is it hardly ever entered my head, and if it did what could I do about it? It was like being hit by a trolley car—that could happen, too. And about Guy and drugs, you should remember that most of his assistants at the Hospice were a generation younger than he and much more self-indulgent and nihilistic, they had grown up sheltered and spoiled and believed simultaneously that they shouldn't be denied anything at all and that the existing power structure, which had given them everything they had, was totally evil. Guy was three years younger than I, but we had both felt the Depression and the war; in fact, as you know from your research, he served in it, two years in the Coast Guard, sitting up in the Aleutians freezing his skinny butt but doing his bit. He didn't talk much about it, but he used to go about every five years to these little reunions of the guys he had served on the cutter with. There was a connection, though you're right, connection wasn't what he was about. Or passion. The artists I first knew were always talking about passion, Bernie of course, and Roger always going on about his *feelings* as he painted, and Onno and Zack pouring this passion onto the canvas, these furious strokes and frenetic overpainting, but I never saw Guy lose his temper or express disappointment or dislike of another person, even the critics in the beginning who were so stupid about the beauty and really stunning variety of what he was doing. He read them but never let on, if anything he acted amused. And he didn't express much rapture, either, when the money began to pour in."

Why is she talking without letup? Because she wants to exhaust this woman on the subject, she wants to hide the humiliation Guy did inflict upon her with his casual abandonment, her and the children, the pain of seeing this, her only set of children, ever, maimed and puzzled by his defection. She is like Guy in being well bred, in seeing the value in a front, in seeing everything as a front, in believing in a controlled finish, for all the incidental dribbles. She had felt in league with his coolness, that calmly considered distance in him which was necessary to his steady good nature, and then she had been spurned, turned out of their little club. She tells Kathryn before the tenacious, clinging girl can think of another question, "Toward the end, as I said, as the 'seventies wore on, I think he began to feel strain, the strain of keeping ahead, of staying sexy for the galleries and the museums. It's not easy, making kitsch and trash seem something else. The tragedy of the modern, or should we say post-modern, artist is that the public's attention span is so much shorter than his normal creative life. Duchamp quit and gained a lot of points, Korgi and Seamus committed suicide, and Zack too in a way, but for a non-self-destructive artist there is just too much *time*. If he hits his vein early, his art is eventually exhausted. Those things Guy was doing before and after leaving me, the huge public statues, the pseudo-billboards, the giant coloring books with hideous colors, were not good. They had the same effrontery but lacked the original—what can we call it?—merriment. He thought leaving me might give him back his merriment." That is how she has framed the abandonment, as a byproduct of the artist's quest.

"There was a certain scandal attached to Guy's work, especially the movies and the happenings, with all their nudity and homoeroticism. How did you cope with that? How did your children, as they got older?"

"It was part of Daddy's business," Hope tells her, slightly lying and not caring; her visitor's inquisitiveness is wearing down her ethical sense. She feels most ethical in the morning, when she paints, and her exaltation crumbles away as the day goes on. She makes an effort to reflect and be honest. "The boys handled it by becoming very square, beginning at Buckley—it was Guy, by the way, who wanted to send them there, I had thought some school more progressive, but he said No, he didn't want his children typecast, he wanted them to have the straight educations he and I had had—and then at Putney, where almost nobody else was square. Dot did her own rebellion, as we've already discussed, off the record. What is hard to remember about those years is that Guy didn't put on a suit and tie like the other men in the building but in his turtleneck and tweedy jacket and blue jeans he *did* go off downtown much like they did and came back at dinnertime, or else called me and told me he was being held up at work and that I should eat with the kids without him, again a lot like the other men. He was dutiful, going to school events and playing softball with the other fathers and sons when they had outings in Central Park, and for the first dozen years at least he tried to be a normal husband to me. We would go together to one of these ballets in the basement of the Judson Church and watch a bunch of young people writhe around naked smearing each other with brown fingerpaints to symbolize filthy capitalist lucre or whatever, and then come home and have a lentil salad and a glass of milk in the kitchen, whispering so as not to wake up the children. Guy was a sensible, mild—"

"Or marmalade and peanut butter," Kathryn interrupts.

"What?" Hope's inner eye had been intent on the domestic picture, focusing on what she needed to say, to be fair, about Guy.

SEEK MY FACE

"I was reminded of the sandwich you just gave me," says Kathryn. "That was sweet."

"Too sweet, I suppose. You didn't finish it. You're all so afraid of sugar." This young woman's presuming to joke about the older one's apparently innocent tastes inflicts on Hope an irritation she resists revealing, because any sign of a quarrel or difference to be smoothed over will prolong the interviewer's already excessive stay. Hope tries again: "A mild, sensible man, and it was easy for all of us to forget that he was a celebrity, a major force in American art when it was still the world leader, and that behind all his family-man obligingness he was fighting for his life. He would wake up at night and not get back to sleep, I would roll over and readjust the eye mask and leave him sitting up under the reading light and find him at the breakfast table with the *Times* all read and refolded and lines in his face I had never seen before. With that effortless intuitive sense of his, he could feel it all slipping away, he was falling behind. In the late 'sixties, it wasn't just Pop and Op and what little was left of Abstract Expressionism, everything was having its start-up then—Minimalism, scatter art, earthworks, conceptual art that used just words, claiming it was a lie to pretend that perception wasn't a matter of language, or of *theory*. Europe was sending us its critical theory to kill our creativity, Guy used to say. It got so that *any* art that still produced paintings or combines that even if cumbersome could be hung on a wall and sculptures that could actually stand or sit in somebody's not terribly immodest living room was in danger of being old hat. No matter how hard Guy worked, no matter how inventive he was, Pop was beginning, with its flags and stacks of Wheaties boxes, while these enraged kids were out on the streets *burning* American flags, beginning to look, I hate to say it, *cozy*, and that was why I couldn't mind too much the drugs down at the Hospice, and the porno films that look so funny and fuzzy now, because they kept his enterprise—let's call it that—trendy; they kept for Guy his edge of being *maudit*. For selfish reasons and the sake of the children, which is selfish at one remove, I wanted him as domesticated as possible, but for him as an artist it wasn't healthy, we can't have Vermeers and Chardins any more, we can't glorify bourgeois life any more, not when it was somehow to blame for Vietnam and Birmingham and colonialism and so on, and it was a *strain*, as I said, for Guy to pretend to be bourgeois, to pretend art can be a business. I half-blame myself for going along with it, Guy's pretense, for my own bourgeois comfort, and that was why when he upped and left I was so half-hearted in resisting. Dot sensed it, and hates me still for being so weak. Don't put that in anything you write, please. But what could I do? I thought it might be better for him, for his art."

"I wonder why," Kathryn muses, "art can't be a business. It used to be a trade, and there was no shame in that."

"I suppose the same way religion shouldn't be a business, or be *only* one. Except that religion has a dependable product, our fear and loneliness, to trade on, whereas art has to convince people that they need it, they need something purer and more authentic than they get elsewhere, in all of life's *other* business. That purity and authenticity are worth having, or witnessing from however far away. The soul—can you stand the word?—can't be sullied by worry and self-interest. Guy had a lovely untroubled productive disinterest when I met him, living in that loft full of junk he'd stolen from the street, and as the money and flattery and awards poured in, he felt it slipping away from him, the purity, the heedlessness that can make something truly new. He began to care too much, because he *had* to care, because all of us around him depended on him; it was cruel. But, I must say, he never did anything that mattered—that had enough soul, enough disinterest to matter—while he was in the care of Little Miss Hardbum. And now she's nursemaid to a man who hasn't a clue as to who she is or he is."

"We should move on," Kathryn has the nerve to tell Hope, when it was her obtuse question that had prompted the monologue. "Tell me about Jerry. The two of you met when? Do you remember the occasion?"

"Oh, it was at one of Guy's openings. Unlike most of the people there, he was trying to look at the works, and I was worn out with making conversation, and we were standing side by side in front of a limp old-fashioned typewriter, twice real size and made of shiny white vinyl, all the round button keys overlapping and jumbled and the keys and carriage return dangling like a newborn lamb's helpless little legs, and we both said, together, 'Beautiful.' Beautiful. What can I say about Jerry that everybody doesn't already know? He was a dear man. He was dear at least to me, divorcing his wife to marry me, a favor I must say I never received from Bernie. Not that I wanted it. Bernie was too . . . too citified, he and Jeanette were too much a team. As we were saying earlier, in the decade after I . . . knew him *well*, Bernie had come up roses, the father of this, the father of that, when they'd had no children actually, Color Field, Hard Edge, the father even, supposedly, of some of the earthworks, those two-mile-long chalk lines somebody drew in the Mojave Desert in the late 'sixties, as I remember, using the desert like one of Bernie's big monochromatic canvases. Those big flat paintings everybody hated for years—Peggy couldn't stand them, and neither could

Betty—they turned out to be the road to the future, while Jarl's huge, scraggly vertical things were an embarrassment to museums he had bullied into buying them, they took up too much wall space, Jarl wanted room after room to himself, and Zack was stuck in his moment, a classic like Ryder or Bierstadt but absolutely fatal to imitate, in fact nobody else knew how to do it, how much to thin the enamel and what stick to use. Bernie was even named the father of Guy's early flat look and lack of impasto, and I've never seen Guy so miffed, it was as if he resented the little part that Bernie had played in my life before, of course I had told him, but that kind of conventional sexual jealousy was the last thing Guy would ever let himself confess to."

"And weren't there, even while you were married, a few younger men," Kathryn asks in the careful, slightly retracted voice with which she hopes to enter Hope's bloodstream without breaking the skin, "performance artists?"

Young male bodies, shadowy, the rounded muscle mass of shoulder and thigh, the flat stomachs and their tender pendants, stir in her mind like bodies buried in mud, faces without marked expressions. Jeb. Randy. They had names, addresses, philosophies, aspirations. They had hoped to use her, but she was hard to use, even by herself for her own benefit. The blacks were an adventure for her, dancers, their touching knobby hardworking feet. Henry. Kyle. They differed from whites in that as soon as you began to talk to them they assumed they knew what you wanted and they were right. She wanted release. They were gentle in adhering and gentle in letting go, too much so for their own benefit, but this was a time when profitless bestowals were the political fashion. "Please, my dear," she protests. "I was in my early fifties. I was a *grande dame*."

"But still very attractive. I've seen lots of photographs.

I've also seen," Kathryn goes on when Hope says nothing, "you described as another of Bernie's disciples. The stripes."

"My stripes are much smaller and more numerous than his," Hope says, her voice firmer on the ground of her art. "I would describe myself as a Hochmann disciple, one of the last. I'm still trying to do the 'push and pull' he taught us, but in a quieter, shallower space." With her bent fingers Hope measures for the girl an inch or less of space, to show how subtle the push and pull have become in her gray mists. "Like the push and pull, scarcely noticeable, of breathing."

She wonders now if any of her infidelities hurt Guy. At the time she felt, or made herself feel, that he wanted it, with that obscure impulse that led him to hide himself in a mass of identities, an outpour of parodies, an art that committed itself to no one personality. Her little band of lovers were her Hospice, her self-effacing haven.

Kathryn decides she is going to penetrate no deeper in this direction and says, "And all this time, you were holding on to your and Zack's place in the Flats." This seems an accusation. Though Hope has tried to sell her interviewer on Guy, painting an affecting portrait of his beautiful fluency and flair and eventual stymied sorrow, the art world cycling even the blithest talent out of fashionability, Zack is where Kathryn's heart lies; Zack has brought the two women together. Her interviewer is implying that Hope betrayed her second and third husbands by holding on to the house where she had lived with the first.

She doesn't deny it. "It was security, I suppose, to have a property that was all mine, that I had inherited. At first I had the paintings he left to deal with and protect. Then, when they became too valuable for me to protect, and I was spending more time in the city, it was easier to leave the old furniture in place, it would have looked like junk mixed in with Guy's and my expensive things. We would spend summers out there, the children loved it—the beaches, the funky feel of the Island out that far—though Guy came with us less and less, he said he hated rich people's parties and sand in his shoes. Zack's ghost oppressed him, I think. The new art crowd was more Fire Island than East Hampton. Off-season, I rented it, for quite little if the renter seemed sympathetic, sometimes a Lemon Drop buddy of Zack's or one of Guy's protégés who needed somewhere to cool off, the money was less important than that the place not be damaged or go to ruin. When Jerry came into the picture, he had his own place in Southampton but never saw any need to sell the Flats, he called it my ace in the hole. The collector in him was excited, actually; he hired a custodian to live in the house, since things were getting broken or stolen under my system, and we both saw that the value of it was to keep the place, especially including the barn, the way it was when Zack lived there."

"And now it's a museum."

"By appointment only. Schoolchildren come, on trips. Documentary filmmakers use the house, I'm the only one left who knows how it isn't exactly right, what furniture is missing and so on, but it's close enough. There are people to whom Zack has become a cult, not as big a one as Elvis's or Marilyn's but like James Dean's, say; Zack was a far more important painter than Dean was an actor but, still, car crashes, and that uneasy cocky look—these people should have a place to visit, and where better than where he did all his important work?"

"Of course," Kathryn says. "And it keeps a part of your life intact, too."

"You object to that?"

"Not at all. I envy it. Most of us live in a place, and then move out, and the landlord moves another person in."

"Don't envy me, my dear. You have your life ahead of you, and mine is behind me. You wouldn't want to be in my body a minute, there are so many aches I've learned to overlook that you would notice; you would find them unendurable." This would be impolite to dispute, though Hope sees that Kathryn is tempted to argue, her long head recoiling as if at a scent or to hearken to the rain that taps at the windows and makes that low groaning harmonic in the gutter, and Hope notices for the first time a beauty to the underside of the other woman's nose: its curve ends in a tip where two small planes meet, the lower facet continuous with the flesh of the septum, which extends lower than is common, so that her nostril flares in profile, tender and avid and redly suffused with blood. This glimpse of live creatureliness brings the girl's other features up into a feral glory: her plum-dark eyes with their curious glassiness, her unpainted lips pursed and unsmiling under the tension of this interview, her somewhat cupped and uncannily white little ears, small for the size of her jaw and fully exposed by the silver combs that flatten her hair against her skull, hair that, left to its own tendencies, would sprawl hugely on the pillow. Hope sees the other woman as one a man could adore, go sick in love of, sink his seed into the groin of as if his life's work would be thereby accomplished. The strange concept, which she heard herself just propose, of this alien young identity seated opposite her transposed into Hope's own body, with its arthritic fingers, passing chest pains, frequent shortness of breath, and abdominal complaints as her shrinking stomach resists the daily meals she force-feeds it, engenders more quick fantasies—the half-dreams that flutter through a weary mind—of their interpenetration, scorpions in a bottle, this girl invading her with her questions while Hope in turn tries to imagine Kathryn's intimate life, the sensate creature beneath the oily pubic curls.

"So," the next question comes, "your relationship with Jerome Chafetz began while you were still married to Guy Holloway?"

"Yes, several years before, but perfectly properly. Jerry had bought a number of Guy's white vinyl sculptures just as the market not only for Pop but for every kind of art was cooling," Hope states. It pleases her to demonstrate that, thanks to her third marriage, she knows how money talks: "The Arabs had embargoed oil shipments to the U.S. because we helped Israel win the Yom Kippur War, and the economy had gone into what they called stagflation for the rest of the decade."

"But Jerome Chafetz didn't starve."

"You can call him Jerry if you like. Everybody did, even his underlings and the help up here. Well before I became his wife, Jerry had reached that lovely point where his money couldn't help making more money. He had been a stockbroker and then a stock analyst for one of the earliest mutual funds; in the early 'sixties, he struck out on his own and set up his own funds, designed to attract small investors as well as the pension-fund managers. He kept it simple, with just three funds in the beginning—Super-Gro, Sur-Gro, and Slo-Gro. Oddly enough, the Slo-Gro was the most heavily subscribed—people trusted it, people with money were still very conservative. The idea that everybody was rich or soon would be was something that Reagan brought in."

"Jerry"—trying it out, with a twitch of that glorious nose—"died in '86."

"Yes. We were married in '77. Nine wonderful years. We

must have had some cross words, but I can't remember them. He was eleven years older than I, and saw me, I think, as the companion with whom he would start to have some fun in his life before time ran out. The funds were in the hands of younger managers, and we were always going away to Europe, or the Caribbean, or up here. We bought it in 1980. He had been a city boy all his life and discovered he loved the soil, the grass, the rocks—he built yards of stone walls, with his own hands. They got calluses, he would show me proudly."

"He was an art collector; there must have been a frustrated artist in him."

"Not frustrated, he always said picking stocks was an art and not a science. People in money are happier, I decided, than people in art. They're not always preoccupied, they can relax without getting blind drunk. Jerry played tennis, he read novels and even poetry, he liked to cook, he read cookbooks, doing all the little measurements exactly, where Guy couldn't have cared less about food, if it wasn't a case of making a hamburger out of plaster or painting a row of cakes in a bakery window. And Zack, well, Zack would have fallen on his face on the stove."

This is unjust, Hope feels as soon as the words are out of her mouth: Zack barbecued steaks those first summers on the Island, and some mornings, waking with a hangover earlier than she, he would scramble eggs or make an omelette with whatever stray vegetables he would find in the refrigerator or out in the garden, going out into the dew in his bare feet. The fence on their garden and the carpentry in the house that Zack did when they first moved to the Flats showed an instinct for order, an instinct fighting his pull toward self-destruction.

"I'm sorry," she confesses to Kathryn, "that's not quite

fair to Zack, he had a handy streak in fact, but Jerry was my first real experience of someone devoted to what you could call the art of living. My Quaker blood distrusted anything of the creature—"

"Creature?"

"Our bodily self. The *world's* bodily self. Color, sex, ostentation. You know, the sins. You've heard of sins?"

"Of course." Kathryn turns her head as if the question were a kind of slap.

Hope repents, tries to explain herself, herself and Jerry. "The artists I had lived my life among could be jolly and witty when they got together, but there was always an anxiety, a lot of jealousy and snide joshing—Zack was the butt of a lot of it, but then he would smash up their living rooms in sheer hostility—and a feeling of, what can we call it, *excessive* fun, as if they didn't quite know what to do with life, the part of life that wasn't putting in a bid for immortality, the daily pleasures that are all most people have. Jerry brought me back to those, the daily joys. He showed me that a day wasted wasn't really a day wasted."

A memory of Jerry arises: his tennis. Hope had played a lot in Ardmore and Maine, and on Long Island there would occasionally be games in which, compared with most of the wives and girlfriends and for that matter the men—physically careless intellectuals without her country-club background—she looked pretty stylish and felt strong; but when she played with Jerry, on the rooftop court of his midtown athletic club, his serve, no matter how he tried to weaken it, kicked up high and right at her head. "Oh, dearest!" he would call out when once again she blooped the return. He had more top spin than she could handle, it was embarrassing yet thrilled her so that she remembers it now, the power effortlessly ejected at her from across the net, sending this fuzzy bullet bouncing up between her eyes; it was typical of him. Where *had* he, with his strictly New York–Jewish background, no Main Line clay courts, no collegiate tennis teams, learned to hit with top spin like that? She smiles to herself, and declines to share the memory with Kathryn. Jerry had a muscular knottiness—bulging hard calves, woolly flat abdomen—his gray business suits concealed. He was fit, a competitor.

"How did your children relate to Jerry?"

"Beautifully. He was warmer than their own father, at least less preoccupied. He would organize outings, get tickets for the Rangers or the Knicks during their school vacations, or take Dot to the Alvin Ailey, she was going through an intense liberal phase and was talking about dropping out of Brearley and serving the city's poor somehow, he would listen to her for hours, I didn't have the patience myself, it seemed to me very pretentious, with an undertone of violence toward the elected government that reminded me of Fascism, simple fallible government not good enough for fine spirits like her. And her vegetarianism made every meal an additional headache for me to prepare. I loved it, frankly, when she would go stay with Guy and Gretchen for some of the summer. The boys were in their late teens, college age, and we saw less and less of them even during summers, but Jerry never let up on his involvement, his genuine interest in them; his own children with his first wife, Pearl—he said he only married women with monosyllabic names—they were grown up and married by then and into what sounded like rather vague and directionless things like Ph.D.s in Mandarin and computer start-ups and holistic medicine and organic farming in Colorado, so I think he was pleased when my two boys began to come to him with questions about the world of finance. Not that you should gather the

impression, or pass it on to your on-line readers or whatever they are, that his and Pearl's children were flops—
they've all landed on their feet, as adult children tend to do
if they haven't hopelessly addled their heads with drugs,
which is what might well have happened with Zack's and
my child if there had been one, but my children with Guy
were born too late for that 'sixties naïveté, and at any rate
had too much of his and my good Protestant sense. Actually, Mandarin turns out to have been a sensible thing to
study, the boy in question lives in Taiwan and is always over
in mainland China for various companies, and his younger
brother did quite well in the computer start-up until last
year's slowdown. But you don't want to hear about all this
domestic trivia, dear, this *Küche und Kinder,* you care only
about painting, just as I did when I was your lovely age."

"What was Jerry's attitude toward your painting?"

"*Very* enthusiastic. Utterly supportive. He demanded I
do a stint every morning, and one reason we bought this
place was to get away from the ringing phone, the idiotic
New York social life. The show I mentioned that I did
when I was still married to Guy had got such tepid notices
I needed to be encouraged; I didn't pick up a brush in
years, and when I did, up here, I tried to forget everything
Hochmann had ever told us and did kitchen still lifes, pots
and kettles on shelves, the shelf edge exactly horizontal
and at the level of the viewer's eye, in beigy grays, nothing
shiny, everything matte like unglazed clay. And windows
again, only country windows now, looking out on nothing
much, rainclouds with fuzzy edges, barely distinguishable
shades of gray but with carefully done muntins and putty, as
if in foreground focus by somebody standing there meditat-
ing, I had to laugh I was getting so Wyethy, everybody had
always sneered at him so, but I was trying to cleanse myself

of abstraction before going back in. I wanted things to look hand-done, but at the same time I had this hunger for the rectilinear and for subdued colors. Jerry, who had built me the studio and would never have said anything to discourage me, did ask me once if I shouldn't be more violent. Zack of course had been violent, these terrible spatters where you can just feel him whipping the brush in the air as if smashing something, and then of course all the dribbles and daubing with which Guy used to unify his combines and to mock the idea of finish, and what Hochmann preached had been violent in its way, swoops and rectangles of raw color having their tussle within the frame, push and pull, and maybe now, with Jerry giving me a sense of being cherished a little like my grandfather used to do, I was free to express a distrust of violence, a fear of color as the Devil's motley as I said in that rather sanctimonious statement you began today by reading to me. *Or,*" Hope quickly interposes when Kathryn makes a little move as if to interrupt, "I was catering to Jerry, just as I catered to my painter husbands by imitating them, but in this instance by giving him something to collect—flat, calm canvases of modest size that wouldn't clash with anything else in the room. You see, Kathryn, there was less and less to collect. Art, Jerry used to say, was off the wall. How do you collect an earthwork? You can't even get to it, except by driving for hours in Arizona. Or a piece of performance art, all the mock blood and mess of it: a young woman gets naked and dips her long hair in a can of paint—latex, let's hope—and crawls backward down a long strip of paper to symbolize menstrual flow or the one-track sexist male mind or whatever. What is there left to keep? The long streak of dried paint means nothing if we don't know it was done with a woman's head of hair. There was in the 'seventies a Japanese body-artist who used to stick the handle of a brush up her vagina and squat and paint a few symbols with it, but there really wasn't too much she could do, a circle maybe or a cross, or some random swings like elephants can be trained to do with a brush in their trunks, and so we had to be told how it meant that all creation comes from the vagina. I've seen Zack called the father of performance art—those movies the bossy German took of him that awful day, it was much too cold to be outside, especially in a black T-shirt, a 'muscle shirt' they say now but they weren't called that then—but his performances, so-called, the dances he did when he was alone, were routes to a product, an absolutely gorgeous abstract painting, as explosive and finespun and empty and full as the cosmos itself. Zack reinvented the sublime. He was after eternity. In his mind he was like a Renaissance muralist, working for forever. Permanence was the very thing that the new artists couldn't abide, and the NEA kept pouring money into all these performances, these videos and light shows and flimsy installations dismantled and trashed the next week. Oh dear, I sound rather Helmsish, don't I?"

"Or like another kind of artist. But why should art be permanent when nothing else is? Why should it privilege itself? You think those cave artists had more in mind than the hunt the next day? And look at the actual state most Renaissance murals are in—Piero della Francesca is almost all restorer by now, and *The Last Supper* just a few glued-on crumbs in an empty room in Milan."

This is the longest continuous speech Kathryn has yet delivered. She is showing her claws, the skulking intellect behind the deference. That deconstructionist verb "privilege." Both women are tired. The two heads of hair, grizzled auburn and tinted raven, are loosening in the humidity as the rain drums outside. Light has ebbed from the windows; the thin panes, with their lavender tint and warping bubbles, give back the room fragmentary reflections of furniture, curved gleams of lamplight on ceramic surfaces, pallid unsteady shadows that are faces and hands. The first time she went to one of Hochmann's classes, there had been this sidelit still life mixed up with reflective cellophane. Hope lifts her chin to repel the invader with a blast of energy: "How can you collect a big tangle of rope hung all over a museum room? Or a heap of used bricks or four square yards of zinc plates on the floor? Or a rolled-up thirty-five-foot sheet of lead—this was somebody's master-piece, I forget whose, maybe that bully who put a big sheet of rusty iron across a nice little park downtown. Jerry did have some Minimalist pieces, some very nice cubes of Plexi-glas, and people kept setting their drinks down on them. How can you collect so-called light sculpture? Or graffiti art sprayed over the entire side of a subway car? It's all so liberal *chic*, so *faux* demotic. And all these photographs artists began to take of themselves, Cindy Sherman and everybody else, making faces or spouting water or rolling in broken glass or riddled with body-piercing, how can you put them on your wall with a straight face? Or basketballs suspended in a tank of Perrier water, or sliced-up cows in formaldehyde? Who would want to own these things?"

"I suppose," Kathryn says, her voice retracted from its surge of assertion, "it could be argued that art has no obliga-tion to honor the concept of ownership. It shouldn't be owned, it should just *be*."

"Well, who is going to *pay* for it to be? What is the point of its being, if all it does is express the grudges and neuroses of the artist? Where is the *transaction*?"

The younger woman, no doubt not wishing her inter-view to deteriorate into a quarrel, or a debate that could be

held in any art school, or any twenty-first-century equivalent of the Cedar Tavern's leathery back booths, declines
to answer Hope's questions and reverts to the personal; she
recrosses her long legs in their black-ribbed mystery fabric,
clears her throat of a dry tickle, and ponders her by now
creased and much-shuffled laser-printed pages before asking in a strengthened voice: "Could it be said that Jerry, in
the absence of things to collect, collected *you?*"

Hope has to laugh, in admiration of youthful nerve and
hard-heartedness. "It *was* said," she says, "no doubt, but
never to my face before."

"It seems rather obvious," says Kathryn, as if Hope is
indeed an object to be dispassionately critiqued and not a
person, a former child, with feelings and a sentimental,
organic view of her own value. "Zack, Guy—in you Jerry
had them both, major artists in terms he could understand,
producers of wall-dressing. You were house-dressing."

"How harsh you are, my dear. We've been so friendly."

Her visitor's pale face, like a sheet of photosensitive
paper, registers a shadow of dismay. The young don't credit
themselves with the power to hurt those older, richer, and
more famous than they are; they think even the faintest
celebrity resides in a virtual realm they cannot touch. "I feel
very friendly," Kathryn weakly says, "so much so I may be
getting careless in how I put things. Also, guilt is gnawing
at me, for taking up your entire day. I'm just trying to *see*
you and Jerry."

"Why strain to see? He was an aging man, I was an aging
woman, we amused each other. And comforted each other;
he was the only one of my husbands I could call *com*forting.
He always knew what I meant to say, even if I had trouble
saying it."

"Did Dorothy like him?"

"He couldn't have been much nicer to her, but, no, I suppose not. She was loyal to Guy, as a way of getting back at me, though it was Jerry and not Guy who put her through Stanford and underwrote all those post-graduate years when she was 'trying to find herself.' Whatever that meant—people didn't use to lose themselves, you were what you were, and that was it, you *couldn't* lose it—she was conducting the search pretty expensively, it seemed to me, she and her beach-bimbo hangers-on. Don't you think she wasn't trading on being Guy's daughter, for all her 'independence.'"

"Your own self-education wasn't exactly un-underwritten, was it?"

Another slap. My goodness. This girl is angry. Hope pauses before responding. "I take your point. Indulging one's creative instincts, one's search for beauty, is a luxury most people don't have. My daughter and I are both willful bitches, yes? My poor respectability-loving parents—Philadelphians, the mousiest elite in the East, my father hated to see his name in print even in connection with a court proceeding—it never occurred to me what an embarrassment I must have been, off in New York doing unspeakable things and then marrying an uncouth boozehound from nowhere. I guess I thought, if I thought at all, that they loved me, and whatever made me happy would make them happy."

"And did it? I mean, were *you* happy?"

"Quite, dear. As much as anyone can be, given our human habit of wanting more than we have. I would love to have a major reputation, instead of being a kind of long-lived footnote."

"You are *not* a footnote," Kathryn tells Hope with a startling firmness. "Not to me or to any number of other younger women. Your work—so balanced and quiet and yet nervy and terribly female—means a great deal to us. That's why I'm here."

"You are? How flattering. I thought you were here to share Zack with me. And Guy. Not Jerry, a mere money-man. But art rides on money, you see." Praise tends to make Hope prickly, awakening a contradictory spirit, the Christian imp of self-negation.

Kathryn fights back. "Graffiti art? Jazz?"

"In the end, yes. It's how word gets out, it's the means of marketing, which is always looking for a fresh product to push. Money took up those poor graffiti boys and confused them and dropped them cold when the fad was over, and let dope and AIDS carry them away. Jerry's money took me to Europe, where my genius previous husbands almost never bothered to. We went again and again, the best hotels, Venice, Paris, London, but Greece and Portugal too, Denmark and Norway, a lot of England and Holland, I saw at last what Henry James was saying—everywhere you look in Europe there is something contemplated and completed, these centuries of previous lives all contributing something of interest, little details like a curving staircase or an old square with a well in the middle of it, a building bent to fit into an odd lot, and the way the Italian towns grow out of their hills like trees on a cliff, and how the centers of cities reached up only so high before elevators were invented, only as many flights of stairs as a healthy person could climb; everything had been cut to human measure, and beauty was just the desire of all those dead people to live decently, they and their parents and their children, polishing the paving stones with the soles of their feet. I know, America isn't so young any more, it has many of the same things, and without the tyranny and class system that put up

the European palaces, but everything here is still compara-
tively hasty and square and so quickly shabby and *démodé*,
it seems; Europe felt, when Jerry would take me there for
weeks at a time, we would rent villas and flats, Europe felt
like an ancient forest, everything grown together, vineyards
and cities and museums, though of course it's all being
swamped now with Americanism of the tinniest sort, 'tinny'
because they haven't had the one thing we have had,
our particular encounter with the wilderness, that tragic
blankness. And the *people*, the way they treat you and one
another, the women in Florence on the street with their
round eyes like actresses, always playing a part, and the very
precise little Frenchwomen, even the traffic cops, in high
heels and stockings and smart dark suits, their decisive gestures, the way the same words are used over and over, even
the way the Europeans snub and overcharge you, it's all so
human, so *practical*, as if it's all been done a thousand times
before and nothing more needs to be invented. In school
they used to tell us that Americans invented everything, and
though of course that wasn't true, you can see why it *should*
be true. *Oh my goodness, so what?*, you're thinking. But it's
about art and money, you still see there the churches and
the palaces, the official market for art we never had, you
feel how it was woven in, instead of added on as it has
always been here, something extra and faintly silly."

The interviewer has not been listening, only the tape
recorder has been listening, the interviewer has been shuffling through her sheafs of questions, looking for strays.
"Here's a personal question, if I may. Why does your house
contain, as far as I can see, so few examples of post-war
art—the art of your life, so to speak? And what of Jerry's
collection? Though you say there was nothing to collect, I
know he did own some paintings by David Salle and Eric

Fischl and kept buying Wayne Thiebaud all along, and owned some smaller sculptures by Jeff Koons and Martin Puryear—not everything in the 'seventies and 'eighties was museum art and propaganda, though it may have seemed . . ." Kathryn trails off wearily. Poor girl, she has come so far, to end in vagueness, in dispersal and let-down.

Hope tells her briskly, trying to pep her up, "In answer to your question: Jerry left all of his collection acquired before his marriage to me to the children of his first marriage. We discussed it, and it seemed fair. His best pieces, that had appreciated most, were in that lot. Then there were estate taxes, nearly half of it all, and cash had to be raised, there was a liquidation when he died—not only the estate taxes had to be covered, but there were some unsuspected debts including more than a million owed to dealers. Lawsuits!— I became quite blasé, a hardened defendant. In the end, after the lawyers had their cut, there was less than anybody had expected. I had to sell my East Seventy-ninth Street co-op and Jerry's Southampton place and his half-share in the Sarasota condo he and Pearl had split in the settlement— they were no good to me anyway. I came up here to live year-round. Where up here would I keep valuable art safe from anybody who wanted to break in? A burglar alarm, by the time the local police answered it, was useless. I sold the few major McCoys I had left, and the Holloways that had been part of the settlement, and put it all in a trust for Doro-thy, a trust in case some conniving woman got her hooks into her, they can be as predatory as men—more so, since they have the excuse of being disadvantaged in this patriar-chal society. The boys don't need money from me, they're doing fine—the salaries and bonuses they pay on Wall Street, you wonder there's any money left for the investor. Often there isn't. So," Hope concludes this whirlwind baring of her divestitures and holdings, "I've made my daughter a rich middle-aged woman one of these days, when I won't hear any thanks for it. I suppose you shouldn't put that into your article either. Let's let Dot be surprised."

"My article won't be as long as I'd like it to be. There's a lot I'll have to leave out."

"I know, I know," Hope reassures her. But she has never learned how little the world needs us to give; its beauty is an impervious beauty, self-absorbed. Her onrushing words have ended by wounding her: they have made realer to her than she wants it to be her own death, which will make Dot rich, though the child will construe it sarcastically, as some sort of payback she had coming, as another attempt of her mother's to court her and break her righteous silence, as a bribe from beyond the grave, proving to her that her mother was guilty as charged. What had been the charge? Hope cannot remember, for all these years she has felt herself the focus of an anger that has almost nothing to do with her, that had to do with some chemicals the child was born with and that kept her awake and that eventually made her furious that her mother was not as obsessed with her as she was with her mother, whose only sin as far as Hope could honestly see was not rejecting the world but too eagerly accepting it, accepting the promise of freedom America gave, accepting her sex as another piece of potential, and believing, what is harder and harder to do for these young people as scientific evidence to the contrary eats religion away, that you are not quite alone, that the voice you hear within is a companion. Guy came, Guy went, an abstracted stab at a father, and she who was always there in the apartment got blamed for being herself, the one sin she could not help committing every living minute. The ungrateful girl had never had a hungry day, had never been sent out in insufficient clothing. Still, this estrangement inhabits the guilty boggy area visited by Hope's thoughts of her approaching death and the memory of Jerry's, which she witnessed. She saw the light die in his eyes. He loved life much as she did and had been so vigorous, yet when death sneaked up on him, in the guise of malfunctioning kidneys and a weakening heart, he went meekly limp in its embrace, a mere seventy-five. He offended her by not fighting harder to stay with her. He would have had to get in line for a kidney transplant, and the wait might be as long as a year, and the doctors were worried that his heart could not take the strain of an operation. They could do a bypass operation in the meantime, but Jerry was dubious and strangely uninterested; he called it a hassle that benefited mostly the doctors and would leave him with an endless caretaking of his own body. He was afraid of it, she realized—he who had been afraid of so little, who had rushed forward into every experience, including his experience of her. They had made love the second time they dated, and the first date had scarcely been that, she was just separated from Guy and still disbelieving they would never get back together, she had remembered Jerry from the time they had stood together and called the same white vinyl typewriter beautiful, and then at other openings they would gravitate toward each other and she began to feel their attraction lighting up over their heads like a neon thought-balloon in a Kienholz tableau, and she had called him, yes, she had made the move, telephoned him at his office instead of at his home and told him her circumstances were changing so that she might need some financial advice, and he took her to lunch downstairs at Lutèce with its two steps down and its skylit back room full of dappled dazzle like a plein-air Bonnard, and he put a warm soft hairy-backed hand, brown from tennis and the beach at Southampton, over hers when the lunch was over and she was done crying and spilling out her shock and insecurity, spurned when she had done nothing wrong, just grown older, presiding over children, not even Zack at his most abusive, at least he had sent her flowers at the end. . . . Jerry's hand gave a squeeze that might have been merely sympathy. But there was an intent, entertained glint in his eyes—her tale of desertion and distress had made him laugh in several spots where she hadn't been meaning at all to be funny—which she felt as a kind of money in the bank, though it was months before their second date; he had waited for her split with Guy to be public knowledge and in the care of lawyers, and for his own wife to be having her winter stay in Sarasota, with him flying down on weekends. That light of interest, of mischief, in his steel-blue eyes, surprising eyes in a Jew, had faded in the hospital to a dull color as if mixed with a fine ash, while his kidneys and heart raced toward total deterioration and the doctors came to him like Job's comforters, salesmen pleading with a tight-lipped customer, tight-lipped or deaf, the life in his eyes and ears and fleshy mouth with its wry little scar seeming to sink as he relaxed into the care of the hospital, its clean white rooms, its gentle night-noises and winking little signal lights as on the bridge of a great gliding ship, its deceptive bustle of young nurses and interns, as if their youth and efficient health could be portioned out to patients as equably and breezily as diet meals and pills and consent forms, there above the East River. His room looked down on the river from eight stories up, the widening wakes of its traffic of tugboats and barges brimming with rusted scrap metal and round-the-island tour boats and speeding police launches and the occasional yacht at half-throttle, its sails furled and two just-about naked young women sunbathing on the bow as the skyscrapers and all their gazing windows floated past. Jerry liked the hospital because it was a city within a city and hummed with impersonal city current around the clock; Hope was furious at him for making himself so at home here, for not fighting harder to stay with her on the outside of this seductive death-factory, for so passively letting the city reclaim him and putting the lie to the Vermont idyll she had constructed, perhaps out of her memory of her youthful self taking Zack to Long Island, bringing Zack out to the light-soaked Flats at the end of the civilized world where he needed to be to make his fame, with five glorious, drudging years, Hope's masterpiece as a wife, there by Gardiners Bay, in sight of McGonicle's Harbor. The Bay merged with the Sound, whose same waters narrowed at last to this so-called river, a river only insofar as its circulating waters were borrowed from the Hudson. But Zack had been a country boy, untamed space was in his veins, whereas Jerry had been a child of paved streets and ceaseless human sounds. "Jerry. Don't leave me."

"What?" The whispered plea brought him back from some haven within, a pocket of drugged peace; his brown eyelids, with their broken capillaries like the tiny red and blue threads embedded in dollar bills, curved around a greater portion of his eyeballs now that his face was shrinking, adhering closer to the bone.

She made her voice more penetrating. "I said, Jerry, please fight harder for me. For *us*. Don't give up."

He struggled to be awake; his eyelids lifted on his irises' ashy blue and kept blinking. "I've had a good ride," he said. "This last leg has been the best. Much obliged, Tiger." He called her Tiger, after one of their first times in bed, when her hunger had startled herself as well. The nickname went oddly with her impression, those first trysts, of his hair, thinning but thick and pungent, matted like sheep's wool. It had become fleecier, whiter, in nine years, but a docile streak had always been his. She had seduced him away from Pearl and now his death was seducing him away from her.

"The doctors want to give you a new heart, Jerry. And dialysis until a kidney is available."

"You don't think," he asked, forcing his eyes to stay open, the effort coaxing a sheepish smile onto his lips, with their crimp remaining from a youthful street battle, "it'd be putting a new engine into a rusted-out chassis? And then a new carburetor. One more bionic man, bankrupting the health system."

"Jerry, don't you want to see your next step-grandchild? And see Piet made partner?" Paul's wife, Kay, was pregnant again, and hoping for a girl this time. Jerry had taken as keen an interest in Hope's children as in his own—keener, since even Dorothy was less fraught for him than his and Pearl's offspring. His stepchildren could be his friends, his children were painful extensions of himself, when he was aware of them, so he did not go out of his way to be aware, and thus saved himself aggravation. Hope urged him to communicate with them more, but he brushed her aside: "We understand each other, they know I'm here if they need me." It was as if she had opened one of those passages of the Old Testament—lineages; dietary laws; the smiting, vengeful, barbaric God—that had nothing to do with a Quaker maiden. Jews in America, for all that they ebulliently conversed with the Gentile world around them, kept something back, there was a room that stayed locked, and in this room their transactions with each other were conducted and, she imagined, their secret kept in its tabernacle. They saw his children rarely; it was hers, their changes of job and apartment, their births and promotions, that kept the aging couple in touch with the elementary adventures of living these nine years they were married, travelling abroad and to Vermont and back to New York and performing the little they needed to perform to keep their positions, in the ever more diffuse and directionless art scene, as painter and as collector. Now she dangled by Jerry's hospital bed these tidbits of vicarious life and he could not conceal his boredom. He closed his eyes, the orb of the eyeball declaring itself beneath its fragile covering, the red and blue threads of broken capillaries never to be mended. She began to cry at her helplessness in the face of our creaturely limits, which included, she could see, a limit in this, the fullest, the least marred, of her relationships. Without a break in his faithful graciousness, Jerry was leaving her. Had there always been something patronizing about his good humor: a disdain of giving her the honor of a fight, equal on equal, as she had given Zack, and Pearl must have given him? He seemed determined to go through with this last bargain and keep any deficits to himself. Hearing her silence, he opened his eyes, and they wore a fishy glaze she had seen before, in Zack's and Guy's eyes when she realized that all that a woman does for a man, all that tending and loving, falls short, for him is secondary, inessential. Art was what these men had loved—that is, themselves. Jerry had picked her up cheap, with a fine provenance. She had become to Zack and Guy dreamlike in her inconsequence, as she was to Jerry now, weeping and begging him to live for her sake. She bored him, she was annoying him, tiny as she had become. He didn't have the strength to swat her away. "Give it a rest, Tiger," he told her. "We'll see how it all looks tomorrow."

Hope tells Kathryn, "I do have some worthwhile pieces

upstairs. Downstairs, I didn't want anybody looking in the window and seeing anything worth stealing. Though whoever looks in these windows isn't apt to know the difference. I think the locals decided long ago, when Jerry and I were going back and forth, that there was nothing here they could resell. Actually, in this room and the dining room around the corner are some paintings that used to hang in my grandparents' house in Germantown. That watercolor of nasturtiums, for instance, near the phone, and the still life in oils on the far wall, and that old wedding certificate over the mantel, above the clock."

"I wondered what that was."

"Pennsylvania Dutch Fraktur. A marriage certificate, in German. As a child I used to study the little doll-like figures, the bride and groom. They seem so unready for marriage, don't they?—more like the paper dolls little girls used to dress in paper dresses. There are some nineteenth-century miniatures of my Ouderkirk ancestors in the dining room, which I never use any more—oval miniatures in velvet-lined box frames. They have rosy cheeks and clear blue eyes, blue like the eyes of two of my three husbands. Some of the fine brushwork and stippling is rather wonderful; they painted on thin sheets of ivory, you know, very precious fine-shaved stuff, and it didn't take the watercolors very readily. Would you like to go around the corner and see them?"

"I don't think I need to. You describe them so well."

"Upstairs, in the various bedrooms—let me think. In the guest room, some old prints, faded, never expensive. Lawrence's *Pinkie* in a tarnished brass frame, and the Vermeer of the woman with the silver pitcher, in the Met, with that marvellous streak of reflected blue on the back of it, away from the window—blue everywhere, really, even on the rod at the bottom of the map, you wonder if it hasn't burned through some other pigments which have bleached out. And on the blank wall of the upstairs landing, a big messy oil of woods that was in my grandfather's study, the only wall without books or a window; when my grandmother used to complain that she couldn't understand how he could look at something so gloomy, he'd tell her, 'That's how woods are, full of fallen deadwood. That painter was an honest man.' And in my bedroom I have a few modern items, worth something to the right collector, I suppose—the first, rougher version of the pastel Ruk did of me that hangs in the Corcoran, and a silk screen Bernie gave me, an intimate version of one of his heroic oils, a nearly square field of blue, as cold as the underside of an iceberg, with a single strip, well off to one side, of rose madder, done in slightly uneven, jabbing strokes. Would you like to go upstairs to my bedroom to see them?"

"I don't think that will be necessary." Aware of possibly seeming unresponsive, Kathryn adds, "You must be tired."

"You too, dear."

Her bedroom—she would have liked to exhibit it to this dark-haired young intruder, the site of her nightly surrender to sleep, her airy cell, the tightly made bed, the pink-bordered Amish quilt turned down to the foot with linear precision, with the fussy primness of the old. The first thing Hope does each morning, once she empties her inelastic bladder and brushes her teeth—crowns and implants, most of them; her smile is a lie—is make the bed, having turned on the classical-music station from Burlington, an affiliate of WNYC. She has never painted to music, unlike Zack and his noisy jazz—once they got electricity out to the barn, he turned it up loud as if to keep her away—but she needs it to make the bed to, with aching finger joints; it lifts her mind up from the ignominy of these daily chores, catering to our own creature comforts, the tedious rites of hygiene. Often, wet from the shower, she makes the bed naked, her ghastly bony and bulging and sagging and spotted old body shining out in the room's fresh light, the Lord her only witness, and He in her mind's eye pleased enough by her Schongauer look; that was Protestant art, God looking at us rather than us looking at Him, every Dutchman and Jew in Holland a saint in darkness to Rembrandt's loaded brush.

"You mustn't think," Hope tells Kathryn, who once more has leaned forward anxiously, her body like a folded black jackknife, to check if the Sony is still running, "and I know I sounded like a terrible grouch and philistine, that Jerry and I disdained everything in art after 1975. Those Photo-realistic sculptures that used to startle you at the Whitney because they looked too much like people, lifesize and made of Fiberglas, with glass eyes and real hair, in real clothes, one of them was even of a museum guard, people kept asking it questions, *oh*, what *was* the man's name. Hanson. Duane Hanson. I should remember it, because he died a few years ago, and he was younger than I am. Even younger, I should say. And there was a young British artist, he might have been Australian if there's a difference, Ron something, he was in that exhibition at the Brooklyn Museum that got Mayor Giuliani all upset, a German kind of name, Monk or Munck, he has the same idea, though he doesn't do lifesize, he did a *perfect* little replica of his dying father no bigger than a housecat, and then a huge one of his own face, with every pore rendered, every stubby whisker. I've always been so grateful—haven't you?—that I don't have to begin the day by shaving, I don't think feminists are appreciative enough of what men go through, even though it's true they don't have to bear the babies, or suffer in love so horribly. When you look at these Middle Eastern men, with these five days' beards so they all look like terrorists, and baseball pitchers too now—to intimidate the batters, I suppose—it makes *me* at least thankful. Mueck: his name just came to me. M-U-E-C-K, I do believe."

Is she rambling to drive this girl away, or because she can't help emptying herself completely into captive ears?

She goes on, "They affect me, these literalist sculptures. They tell us something about being human—our vulnerability, mostly. Just our skins—so bald, so easy to puncture, even without a gun. The fingernails, the eyelashes, even the earwax, all the tiny touches that at some point in evolution apparently enabled some people to survive better than others, or to find mates, though I'm not sure how earwax would help with that, not to mention all the molecular niceties that we notice only when we get so sick because they are going just ever so slightly wrong. Looking back," Hope confesses, "it's hard to remember why we all looked down on representation, regarded it with such contempt—we didn't want painting to be *anecdotal*, that was the scare word, Clem would get quite livid at the thought, so he had to take another drink to steady himself, and Hochmann, too, utterly scornful, in that way Germans have of wishing something out of existence, but I wonder now if all painting isn't anecdotal, a story the painter wants to tell. What he won't do, what he *will* do, what he is dying to try, what he is working out from within himself toward some kind of—what?—ultimate economy, let's say. The canvas is an adventure, Clem was right about that, and the artist is the adventurer, telling his story as he goes. I'm sorry, Kathryn, I fear I'm not saying this very well, it's clearer when you go back to near the beginning, to Giotto and Cimabue and the Sienese beginning to grasp at perspective and human expression, and then see these skills so triumphantly mastered in the High Renaissance, where the artist keeps boasting what he can do, Michelangelo telling you he can do *any*thing, Raphael too, in a softer voice, and then these skills becoming so common that art gets bored with them finally, think of Ingres and Copley, that sickly finish, and then, in the 'twenties and 'thirties, magazine illustration and Soviet social realism, terribly skillful really, with this leering sort of *flair*, you see it in Rockwell, who God forbid is marching through the country's museums even as we sit here, while the mainstream of course since Impressionism has been running the other way, dissolving the image, letting it feather and jiggle away, until you get to Zack and Onno and Bernie and there's nowhere left to go but parody. I know you've thought a lot about decadence—how can one not these days? a whole millennium just went to seed— but it seems as though art has to fumble not to be decadent, it has to be just on the cusp of the possible, or we can't respond to it as something . . . something, do you mind if I say, 'heartfelt'? It has to be about us, just a skin away from being nothing. Not nothing perhaps, I don't know what your religion is, but tumbling back into the radiance."

The black windows tell them that behind the veil of steady rain the day has moved beyond twilight. The nearly invisible hands of the mantel clock say twenty to seven. If she started right now the girl would get home to New York by midnight at best, bleary and sandy-eyed from squinting through the swishing windshield, deafened by the thud of the wipers and the onrushing of the wet tires and the tinkle of the radio, something Michelangelo didn't have to keep him company on that scaffold, voices and songs beamed from a cramped, sealed cave lined with insulation, electromagnetic waves what we have now instead of messenger angels, disk jockeys lulling Hope's visitor, senses swaddled, her legs cramped, an ache across her shoulders from holding on to the steering wheel with her long white hands— *Mona Lisa* hands, early studies for which can be seen in the portrait allegedly of Ginevra de' Benci in the National Gallery and that of Cecilia Gallerani in Kraków, but without Kathryn's black or, better, eggplant-colored nails. As if feeling the car's confinement already, Kathryn stiffly shifts in the wide-armed plaid chair and gazes down at the Sony. Digital is the coming technology, Hope has read, with virtually infinite storage, but who will listen? Who will transcribe and read the infinity of digits?

"You must go," Hope tells her.

"Yes. But we haven't really talked about the fifteen years since Jerry died, and the remarkable way you've resurrected yourself, with your paintings of course. You've created a new reputation for yourself."

"Have I? What does Shakespeare call it—'the bubble reputation'? It amuses people that the old lady keeps at it. Critics talk about the gentle Quaker spirit of my abstractions, but I feel more what Bernie used to insist on, the passion. Those big monotone canvases of his, with a stripe or two in a different color, sometimes only slightly different, people wondered how there could be passion in them, even I wondered, but there it was, a terrific tautness, like the surface created when a big stone basin is filled to the brim, or that neo-Minimalist—on the West Coast, I think—who filled a black cube with black ink so that it looked like the top side, perfectly rigid, and you're dying to touch it but of course don't dare. Do you know, my young ophthalmologist—they're all young now, everybody who used to be old, your doctors, your lawyers—my ophthalmologist explained to me, I found it *fascinating*, that our eyes achieve the fine resolution they do because on top of the film of water, which smooths out some of the cornea's microscopic irregularities, little sebaceous glands along the edge of the lids, literally *hundreds* of them, secrete a coating of oil which smooths it out even further. A hawk's eye is five times finer than ours—five times oilier, it may be. Seeing *is* the predatory sense, isn't it? We listen and sniff to protect ourselves, but we see to capture and kill."

She doubts, as soon as she says it, that this is quite true; her interviewer's forward-leaning, anxious-edged voice cuts across her doubts with another question: "Do you think men and women see the same? Do they paint the same?"

Hope winces, beginning to feel bruised by the demands of this encounter. The question is feminist but not necessarily stupid; she wants to answer it the best she can, and closes her eyes, as if what the Elizabethans called the beams of her eyes can worm in the reddish darkness toward an honest response. "We look," she says, "at what interests us, what pertains to us. A woman, for example, entering a room, because she is a housekeeper, sees dirt to which men are blind. She sees how the other women have dressed and painted themselves to set off their best qualities. Women fear danger from a greater variety of directions than men, so I suppose there is less, what can I call it, *frontality* in their work. Women in theory should be interested in phalluses, and there is—correct me if you don't agree—a physiological moment when we are, but there is much more phallic imagery in men's painting than in women's. Since O'Keeffe and her damn flowers, rather the opposite. We paint ourselves. So no, not quite, but much the same, would be my answer. The human species is less differentiated by gender than many—the male and female of certain intestinal parasites, I believe, don't look at *all* alike. We, men and women, are both made to run, and to hang on to branches, and to eat nuts and berries."

"How interesting."

"Well, is it? I've been thinking about my painting ever since you hit me over the head with that statement I gave five years ago. I was in a rather distinctly religious frame of mind, it seems. Color equals the Devil—what a wild thing to say! I mix *lots* of colors into grays, to produce just hints of lilac, of beige, of pink even, to set up the vibration between the stripes, the *activity*, the atomic activity that is in everything, apparently even the flattest-seeming surface, if you can believe the microscope, this *seethe*, like Zack's spatters and swirls, in a way, or Guy's dribbles in that era when I was drawn to him, before he became a factory, declaring we can't take the imperfection out of art, that's part of the perfection."

"Are they your concluding statement? Your recent paintings. They seem darker, richer."

"They have, I supppose, the terror and sadness of last things, of death—why not say it? Even though it's impossible to grasp, to picture." Involuntarily she pictures her bedroom, for which she longs. On the bedside table, spare reading glasses in a paisley cloth case, a copy of the latest little Muriel Spark novel, a square black Braun clock with its face averted so she won't see its glowing hands if she awakes in the night and have them frighten her into insomnia, an eye mask to keep her asleep as the spring light slants in around the shades earlier and earlier, wax earplugs in a plastic case—four blobs squeezed in a row as in a painting by Roger Merebien—to shut out the Vermont owls and invading coyotes and the murmur of traffic, oddly audible at night, somehow come closer, from Route 89. On her bureau sit silver-backed brushes that had belonged to her mother and small color photographs of her grandchildren, including the three born since Jerry died. And then in the 'nineties Dot and her giant Dutch housemate adopted a Vietnamese girl; Hope learned of this from Paul, who gave her a color copy of a photograph Dot had sent him, since she had not sent her mother one. The girl, about four in the photograph, looks bony and apprehensive in the glare of the flash but gamely smiling, game to become one more American. "On the other hand," Hope continues, "when I'm actually at the easel I don't think of the one I'm working at as at all my last painting, nowhere near it, there is in my mind's eye a whole string of them, an infinite domino-row, ahead of me."

"How lovely," Kathryn says, having waited for the image to continue. *How interesting, how lovely*—the girl has run dry, the way men do. Men do what they came for and then leave, and for the longest time this seemed heartless to Hope.

"You should go now," she tells her guest.

"I really should. But it's so pleasant here, I have this—"

"Inertia."

"Yes. Exactly."

"You must get back to your life. You tell that young man of yours to open himself up when he goes with you to a gallery. If he can't see the fun of it he may not be the right man for you."

"I think it's hard for Alec to have fun with so much of life—his career and all—undecided."

"By the time everything is decided, it will be too late. The moment is always *now*. There is no *then*, it turns out. Everything real is a kind of now."

"You tell *him* that," Kathryn says.

"I'd be happy to. I was born too long ago to be ashamed

to learn from men, but there are things they can learn from us, too, and the smarter of them know it. Men see what's in front of them but not always all the rest." Kathryn is in front of Alec, Hope's impression is, and he does not quite see that she might not always be, that she is ripe and should be plucked.

The two women hesitate at the threshold before them: the end of words, a resumption of their burdens. "Before I switch off the machine, is there anything you still wanted to say?"

Hope holds her mouth open and looks at the far edge of the slightly sagging, here and there discolored ceiling as if at something astonishing. "It feels as though there is, but I can't imagine what it would be." She adds, "I've been a fortunate woman. I don't really believe the world is the Devil's. Or *only* the Devil's."

Kathryn leans forward with that awkward impatience of hers, as if overcoming a mechanical tendency to get stuck, and touches into silence the tiny Sony, dove gray, the third presence in the room, motionless, unsleeping, all-aware. With a snuffly sigh of effort the interviewer stands, and Hope rocks back in her chair of many woods at the splendor of this unfolding—the long black legs; the fine-ribbed pants tight around the thighs and flared above the boot tops; the brief jacket of soft black imitation-leather, which the girl has never removed, in silent comment upon the chilliness of the room compared with almost any New York apartment. The contrasting white turtleneck protects her throat, and above her small cupped ears two curved silver combs pin the long glossy hair tinged with henna flat against her skull. From her square-toed boot soles to the top of her skull she must be fully five foot ten; one of Alec's holds over her is presumably that he is as tall or taller.

Hope, being short, had her pick of men. Both women affect the pulled-back, quickly assembled hairdos of art's camp followers, of those pursuing, through thickets of commerce, neglect, and personal entanglement, a glimmering activity disinterested, incorruptible, and ardent. Kathryn thrusts the Sony and her printed notes into the big black pocketbook, almost the size of a tote bag, which has waited beside the armchair, on the rug of braided rags.

Hope asks, "Would you like your half-sandwich for the trip? And I could make up a little Ziploc bag of nuts and raisins and dried fruit. I worry about you; there really aren't many places to stop between here and the New York Thruway—those terrible convenience stores that sell mostly stale candy and *National Enquirer*s. Don't you love the headlines? *Julia's True Love Kidnapped by Space Aliens. Whitney's Weight Loss Horrifies Fans.*"

"No, I'll be fine, Hope. It's Alec's car, and if I got the wheel sticky with marmalade he'd kill me."

"Oh my. He sounds not easy to please."

"He's sweet, basically. But as I explained he's at a difficult time of life."

"Well, aren't we all? What would an easy time of life look like? Goodbye, Kathryn. I've stupidly forgotten your last name."

"D'Angelo. With an apostrophe."

"Of course." It rings a very faint bell, from their introductory phone conversation, a distant rustle in her ear. How stupid she had been, sitting here all these hours assuming the girl was Jewish. Well, she *is* a child of the Mediterranean, the middling mother of wine and of olive-skinned races and of all the ideas we still live by, we children of the Northern mists.

"Thank you *so* much," the intruder says. "You've given

me so much, more than I can possibly use. I feel guilty about taking your whole day."

"I did my hour or two at the easel before you came. After that, my time is worth very little, and there seems a lot of it. I fear I talked your pretty ears off. I go many days up here talking to no one except over the telephone—not that it rings every day."

"You should have a pet."

This directive takes her aback, but perhaps she asked for it, seeming more helpless than she felt. "Jerry and I did have dogs up here, lovely good-natured goldens, we'd haul them back and forth to New York and put them in a kennel down toward Bolton when we went to Europe, they would look so *wounded* as we drove off, and be so frantic to see us when we came back, I feared their hearts would burst with happiness, talk about passion! After Jerry died, Jupiter, the last of the goldens, died too, he wore himself out going to the door looking for him. Dogs don't really respect women the way they do men, and I thought of getting a cat, but then decided it was purer to have no pets, and not to leave my boys the problem of how to dispose of it. The creatures of the wilderness are my pets. Even the bears, though I don't like seeing their claw marks in the woods too close to the house. There are more bears in these woods now than since the early nineteenth century, you know."

"I didn't know."

There was something Hope had been on her way to say when interrupted, and now she says it: "It's been a gift to me, to be allowed to tell so much. To look at my poor little life entire."

Kathryn matches this somewhat stilted declaration with one of her own: "It's so unusual for someone of my generation," she says, "to talk with anybody so pleased with her life. My friends, they're well fed, and make good money, some of them, and have enough sex, I guess, but they're not really *pleased*. They don't have that capacity. You *are* pleased, aren't you?"

Hope laughs, it has become so oddly formal again. "I'm pleased to meet *you*, Ms. D'Angelo. And I'm pleased I guess that every time I was left alone in my life I still had a reason to keep going. Art, if you have any vocation for it at all, doesn't desert you. It's always willing to flirt. Now, really, before you rush off, you *should* use the bathroom. That I insist on. It's so hard, even not in the rain, to find rest rooms along the road that don't humiliate you by making you ask for the key."

Even while Hope is saying these things to her, Kathryn has stalked across the parlor floor to the front hall and in one large swift gesture dressed herself in the purple cashmere cloak she came in and deposited on the spindle-back settee. The hood makes her look sinister yet winsome, her long nose jutting now from shadow, her big black purse dangling from a bent forearm. She reflects and decides, "Yes, that I *will* accept. Thank you."

Again, then, in those noisy boots, she visits the bathroom under the back stairs. In the kitchen, Hope quickly, furtively extracts a medium Ziploc bag from its box in a drawer and, opening the refrigerator, from a set of plastic containers on a door shelf, portions out a modest quantity of Brazil nuts, raw peanuts, lightly salted roasted pecans, raisins, yogurt-covered baby pretzels, and dried apricots. She seals the Ziploc with a painful squeeze of her fingers; Kathryn accepts the fat package of snacks without protest or a word of thanks, like a child hurriedly going off to school. Her mind is on the journey ahead; her eyes are already looking through the windshield, its beating wipers.

"You've been very kind," she says in her daze of departure. "Shall I send you a transcript when I have one made?"

"Oh my goodness, no. I couldn't bear to read it."

"Would you like to approve of the quotes I use in my article? As I said, you've given me much more than I can use."

"Not really, dear. I'm sure you'll get them right enough. You had the tape recorder. And I honestly can't picture who the reader of this article is going to be."

"There might even be some print options, depending on the slant I give it. My agent is very enthusiastic about the possibilities."

"I've never had an agent, I suppose it's their business to be enthusiastic. If you begin to feel tired, and your eyes start to close, and having a dried apricot doesn't help, dear, you must promise me to pull over, and not just to the side of the road or in one of those vast truck-rests where dreadful things happen, but next to a restaurant with its lights on and people coming in and out."

"I'll be fine, honest. Goodbye again, Mrs. Chafetz." Kathryn tugs at the front door handle but has no success; Hope, who knows all the tricks of this latch, in damp weather or dry, yanks it open for her. The live wet breath of the rain, the sound and stir of it in the dark, the glimpse by doorlight of its thin vertical rods sparkling with reflections, its towering presence stretching up out of sight into the darkness from which it falls: the beast confronts the two women. The lamps of the living room reveal only a few strides of dead lawn, plus the spangled tops of the bushes planted close to the house, soaked white spiderwebs spread on the flat-cut yew like doilies on a table. The irregular flagstones dimly lead into the whispering, pattering dark-ness where the visitor's car is hidden. "Oh, don't come out!"

Kathryn cries, when Hope steps with her out of the shelter of the little roof here, over the porch of flagstones that twenty years ago had replaced rotted porch boards. "You'll get wet!"

"Only for a minute. It will do me good. Jerry always saw guests to their cars."

Having no choice, unless she uses her greater size and youthful strength to push the older woman back into the house, Kathryn turns with a perhaps humorously despairing sweep of her arm, leaping in black from its cape, and heads down the flagstones with at first firm and then, in the dark, groping footsteps. Hope, who knows each tilt and gap in the walk, takes Kathryn's arm, feeling through cashmere the other's tense, resilient flesh, flesh hardened by "working out," running on pavement; rain, cold and lightly wind-tossed, coats Hope's face with delectable sensation. Under the beech, the drops are bigger, gathered and released by bare branches. They hit hollow metal noisily; the borrowed automobile, its unpainted fender glimmering, forms a shape in the night less distinct to the eye than to the ear as Kathryn arrives at its side and scratches with her key at the door, which she absurdly locked out of city habit, here on this Vermont hill where seldom more than six cars a day pass. It is an aging cheap car, not equipped to lock and unlock at the squeeze of an electronic remote, as does Hope's royal-blue Caravan. Oh, she knows that her SUV guzzles gas, yet the space inside, enough for canvases five feet by six, and the exaltation of sitting up so high on the road seem luxuries she owes herself near her life's end: let the young inherit a depleted world. Methane is coming, and hydrogen separated from water by windmill-generated electric power, she heard about it on the NPR station on a Science Friday.

Under the beech she feels her face flood with an excited warmth of pity and envy, as if encountering in the dripping dark a younger self; when Kathryn turns, having unlocked the door, to say a formal final goodbye, holding out a long white cold wet hand, Hope instead embraces her, though being so much shorter she lands her lips not on the other woman's cheek but on the bony curve of her jaw. Still she hangs on, relishing this muffled, impatient other body, naked and savory beneath its clothes, warmer than the air: amid the rods of rain, a scent of thick black hair. "*Have* your life," she says, in a whisper pushed from within like a shout, "go and have it, dear. It won't be mine, it can't be mine, we were all so naïve in a way, thinking we were so important to the world, but it will be yours, your own. Don't hang back. Don't let this Alec or any man take it from you."

Kathryn, rigid for a moment, returns the hug, perhaps more crunchingly than she had intended, and lowers her face enough to promise, "O.K., I'll try not to." The peck of a kiss her wet face gives the older woman's wet face has the stern, statuesque quality her mouth has: hardened by seriousness, by concentration on the effort of an interview, denying itself all but a few smiles. Now it does seem to smile from within the drenched hood of soft wool. The invader says, "*Thank* you for being so generous with your time, and so frank. Please, you *must* run inside."

"Thank *you* for letting me go on and on, making it real to myself again." *Had* she been frank? Too frank? About Dot? About Zack? No matter. So little matters, it turns out. Why do we get so fussed? Hope quits the embrace; she feels the rain seeping through her thick wool shirt to her skin and beyond, into that layer of her where death will one day settle. "Catch your death" was a phrase of her childhood, used by grown-ups of colds, which lurked in the air like ghosts and polio and radio waves. Our African ancestors thought we walked through swarms of spirits and it turns out we are in fact wreathed in invisible microörganisms.

Kathryn finds the door handle of Alec's car; the dark and rain release the concussive pang of the driver's side opening, spilling a wedge of light onto Kathryn's square-toed boots, the patch of ground turning to mud beneath them, some flattened blades of grass here at the lawn's edge, and a scattering of pebbles each with its sharp projection of shadow, like something Mr. Hartz would have wanted Hope to see. What would he think seeing *her*, approaching eighty and as blind now as when ten! Not daring to run, she makes her way back along the flagstones, whose placement her feet know by heart, though still she is grateful for the growing visibility as she nears the house's lit windows. Kathryn's headlights come on and then swing in the start of a three-point turn, so that the earth beneath Hope's feet seems to wheel, to tilt on a wave of raking illumination that exaggerates each contour and pocket of shadow in the colorless lawn; it rises toward her like the lunar surface to a moon lander, but subsides as the visitor's automobile turns farther, changes gear, and heads down the dirt driveway with red taillights blinking like angry dragon eyes. The horn honks once, the headlight cones full of sparkling rain pause and then disappear behind the stone wall at the upper side of the public, macadamized road. Hope has reached the half-dry porch, gives an unseen wave, and lets herself into her house.

You should have a pet. A cat would kill the birds that come to the feeder. A dog would inflict upon her the oppression of love and a need to be walked, to be fed, to be humored, to be accepted as a fully qualified though frequently puzzled person. After talking so much, Hope feels disgusted with herself, as if after eating too much. Nothing to do but let it work out of her system; it takes days. The thread-thin hands of the mantel clock say seven-forty-seven, a little early for bed, even for her, but her moss-green shirt is wet, along with her hair and Birkenstocks and lint-colored socks, and she doesn't want to catch her death. Pneumonia is how it happens if cancer or arterial stenosis doesn't close the deal. When she tries to personify death, she pictures a gallery owner, who always has the advantage, small and humpbacked and deferential as he is. She reaches behind her head and pulls off the candy-colored elastic from the Montpelier five-and-ten that has been holding her gray ghost of a ponytail in place, and absent-mindedly slips it onto her left wrist as she walks into the kitchen, where she vigorously rubs her wet hair over the sink with a checkered blue dish-towel. She unbuttons the wool shirt, heavy with absorbed rain, and moves about in her wheat-yellow turtle-neck, which is wet only at the neck, and with one hand on the marble counter works off her Birkenstocks and soaked heavy gray socks. She boosts up the kitchen thermo-stat two degrees. She opens the refrigerator, its obedient little light that automatically comes on reminding her of the light that splashed down on Kathryn's expensive, uncomfortable boots. After contemplation of the meagre fare on the shelves of parallel rods of chrome, she lifts out the half-sandwich that she had wrapped in aluminum foil for Kathryn to take with her but that the girl had snubbed. As Hope unwraps it, glimmers reflected from the crinkling Reynolds Wrap swim unnoticed across the tex-tured composition panels of the dropped ceiling with its inset, rheostatted lights. Snubbed the sandwich, she thinks, snubbed her instant coffee, implied she loved Zack more than Hope ever did, and after all that, a whole day of assault, gave her rather perfunctory thanks. Hope bites one corner of rice-pecan bread, tasting first the sugary marmalade, then the oleaginous peanut butter, and walks down the corridor to her studio, eating as she goes, making crumbs. Feeding the mice. A cat would kill the mice, too, another unpleasantness, bringing the little furry, chewed bodies to her for praise, or to teach her how to kill mice also, as if she were a kitten. Her days of kittenhood are by. Surely, having given the girl a whole day of her dwindling time on the planet Earth, she can give the mice a few crumbs. Mildred Warren is coming tomorrow to clean. Tomorrow is an eventful day—the cleaning lady and a dental appointment in Burlington with Dr. Weiss, a cavity where her gumline has receded from a crown on a bicuspid, exposing the root to decay. Perhaps filling it will take away the bad taste in her mouth, which no amount of brushing and rinsing with Listerine seems to alter. Her mouth is such a patchwork of crowns and root canals and implants, in any earlier era she would have been one of those grotesque crones such as Leonardo in his cool and unearthly way would draw, with one or two teeth left and the profile all sunk in. Poor man, the genius of geniuses, the first man since the Greeks and Romans to dare to look at everything, the body and its bones and bowels and the watery corkscrews of the winds and river currents, but he had never seen a vagina, evidently, at least the one in his notebooks is clearly that of a female corpse, insensate and agape.

Hope had forgotten to turn off the fluorescent studio lights since briefly entertaining her interviewer here. Their overhead tubes pour sharp blue light into every corner of the great space, a cold unnatural light she prefers not to paint by; even on an overcast day the northern light as it falls, with its hidden rainbow, through the two high windows and the domed Plexiglas skylight, is better, truer. The skylight drums with the sound of rain like a demented man alone in a room talking to himself. She has always been afraid of its leaking but it hasn't yet, Jerry assured her it wouldn't when he had this studio built for her. He left her snug. He knew she would be alone again. The space is too big, he didn't understand that her kind of painting happened in the inches between the hand and the eye, she would have been content to work in the spare upstairs room just as she did in the Flats house until the barn had become hers. Along the walls, behind her, several easels—for she likes to work on two or three paintings at a time, each with its own gray music like harps being strummed in the fog, the gray of graphite and that of pigeon feathers and of silver and stone and dirty soapsuds—canvases lean stacked with their stretcher sides outward, her own, dried and hardened and waiting for their ride to New York and her next show, a retrospective in honor of her eightieth birthday in the year 2002, and a few by her first two husbands, by Zack several scraps of sized cardboard so casually dripped on that she never offered them for sale, in his chaotic way he was a perfectionist and destroyed what he considered failed work, work that lacked the impetus from the Jungian depths, and by Guy a few playful small works, in paper and pastel, one of acrylic and wood and wire and colored paper forming a Pop bouquet interwoven with the words on a ribbon SPRINGS ETERNAL, works given to her at family occasions, anniversaries and birthdays in their seventeen married years. Both men, it occurs to her now, believed that order and beauty must be man-made, achieved by a titanic conscious effort like that shown in the musclebound 'thirties murals propagandizing the tragic vision of humanistic Socialism, whereas she sat at her easels hoping that by modestly holding still she would overhear a music from beyond manly noise. How silly, perhaps. But all the excuses for art are flimsy and fade; what endures is the art itself, the paint keeping intact whatever hope or intention worked for that perilous moment.

She forgot to turn off the lavish lighting Jerry provided and now forgets why she came in here, wet and weary and slightly missing her visitor, that brave, tenacious, aggravating girl, and then remembers: to replace the wall phone on its cradle. She has a machine to pick up messages in the kitchen, but Hope knew she would strain from the living room to hear what they were saying into the device; and it would have been further impolite to make the disconnection there or in the living room and inflict upon her visitor that periodic squawking with which the phone company tries to tell you that your phone is off the hook. Better it squawked unheard in the studio, amid the unseen paintings. The receiver—so much smaller than the old-fashioned ones, which reached from your ear to your mouth as in those old Petty-girl pinups, whereas these new receivers and the flip-open cell phones suggest it is just enough to be in the vague vicinity of the speaking lips, inches to the side, part of the general blurring of attention perhaps, the movies and TV shows where the crucial lines are thrown away with Method acting and the CNN screen tries to give you three news stories at once, talking head and headline crawl and sports score—reminds her, as she settles it back on the upright cradle, of Guy's old-fashioned pay phones in limp vinyl, limp as Chardin's dead rabbits, though at the time he was making them she was too thoughtlessly alive to wonder if death was Guy's intended metaphor, and now he is too gaga, his brain hardening into useless gristle as the medical journals describe, to answer if she asked. Watching herself daily for signs of the same fate, she often wonders how it feels to know less and less and always arrives at the riddle that one does not know what one does not know, any more than a dog understands the superstructure of language and political and economic arrangement behind the human presences to which the animal is so alert, his nostrils packed with layers and tints of human odor. The obvious analogy is with us and the mind of God, we don't have a clue, or, rather, clues are all we have.

So. The phone reconnects her with the world, with Mildred, who might have been calling to cancel—she is all friendliness, with her valley gossip and gifts of pies and apple butter in apple season and repeated offers of a Labrador puppy almost for free, but she keeps her own schedule, and has a proud streak, treating Hope as an equal she is doing a favor for—and with her own sons if Paul or Piet had wanted to share news or assuage their filial consciences, though they usually called on weekends; Hope is potentially reconnected with telemarketers and fundraisers and alarmists and gossips, with the several other elderly women of the region with not dissimilar metropolitan pasts and predilections who check in on each other, and with those occasional younger voices, eager opportunists or the children or grandchildren of old friends—Jarl Anders' granddaughter showed up last summer, with his high Scandinavian coloring but Frieda's thin sharp features and a wispy do-gooding air that was what remained of Jarl's terrible prophetic transports—or young art-grant hustlers hoping to cash in on even a little attention or blessing from anyone with a slightly famous name from the past. She is plugged in again to all this, though she doubts that the phone will ring now that it is after eight. Turning off Jerry's excessively bright fluorescent lights, leaving her canvases to darkness and the muttering monologue of the rain on the skylight, Hope feels a weight rolled away, the tall dark girl gone, swallowed by the storm, lost in the vortex now that the damp moment is past when she felt her solid in her arms, like Dot in those faraway days when the infant lay wriggling in her lonely cot on the floor dying to be plucked up and held, and delivered that cold wet kiss that made her stiffen there by the pale car fender; Hope is relieved to be alone but the long interview has left her with the disquieting sensation that the events of her life have been too close together, compressed into a single colorful slice of time rather than unfolding in an organic sacred slow procession of nights alternating with days, phases of solitude and uncertainty and desolation but also of fruitful dreaming, daydreams alternating with stripes of activity, of sociability, dancing invitingly around a beautiful man and spending the energy built up in stymied idleness.

A little laundry room was added when Jerry built the studio wing for her, and in its small space, snug as an ice-cube tray holding two huge cubes, the twin white appliances and shelves of detergent and spare light bulbs and spray cans of sizing and Bounce sheets/feuilles/hojas of fabric softener, Hope drops the wet lumberjack shirt and removes the yellow cotton turtleneck, its soaked neck like a slimy garrote, and her brown corduroys made baggier by being out in the rain, and puts them all in the washer without getting down the orange jug of Tide or touching the controls—the wash cycle would be twenty-five minutes and the drying could take forty or fifty, but if left in the dryer overnight everything gets wrinkled, and she doesn't want to come down again or be barred from falling soon asleep if the little Spark novel lulls her. Mildred can run a load tomorrow, while she pushes the vacuum around where she pleases and dusts the surfaces that are easiest to reach, never getting the cobwebs around the chair rungs or in the high corners. The woman still smokes, as so many of these "real" Vermonters do, and the rasping don't-give-a-damn smell in the house reminds Hope fondly of the days when everybody smoked, at the Cedar on University Place or the Waldorf Cafeteria on Sixth Avenue, at the Artists Union loft parties at Sixteenth and Sixth, thick drifts of it, atmospheric effects out of Whistler, fumes of depression and war and reckless artistic aspiration. Hope feels the air on her bare skin, bringing up goosebumps. If any prowler or long-clawed bear looks in the side windows he will get what he deserves, the sight of a barefoot old lady in her underwear—white underpants, the broad un-bikini, un-thong style, and so-called flesh-colored bra, though not the flesh color of Titian or Fragonard or Bonnard or Modigliani.

Her mouth feels dry and loose from all that talking. She sucks at her teeth to see how bad her breath is; she can never quite tell. She licks her fingers, still sticky from the marmalade sandwich, and from the breadbox takes out two brittle Carr's Hob Nobs and pours herself a small tumbler of fat-free milk, first checking that there is enough for tomorrow's breakfast cereal plus a splash into the mug of tea she carries with her in the mornings into the studio. She sees herself doing this so vividly it is as if the night has already passed. The sense of compressed simultaneity hangs in her head like the cerebral displacement the morning after a night of drinking wine and smoking pot, a kind of sideslipped hangover. For fear of addling their heads, she and Guy quit dope, at least inside the Seventy-ninth Street apartment he did—undoubtedly, as Jeanette Nova maliciously hinted, more may have gone on down at the Hospice than she ever realized, events out of sight like water seepage that finally undermines the foundations of a house—but she and Guy, descendants of radical Protestantism, were alike in distrust of gilding the lily of earthly existence, being alive was itself the trip. In her mind's eye Zack feels more distant than Guy, a woeful ogre who upset tables and crashed cars, tucked into that far corner of the Island where she had taken him; she should feel close to him since he left clear and dynamic traces of his hand in his drip paintings, but those canvases poured and spattered in a shaman's dance have become monuments as rigid as those of Egypt, built of blocks of hand-smoothed stone.

In the living room, where Hope wanders with the day's last handful of unsalted almonds, her attention gravitates to objects salvaged from the Germantown and Ardmore houses, ones her surviving brother did not claim. On the top of a simple square curly-maple sewing table she sees a worn blue-and-red cotton runner whose faded threads still describe two stylized Arabian birds whose exact anatomy her childish eyes had puzzled over, and a peened copper ashtray still holding the smudge of her father's stubbed-out Chesterfields, and a crude ceramic candlestick with a celadon glaze and jaunty handles like the arms of a man with his hands on his hips: meaning had inhered in these objects before she had words to weaken meaning, her hands and eyes had explored them in the silent anteroom just this side of her entry into the world. At the back of the next-to-top shelf of a glass-fronted breakfront there are two curious vases that she tried to paint in watercolor when she was taking lessons from Rudolph Hartz. One was heavy and brown, so heavy it felt full though it was always empty, with a dumpy waist and purple streaks in its glaze, and the other vase cylindrical and diagonally streaked somewhat like a barber pole in strands of muddy color, reminding her of marbled endpapers in a fancy book or, now, of the colors in the wings of the angel kneeling in the Annunciation Fra Angelico had painted on the gallery wall at the head of the stairs in the Convent of San Marco. It was a deathless work but showy, in its feathers and pillars and flowers, the cloistered painter guilty of virtuosity; Hope preferred, when she toured the convent with Jerry two decades ago, the severer Annunciation in a monk's cell, two feminine creatures transfixed in a bare room.

How she had stared at those vases in the light of the Ardmore side porch!—stared and mixed colors in the indentations of the lid of the watercolor set, its rainbow broken into concave squares, stealing with her wet brush from one square a lick of red and from another a trembling drop of blue, seeking in dabbling them together the equivalent of the gleaming purplish-brown of the waisted thick-skinned vase, or of the muddy many-colored swirl on the straight-sided other. The world was all colors but never unmixed ones. This vanished world held pieces of furniture that she can still picture—a red-stained pine corner cupboard; a coal stove her grandmother had cooked on in the German-town house, pulling with a flowered asbestos mitten a sheet of raisin cookies from its clanking black belly; a four-postered bed that supported its mattress on ropes and creaked instead of bounced when you jumped on it; the has-sock, with its long triangular pie-slices of colored leather for a top, that "lived," the expression was, in Grandpa's sun-room, along with the potted philodendrons and the maple magazine-rack subdivided in the middle by a partition with a wide hole near the edge for fingers to lift it by. It stood, loaded with magazines which went out of business half a century ago, next to her grandfather's plaid chair; he faithfully read *The Saturday Evening Post*, romance stories and all, his head tipped back to get the benefit of his bifocals.

In her underwear, Hope sits on the broad-armed plaid chair and spreads the fingers of one hand on the curved oak. Her thumb and little finger easily reach from side to side. The back of her hand is mottled and scarred by sun and age as if once scalded, the more prominent veins making patterns like wiggly letters she can almost read, random little rivers that have stayed in their courses all her life. The swelling of arthritis in a number of joints has caused the top segments of her fingers to deviate from the straight. She marvels that this gnarled crone's hand is hers.

Her grandfather enters the room with his soft, sly tread. Though not tall, he moves about his big house in a stealthy crouch, the proprietor's artful pretense of being the meekest of men. Hope starts guiltily at being discovered in his chair, but he appears amused, his eyes jumping from one degree of magnification to the other as he moves his tidy gray head up and down, surveying her. He looks to her gray all over, his straight hair parted in the middle and much mixed with white, his sweater-vest gray over his collarless striped shirt, his trousers once black in color but so often ironed and worn back into baggy knees that they are dull as a shadow, his hightop shoes so creased they take their shine in stripes. The hole where the collar button should go shows, and his long-cuffed sleeves are held in place by black elastics above the elbow. A smell comes off him like that of the winter clothes kept all summer in the tall cedar closet. With comical formality he lifts a hand as if to halt the traffic of her mind to give his words passage: "Do not unsettle thyself. What wast thee measuring with thy hand?"

The child she long ago was lacked the words to explain. "Just seeing something," she began, and stopped.

After a pause he offered, "That is a pleasant seat from which to view Creation. My plans had been to sit with yesterday's *Evening Bulletin*, searching for tidings I may have missed, and to wait for the afternoon mail. The good Mr. Brubaker generally delivers by three-thirty o'clock, if he omits to tarry in conference with the Widow Kendall up the street. It is written in the Constitution, evidently, that the foremost duty of the Post Office Department is to gather the gossip of every domicile."

"It is?"

"In a manner of speaking, child. As it seems, so it becomes. I made what in common parlance is called a joke. Tell me, is there, for young ladies, no playing today, no visiting playmate?"

He saw into her life. Flattered, Hope rendered a full report. "Freddy Traphagen came over but had to go home. Gramma walked to the butcher shop to buy a roast and scrapple but I didn't want to go along, I hate all the blood and the way the man in the big apron smiles at me. Mama is taking a nap and said I wasn't to make any noise. You and I could play Fish." Her face felt hot from trying to rise to this attention he was paying her, in such grave and courtly fashion.

"Indeed we could, though I would slightly have to readjust my aforesaid plans. Instead, we might hunt for treasure."

"Hunt for treasure?"

"If I close my eyes, I have an inkling where some might be hidden. But thee will have to readjust thy position on our chair. Thee will have to kneel beside it. Thy hand is so slim and small compared with my own; do me a kindness, granddaughter, and squeeze it down between the two cushions."

She looked at his hand, hanging half curled at the level of the trouser pocket that held his bone-handled pocket-knife, with which he not only pared apples and peaches in long spiralling strips but cut his own fingernails; when he pared his fingernails, his mouth, more flexible than hers because his teeth could come out, shrivelled in concentration, and his eyes got enormous in the lower half of his glasses. She saw that he was right, his hand was lumpy and wrinkled, brown like newspapers kept for years at the bottom of drawers, and his fingers had edges like the rounded backs of books or chocolate fingers where they had hardened on the candy-maker's tray. Hope had watched from the pavement on Chelten Avenue candy being made through the big window near the shoe store when she shopped with Mama; the chocolate came out of the big pot steamy and gooey, but hardened, very quickly, giving the fat woman sitting surrounded by of all this sweetness just time to scribble a design on top with her spoon, fast as light.

Obediently Hope knelt beside the chair and pushed her own hand, small and round with fat between the joints, into the crease, which was scarily tight at first. She felt around in a secret clothy space, praying no spider would bite or centipede with its horrible wavy legs would fasten on. Under the flat cloth were the bumps of metal that held it firm from beneath, and over on one side, when she was about to give up, her arm feeling squeezed as if by a mean boy, her fingertips met the curved hard edges of one—no, two—circular small objects. Carefully pinching, she brought them up and showed them on her palm: two coins, one big and silver and the other small and brown. The brown one she knew was a penny, but the larger she had never handled before. "What is this?" she asked her grandfather.

"Canst thee not read?" he asked.

"Not words yet. The kindergarten teacher told us that comes next year, in first grade." Miss Fox had big teeth that overlapped and spoiled her natural beauty, Mama said. Mama knew about beauty and told Hope she would never be beautiful but a radiant spirit could make up for it.

"Not even numbers and the alphabet?"

"Maybe," she said, not sure if she was lying.

Her grandfather's voice had acquired a pleading wheeziness. "Take the big coin to the light at the window, young lady, and tell me what thine eyes detect."

The air over here borrowed a blue tinge from the hydrangeas outside the window, crowded head upon head as if jostling to look in, to get out of the sun that was bleaching their blue. "There's a lady walking into a big ball, the sun is setting—"

"Or rising, some would say."

"And under her feet are some little numbers—one, nine, two, two."

"That is the year it was minted, the same as thyself. And what is on the other side?"

"A scary bird, walking the same way."

"A warlike eagle. Our national emblem. Benjamin Franklin thought the wild turkey would be more suitable."

"There are a lot of words around him."

"At the bottom, can you spell those letters?"

This was hard. Why did they make these coins so they looked so old-fashioned and jumbled? She felt a crabbed divine force pressing on the design, making it obscure. " 'H,' I think, like in my name, and 'A,' and—it's the one with the single foot—"

" 'L,' " he said. "Unsounded, in the illogical way of the English language. A half-dollar, my child. A fifty-cent piece," her grandfather announced, his voice changed again, more settled in his chest. "It is thine, with my blessing."

Hope turned from the window and saw that he had sat in the broad-armed chair. That was why his voice had sounded slightly different. He had stolen her place. Already he had eased his weary shoes up on the hassock with the fancy leather pie-pieces, though Hope has more than once heard Gramma tell him not to do that, it put dirt in the seams. "Hey," she said. "That was *my* chair."

Her grandfather didn't seem to hear. He met her protest with a serene gray-blue gaze split by his bifocals, a gaze into which her child's eyes read total approval, a bifocal love from both near and far, up close and everlasting.

Hope smiles, recalling the old man's trick, and realizes that he had planted the coins there, for her to discover one day of his choosing. The half-dollar and the penny had a suspicious symmetry; the date on the bigger coin was too fortuitous. From that day on she searched between the cushions so faithfully that sometimes there were no coins—they had not had time to grow—and rarely more than a dime. Sometimes there was a paper clip, another time a black Smith Brothers coughdrop with the raised star on it, and once his pocketknife, which had slid from his pocket into the crevice. When she returned the bone-handled knife her grandfather's gray eyebrows shot up in surprise and he rewarded her with a quarter. Hope thinks of exploring between the two big plaid cushions right now, but her back and hip hurt in anticipation of getting down, grunting, on her knees on the oval rag rug, and she is afraid of finding nothing.

JOHN UPDIKE was born in Shillington, Pennsylvania, in 1932. He graduated from Harvard College in 1954 and spent a year in Oxford, England, at the Ruskin School of Drawing and Fine Art. From 1955 to 1957 he was a member of the staff of *The New Yorker*. His novels have won the Pulitzer Prize, the National Book Award, the National Book Critics Circle Award, the Rosenthal Foundation Award, and the William Dean Howells Medal. In 2007 he received the Gold Medal for Fiction from the American Academy of Arts and Letters. John Updike died in January 2009.

Printed in the United States
by Baker & Taylor Publisher Services